THE
AUTHENTICATOR

Also by William M. Valtos

Resurrection

THE
AUTHENTICATOR

William M. Valtos

HAMPTON ROADS
PUBLISHING COMPANY, INC.

Copyright 2000
by William M. Valtos

All rights reserved, including the right to reproduce this
work in any form whatsoever, without permission
in writing from the publisher, except for brief passages
in connection with a review.

Cover design by Grace Pedalino
Cover/spine photos by Grace Pedalino
Author photo by RoseValtos

For information write:

Hampton Roads Publishing Company, Inc.
1125 Stoney Ridge Road
Charlottesville, VA 22902

Or call: 804-296-2772
FAX: 804-296-5096
e-mail: hrpc@hrpub.com
Web site: http://www.hrpub.com

If you are unable to order this book from your local
bookseller, you may order directly from the publisher.
Quantity discounts for organizations are available.
Call 1-800-766-8009, toll-free.

Library of Congress Catalog Card Number: 99-95407

ISBN 1-57174-149-6

10 9 8 7 6 5 4 3 2 1

Printed on acid-free paper in the United States

DEDICATION

*For Rose,
who showed me
the world*

---

*and for
Jake and Mary,
who are waiting
to show me
the Other Side*

Riker's Island
New York:

My legal counsel has advised me against seeking publication of this account. It is his opinion that any perceived profit motive would prejudice the jury in my upcoming criminal trial.

In addition, any manuscript I submit to a publisher would be subject to an immediate subpoena by the New York District Attorney's Office. The manuscript will be carefully analyzed for discrepancies and contradictions that can be used against me when I testify in my own defense.

I have nevertheless decided to take that risk, because it is the only way to fulfill the promise I made to Laura Duquesne.

It was her desire that I tell the world what really happened to her. It is a story which I will not be allowed to tell in its entirety during my trial, yet one which begs for documentation. I have attempted to reconstruct events exactly as they unfolded before me. I am by nature a skeptic and by training a psychologist. But nothing in my background could have prepared me for the extraordinary events to which I was witness.

Theophanes Nikonos

ONE

The first time I saw Laura Duquesne was six months after she died.

All the way up from New York, I had been dreading what awaited me. Normally in a case like this, I'd expect to find massive physical disfigurement. Or at least some mark left behind by the doctors who worked on her before she died.

But instead of a mangled body, I found a lovely young woman who looked as if she had fallen asleep just moments before I arrived. She was laid out in a small, dark room, as if she were on display. A white sheet covered her body, revealing only her face. Her flesh had an opalescent pallor, which made the shadows beneath her eyes appear darker than they really were. The sharp smell of antiseptic served as her perfume.

My flashlight revealed no visible reminders of the cause of her death, nothing in her face to indicate the violent events that brought her to this resting place.

She deserved better than this, I thought as I looked around the otherwise empty room. They were keeping her below ground level, in a concrete bunker. At some point in the past, water must have seeped through a crack in the foundation, leaving behind a damp, earthy odor. It was a dismal setting for a woman as beautiful as she was.

I knew I could be arrested for what I was doing. The security people had turned me away earlier in the day. They denied any knowledge of what happened to Mrs. Duquesne, just as I had been warned they would. But I had traveled too far and I needed the money this job would pay, so I wasn't ready to give up easily. I had returned after dark, slipped past a dozing guard, and made my way down to the bunker, where the crudely-drawn map indicated I would find her.

I leaned in closer to examine her more carefully. There were no scars that I could see. No sign of any stitch marks on her flawless skin. No unusual lumps on her cheekbones that would suggest underlying fractures. No telltale X to reveal where a tracheotomy might have been performed at the base of her slender throat.

My practiced eyes searched along the edge of her hairline, where her flowing blonde hair might have covered some disfigurement. I could find nothing.

It must have been internal injuries, I thought, still not quite believing the remarkably good condition in which I found the body of this woman whose death I had come here to investigate.

Seeing the aftereffects of vehicle accidents normally was the most unpleasant part of the work I did for the Institute. The drownings weren't that bad, because the water never left any marks on the victim's faces, and the ones I saw were never in the water very long. The heart attacks could be surprising. They weren't always overweight middle-aged white males as the newspapers led you to believe. The previous month I had a high school basketball player, and the month before was a female executive from a fashion magazine. The comas and the long illnesses were usually pretty grim, the victims always appearing gaunt and hollow-eyed, after wasting away for months.

But none of those cases bothered me as much as the vehicle accidents, because usually the victims were horribly disfigured, missing major body parts, or had suffered unusual grotesqueries, like the twenty-year-old Connecticut seminary student who fell off the back of his friend's Harley-Davidson and skidded sixty feet on his face across an asphalt road.

I had wanted to quit after that particular assignment, but Professor DeBray had talked me out of it. The Professor explained that it was a natural reaction, that I was over-identifying with the suffering the victims had endured. It was similar to the problem I had encountered on my previous job, when I was an auto insurance claims adjuster. My sympathies for the victims and their families resulted in my dismissal when the claims supervisors discovered I was approving damage awards far in excess of the company's guidelines. The Professor knew about this weakness in my character when he hired me. But he assured me I'd conquer this sensitivity in time.

I wasn't entirely convinced about that. Which was why I was relieved to find Laura Duquesne in such flawless condition.

I wished she would open her eyes.

It unnerved me to be so close to this lovely woman, so close I could count the number of gently curled hairs on her eyelashes, so near I could examine the exact line where the fleshy mound of her lower lip swelled out of the pale skin below. The only indication that anything unusual had happened to her was the sad smile that lingered on her mouth.

I had a sudden, irrational urge to touch her, but I had been cautioned to avoid physical contact with the people in these cases. I had to maintain a professional objectivity. My report would have to reduce her beauty to clinical terms, following the format developed by Professor DeBray. The Institute required me to observe a rigid protocol, so the data I collected could be easily loaded into the Professor's computer for analysis and comparison with the thousands of other cases investigated thus far.

While I waited, I reviewed the data that had already been entered in the Preliminary Assignment Sheet.

The information had come from a newspaper clipping and a short letter sent to the Institute. The letter gave detailed instructions, including a rough map showing exactly where to find her. The newspaper article contained a photograph of some burned-out wreckage, all that remained of the BMW in which Harrison Duquesne died. It also included a photo of Laura Duquesne, with an explanation of how she was taken to Scranton Evangelical Hospital, where she died on the operating table. It was the rest of the story, a single paragraph circled in red at the bottom by the letter writer, that was the reason I had been sent on this assignment.

I looked up from my notes just in time to see Laura Duquesne open her eyes.

At last, I thought. Now we could get started.

PRELIMINARY ASSIGNMENT SHEET

CASE NUMBER: 3248

INVESTIGATOR: Theophanes Nikonos

SUBJECT: Laura Lehman Duquesne

SEX: Female   RACE: Caucasian

HEIGHT: 5' 4"   WEIGHT: 118 lbs.

MARITAL STATUS: Widow (see addl. notes)

RELIGIOUS PREFERENCE: Roman Catholic

DATE OF BIRTH: August 18, 1969

DATE OF DEATH: October 15, 1995

TIME OF DEATH: 10:18 P.M.

PLACE OF DEATH: Trauma Center, Scranton Evangelical Hospital, Scranton, Pennsylvania

ATTENDING PHYSICIAN: Dr. Ranjeet Subdhani

CAUSE OF DEATH: Cardiac arrest due to complications resulting from massive blood loss and trauma to upper thoracic region sustained in automobile accident

ADDITIONAL NOTES: Subject's husband (Harrison Duquesne) died in the same accident

TWO

Her eyes appeared dull and she seemed to be having trouble focusing. When she finally spoke, her lips barely moved.

"Who are you?" she asked. Her voice was hoarse from disuse.

"A friend," I said. "My name is Theophanes." I quickly added, "Most people call me Theo."

Her eyelids slowly closed. I waited patiently, not wanting to say anything that might upset her. When she opened her eyes again, her vision seemed to have cleared, although I noticed the pupils were dilated. I could sense she was frightened by my presence.

"Don't be afraid, Laura," I tried to reassure her. "I won't harm you."

She studied my face, as if she were trying to decide whether I was telling the truth.

"How did you get past the guards?" she asked, speaking slowly, slurring her words almost drunkenly.

"I slipped in through the back. They don't know I'm here."

She nodded almost imperceptibly, apparently satisfied with my answer.

"What day is today?" she asked.

"Sunday," I said softly. "The eighteenth of April."

She closed her eyes again.

"Six months," she sighed. "It's been six months since I died."

"I have some questions about what happened to you that day, Laura. Can we talk about it?"

"You're wasting your time."

"What do you mean?"

"I don't know where he is."

"Who?"

"My husband. That's why you're here, isn't it?" Still slurring her words. "To try to find out where he is?"

Apparently they still hadn't told her about Harrison Duquesne's death. It didn't seem right for them to withhold the truth for so long, but I certainly wasn't going to be the one to break the tragic news to her.

"I'm here to talk about what happened to you, Laura. Not to ask about your husband."

"I keep telling them I don't know where he is," she insisted, an edge of anxiety creeping into her voice. "Why don't they believe me?"

"I believe you," I said as gently as I could. I wanted to keep her calm, so she wouldn't alert the security people.

"Do you?" She didn't sound convinced.

"I do." Technically, it wasn't a lie. After all, I had no reason to disbelieve her.

"This isn't a trick of some kind?"

"I came here because you had a very unusual experience six months ago," I said. "The people I work for want to find out more about it."

"Six months ago? You mean when I died?"

"Yes."

"Will you tell me what happened?" I asked.

"The car went off the road, that's what happened," Her voice was flat and lifeless.

"I don't mean about the accident," I said, "I want to hear what you remember about the process of dying."

She turned her head on the pillow to look at me again. There was no room on the questionnaire to describe the incredible clarity of the blue eyes that studied me.

"Why?" she asked.

"It's my job," I said. I tried to make it sound more routine, as I had been instructed. "I work with the Institute for the Investigation of Anabiotic Phenomena. We study cases like yours."

"Who told you about me?" she asked.

"A woman wrote to us. We run little ads in the tabloids offering a fifty dollar reward for every case like yours that can be verified."

"Was it someone from the hospital?"

"I'm sorry, but I can't reveal that information."

"I guess it doesn't make much difference, does it?"

She frowned when I placed the tiny Minolta microcassette recorder on the pillow beside her. I never liked the idea of using the recorder. It tends to put people on guard when they see those little wheels of audiotape turning, recording every word for posterity. If it were up to me, I'd use a hidden body wire and accomplish the same thing without the distraction.

"I'd like to ask you some questions about your death, if you don't mind," I said.

I switched on the Minolta and tapped it once to be sure the little green recording needle jumped.

The Institute's official procedure was for me to turn on the recorder and place it in plain sight before asking the subject's permission to tape the interview. The idea was to present it as a standard research routine and at the same time record the subject's agreement, in case there were any future objections raised by relatives or other third parties such as lawyers or in some cases agents for book or movie deals.

"We record every interview," I said, continuing to keep my voice casual. "We want to get your exact words. Is that okay with you?"

"Why do you need my exact words?" She still seemed suspicious of me. "Why is that so important?"

"I assume the tapes are examined for patterns, things that keep coming up over and over again. I don't really know. I only do the interviews."

"You mean there are others like me?"

She was rousing slowly from her lethargy. Her eyes stayed open for longer intervals.

"What do you think?" I countered. I tried to avoid giving her a direct answer. It was important not to taint the interview by giving the subject information about other cases.

"I don't know what to think," she said with a sigh. "That's why I'm asking you."

"You haven't heard about other people who went through similar experiences?"

"No."

Her answer qualified her for a special category. In Professor DeBray's terminology, she would be described as a "virgin": a subject with no previous knowledge of similar experiences. It was a lucky break for me. The Professor paid a hundred dollar bonus for every virgin. That would make this interview worth four hundred fifty dollars, plus mileage from New York.

Since bonus money was involved, I wanted to make sure her disclaimer was repeated on the tape.

"You have no such knowledge at all?" I asked.

"No. But if there were others, tell me about them," she said. "What happened to them?"

She tried to strain her head closer to me. She seemed unable to move the major portion of her body, whose provocative contours remained motionless under the tight white sheet.

"I can't," I replied. "Not until later."

"At least tell me how many others there are."

"I honestly don't know."

"But you said you do the interviews. How many did you talk to?"

She was close enough for me to see the delicate tracing of blue at her temple, where a small vein throbbed with life.

"They come in clusters," I finally admitted. "Sometimes, we go for weeks without a report, and then we get three or four at the same time."

"Tell me about them," she pleaded. "Are they all treated like me?"

I was so close to her, I could feel the warmth of her breath on my face. I wished I could tell her what she so desperately wanted to hear. But I had been warned by the Professor to avoid talking about other cases. Especially with a subject who claimed no previous knowledge of similar experiences. If it could be proven that the Institute's subjects were picking up verbal cues or responding to prior knowledge, it would destroy the integrity of the data. More important, it would damage the reputation of Professor DeBray and the work of the Institute.

That was probably another reason for the tape recorder, I suspected. The little Minolta was there to insure that I follow the

Institute's guidelines. Professor DeBray personally reviewed every interview tape, evaluating the interviewer as well as the subject.

"I can't tell you any more," I said, pulling myself out of the spell of the earthy aura that surrounded her. I tried to think of what the Professor would allow by way of explanation. "I'm not permitted to discuss other cases before the interview is completed. We're conducting a carefully controlled study of anabiotic phenomena, and we can't allow prior knowledge to affect your responses."

"That's the second time you used that word," she said.

"Anabiotic."

"Yes. What does it mean?"

"It's the scientific term for what happened to you," I explained. I was pleased that my use of the word impressed her. "It comes from the Greek word *anabioein*, which translates roughly as reanimation or returning to life. In the popular press today, they call it a near-death experience. You're sure you haven't read about it anywhere, like maybe in the tabloids or magazines?"

"What happened to me wasn't a near-death experience," she said. She still spoke slowly, but was no longer slurring her words. But she appeared to be growing more lucid. "I really died," she said. "I had no pulse, no heartbeat, no brain activity. My pupils were fixed and dilated. My brain scan was flat. I wasn't near death. I was dead. Clinically and officially dead."

That was better, I thought. The Professor always preferred subjects who got upset when their claims of death were challenged.

I made a notation of her response under General Observations and turned to the second page of the interview guide. Twenty-four separate items were listed on the page, arranged in the order Professor DeBray found to be the most common sequence. In his famous book on the subject, the Professor identified the twenty-four items as near-death experience Reference Points. In conversation, he referred to them as N-DERPS. These were the most common elements that people recalled from their purported journeys to the other side.

Evidence of clinical death wasn't one of the reference points, since it had to be substantiated by qualified medical authorities.

However, determining the availability of death information was the entry point for every interview.

"I'll need a written release from you," I said. "So I can get copies of your medical records, and I'll also need your permission to interview the attending physician."

"What if I refuse?" Still wary.

"In that case, there'd be no point in continuing. The Institute requires medical confirmation of clinical death." I made another note while she thought it over. It was considered a good indicator of credibility when a subject wasn't too eager to talk about the experience. "Unless you agree to a release, I'll have to terminate the interview."

It came out sounding harsher than I intended. Maybe I was overcompensating, trying to fight against the strange emotions this woman aroused within me. While I waited for her response, I tried to keep my face as impassive as possible, hoping not to display any hint of the effect she was having on me.

"If I agree, will you help me?" she asked.

"In what way?"

"Get me out of here."

"I'm sure they'll release you when you're fully recovered," I said in a cautious voice. It was strictly against policy to offer any inducements, monetary or otherwise, in exchange for an interview.

"They don't want me to recover," she said. "They give me drugs. They keep me unconscious for weeks at a time. And then what they do . . . what they do to me . . . ."

The sentence was left unfinished as her jaw started to tremble and tears gathered in the corners of her eyes.

I hoped she wasn't going to become hysterical on me. It happened occasionally. The near-death experience was a powerful emotional event, and some subjects had difficulty working through the psychological aftermath.

"I'm sure they're doing what they think is best for you," I said.

In fact, I wasn't sure, but I had to be careful what the tape recorder heard me say. I particularly wanted to discourage any talk about drugs, even though her physical symptoms were consistent with someone struggling to communicate through the fog of drug intoxication. That sort of thing could bring the credibility of the interview into question.

"You have to help me," she pleaded. "I have to get out of here."

I thought about the menacing security guards, and how they had refused me entry earlier in the day. But that could be explained away as the precautions taken by an overly-cautious health care facility, trying to protect the privacy of its patients. I didn't understand why they were hiding her down here in this tomb-like chamber in the basement of the Walden Clinic, but there was probably a logical explanation for that, too. I had to remind myself that I was here simply to get an interview.

"Will you help me?" she asked again.

"I'm afraid I can't."

"You don't care what they do to me, do you?"

"I'm not here to make judgements, Laura. I'm just here to interview you, to hear what you have to say about your death. But I need your permission to review your medical records and speak to your doctor."

"You want me to do something for you, but you won't help me," she said. She closed her eyes and let out a deep sigh. "All right, I give you my permission. You're so interested in documentation, go ahead. Read all the reports. Read all about what happened to me during the hour and twenty minutes I was officially dead."

Had I heard her right?

None of my other interviews claimed to have been dead more than twelve minutes. Brain damage normally occurs after four minutes without oxygen, although in hospital settings, the new heart-lung machines have largely overcome that problem. Still, after one hour and twenty minutes of what she had earlier claimed were flat brain waves, it was impossible for this woman to be lying here carrying on a normal conversation with no apparent damage to her mental faculties.

"One hour and twenty minutes?" I quickly leafed through the case folder, rechecking my background notes. "They didn't report the length of time in the newspaper article."

"Is it important?"

Hell yes, I wanted to say. She had been clinically dead more than twice as long as any case I knew about. One hour and twenty minutes of flat brain waves was a new record. Either that, or a flat-out lie.

"I'm just curious why people at the hospital didn't tell the reporter how long you were dead."

"Maybe they were embarrassed," she said. "Or maybe they were afraid of a malpractice suit."

"I'd think they'd be proud. Bringing you back to life after all that time."

"No," she said. "They gave up on me. They stopped trying to revive me and sent me down to the morgue. That's where I came back to life."

"That wasn't in the article, either. But I guess it'll be in the medical records."

"Is that all you care about? Newspaper articles and medical records?"

She was wide awake now, her mind apparently functioning normally. How long it would last, I wasn't sure. Patients on medication often float in and out of consciousness.

"I need the documentation," I said.

"The documentation will prove I was dead for one hour and twenty minutes. But it won't tell you why I came back from the other side."

"We'll get to that," I said.

Most near-deathers felt there was a reason for their coming back from the other side. The topic was listed under N-DERP #20, on page two of the questionnaire, with instructions to query the subject if the information wasn't volunteered freely.

"I want to talk about it now," she insisted.

"All right, Laura, if it makes you feel better. Why do you think you came back from the dead?"

"To find my husband."

There it was again. Another mention of her husband. This time I couldn't let it pass. If she continued referring to him as if he were still alive, her credibility would be destroyed and the interview dismissed as the wishful fantasy of an irrational woman.

"Didn't the doctors tell you about your husband?" I asked.

"They said Harry died in the accident. But they're wrong. I know they're wrong."

"The police identified the body," I said, phrasing my words as gently as I could.

"It must have been someone else's body. If he was dead, I would have seen him on the other side," she argued. "My dead relatives and friends were all waiting there for me. But I couldn't find Harry."

After conducting hundreds of near-death interviews, I was accustomed to hearing bizarre stories. But nothing I heard in the past could have prepared me for the chilling words that came next.

"They told me he was still alive," she said.

I was unable to speak for what seemed like a long time, but was probably only seconds. She stared at me, as if daring me to challenge her.

"Who told you he was still alive?" I asked, knowing in advance the only answer she could possibly give, but wanting to hear her say it, needing to get the words on tape for the Professor. This was going to be the most preposterous near-death interview ever conducted.

Or the most important.

I checked to make sure the tape recorder was working, and repeated my question.

"Who told you your husband was still alive?"

She gave me a quizzical look.

"Haven't you been listening to me?" she asked.

"Yes, I have. But I'd just like to get confirmation of the identity of these people you're talking about."

"It was the people I met on the other side," she said. "The dead people."

THREE

At first, I treated Laura Duquesne's claim with my usual skepticism. It had been almost two years since I started interviewing people who claimed to have returned from the dead, and I was accustomed to hearing some fairly outlandish descriptions of what awaits us all on that final journey.

Almost all the near-deathers I interviewed seemed totally convinced they were telling the truth about their experiences. However, I had learned in my psychology training how easily the human mind could deceive itself. Although there was no way for me to ever be certain how much of what I heard was true and how much was fantasy, I found the work fascinating. The people I interviewed were invariably pleasant and friendly, most of them claiming to have been somehow transformed by their encounter with the afterlife.

The Institute was founded by Professor Pierre DeBray, author of the international best seller, *The Life Beyond*, which had sold twenty million copies in eighteen different languages. In addition to his writing, the Professor gave dozens of lectures a year at five thousand dollars an appearance. He was the darling of the TV talk shows and supermarket tabloids.

When DeBray offered me the job, I didn't really believe in his theories. As far as I was concerned, he wasn't any different from the authors of those diet or self-improvement books that were always at the top of the New York Times best-seller list. He was just cashing in on the latest fad, which happened to be the current fascination with life after death.

Doing the fieldwork for what I thought was simply another new age guru wasn't the prestigious career in psychology for which I once thought I was destined.

My track record in college, where I had first met Professor DeBray, suggested a golden future awaited me. I was considered a brilliant student, with a remarkable talent for research. I graduated *cum laude* from Columbia, with a major in abnormal psychology and a minor in philosophy. I took my master's in applied psychology at New York University. And up until a few years earlier, I was a teaching assistant there while I worked on my Ph.D.

Some of my friends considered me an intellectual drifter, a gifted student aimlessly seeking out those courses in which it was easiest for me to excel. That was probably true. I had always exhibited a lack of purpose, an absence of goals in life. But whether by chance or not, I was well on the way to fulfilling the educational and economic aspirations of my Greek immigrant parents. My future seemed assured. The only question was whether I would drift into the lucrative anonymity of private practice, or continue in the academic world, settling into the comfortable routine of teaching, research, and writing.

Although I excelled in class, I was relatively unsophisticated in social matters, and thus particularly vulnerable to the first female who showed any real interest in me. Her name was Elizabeth Ann Maletesta. She was a receptionist at the bank branch where I was renegotiating my college loans. Elizabeth was a wild Italian beauty with black hair, big dark eyes, and a hungry mouth, with whom I immediately fell madly and irrationally in love. From the start, we were an ill-suited pair. She was far too exotic a creature for an introspective Ph.D. candidate like myself. When I wrote about her to my parents in Florida, my father warned me that her Italian family name can be translated to mean "evil head" in English. To the superstitious old man, it was clearly a bad omen.

But with the hubris of youth, I dismissed his warning, suggesting it was time for him to forget the ancient Greco-Roman feuds. I found Elizabeth utterly irresistible, and we were married within five months.

In the beginning, things went surprisingly well. Elizabeth was an ambitious woman, and she wanted only the best, I thought, for both of us. She seemed to have a better understanding of the monetary value of my degrees than I did. And, never having set any particular goals for myself, I found myself bending to her will.

It didn't take much effort for her to convince me that I was terribly underpaid as a teaching assistant. Soon we were both searching the New York Times employment ads, looking for the right opportunity for me. A very short job hunt turned up a lucrative position in the human relations department at Grumman Aircraft on Long Island. In addition to the standard benefits package, the company encouraged me to continue working towards my Ph.D., agreeing to underwrite all expenses.

Elizabeth transferred to the Trust Department at her bank, and with our combined salaries, we were able to qualify almost immediately for a mortgage on a one-bedroom condo on the Upper West Side in Manhattan. Things looked great for about six months.

It all came crashing down just like the Berlin Wall.

I remember watching those exhilarating TV pictures of the young Germans waving flags and holding hands and dancing as the Wall between capitalism and communism was destroyed. I didn't realize at the time that what they were celebrating meant the destruction of my career.

I lost my job in the first cycle of defense cutbacks.

It happened at the same time New York City was going through a mini-depression, with thousands of jobs disappearing in the restructuring of the financial and advertising industries. Formerly highly paid holders of master's and Ph.D. degrees clogged the New York City unemployment lines.

After three months of looking, I found a job as a claims investigator for Capitol Casualty and Auto Insurance. It was a depressing career move for a man with my education, but at least it was a job. I soon discovered it was impossible to live like a normal person in Manhattan on an insurance investigator's salary. I had to pay the mortgage, pay the condo assessment, pay the real estate tax, the Federal income tax, the State income tax, the City income tax, add in the utilities, and if I wanted to eat, too, I had to go on overtime. As much overtime as possible. And then moonlight as a comparison shopper on my days off and during vacation and even sick days. All because of the damn condo.

Elizabeth took a higher paying job as a legal secretary so she'd still have enough money to feed Bloomingdale's and Lord & Taylor, with maybe a little left over for Macy's.

Meanwhile, I was starting to actually enjoy the investigative part of my work. I was using my psychology training in an unexpected arena: uncovering fraudulent claims from among the hundreds filed against our company every month. Although the money wasn't good, the work was a lot more exciting than academia or human relations. And with my talent for research, I began to wonder aloud whether an investigative career might turn out to be a good career move for me.

That was when Liz must have realized I wasn't going to be able to keep her in the style to which she wanted to become accustomed, and decided to trade up in the husband department. While I was enduring sleepless nights working two jobs, Liz was enjoying her nights sleeping with Milton Goldman, one of the partners at the law firm where she worked.

By the time our divorce was final, she had run through everything in our joint bank accounts, piled up nearly fifteen thousand dollars in credit card debt, and forced me into personal bankruptcy. In the final settlement, she offered to sign over her share of the condo in exchange for me agreeing to pay all our joint debts. Unfortunately, I had been too busy investigating insurance fraud to pay much attention to what was happening to Manhattan real estate values, and I discovered that the condo was worth twenty-two thousand dollars less than what I still owed on the mortgage.

Liz married Milton three days after the divorce came through. A few months later, the condo was repossessed and as a personal favor, Liz's new husband helped me file for bankruptcy to get out from under the bill collectors.

The people at Capitol Casualty and Auto Insurance didn't like the idea of someone with money problems handling expensive insurance claims. So they dredged through my records, decided I was approving damage awards that exceeded the company's guidelines, and proceeded to fire me.

In the new era of corporate downsizing and restructuring, there seemed to be no more jobs available for someone with my background, as at every interview, I was competing against a huge pool of unemployed MBA's looking for work. They made my master's in psychology seem superfluous.

I reached the low point of my life within a year of the divorce. I was living alone in a slum building on the Lower East Side, my only income slim checks from unemployment insurance. When word came that my mother had passed away, I had so little money that I was forced to hitchhike to Florida to attend her funeral. I was too ashamed to let my father know how far I had fallen, afraid of what the disappointment might do to his already broken heart.

The loss of self-esteem affected me on most days like a low-grade fever, dulling my senses and deadening my interest in the outside world. The depression wasn't severe enough to trigger suicidal impulses, but it was enough for me to surrender, to give up the effort to succeed at anything meaningful, for fear that once again I would see it all come crashing down upon me.

That was when Professor DeBray reentered my life.

At Columbia, he once taught a course in The Psychology of Death. For me, it had been one of those no-brainer courses I signed up for to pad my credits. I never expected to develop a rapport with this stuffy old man who had such eccentric ideas about mortality. Nevertheless, we got along well, and kept in touch, even after I moved on to NYU.

I'm not quite sure how he found out about my desperate straits. Perhaps it was the academic grapevine. More likely, knowing the Professor, he had been monitoring my progress for some reason known only to him.

Still, if not for my desperate circumstances, I probably never would have accepted DeBray's job offer. It was freelance work. No benefits. The pay was two hundred dollars for each valid interview, plus a daily rate, plus mileage charges and motel money when I had to stay on the road overnight. It wasn't much money, but he promised I would be pretty much on my own, following up the leads he gave me. And I would be using, on a regular basis, both my psychology training and investigative experience.

That's how I ended up breaking into this darkened chamber in Northeastern Pennsylvania to hear Laura Duquesne's incredible story.

FOUR

If what she said could be proven, if some mistake had been made, and Harrison Duquesne turned up alive just as she claimed, it would be the paranormal equivalent of bringing back rocks from the moon.

DeBray was going to be delighted when he heard the tape of this interview, I thought. It was the Professor's dream: a clinical subject who came back with otherwise unobtainable information acquired while she was brain-dead.

There'd be another best-selling book in it for the Professor.

And even if it didn't turn out to be true, there'd definitely be extra money in it for me, maybe quite a bit, depending on how long the investigation took.

"I think we'd better go back to the beginning," I told her.

I had to be careful now, follow the proper methodology, get it all on the tape. Lay the proper foundation, the Professor always instructed me. Follow the format. Gather the basic data first. Avoid asking leading questions. Keep the subject on track and avoid digressions.

"I thought you wanted to know what happened to me on the other side," she said.

"Of course I do," I assured her. "I want to hear everything you remember about your experience. But it's better if we take it in sequence. I want you to tell me everything you remember about the accident. Not only the factual aspects, but your feelings and emotions at the time. The more specific details you can recall, the better."

"I don't remember much about how the accident happened," she said. "My husband was driving and I was asleep at the time. I think he must have fallen asleep, too, and the car went out of control."

"That's okay, just pick it up from wherever you remember."

I sat back, ready to check off the correlating N-DERPs on the interview sheets.

No two interviews were ever identical, but with all the interviews I had done, there always seemed to be a common sequence of events that emerged. It didn't seem to matter whether the subject had deep religious beliefs or not. I had interviewed professed atheists, and their experiences were just as intense as those of the Born-Again Christians who quoted Bible passages from memory and tried to convert me. It also didn't matter how their deaths occurred, whether from shootings, natural causes or accidents. The same patterns always surfaced. Male or female, young or old, they all described basically the same experience. Similar results have been reported by NDE researchers in other countries, which indicates that the near-death experience is a cross-cultural phenomenon.

The average subject describes four or five events that match DeBray's Near-Death Reference Points. Seven or eight matches is considered the high range. Very rarely does anyone get a correlation over nine. The most I ever heard about was twelve. That was the famous case of Bridgette Andrews, whom the Professor singled out for special analysis in his book.

"Like I said, I must have dozed off," Laura began her account. "When I woke up, the car was bouncing over the median. I guess it was the bumping that woke me. I looked over at Harry, but it was dark and he was slumped over the wheel. I remember screaming, but not even hearing my own voice. Everything seemed to happen in slow motion, the car slamming into the guardrail, the door on my side popping open from the impact, and my body being thrown from the car. I hit the guardrail and it felt like my chest was caving in. The car kept going. I found out later that the car smashed right through the guardrail and fell two hundred feet into a dry stream bed, where the gas tank exploded."

"So the last you saw of your husband was when the car went over the cliff."

"But that doesn't mean he's dead."

"Of course not," I pretended to agree, knowing it was best not to argue with a subject, especially this early in an interview. "I'm sorry for interrupting you. Please go on."

"I found out later someone called 911 from a car phone," she continued. "If it wasn't for that call, I would have died right there on the side of the road, long before the ambulance arrived."

"Would that have made any difference, dying on the road instead of dying in the hospital?"

"I don't think so."

"But in the hospital, you were surrounded by doctors and nurses," I pointed out. My background in insurance investigations made it hard to conduct an interview without trying to trip up the subject. DeBray sometimes accused me of acting like a cop in an interrogation room, but I think he secretly liked my efforts to weed out the phonies.

"They did everything medically possible to bring you back."

"They didn't bring me back," she said. "I told you they gave up on me. The only reason I came back was to find my husband."

At least she was consistent.

"Sorry again," I murmured. "Please continue."

"I was still conscious when the paramedics arrived," she went on. "They wrapped something around my neck, slid a board underneath me, and tried to stop the bleeding. They hooked me up to a telemetry unit that sent my vital signs to the hospital. I found out later that I lost almost three pints of blood before the paramedics arrived. Half of that turned out to be internal bleeding, which nobody realized until I was at the hospital."

I wondered about the injuries described in her file. If she hit a metal guardrail at seventy miles an hour, she would have suffered severe damage to her chest muscles, upper rib damage and probably a ruptured lung, possibly a collapsed heart. She didn't appear to be suffering any residual pain. But she seemed to be immobilized. The only part of her body that exhibited any movement was her head. I made a note to question her about it later.

"Did they give you any medication at the scene?" I asked. It was important to keep track of any drugs she might have been administered. Some critics of NDE research claimed the experiences were simply the result of pharmacological reactions.

"They hooked me up to an IV," she said. "And by the time I was in the ambulance, they were giving me plasma, too. But they said they couldn't give me any painkillers until the doctors examined me, because it might mask internal injuries."

"Were you in shock?"

"If you mean was I hallucinating, the answer is no. I was in pain. I knew things were bad when they wouldn't do anything to kill the pain. I was conscious all the way. They were talking about my husband being dead, as if they thought I couldn't hear them. I remember them wheeling me into the Emergency entrance, and everybody staring at me, even the admitting nurse. I knew I was a horrible sight, all bloody and dirty. I was really embarrassed to have people see me like that. That's funny, isn't it? To be thinking you're going to die and still be worried about how you look?"

She broke into a smile as she admitted to that fleeting moment of vanity. It was hard for me to picture her ever looking anything less than lovely, even with IV and plasma drips attached to her.

"I was so happy to be there," she continued.

"You mean in the operating room?"

"Yes. It's odd, but when they wheeled me into the operating room, I had an intense feeling of well-being, almost as if I had come home from a long trip. And the feeling kept growing inside me. I just felt . . . overwhelmingly happy."

Bingo, I thought. That was the first N-DERP on the Professor's list, and she hit it right on cue: *Sudden Feelings of Peace and Happiness.*

"The Doctor bent over me, and I'm sure I must have smiled at him," she said. "I wanted to tell him the pain was gone, but I couldn't move my lips. I couldn't talk, but I didn't care. I didn't care about anything. I just gave myself up to this wonderful feeling. The pain was gone, and I felt such joy, it was the most exquisite feeling you could ever imagine."

I checked the little square for N-DERP #2: *Total Cessation of Pain*.

"I heard one of the ER nurses say, 'We lost her.' I knew she meant I was dead. But I couldn't understand why, if I was supposed to be dead, I could still hear her voice. I heard the doctor's voice, too. He got really excited and started shouting for some drugs. The other nurse said my heart stopped beating, and she, too, said I was dead. I felt sorry for them that they weren't able to save me. But I didn't mind being dead. The pain was gone, and I felt so peaceful, as if all my troubles were finally over. I felt free."

I checked off reference point #3: *Hearing The Announcement of Death*.

"You could still hear them talking?" I probed.

"I know it sounds strange," she said. "But that's how it happened. For a while, I was convinced they were making some sort of mistake. I thought their machines weren't working properly, or the nurses were playing some kind of joke on the doctors. Because you know, I could hear what was going on. How could I be dead, if I could still hear them, right?"

That was N-DERP #4: *The Moment of Disbelief*. So far, she was tracking perfectly through the Professor's reference series.

"But then," she frowned. "I couldn't hear what they were saying. There was this noise . . . it was terribly irritating, like, I don't know . . . like a buzzing sound that kept getting louder and louder."

Only about one out of every ten subjects claimed to hear the sound. Some describe it as a clicking noise, others hear it as a low hum. I had never heard it described as a buzzing sound, but I checked off N-DERP #5: *The Strange Sound*.

"I felt a little lurch, as if something inside me came unglued, and then I had this weird sensation, as if I was actually drifting out of myself, not straight up, but through the top of my head."

I nodded. It was the standard exit point subjects reported for N-DERP #6: *Separation from the Body*.

"The next thing I knew, I was floating up near the ceiling, looking down at my body. I felt sorry for myself, because they had all those tubes in me. There was a respirator tube down my throat, plus the IV bags and the blood plasma, and one of the doctors was sticking a big needle into my chest."

That would have been the adrenaline, I knew, injected directly into the heart to revive it. For a moment, I felt angry at the doctors for defiling her body with their instruments.

I quickly shook off the thought and checked off N-DERP #7: *Looking Down on the Body*. I noticed that Laura's responses were already moving into the high range of correlation on DeBray's profile, and we were just getting started.

"And then the nurse handed the doctor two round paddles with plastic handles. He pressed them against my chest, and my whole body jumped on the operating table. He did it again and again, and I watched my body jump and my legs and arms thrash around like a rag doll being shaken. It didn't bother me, because I wasn't in my body, and I couldn't feel anything anymore. I tried to tell the doctor it was useless, but he didn't hear me. Somehow I floated down from the ceiling and tried to get his attention by touching him on the shoulder, but my hands seemed to go right through him."

She paused for a moment, reconsidering.

"I'm not really sure about that part," she corrected herself. "I'm not sure if I really had hands at that point, or if it was just something that looked like hands, but whatever I tried to touch him with, I couldn't seem to make contact. It was like I was a ghost."

That was N-DERP #8: *The Ethereal State*. I was beginning to feel uneasy with her story. She was using her own words, which made her narrative slightly different from the other interviews I conducted, but she was hitting each of the N-DERPs precisely right. She was going through them in the same sequence Professor DeBray had formulated from his years of research. And she hadn't missed a single reference point on his list yet.

"All of a sudden, I seemed to get pulled into a long, dark tube. It was like I was in a vacuum, and I was just being sucked through it at a tremendous speed."

This was the single most universally agreed-upon aspect of the near-death experience. It was described in similar terms by every one of my subjects and those of other interviewers around the world: it was N-DERP #9: *The Tunnel*.

There were questions I was supposed to ask, points of clarification suggested in the Interview Guidelines. But as she continued to talk, I forgot about them. I forgot about my own usually skeptical comments. I was by now caught up in how seamlessly and effortlessly her recollections flowed from one reference point to the next.

She described #10: *The Awareness of a Higher Presence*, #11: *The Golden Glow*, and #12: *The Appearance of a Guide*.

My hand trembled with excitement as I checked off #12. At that point she already matched the famous case of Bridgette Andrews, and she still had twelve more N-DERPs to go. Her voice grew hushed and reverent when she moved on through #13: *Entering the World of Light*, and #14: *Meeting The Being of Light*.

I checked the input needle on the tape recorder to be certain everything she said was being preserved. This interview was too perfect to risk losing it through some stupid error.

She described N-DERP #15: *The Life Playback,* in greater detail than I had ever heard before.

At this point, I no longer cared whether she was telling the truth or not. I just wanted to get it all down and get the tape back to the Professor. There was bound to be a bonus for this interview.

She went on with N-DERP #16: *The Revelation of All Knowledge,* which to me was always the most intriguing of all the reference points, and one which less than ten percent of near-deathers reported.

"I suddenly understood the entire plan of the universe," she said. "I knew when the world was going to end, and how it was going to happen. I knew the entire master plan. And the strangest thing is that it seemed as if I was simply remembering something I had known before I was born, but had forgotten. Does that sound strange?"

Not to me. There was N-DERP #17: *Recalling Lost Memory.*

In N-DERP #18: *Return of the Senses,* she gave one of the most detailed descriptions I had yet heard of the verdant meadows and flowers, the sparkling rivers and the apparently incredible luminosity of the colors with which the other world was drenched.

And then we came to the part of the interview that she had alluded to at the outset. Here, verbatim, is what I recorded on N-DERP #19: *The Reunion with Loved Ones:*

"I was taken to a lovely white Cape Cod house with a cedar shake roof and a big bay window in front, just like the one we lived in when I was a child in Binghamton. My father came out of the house first. He died almost ten years ago, after a long illness. The left side of his body had been paralyzed from a stroke, and he was confined to a wheelchair before he died, but when he came out of that white house, he was walking normally again. He looked healthy and happy, and so did Mom. They were so happy to see me. We hugged and kissed. All my grandparents, who are dead, were inside the house. I could see them through the front window. And my little cousin Betty, who was killed in a gun accident last year, she came running out of the house to meet me."

Her voice faltered. I was afraid she going to be overcome with emotion, but she swallowed, caught her breath, thrust out her chin, and continued the narrative.

"There were so many people in the house, I don't know how they all fit. Dead aunts and uncles, cousins, friends, even Mrs. Enright, my favorite high school teacher. It was like a big welcoming party, all these wonderful people who died before me coming to greet me. There was only one person missing."

I had seen other subjects break down and cry during interviews, but I had never felt as much anguish as I did when the tears began to well up in Laura's eyes.

"There was only one person missing," she repeated.

I wanted to take her hand in mine, wipe away her tears and tell her everything was going to be okay. But that would violate the Professor's warnings against involvement. And this interview was potentially too important to screw up by violating the rules.

"Who was missing?" I asked in a gentle voice, already knowing, of course, what she was going to say, but needing to get it on the tape.

"My husband was missing." She choked on the words. "I kept looking for my husband, but he wasn't there."

"You're certain of that?"

"I'm positive," she said, her chin still trembling. "All the people I ever knew who had died were in that house, except for my husband. I couldn't find him. I ran through the house and out into the back yard, but he wasn't there."

Up until that moment in her account, everything she said had been consistent with previous NDE research. This was the first deviation.

"Why do you think you couldn't find him?" I asked.

"The Being of Light said he hadn't arrived yet. He said Harrison was still alive."

"But you thought your husband was dead, didn't you?"

"At that point, yes, I thought he was dead," she agreed. "I heard the paramedics talking about his death in the ambulance, and also at the hospital, when they were working on me. But the Being told me Harrison was still alive."

"Maybe the Being of Light made a mistake," I said, feeling foolish as soon as the words came out of my mouth. What were we talking about here? Hallucinations? Dreams? Illusions? It certainly couldn't be ghosts, no matter how believable Laura's story was, because a ghost would surely know who was dead and who was alive.

"No," she insisted. "Everyone I met on the other side told me the same thing. That's when the Being of Light told me I had to go back. It wasn't my time yet."

I checked off N-DERP #20: *The Order to Return*.

"I didn't want to go back. I wanted to stay there, where it was so peaceful."

That was #21: The *Desire to Remain*. She had achieved a perfect score so far, and incredibly, she still had more to say!

N-DERP #22: *The Assignment* is something that near-deathers often feel they were given when they were told to return. Although most of them report some form of a spiritual transformation, and subsequently alter their lifestyles to better serve humanity, less than two percent of all DeBray's subjects can ever put into words the specific assignment with which they were sent back. Laura seemed to understand her assignment perfectly.

"They all seemed sad to see me go," she continued. "But the Being of Light said I had to go back, that I had to find the man I love, that he needed me, that I had to save his life."

This, I knew, would be the the most exciting aspect of the interview for Professor DeBray. In spite of the protocol I was supposed to follow, I was certain he would want me to pause here, to challenge her, to test her conviction and credibility on this point.

"Your husband is dead," I challenged her, wanting to be gentle, but knowing I had to state it as bluntly as possible to eliminate any ambiguity on the tape. "He died in the car crash."

"There has to be some sort of mistake," she said firmly. "Otherwise, why would I have been sent back to find him?"

"The coroner identified your husband's body," I said. "It's all in the newspaper clipping that was sent to us."

"The coroner was wrong," Laura insisted.

Her eyes were dry now. Dry and clear and strong and convinced of the truth of what she was saying. In that respect, she was just like all the other subjects I had interviewed. Once they told their stories, they'd never budge, never admit that there might be some other explanation for what they thought they had experienced.

"You don't believe me," she said. "I can see in your eyes that you don't believe me."

"I told you, I just do the interviews," I responded. "It's not up to me to decide what the truth is. All I know is that your husband is officially dead."

"So was I," she countered. "I was officially dead too. But here I am, talking to you."

"They found your husband's body in the wreckage," I said softly. "His body was badly burned, but they were able to come up with a positive identification."

"If he was dead, I would have seen him on the other side."

"Maybe you just missed him," I tried to humor her. "Maybe he was visiting with his own dead relatives, while you were visiting with yours."

"No," she insisted. "If he was dead, I would have seen him."

Logic, such as it is in matters as speculative as these, was on her side. Being greeted by dead relatives was one of the more consistent elements in the NDE stories. There were even some cases in which the subjects were shocked to meet relatives whose deaths they hadn't previously known about. I had no answer for why she didn't see her dead husband among the other relatives.

In any event, I felt I had enough on the subject, so I went on to N-DERP #23: *The Return to the Body,* and wrapped up the interview with N-DERP #24: The *Loss* of *Mystical Knowledge.* Unfortunately, all responses so far indicate that all that wonderful knowledge revealed to near-deathers has to stay on the other side, where it presumably awaits their return.

When the interview was over, I felt I had participated in an historic event. Never before, to the best of my knowledge, had anyone ever achieved a perfect score on DeBray's Near-Death Reference Points. I slumped back in my chair, exhausted.

But Laura wasn't done yet.

"Now I want to show you something," she said.

I watched her right hand struggle awkwardly with the tightly wrapped sheet, until she finally succeeded in pulling away part of the fabric. It revealed a heavy leather restraint circling her wrist. With a shock, I realized that was why she hadn't been moving. A quick examination revealed other restraints circling her legs and waist and upper body.

"Do you see what they've done to me?" she asked.

Her eyes pleaded with me, and her fingers motioned for me to take her hand. Knowing it was wrong, I nevertheless reached out to her. Her palm felt warm, her fingers were small and delicate. Her soft flesh made my own hand seem crude and heavy to me as she squeezed.

"Please help me get out of here," she begged.

I wanted to pull my hand away, afraid of getting involved, wondering how this was all going to sound on the tape. But as strong as I was, I couldn't seem to release my hand from her gentle grip.

"I have to find my husband," she pleaded. "I came back from the dead to look for him. But they won't let me out of here."

"I'm sure they'll release you when you're fully recovered," I said in a cautious voice. I didn't like having this part of the conversation recorded.

"They don't want me to recover," she said. "As soon as you leave, they'll drug me again. They keep me unconscious for weeks at a time..."

She stopped speaking when the door behind me opened. For a moment, the room was flooded with light from the hallway. I turned in time to see a massive shadow slowly move in front of the entrance, blocking off most of the light.

It was one of the two "enforcers" I had been warned about. Even now I can't begin to estimate his weight. He was bigger than any human being I had ever seen up close. His enormous bulk made the doorway look small. I remember wondering where they ever found a white uniform big enough to fit him.

With the placid assurance of a man who knew his sheer size gave him an advantage over ordinary human beings, he didn't even attempt to enter the room. Simply by positioning his bulk in the doorway, he eliminated any hope I might have of escaping.

Without saying a word to me, he flipped open a compact cellular phone. It looked ridiculously small in his massive hands. The buttons on the keypad were obviously not designed for fingers as thick and clumsy as his. He had to use the tip of a pencil to activate the pre-programmed numbers he wanted.

His voice was calm and unemotional as he spoke into the phone.

"We've got an intruder down here," he said.

FIVE

It isn't unusual for an institution whose patients are prone to violent psychotic episodes to employ an "enforcer," an attendant of such size and strength, his very presence can be intimidating.

In most institutions, they serve a benign purpose. Their job is protect the staff and the patient population from harm, whether self-inflicted or otherwise.

There were supposed to be two Samoans working as "enforcers" at the Walden Clinic, according to our informant. The one blocking the doorway seemed capable of controlling any problems short of a full-scale riot. Why they needed two of these South Sea giants was a mystery to me.

Somewhere in the distance, I heard a door open and close, followed by the rapid approach of footsteps and anxious voices. Help was on the way, as if he needed it.

I turned away from the waiting enforcer. With my actions thus shielded from his view, I carefully removed the tiny cassette from the tape recorder. Laura watched with frightened eyes as I hid the tape.

Afraid of being overheard, her lips mouthed a silent plea for help.

Behind me, the reinforcements had arrived. I turned to see a giant who could have been a brother to the first, the only difference being the gold earring in the second Samoan's right ear. A third man stepped between them, switched on the light, and entered the room. He was dwarfed by the size of the enforcers, but he was still a few inches taller than me. He was well-muscled, and had a square block of a head topped off by a Marine-style crew cut. His name tag identified him as Roland Metzger.

"We've been waiting for you," he said in a menacing voice.

The two giants followed him through the doorway. The room suddenly seemed a lot smaller.

"Son of a bitch has a tape recorder," the first enforcer said.

I tried to retreat, but my way was blocked by the hospital table to which Laura was secured. Behind me, I could feel the thick leather restraining bands that immobilized her body. Somehow, my hand found hers. Our fingers wrapped themselves tightly together in a foolish gesture of solidarity. There wasn't much I could do. I worried that, simply by coming here, I might have provoked later reprisals against her.

"Get him," Metzger commanded.

Moving with a speed that belied their size, the Samoans tore me away from Laura and dragged me into the light. One of them grabbed my hair, snapping my head back. His partner extracted my wallet. My chin was turned from side to side. Some sort of examination was taking place.

"Bring him closer," said a voice. Not Metzger. It was a fourth person, someone speaking from the other side of the doorway. "Hold him under the light."

The giants hustled me forward.

"No," said the voice. "It's not him."

The owner of the voice stood in the dim hallway. He was a tall man, probably around six-three, and much too thin for his height. He was wearing a dark, double-breasted business suit. Much of his face was lost in the shadows, but there was enough light to reveal a sharp nose and a narrow Van Dyke beard.

"Who are you?" the voice asked.

"My name is Theophanes Nikonos."

"An unusual name."

Beside me, Metzger was examining the contents of my wallet. He nodded to the voice, indicating that I was telling the truth.

"It's Greek," I said. "They call me Theo for short." I was trying my best to sound friendly and non-threatening.

"What are you doing here?" the voice asked, still cold and unemotional.

"I came to see Mrs. Duquesne."

"Why?"

"I'm a researcher. I wanted to ask some questions about her near-death experience."

Metzger handed my interview file to the voice.

"He had this stuff with him, Doctor Zydek. He was taking notes."

Zydek. At least I had a name to go with the voice.

"I'm sorry about sneaking in here," I apologized, hoping it would defuse the situation. "I guess I got a little too eager."

He ignored my apology as he leafed through the papers in the folder.

"Who sent you?" he asked, without looking up.

"The Institute for the Investigation of Anabiotic Phenomena."

"I never heard of them."

"It's a research group in New York. You can call them and confirm that I work for them. The telephone number is in the file folder."

"How did you find out about Mrs. Duquesne?"

"From a newspaper clipping. It's in the file, too."

"I mean about her being down here, in this specific room. How did you find out about that?"

"Guesswork, mostly. I didn't think you'd have her in with the rest of your patients."

Fortunately, the photocopy of our informant's letter wasn't in the file, a standard precaution we took to prevent curious interview subjects who might get their hands on the file from discovering who had reported them to us.

Doctor Zydek read through the file, flipping the pages slowly.

"You know you're on private property?" he said, again without looking up.

"I'm sorry, I really am," I apologized again.

"You were warned away earlier, weren't you?"

"Yes."

"I could have you arrested. I could call the police and have you thrown in jail."

I thought it was an idle threat; if he actually dared to call the police, they'd find out he was keeping Laura here against her will. I awaited his next move in silence, a silence dictated by cowardice rather than defiance. Because of my life as a typically desk-bound intellectual, I was ill-equipped for physical confrontation. Although I inherited a six-foot frame from my Greek ancestors, that same genealogy endowed me with a gaunt physique more suited to running the marathon than lifting weights. And since I'd spent most of my adult life in the lecture halls and libraries of academia rather than in health clubs, my rather limited physical gifts remained underdeveloped.

"Get rid of him," Zydek finally said.

"But he was recording what she said," Metzger protested.

"Keep the tape," Zydek said as he walked away. "I'll listen to it later."

Metzger fumbled with the tape recorder until he found the eject button and the door popped open, revealing the empty tape compartment.

He sneered, and his eyes were drawn to the small bulge in my shirt pocket. Two meaty fingers removed the tiny cassette from my pocket. With a smile he placed the cassette in his own shirt pocket, and then dropped the empty tape recorder to the floor and crushed the fragile plastic under his heel.

"Now get him the hell out of here," Metzger commanded. "I'll take care of her."

The twin giants, who hadn't relaxed their grip on me in all this time, dutifully shoved me towards the door. I twisted my head for one last look at Laura. I'll never forget the expression of terror on her face as Metzger reached out for her.

Nothing in my academic background prepared me for what happened next. They took me into the alley behind the clinic. The one with the earring slammed me against a wall and drove a fat knee into my groin, the force of the blow lifting me off my feet. My body seemed to explode with pain. Overcome by nausea, I watched the asphalt gutter fly up to hit me in the face. I remember my cheek bouncing when it hit the asphalt surface, but I didn't feel the impact.

Instinctively, I curled up into a protective fetal position. I lay there, gasping for breath and trying to vomit at the same time.

Strange shocks attacked my body. It took me a while to realize they were kicking at me.

How long the mauling went on, I don't know. I lost count of the blows, lost consciousness, and drifted off into the blessed peacefulness that comes when the body can no longer cope with pain.

All this was accomplished without the giants throwing a single punch. They had disposed of me with their feet, the way they might kick away an annoying clod of dirt. Fortunately for me, they were wearing rubber athletic shoes, which cushioned the shock of their blows. Although every inch of my body would ache for days, I wouldn't suffer any broken bones from the beating.

When I finally regained consciousness, it hurt too much to move. I lay in the gutter for what must have been an hour, waiting for the worst of the pain to subside. While I tried to regain some strength, my thoughts went back to Laura. Despite my own pain, I couldn't forget that last desperate look she gave me.

Near-deathers have always been the most fearless individuals I've ever met. Having already endured the process of dying and finding it to be a pleasant experience, they normally lose all fear of death or the pain that often precedes it.

But if Laura was no longer afraid of death, which for most of us is the ultimate terror, then what horror could possibly account for the fear I had seen in her face?

SIX

If what she said was true, Laura Duquesne had traveled deeper into the mysteries of death than any other human being.

The problem was whether to believe the story she brought back from her Stygian journey.

"Extraordinary. Absolutely extraordinary," the Professor said after I described the night's events. "I've been waiting ten years for this."

I was calling him from a pay phone at a Shell station, in downtown Scranton. Normally, I wouldn't file a report until I got back to New York, but I was in too much pain to drive back to the city that night.

"And you still have the tape?" DeBray couldn't conceal the delight in his voice.

After destroying my tape recorder, Metzger and the Samoans took all my paperwork and the NDE questionnaire. But the cassette they took from my pocket was a spare I always carried for longer interviews. The cassette on which I recorded Laura's interview was still safe inside my shirt, where I had slipped it when I turned my back to my attackers.

"That was very quick thinking," DeBray said.

I had expected the Professor to be furious at me for risking arrest to get the interview. His theories made him an easy target for the press, and the arrest of one of his employees could damage the Institute's reputation. But when he heard about the information Laura claimed to have brought back from the dead, he was too excited to worry about any possible illegalities.

"I'm not sure we should believe her," I cautioned him. "She might be making it up. Not all of it, maybe, but part of it. At least the part about her husband."

"But what if it turned out to be true?" he challenged me. "Do you realize the significance of what she told you?"

I could picture DeBray in the Institute's Greenwich Village office: a cluttered five-room condo on West Eighth Street that doubled as his living quarters. The Professor was overweight and tried to disguise his portly figure by wearing dark three-piece suits with the vests always tightly buttoned. He kept his grey hair long, spilling over his shirt collar and covering his ears. For a man well into his sixties, he had a remarkably strong, authoritative voice whose resonant tones enthralled countless audiences in lecture halls.

"If the information about her husband turns out to be true," he said, "it would prove once and for all that near-death experiences really are glimpses beyond the curtain, visits to the place where our souls live on after death."

The Professor had a way of overstating things. He'd take simple events and try to turn them into eternal truths. It always made me feel uncomfortable, but I knew his flair for exaggeration was one reason why his books and lectures were so successful. From the tone of his voice, I could tell he was already dreaming about another best-seller, probably jotting down notes even as we spoke.

"You're putting a lot of faith in her story," I cautioned him. "Wanting it to be true doesn't make it true."

"That's exactly the point," DeBray responded. "People buy my books, listen to my lectures, and walk away wondering if it's all true. They all want to believe there really is life after death. But I'm not foolish enough to think they're totally convinced, except for a few devoted followers. Most people are like you, Theo, like the disciple Thomas in the Bible, who wouldn't believe the claims of Jesus Christ until he could touch the wounds himself."

"It's human nature," I said. "You'll never convince most people."

"Unless you can prove Harrison Duquesne is still alive."

"I feel sorry for the woman, Professor. I really do. I'd like to help her. But this business about the husband being alive is just a fantasy on her part. A wishful fantasy."

"How can you be so sure?" DeBray asked.

"Well, for starters, the newspaper article said he died in the crash."

"Do you believe everything you read?"

"His body was positively identified."

"Why are you fighting me on this, Theo?"

"I'm not fighting you. I just don't believe the husband is alive. All the information we have indicates he's dead. Even she herself admits no one believes her."

"That's exactly my point, Theo. She's given you a piece of information that no one believes except her. And why does she believe it? Because the information was given to her on the other side."

"That doesn't mean the information was authentic."

There was a long sigh at the other end of the line.

"Listen, Theo, the Institute has conducted more than three thousand interviews over the last ten years. That's a tiny fraction of the twenty-five million people who claim to have had NDE's." Like most self-promoters, DeBray had the habit of repeating the same key facts in every conversation. "We've been looking for patterns, similarities in the responses that would demonstrate a common reality experienced by diverse subjects. And we've been successful. We have thousands of cases that correlate with similar experiences that have been documented since the beginning of recorded history."

"I know all about it, Professor." I said, tired of hearing the same old speech.

"Those three thousand cases form the largest database in NDE research," DeBray continued, ignoring my comment. "We have the names, the dates, the documentation, the N-DERP profiles, the psychosocial characteristics of the subjects all loaded in our computer, where they've been analyzed, cross-referenced, and broken out by every conceivable characteristic. It's all been done very objectively, with much of the field work performed by skeptics like yourself. All very scientific. We've got everything we ever hoped to get. Except for one element."

"A verifiable fact brought back from the other side," I said, recalling the final blank space on the back of the questionnaire.

"Exactly! All these years, I've been waiting for an interview to produce a single confirmable fact that would have been impossible to obtain except through communication with the dead. Thanks to your initiative in breaking in to see the Duquesne woman, I think we finally have one."

"Her responses were too good to be true," I said. "It's the first time anyone had a perfect score on the N-DERP profile."

"That's another reason why this is a landmark interview."

"It's also another reason to be skeptical," I said. "Her story was too perfect. She had all the details worked out. There weren't any loose ends."

"You think she was overcompensating, working too hard to convince you?"

"Yes I do. She must have read your book and was playing it all back, almost verbatim in some places."

"Before I ever wrote a book, people were describing near-death experiences in the same terms as Mrs. Duquesne. There's nothing unique about the terminology. It goes back to the days of the ancient Greeks."

"I know, I know," I said, cutting him off. "But she didn't miss a single one of your reference points. Not one. Doesn't that raise any red flags in your mind?"

"Not when you consider how long she was clinically dead. All the research indicates the depth and intensity of the near-death experience can be directly related to the length of time the subject's vital signs were extinguished. That would explain why she scored so well on the N-DERP sequence."

"She's claiming one hour and twenty minutes of flat brain waves," I said.

"That means she was dead longer than any other subject in our records. Therefore, she had more time to experience the complete sequence."

"But an hour and twenty minutes of flat brain waves? That's impossible, isn't it?"

"The only similar cases have been patients who remained in a persistently vegetative state. Which is why the attending physician's statement is critical."

"You're assuming he'll back her up."

"If she was so intent on fabricating a story, as you keep insisting she did, why would she lie about the one fact that can be most easily checked? Have you made an appointment with the doctor?"

The teen-age girl at the cash register inside the Mobil station was watching me. Her expression suggested she was trying to decide whether to call the police. She was safe behind her bullet-proof glass partition, but I obviously looked like trouble. My shirt and pants were covered with mud, and there was some blood still oozing from the side of my head, where it had struck the curb.

"It seems to me the physician who attended her when she died is your most important follow-up interview," the Professor said. "Be certain you get the doctor to sign his statement, and get a copy of all the relevant hospital records. We'll need them if he tries to deny anything later on. Doctors have a tendency to get embarrassed about being quoted in these cases."

"I hope we're not the ones who get embarrassed," I protested. "I'm really uneasy about the whole situation."

"I can appreciate the way you feel," DeBray said. "But perhaps you're being a bit hasty with your judgment. When you investigate further, you may change your mind. Speak to the doctor, find out more about the woman, and then check out what really happened in the accident. You were an insurance investigator, Theo. You know what to look for."

"That could take some time."

"Stay there for a week," he quickly said. "Stay there as long as it takes for you to prove conclusively that she's telling the truth."

"Or that she's lying."

"I'd prefer to think she's telling the truth."

"If I'm here for a week, it could cost you an extra thousand dollars in per diem and motel expenses, and I might end up proving it was all a fantasy on her part."

Assuming, of course, I would be able to avoid the Samoans. Since I was still able to stand and breathe normally, I was guessing I didn't suffer any serious injury from the beating they gave me. But every part of me ached, particularly my ribs, which seemed to have absorbed most of the punishment. And the

Samoans were probably going to come looking for me again when they discovered they had the wrong tape.

"It would be well worth a thousand dollars to learn the truth," the Professor said. "Maybe I should drive up and join you. I'd like to meet the young woman, talk to her myself."

"They'd never let you in to see her. After tonight, they'll probably increase their security."

"A shame," DeBray sighed. "But maybe it's for the best. At least she won't be giving any other interviews. I wouldn't want word of this to leak out."

We talked a while longer, but one thing seemed clear. The Professor was interested in everything about this case except for the one aspect that troubled me most: why was Laura Duquesne strapped to a table in a guarded room, cut off from any contact with the outside world?

SEVEN

Classic psychology might explain Professor DeBray's role in my life as that of a surrogate father figure. My own father, after the death of my mother, fled the dangerous environs of Miami and went back to his native Greece, where he now drinks ouzo and plays dominos with his friends in the shadow of the Parthenon, happily oblivious to the problems of his son.

Certainly DeBray had come to my rescue, as any good father would, when there was no one else to whom I could turn. He had provided me with work, an income, even a measure of respect.

But what was more important, and was the single most defining aspect of our relationship, was that he had engaged my mind. I felt comfortable with him, not because of any particular emotional bonding, but because of the teacher-student relationship which had soon developed. For reasons I am only now beginning to fully understand, he seemed intent on educating me in the area of his expertise far beyond the requirements of the work for which he had hired me.

At first, of course, there were intellectual conflicts. I initially approached NDE research with the same skeptical attitude I had towards the existence of God. Despite my upbringing in the Eastern Orthodox Church, I was an agnostic. I neither believed nor disbelieved in such articles of religious faith as the concept of an afterlife. This attitude was reinforced by my academic training, which emphasized the Newtonian approach. Like any good empiricist, I believed only that which could be proven, whether by experiment, by observation or by logic. And to me, what the Professor was engaged in bordered on tabloid science.

Knowing this, DeBray supplied me with mountains of data, including the raw, unedited research material he used for his books and articles. He assigned me an enormous reading list; some books came from his personal library, and others I had to track down in various university and public libraries. Before long, I was spending all my spare time in the familiar company of books and research papers. It was exactly the kind of activity I needed to take my mind off my personal problems.

I started out, at the Professor's direction, by reading the complete works of Raymond Moody, who coined the phrase "near-death experience;" psychologist Kenneth Ring, who did the first statistical analysis of NDE's; Dr. Elisabeth Kubler-Ross, who studied the processes of dying; Melvin Morse, who studied NDEs in children; Dr. Michael Sabom, the eminent cardiologist who did his NDE research in hospitals where he could also interview the attending nurses and physicians; and dozens of other modern researchers, including Wilson, Rawlings, Barham and Zaleski.

Soon I was moving back in time on the Professor's reading list to famous figures such as the great psychologist Carl Jung, who described his own NDE in his *Memories, Dreams and Reflections*; the English essayist Thomas DeQuincy's account of his mother's NDE in *Suspira De Profundis*; as well as obscure 19th-century researchers such as the Swiss geologist Albert Hein, who interviewed thirty mountain climbers who had survived near-fatal falls.

The more I studied, the more fascinated I became with the enormous amount of documentation available. I read the accounts of the Native American visionary Black Elk; the death legends of the Hopis, the Aztecs, the Lakota Sioux. I found amazing parallels between their beliefs and those of the Polynesians, the Nigerian Yorubas, the ancient Essenes, and hundreds of other tribes, indigenous peoples and religions, some of them so remote and primitive it would have been impossible for them to be influenced by other populations. In every one of those cultures there is a belief that the spirit leaves the body at death, remains nearby for a time, (which varies from moments to weeks, depending on the culture) and occasionally returns to the body, much to the amazement of observers.

The course of study the Professor laid out led me through Medieval times, and some source materials which were difficult to locate, such as Drythelm's Vision, as related by the Venerable Bede in the *Ecclesiastical History of the English People*. I had an easier time finding Book Four of *The Dialogues of Gregory the Great*, in which a young soldier brought back with him from the dead descriptions of meadows and strange light.

Part of my research involved a comparative study of religions, which duplicated some of the work I had done in college. I reread Saint Paul's Second Letter to the Corinthians, which contained his stunning description of an NDE and apparent out-of-body experience. I studied the Kathin Upanishad, the works of Lao Tzu, Buddhism's description of the Land of Amitahbe, the Zoroastrian Book of Arda Viz, the Book of Mormon, the Talmud, the Bible and the Q'uran.

But for me, by far, the most fascinating material was also the most ancient. These included the Tibetan Book of the Dead, the Egyptian Book of the Dead, the Pyramid Texts, Setme's *Seven Halls of the Underworld*, the *Descent of Innana*, the *Story of Gilgamesh*, and the famous account of the resurrection of Er in Plato's *Republic*.

I studied the scientific explanations for the NDE, starting with the most easily dismissed. Drug-induced hallucinations, for example, can be discarded as a cause for all those thousands of NDEs that took place *before* such drugs were even invented. In addition, some of the strongest NDE recollections are reported by those subjects who died in accidents and were never administered drugs before their recovery.

The most common current explanations revolve around medical theories such as hypoxia, in which deprivation of the brain's oxygen supply creates a brief burst of light before death. But the light reported by near-deathers apparently never goes out, as would be the expected outcome, but instead continues growing in intensity. Each of the theories, as convincing as they may sound, has an equally convincing rebuttal. And then of course, there are the more extreme theories, such as Sagan's birth-canal syndrome, which, to me, are just plain laughable.

What the Professor put me through was the equivalent of a four-year college course, compressed into a year of reading, discussion and study. If it seems like an extraordinary accomplishment, remember that I had no other friends or activities to distract me. All the money I earned from the near-death interviews went for food, rent and accumulated bills. And research and the accumulation of knowledge had always been my favorite pursuit.

But even after completing the research the Professor assigned me, my attitude toward NDEs remained basically agnostic, the position favored by most scientists when confronted with any unproven concept. I neither believed nor disbelieved.

Nevertheless, the deeper I delved, the less convinced I was that the NDE was purely a death fantasy. Something was clearly happening. How else could I explain how a five-year-old girl in Ulster County, New York could come back from an NDE describing the same meadows and crystalline light as Gregory the Great, the same bejeweled trees as those of the Zoroastrian legends?

Yet, like my inability to believe in something as elusive as the nature of God, the truth about the near-death experience always seemed to be just beyond my reach.

EIGHT

When I opened my eyes in the morning, it seemed as if all the connective tissues in my body had congealed and stiffened, turning into an aching glue that immobilized my joints. The slightest movement became a painful ordeal. Every kick that had been administered the night before had left its own individual, residual ache. My arms hurt more than my ribs, especially my left arm, which had taken three or four direct hits on the bicep. It took an hour soaking in a hot bath before I could move about with anything approaching normality.

Following the Professor's advice, my first stop after breakfast was to interview Doctor Ranjeet Subdhani, the physician who had attended Laura at the moment of her death. Since I didn't have an appointment, the receptionist made me sit in the waiting room until the doctor was finished with all his scheduled patients. That took most of the morning. Shortly before lunchtime, when she was certain there would be no more last-minute walk-ins, she finally gave me grudging permission to enter his office.

Doctor Subdhani greeted me with a gentle, almost feminine handshake. His words were soft-spoken, pronounced with the peculiar British colonial accent that was common on the Indian subcontinent. With his custom-fitted grey silk suit, he looked more like the manager of an expensive Indian restaurant than a small-town doctor. He wore thin, wire-rimmed glasses, the kind

Ghandhi used to favor, and a thick gold-and-diamond Rolex wristwatch. A blood vessel in his left eye had burst, flooding the eyeball with red. Like a lot of immigrant doctors I had met, he was probably working too hard at getting rich.

Subdhani seemed friendly enough until I told him I had been talking to Laura Duquesne. His manner stiffened when I handed him the Institute's standard release form granting me full access to her medical records. Technically, I could be charged with forging her signature on the document. But since she had given me verbal consent, I didn't think there would be a problem.

"For what purpose do you want this information?" Subdhani asked. "Are you her lawyer?"

"We need the medical records to corroborate her story." I gave him my business card and explained the work I did for Professor DeBray. "The Institute insists on third-party verification of the physical facts in these matters."

He shook his head in rapid and emphatic denial.

"DeBray is a fraud. I will not allow my name to be exploited by him. Neither my name nor that of the hospital."

"The name of the hospital is a matter of public record. You can't prevent the Institute from identifying the hospital."

"But I can stop you from using my name or any statements attributed to me." He slid the document with the forged signature back across the desk. "In spite of what you think, this form is nothing more than a request. Legally, I am not required to provide any information to you."

"You can't hide your role," I said. "You were identified in the newspapers as the attending physician."

"I never signed a death certificate for that woman."

I jotted down his comment in a small notebook. Until I was able to replace my tape recorder, the Professor would have to settle for handwritten notes.

"But you pronounced her dead," I said.

"There were five people involved in the decision to remove life support from Mrs. Duquesne. It wasn't my sole decision, nor was it my sole determination that the patient's vital signs had ceased. As a matter of fact, it was one of the nurses who first announced that the patient had expired."

"Laura remembers it the same way you do, Doctor."

He tilted his head slightly, as if he hadn't heard me right.

"I don't understand," he said.

"In the statement Laura gave me, she remembers very clearly a nurse with blue eyes saying 'I think we lost her.' At that point, she remembers you calling for three specific drugs."

"Impossible," Subdhani shook his head again, firmly dismissing the idea. "At that point in the procedure, she was already in full cardiac arrest. With the cessation of cardiac activity, the autonomic nervous system quickly begins to shut down. Although there might be some residual activity of the various senses, such activity would normally be overpowered by the massive shock to the nervous system produced by impending death. In my professional opinion, it would be impossible for her to hear, much less remember, any statements made in the operating room."

He was throwing out the usual smokescreen of medical jargon, the kind of technical terms doctors use as protective camouflage.

"Did you in fact ask for those drugs?" I pressed.

"Medications are routinely used to alter the chemical environment of the heart muscle so that it will respond to an electrical charge."

"So the answer is yes."

"Correct."

"She said you injected the drugs just below her left breast."

"When a patient suffers cardiac arrest, the standard procedure is to introduce all medication directly into the heart. Injection at any other location would be futile, since the circulatory system ceases functioning."

"A simple yes or no answer will do, Doctor."

He folded his hands on the desk in front of him. His fingers were narrow and carefully groomed, a surgeon's fingers.

"I was reviewing my procedures for you, Mr. Nikonos. I did nothing out of the ordinary. Nothing that any reasonable doctor wouldn't do."

"I'm not here to question your procedures," I said. I put away the notebook, hoping he might talk more freely if he thought he wasn't going on the record. "Nobody has even suggested you did anything wrong."

He ignored my attempt to set him at ease. He maintained his stiff, formal posture, and continued with his procedural review.

"After administration of the drugs, the EKG readings continued to register a total absence of cardiac activity. Blood pressure readings were flat. Carbon dioxide levels in the blood were elevated. The electroencephalogram was registering a flat brain wave. In a final attempt at resuscitation, I applied electrical stimulus to the patient."

"She remembers all of that, Doctor. Every bit of it."

"After three applications of electric shock, there was still no response on the part of the patient. All of us in attendance concurred that any further efforts would be useless. All medical indications were that the patient had expired."

"I'm sure you did the best you could," I agreed.

He acted as if he didn't hear my comment. He stared at a fixed point on the wall behind me, as if he didn't want to be distracted while he continued his recitation.

"The body was covered and removed from the operating room. An attendant transported it to the morgue, which is on the basement level of the hospital. Normal procedure in deaths of this type is to transfer the corpse to a compartment where it can be stored and maintained at a constant temperature of forty-five degrees Fahrenheit until an autopsy can be performed."

The stilted language flowed so smoothly, he could have been reading from the medical report he was required to dictate after every procedure. This particular report was probably burned into his mind from the number of times he reviewed it with the hospital administrators, as they tried to find a way to hold themselves blameless in the event of a malpractice suit.

"I understand that's when she came back to life," I said.

Subdhani continued as if he hadn't heard me.

"The patient displayed activity of the reflex system when the attendant was placing the body on the slide-out shelf. A sudden lateral reflex movement of the patient's left leg was observed when the left ankle was accidentally struck against the metal door. Closer examination by the attendant revealed a resumption of respiratory activity, although shallow and agonal in nature."

"That's the part I'm interested in," I interrupted. "According to my information, she was clinically dead for an hour and twenty minutes before anyone detected signs of life. Is that correct?"

"There are many definitions of death," Subdhani said. He was still hiding behind the protective wall of professional argot. "Clinical death simply means the absence of clinically detectable signs. As we can see in this case, it doesn't necessarily mean the indefinable spark of life has been extinguished. There have been many instances in which patients declared dead have actually been in some strange state of suspension, some sort of limbo between living and dying."

"According to the electroencephalogram, she was brain-dead," I reminded him. "People who are brain-dead don't usually regain consciousness."

"In my experience, they never do." He shook his head slowly. Some of the earlier arrogance was missing from his voice. "The only conclusion I was able to reach was that there must have been something wrong with the EEG equipment. Perhaps it was improperly calibrated. Perhaps brain activity was continuing at a level below the threshold of the equipment."

I was getting a little exasperated with his evasiveness.

"You seem to have a very flexible definition of death," I said. "A woman appears to be dead, but she's not. If she's not, maybe it's the fault of the equipment. How do you really know? How can you ever tell with total certainty when a patient is dead?"

"There are two definitions of death that I'd consider to be absolute," he said. "The first definition would be the total and irreversible loss of all vital functions. And by that, I mean more than the dilation of pupils, cardiac arrest, the loss of blood pressure, or pulmonary collapse. I refer to the chemical changes that take place inside the cell structures, causing individual cells in the flesh, the blood, the eyes, the brain, to switch off and cease functioning. The result is irreversible. Once those cellular changes occur, the process of decomposition begins."

"And the second definition?" I asked.

"Much more difficult to determine," he said in a more subdued voice. "That would be the religious definition. The separation of the soul from the body. I'm afraid I have no way of knowing when religious death occurs. There are some medical ethicists who claim it takes place with the death of the brain, even though the body may still be functioning through the help of life-support systems. Other experts, particularly those who interpret the Bible literally, believe the soul separates slowly, while the body is cooling."

"No vital signs for an hour and twenty minutes," I said. "If that isn't death, what is it?"

The doctor let out a deep sigh. The red cloud in his left eye seemed to be spreading.

"I don't know," he said. "I've checked the medical literature. There's not another case that even comes close."

It was a remarkable admission, suggesting that he was more unnerved by this case than he had at first appeared.

"Have you talked to her recently?"

"No . . . the hospital's lawyer thought it would be best not to . . . ." He shook his head, his tone of voice becoming apologetic. "You know how lawyers are."

"Are you aware of how she's being treated?"

"My understanding is that she's in a convalescent facility in a nearby town."

"It's a detox center for alcoholics and drug addicts."

"You're getting into semantics now. Detoxification is simply another form of convalescence. I'm sure she's being well cared-for."

"They won't allow anyone to see her."

"That's not unusual."

"She wanted to talk to me, but the security people threw me out."

"Those decisions aren't made by the patients. It's up to the medical staff in any facility to determine when a patient can have visitors."

"But it's been six months," I argued. "Six months since the accident, and they're keeping her in a tiny room with no windows or furniture and not even a TV in the room to keep her company."

"Some patients require solitude."

"She said they drug her for weeks at a time."

"I'd expect a convalescent facility to use medications on their patients."

"They keep her in restraining straps. She can't move anything except her head."

"Perhaps she has violent episodes. Restraining straps are normally used to protect a patient from self-induced harm."

"She said they're holding her against her will."

"Human nature being what it is, patients resent being confined for long periods."

I couldn't get him to admit Laura was being mistreated. And of course each of his rationalizations made perfect sense, except that I had seen the fear in her eyes, and there was no way for him to explain that away.

"She asked me to help her escape."

Subdhani tried to act calm, but his inflamed eye started to flicker nervously.

"I think any attempt on your part to interfere with her treatment would be a dreadful mistake," he said, his voice suddenly sharp. "Mrs. Duquesne obviously has a mental problem. Removing her from medical supervision could cause her irreparable psychological damage."

"You don't know that. You said you hadn't talked to her."

"Why else would they confine her in the manner you described? It has to be some form of mental problem."

"I've been to mental institutions, Doctor. They don't strap people to beds and leave them in dark rooms for six months."

"You're talking about a woman whose vital signs were undetectable for an hour and twenty minutes. Brain damage is common in such cases. They might be using sensory deprivation techniques as part of her rehab." His voice brightened. "Don't you see? There's probably a simple explanation for what appears so sinister to you. That would also explain why the guards were so eager to get you out of the room."

"Except for being sleepy, she sounded perfectly normal to me. More normal than most of the near-deathers I've interviewed."

"Ah, but the trouble with brain damage is that it isn't always as obvious as most people think. The damage can be isolated, and it can take very subtle forms. Selective memory loss. Problems of comprehension. A general lowering of sensory acuity. You could be talking to a person, and they might act as if they understood every word you were saying, and yet a moment later, they wouldn't remember speaking to you at all. And of course there are many recorded cases where a patient retains all the intellectual faculties, but loses the moral values. Women become nymphomaniacs, men become random killers, yet they function normally ninety-nine point nine percent of the time. I don't think you're qualified to determine whether Mrs. Duquesne has indeed suffered brain damage."

"Maybe so. But why did they get so upset when they found me in her room?"

"Obviously, you were an intruder. Perhaps they thought you meant to harm her."

"And why did they destroy my tape recorder?"

"Perhaps they were protecting her privacy."

"They beat me unconscious."

"You were lucky," Subdhani smiled. "They could have had you arrested."

"You have an answer for everything, Doctor."

"It's not as complicated as you pretend it is."

"You think I'm overreacting."

"Yes."

"You think I should go back to New York and forget about Laura Duquesne."

"I think that would be an excellent idea. You're here pretending you want to help my patient, when you're simply trying to exploit her misfortune for your own profit."

"Your patient? You have the nerve to call her your patient? You don't see her, you don't talk to her. You don't really care what they're doing to her, as long as she doesn't sue you. You don't care about Laura. All you care about is your own damn reputation."

I wanted to tell him to go to hell. But I needed his cooperation to do my job, so instead I apologized.

"I'm sorry," I said, lowering my eyes. "I was out of line. I shouldn't have said that."

"No, you're right," he responded. He took off his glasses and rubbed his eyes, seeming suddenly tired and anxious to be rid of me.

"It was the worst mistake I ever made," he sighed. "If the attendant hadn't seen that slight movement of her foot, he would have locked her in the storage compartment. She would have died from the cold and the lack of oxygen."

When he replaced his glasses, the prosperous, confident look of the successful doctor was fading, replaced by the doubt and fear of a troubled man. He seemed to shrink back in his chair, becoming smaller, more vulnerable.

"An autopsy would prove that I was to blame," he said, his voice dropping to a defeated whisper. "By making a faulty diagnosis, I almost killed Mrs. Duquesne."

His abrupt admission of remorse caught me by surprise. I felt compassion for the feelings of guilt he must be suffering.

"She was already clinically dead," I reminded him. "You'd never be held responsible for killing a person who was already dead."

Subdhani shook his head slowly. The red cloud in his left eye now totally surrounded the pupil.

"Perhaps she was," he said. "And perhaps not. I do not know any more. Maybe you can make some sense out of it."

"I'll need a copy of the post-op report."

"I'll call the hospital. They kept all the records on the case."

Watching him struggle with his emotions, I thought I understood why he came up with all those facile explanations a few moments earlier. This wasn't a doctor worried about a malpractice suit. This was a man who was haunted by his encounter with a mystery that all his medical training couldn't refute or explain.

NINE

The medical records clerk at Scranton Evangelical Hospital was a friendly middle-aged woman wearing a pink jacket and a badge that identified her as a volunteer. The name Anita was embroidered over her right breast pocket. She had brown hair showing the first tinges of grey. Red-framed reading glasses hung from a pink cord around her neck. She raised the glasses to study the release form I gave her, the one with Laura's signature forged on the bottom.

"You're Mr. . . ." She paused, as most people do, before figuring out how to pronounce my name. " . . .Theophanes Nikonos?"

"That's right."

"Can I see some identification?"

I flipped open my wallet to show her my driver's license.

"That's you, all right," she smiled sweetly as she compared my face with the tiny laminated photograph. "They tell us to always check identifications before we release any records."

"You can't be too careful," I agreed.

"It's twenty cents a page for each copy," the clerk said. "Plus a five-dollar administrative charge."

She smiled again before disappearing into the maze of wall files that filled the room behind the counter. My experience with hospitals was that the unpaid volunteers were always more pleasant to deal with than the staff. It was a welcome change after my experience with Doctor Subdhani. The encounter had left me with an unsettled feeling, particularly since I hadn't yet managed to get his signature on any medical records, as the Professor had instructed.

The records clerk soon returned from the file room. A puzzled frown had replaced her smile. I got the feeling I was going to be her first problem of the afternoon.

"Are you sure you've got the right spelling on this patient's name?" she asked. "It's hard to tell from the signature."

"D-U-Q-U-E-S-N-E," I spelled out Laura's last name.

I waited at the counter while the woman disappeared once again into the back room. This time, I heard another voice. There was a brief hushed argument, and then the clerk sang out in her friendly way.

"I'll be right with you, Mr. Nikonos."

Leaning over the counter, I could see one of the buttons light up on the desk telephone, indicating that another extension was being used. My instinct told me to leave, that maybe they had discovered the signature was forged, but my curiosity kept me rooted to the spot. The call on the extension was brief. The light soon went out, and the clerk reappeared, meekly following a tall, slim woman in a brown business suit. A matching brown plastic name tag on her lapel identified her as Ms. Eva Hillier. She was carrying the forged records release form.

"I'm the records supervisor," she said. "I'm sorry, but I'm afraid we can't help you with this request of yours."

"What's the problem?" I asked. "That's a perfectly legal document I gave you."

Ms. Hillier looked over my shoulder at the hallway behind me.

"Perhaps you should discuss the matter with Mr. Renshaw," she said.

I turned to see an officious little man in a blue blazer and tan slacks hurrying down the hall towards us. A hospital security guard was behind him, long loping strides easily keeping up with the little man's shorter steps.

Renshaw took the form from the records supervisor.

"Where did you get this form?" he demanded. "It's not one of ours."

"Our lawyers drew it up in New York," I said. "It's a standard consent release, indicating that the patient grants us complete access to her medical records. It's legal in all fifty states. Do you have a problem with it?"

"I thought you'd have a subpoena. Usually in these situations, the procedure is to secure a subpoena."

"Why would I need a subpoena? I've got her signature on the release."

I was about three inches taller than Renshaw, putting the top of his head on a level with my eyes and giving me a close-up view of a bizarre sight. Renshaw's hair grew in precise little clumps that lined up evenly atop his scalp like tiny rows of wheat. It took a moment before I realized I was looking at hair implants.

"What firm do you represent?" Renshaw asked.

I snapped a business card out of the pack I kept tightly bound with a rubber band. Renshaw seemed puzzled by the name on the card.

"Is this some sort of public-service law firm, this Institute you work for?" he asked.

"All we do is research work."

I had a hard time keeping my eyes from wandering back to Renshaw's expensive crop of transplanted hair.

"Is any of your research work done for law firms?"

"If you're worried about a malpractice suit, you can relax," I said. "That's not why I'm here."

The little man frowned at the mention of the M-word.

"Evangelical Hospital has no fear of a malpractice suit in this case," he quickly said. "The procedures used on Mrs. Duquesne were medically correct."

"I don't want to argue about her treatment. I want to find out more about what happened to her. The facts surrounding her death."

"Mrs. Duquesne didn't die," Renshaw corrected me, just as Doctor Subdhani had done earlier. "It was due to the alertness of a member of the hospital staff that she was determined, in fact, to be alive."

"The attendant in the morgue," I nodded. "I know about him. All I really want is a copy of her medical records."

Renshaw's eyes darted back to the slim woman in the brown suit. She shook her head. He made a sour face.

"I'm afraid we can't help you," he said.

"I gave you a legal request from Laura Duquesne to release her records to me," I insisted. "You have no right to refuse me."

"Perhaps if you come back tomorrow," Renshaw said as he studied my card.

"You're stalling me."

"Really, we'd like to cooperate."

"Maybe I *should* get that subpoena," I bluffed.

"It wouldn't do you any good." Renshaw sighed. "Even if you had a subpoena, we couldn't produce the records you want. They seem to be temporarily unavailable." He glared at Ms. Hillier, as if it was all her fault. The friendly volunteer in the pink jacket had disappeared, leaving the supervisor to handle the problem.

"We can't find the Duquesne file," Ms. Hillier told me.

"It's probably just misplaced," Renshaw tried to explain. "We'll conduct a thorough search of the files and contact you when we find her records. Is this a current address on your business card?"

"Maybe I could talk to one of the nurses who was on duty when Mrs. Duquesne was brought in," I said. "I'd like to get confirmation on a few items."

"Without the records, we have no way of determining who did the procedures on her. We have dozens of nurses who rotate through the Emergency Room."

"All you have to do is check the date and time she was admitted," I pressed him. "Then you can double-check your Personnel records."

"I'm afraid that won't be possible, either."

"Why not?"

"We seem to be having a problem with the computer system."

"It's strictly a software problem," Ms. Hillier tried to reassure me. "The electronic file on Laura Duquesne is giving us garbled responses. We've already called our computer people. I'm sure they'll be able to correct it."

"How much time will that take?"

"A day or two, that's what they tell me," the woman said.

"Maybe what I should do is go down and talk to that morgue attendant," I said. "At least I know he was on duty."

"I'm afraid that won't be possible," Renshaw said. The corners of his mouth curled up in a cold smile, "The form you brought is simply an authorization to release Mrs. Duquesne's medical records. It doesn't give you any authority to question members of the hospital staff."

"Considering the way your hospital staff lost her records, I thought you might want to show a little cooperation in the matter." I knew it wasn't going to work when the smile remained frozen on Renshaw's face.

"I'm afraid not," he repeated what was apparently his favorite response. "Everyone involved with the Duquesne case has been instructed not to discuss specific details of the treatment and handling of Mrs. Duquesne pending any possible litigation in the matter."

"You know, Mr. Renshaw, I'm beginning to wonder if those records might have been lost on purpose."

"That's ridiculous. Why would we purposely lose our own records?"

"Maybe there is information in the file you don't want anybody to see."

"It was purely a clerical error," he insisted.

"If I was standing here with a subpoena, this could be considered obstruction of justice."

"I'm sure the records will turn up."

"Tomorrow?"

"Perhaps. And if not tomorrow, then certainly the next day."

"And the same thing with the computer files?"

"Our people are working on the software right now."

"I'm sure they are," I said. "I'm sure they are."

I decided not to mention my conversation with Doctor Subdhani. If I was going to use him as a source, I didn't want Renshaw to know about it. But I was puzzled that no one said anything about receiving the phone call Subdhani promised he would make. I hurried back to the doctor's office, hoping my intuition about him was wrong.

TEN

I was too late.

By the time I got back to Doctor Subdhani's office, he had already fled. His receptionist was calling patients to cancel their appointments. She had narrow eyes, thin lips, and a tight, selfish mouth and she did her best to ignore me, while she told one after another of his patients that he had been called out of town unexpectedly. I listened to her explain that she couldn't reschedule any appointments until she knew when he would return. I didn't hear her apologize to any of the patients for the inconvenience caused by his sudden departure.

I stood right in front of her and waited while she completed four more calls before she acknowledged my presence. When she finally looked up at me, she kept one finger poised on the keypad, and the receiver at her ear.

She waited for me to speak first.

"When did Doctor Subdhani plan this trip?" I asked.

"Why?"

"I was here two hours ago and he didn't mention anything about leaving town."

"So?"

"It must have been something very sudden."

"I guess."

"Where did he go?"

"I don't know."

She punched in a series of numbers and telephoned another patient, running through the same routine about Subdhani leaving town. I let her make two more calls, but when she was punching in the numbers for the next one, I placed my finger on the cut-off button.

Most women would probably react with fear, but her reaction was immediate anger. She tried to pull the phone away, but I held tight.

"I'll call the police," she threatened.

"Not while I'm holding the phone."

"There are other phones," she said, edging toward Subdhani's private office.

"They all go through this board," I ran my fingers over the buttons for the extra phone lines. "I can cut off any of them right here."

"You're going to get in trouble," she said.

"No. You're the one who's going to get in trouble, when Ranjeet finds out you refused to talk to me," I said, using his first name, to mislead her into thinking I was a friend of Subdhani's.

My bluff seemed to work.

"What do you want?" she asked in a suspicious voice.

I hadn't been making much progress lately with the honest approach, so I decided to bend the truth a little more. "I came to pick up copies of some medical records," I told her. As long as Subdhani was out of town, there was no way for her to verify my story. "He said they'd be ready for me when I got back."

She looked dubious. "He didn't tell me anything about it."

"He must have been in a rush," I said. "Maybe he left them on his desk."

"No, he didn't."

"The patient's name is Duquesne. Laura Duquesne. Didn't Ranjeet tell you about her?"

"Who are you?" she asked. "How do I know you're legitimate?"

I decided the fastest way to get at Subdhani's records would be to assume my former persona. I gave her one of my old business cards from Capitol Casualty & Auto Insurance. It was like displaying a police badge. My experience as an insurance investigator taught me that people were often willing to turn over the most confidential personal and financial data to the representatives of insurance companies.

"Well, I guess you're okay," she frowned, handing back the card. "But I still don't know about any copies that were supposed to be made."

"Here's my authorization from the patient." I showed her the document with the forged signature. "Ranjeet said that was all he would need."

"Usually it's the hospital that provides copies of medical documents," she said. "Maybe he talked to them. I'll call the hospital and see if they know anything."

She reached for the phone.

"Ranjeet didn't want Scranton Evangelical to know about this," I quickly said. "At least, not yet. There's a question of possible malpractice claims, and he wanted to keep them out of it as long as he could."

It was surprising to me how easily the lies came out. Normally I was a relatively honest person. But the Professor would be furious if I didn't get those records.

"I was just doing your boss a favor," I elaborated on the lie. "It doesn't make any difference to me whether I get the records here or at the hospital, but I know it would make a big difference to Ranjeet."

"Well . . ." she wavered. "Let me check his files."

I followed her into Subdhani's office, which is what I assumed would be the proper way for a friend of his to act. I leaned against his desk while she unlocked a grey metal filing cabinet. The D's were in the second drawer. She quickly went to the middle of the drawer, snapped through a few files, and then started going through the entire drawer methodically, one file folder at a time. Just to be sure, she went through the top drawer and the bottom drawer before giving up.

"No Duquesne file in there," she said, slamming the last door shut. "Maybe he left it in his desk. He does that sometimes."

She went through all the drawers of Doctor Subdhani's desk, only to end up with the same results.

"Well, there's always a back-up file in the computer," she said. "I can print out a hard copy for you."

Amber characters lit up the monitor as the computer came to

life. She punched in commands, replaced disks, and ran through the computer files until she exhausted that possibility, too.

"You're sure she was one of his patients?" she asked. "I can't find a reference to a Laura Duquesne anywhere. Not even in the billing file."

"We talked about her case in detail," I said. "He reviewed all the procedures he performed on her."

"I don't remember her name at all."

"You wouldn't have any reason to. She was an ER patient, strictly hospital treatment. She never came to the office."

By now, the receptionist was as mystified as I was. "I don't know what to tell you," she shrugged.

"Do you know where Ranjeet is?"

"No. He left a note on my desk when I was out to lunch. He wasn't sure when he'd be back, and wanted me to cancel his appointments for the rest of the week."

"Has he ever done this before?"

"He never missed an appointment that I know of."

"How long have you worked for him?"

"It's going on three months."

That explained why she never heard of Laura. But it didn't explain the missing files.

"Just in case he contacts you, I'm going to give you a phone number to call." I wrote down DeBray's unlisted number.

"Is this the insurance company where you work?" she asked.

"It's a consultant who's working with me on this case. He'll be able to reach me faster than if you went through the insurance company swtichboard."

"Does this mean you're not going to get the hospital involved?"

"Not for the time being," I expanded on my earlier lie. "I'd like to help Ranjeet, but I'll need your cooperation."

"I don't want to get in any trouble."

"Neither do I. That's why I want you to call that number if he gets in touch with you."

"Is he going to be arrested, or anything like that?"

"I'm not a cop." It was the first honest thing I said to her. "I just want those records."

When I left Subdhani's office, I wondered how I was going to explain all this to the Professor. Last night, he was so excited about Laura's story, he thought he could build another best-seller around it. It was going to be the culmination of all his dreams, the validation of a lifetime of research into NDE phenomena.

And now I had the feeling it was all slipping away. I didn't have a signed statement from Subdhani. I didn't have anything at all from the hospital. I had come up with no medical documentation of clinical death, no evidence of any kind except Laura's taped interview.

The only fact I could report to DeBray was that all the files on Laura's death had disappeared.

I was beginning to wonder whether she was a beautiful fraud, or whether I had stumbled into an elaborate coverup.

ELEVEN

Since I wasn't making any progress locating Laura's medical records, I decided to turn my attention to authenticating the death of her husband. That meant a visit to the Lackawanna County morgue, the modern concrete-and-glass necropolis where Harrison Duquesne's last remains had been examined and identified.

The way things were going, I wouldn't have been surprised if I ran into another roadblock at the morgue. Instead, I was immediately escorted to the third floor, where I was offered a cup of coffee, and after a short wait, was taken in to meet Doctor Frederick Zimmer.

The last place I expected to find a confirmed NDE believer was in the office of the Lackawanna County coroner.

The processing of human remains certainly wasn't conducive to a belief in the afterlife. Yet here in this citadel of forensic medicine, the coroner himself had a copy of Professor DeBray's book on his shelf, and was greeting me with the enthusiasm doctors usually reserve for each other.

"It's a pleasure to meet you, Mr. Nikonos," he said as he came around the desk to shake my hand. "A genuine pleasure. This is the first time we've ever had a near-death investigator visit our facility. Have a seat, have a seat."

He motioned me to a black leather couch and sat down beside me.

Doctor Zimmer was a small man with a high level of nervous energy. His hands were constantly moving, adjusting his tie, smoothing his hair, folding and unfolding his reading glasses, and when all else failed, simply tapping his fingers in time to some unheard rhythm. He had silvery hair and black eyebrows.

"I've always been fascinated by Professor DeBray's work," he said. His hands busied themselves straightening the cuffs on his shirt. "What can I do for you?"

"I'm following up on a car crash fatality," I said. "The accident occurred on October 15 of last year. The victim was identified as Harrison Duquesne."

"Ah yes, I should have known," his eyes lit up. "You're really investigating the wife, Laura Duquesne, aren't you?"

"It's just a routine follow-up," I said.

"There was nothing routine about what happened to her," he responded. He jumped up and started pacing the floor, too nervous to sit still for long. "It was a classic near-death experience. When I first heard the details, I was tempted to call DeBray myself. I knew he wouldn't be able to resist the Duquesne case. I just knew it."

"I'm really here to talk about the husband," I said, not wanting to get sidetracked.

"Of course, of course. I'll get you the records."

He pressed the intercom button on his desk, and asked his secretary to locate the Duquesne file.

"It was fascinating, absolutely fascinating, what happened to that woman," he said, rubbing the palms of his hands together. "They said she was dead for an hour and twenty minutes. That might well be the longest recorded clinical death from which anyone ever recovered."

"That's what I'm told," I said. "But I haven't been able to come up with any medical documentation yet."

"I guess you know she was already on a morgue slab when she woke up. It's amazing. We process about eleven hundred bodies a year, and we've never had that happen. There are one or two local undertakers who claim they had people recover on the embalming table, but we've never had that happen here."

It sounded to me like Zimmer was sorry that he had missed out on the experience.

"It's happened before, in other morgues," I assured him.

"I'm still waiting for my first one," he grinned, adjusting his necktie for about the tenth time. "I've left standing instructions to call me if any of our incoming cases exhibit anabiotic activity."

It was the first time I ever heard anybody other than the Professor or myself use the word *anabiotic* in a sentence. Zimmer was obviously well-read on the subject. In addition to *The Life Beyond*, his bookshelf held Raymond Moody's pioneering works on NDE, both volumes of Kenneth Ring's more scientific approach to the subject, and Kubler-Ross's thanatological research studies.

"I know it's unusual for someone in my field," he said. "But I'm really fascinated by the near-death phenomenon. I'd really enjoy seeing someone actually recovering from the experience."

He was right about his attitude being unusual. Although most reputable surveys show that sixty-nine percent of the general population believes in some form of afterlife, the percentage is significantly lower among medical professionals. The percentage drops even further when it comes to that subset of doctors who deal most intimately with our discarded mortal coils.

Before I could comment, Zimmer's secretary brought in the Duquesne file. The coroner put on his reading glasses, and sat down behind his desk. He flipped through the pages quickly, familiarizing himself with the contents. Apparently satisfied with his review, he took off his reading glasses and sat back in his chair.

"Now, what can I do to help you?" he asked.

"Convince me that Harrison Duquesne is dead."

"It's all in here," Zimmer tapped the folder with his reading glasses. "Death certificate. Autopsy results. Confirmation of identity."

"Can I get a copy of the file?"

"Certainly. It's all a matter of public record. The right to privacy terminates at time of death."

"You're sure it was Harrison Duquesne? There's no possibility a mistake was made?"

"So you heard the rumors, too?"

"That's why I'm here," I said, careful not to reveal that I had talked to Laura.

"Of course you have your informants," he said. His hands were busy wiping his reading glasses with a lens tissue. "After all, I almost called DeBray myself."

"People pass on all sorts of rumors to us. The near-death community is fairly small and stories like this one travel quickly."

"Do you believe it could really have happened?" he asked. "I mean the part where she was told her husband was still alive?"

"I'm just here to gather information," I said. "It's up to Professor DeBray to decide whether to believe her."

"It would be a breakthrough in NDE research if anything like that ever turned out to be true."

"I guess it would be," I agreed.

"Well, you can tell DeBray that I'm sorry to disappoint him," Zimmer said. He was swiveling from side to side in his chair. He was starting to make me nervous with his constant motion. "I was really excited when I first heard about the story Mrs. Duquesne brought back. I never talked to her myself, of course, but the word got around. And people were asking me questions. So I immediately double-checked every aspect of the process used to identify her husband's remains. Based on my investigation, I can assure you that Harrison Duquesne is dead."

Zimmer got up and started pacing the floor again.

"As I told you earlier, I'm fascinated with near-death phenomena, and what they might reveal to us about the possibility of the afterlife. So I was approaching all this from the point of view of a believer. I actually wanted to prove that we had made a mistake. That we had misidentified the corpse. I *wanted* Harrison Duquesne to be alive. I didn't care about any possible embarrassment my office might suffer. I knew enough about NDE research to understand the significance of what I was doing."

Zimmer stopped in front of the window. The dying afternoon sunlight glowed gently in his silvery hair.

"But I failed," he said with a sigh. "I wasn't able to find any errors. I went over everything we had and went over it again. Of course, there wasn't much to work with, as far as the remains were concerned. When the car crashed, the gasoline tank ruptured and caught fire. The corpse was burned beyond recognition. Visually, we couldn't even tell whether the remains were male or female. The autopsy revealed that the victim was a male Caucasian, five feet nine inches tall, weight before death approximately one hundred seventy-five pounds. That matched up with the height and weight measurements on Harrison Duquesne's driver's license, a copy of which was supplied to us by the New York Motor Vehicle Bureau. The structure of the skull was consistent with the facial features in the driver's license photograph, although that's pretty subjective. We also tracked down the victim's personal physician in New York, who confirmed the height and weight information, and also gave us Mr. Duquesne's blood type, which was O Positive. That matched, too. And of course we had the dental records. I even called in a forensic anthropologist to review our work. He reached the same conclusion we did."

"The dead man was Harrison Duquesne?"

"Absolutely no doubt about it," Zimmer said.

"That's too bad," I said.

Inconsistencies often turn up in NDE interviews: details of time or place that aren't supported by the facts. But this wasn't one of those minor details. The coroner's report totally contradicted the single most important element of Laura's near-death experience. Finding a living, breathing, Harrison Duquesne would have been astonishing proof of DeBray's theories. Instead, my investigation proved the exact opposite. Although I had already expressed my own skepticism, it was going to be awfully hard to give him the bad news.

That was one reason why I wasn't in a rush to go back to New York.

The other reason was my curiosity about the lovely young lady who told me a story that could so easily be disproved.

TWELVE

It wasn't going to be easy getting back in to see Laura. The enforcers would be expecting me, ready to avenge themselves for the way I fooled them with the tape recording. I wasn't sure whether I would survive another of their beatings.

What I couldn't figure out was why the Walden Clinic people were so brutally committed to barring Laura from all access to visitors. What were they doing to her? And what did it all have to do with her near-death experience?

The clinic where she was confined was in Dickson City, a worn-out little town just north of Scranton, off Route 81. It was one of those places that never managed to keep up with the changes in the American economy. The factories around which the town was built were now abandoned. Vacant storefronts lined the Main Street. There were hundreds of towns like it in the Northeast, and I had been in dozens of them during the last year.

Eventually I found the municipal building. It was a homely single-story brick structure that could have been mistaken for an overgrown hamburger restaurant. Like most of the buildings in town, it was poorly maintained. A few shingles were missing from the roof. There were large cracks and small potholes in the asphalt parking lot. A piece of plywood covered the bottom section of the front door.

I sat in my parked car for what seemed like half an hour before I finally worked up the courage to go inside. I knew I was taking a risk. Any time people get involved with the police, they're putting themselves in jeopardy. But in this situation, I didn't feel there was any other alternative.

A narrow corridor bisected the interior of the small building. It took me past the tax collector's office, the mayor's office, and the zoning commissioner's office, ending at two connecting rooms that housed the police department. A grossly overweight but pleasantly smiling woman wearing a dispatcher's headset looked up from her work as I approached. According to the engraved brass plate that hung from the side of her computer terminal, her name was Marie Krisloski, and she was the "official police department receptionist-dispatcher-secretary-typist-filing-clerk-coordinator-and-general-administrative-assistant-and-person-who-doesn't-get-paid-enough-money." Behind her, gold lettering on a frosted-glass door indicated the office of Chief of Police Pat Greer.

I waited while Marie had a brief conversation with a patrol car. In a town this size, I guessed there was probably only one patrol car, not counting the police chief's personal vehicle. The chief would be on duty days and during emergencies. At night, the patrol car was probably parked out front while the duty officer watched David Letterman and the endless stream of late movies in the the back room.

It was probably a good place to be a cop, I thought. In a town like this, the teenagers were far more likely to be vandalizing mail boxes than spraying the neighborhoods with bullets from a MAC-10.

"I'd like to see the Chief," I said.

"You don't have an appointment."

"What about professional courtesy?"

I showed her my New York City Patrolmen's Benevolent Association card.

"You can get those cards just for making a donation," she said. "If you're really a policeman, you'd have a badge."

"So would you," I said, mildly irritated.

"Don't get your hackles up," she said. "I was just making a comment about you not having an appointment. You want to see the Chief, that's okay with me."

"I'm sorry," I apologized. "I guess I'm a little tired. Can we start over?"

"You want to tell me why you want to see the Chief?"

"I'd rather save it for him. Is he in?"

Her plump lips parted in a playful expansion of her smile. "You ever met our Chief of Police before?"

"I never had the opportunity. Is he in?"

"The office right behind me," she said sweetly, waving me past her desk. "Just have a seat," she called after me. "The Chief is in the . . . rest room."

The Chief's tiny office was filled with clutter. Stacks of reports filled one side of an old wooden desk, a computer keyboard and monitor occupied the other side. On the shelf behind the desk were an eight-volume set of Commonwealth of Pennsylvania statutes, a paperback edition of Lackawanna County ordinances, and a bowling trophy. The side wall was covered by a huge map of the town. Hanging on the other wall was a diploma from the University of Scranton and a class picture of the FBI Police Chiefs Training Class at Quantico.

I was beside the desk, trying to get a closer look at the photograph when I heard footsteps behind me.

"Your visitor's name is Theophanes Nikonos," I heard Marie say. "He's the guy was sitting out front in that blue Honda with the New York license plates that you asked about."

I turned and tried to cover my surprise with a friendly smile and an outstretched hand. The Chief of Police was about five-feet-four, wore a custom-tailored, figure-hugging tan uniform, had brown hair, sparkling brown eyes, plucked eyebrows, a minimal amount of mascara, and a light shade of pink lipstick.

"What can I do for you, Mr. Nikonos?"

Her voice was warm and friendly, not at all like the hard-edged accents favored by New York City policewomen.

I was going to tell her I didn't expect a female Police Chief, but the look in her eyes warned me not to. "I want to file a charge," I said. "Assault and battery."

"Were you the victim?"

"Yes."

"I don't see any bruises."

"They were careful not to hit me where it shows. I might have a broken rib, I'm not sure."

I started to unbutton my shirt to demonstrate, but she stopped me with a wave of her hand.

"That won't be necessary," she said. "Who attacked you?"

"I don't know their names. It was a couple of big Samoans at the Walden Clinic."

"Both of them?" Her eyebrows registered surprise, probably that I was still alive after tangling with the Samoans.

"Yes."

"And it happened inside the clinic?"

"That's where it started."

"What were you doing there?"

"I was just . . . working."

"What kind of work do you do?"

"I'm an investigator from New York," I said, offering her one of my Institute business cards. "I'm up here looking into an auto accident."

She motioned me to a seat while she studied my card.

"The Institute for the Investigation of Anabiotic Phenomena?" she read from the card. "Sounds interesting. What is it, and what does it have to do with the Walden Clinic?"

"It's a research organization," I said. "We study death events of various types. Not just auto accidents, but drownings and shootings and medical problems, any incident that results in a fatality. I do the field interviews with the survivors."

"You mean the relatives, other people who were on the scene at the time?"

"I do that, too," I said. "But my primary assignment is to interview the people who died."

She gave me a puzzled look. "You said survivors."

"Yes. People who survived their own deaths," I explained. "We're trying to establish the validity of the near-death experience."

Her eyes widened in amazement. Or was it amusement? For a brief moment, I was afraid she might categorize me as some sort of weirdo who shouldn't be taken seriously. It happens occasionally when I explain my work to strangers.

"They did a story on near-death experiences on *20/20*," Chief Greer recalled. "People claiming they died and went to Heaven. Is all that stuff really true?"

"I just do the interviews," I said with a shrug.

"So who are you in town to interview?"

"A woman named Laura Duquesne."

The Chief's eyes narrowed with suspicion, the long curling lashes nearly touching.

"You came all the way from New York to see her?"

"That's what I do. I travel around, interviewing people."

"How did you find out about, what's her name, Laura Duquesne?"

Behind me, I heard an electronic printer begin its mindless clatter.

"We run ads in the tabloids looking for subjects. Someone wrote to us, suggesting we look into the Duquesne case."

"Somebody local?"

"I'd rather not say."

Behind me, I heard Marie tear a sheet of perforated paper from the printer. She squeezed her huge hips around the side of the desk and handed the printout to the Chief, smiling sweetly at me the entire time.

"Auto accident on Route 380 . . . October 15 . . . 9:30 p.m. . . ." the Chief started to read excerpts from the computer printout she had just been given. "BMW was heading westbound around Bald Mountain Curve . . . driver lost control . . . vehicle crossed over median strip and eastbound lanes . . . crashed through guardrail . . . three-hundred foot cliff . . . gasoline tank ruptured . . . ensuing fire . . . driver's body recovered . . . identified as Harrison B. Duquesne, 128 East 63rd Street, New York City . . . ." She paused momentarily. "Ah, here we are . . . passenger was thrown from vehicle upon impact with guardrail . . . identified as Laura Lehman Duquesne, wife of driver . . . Scranton Evangelical Hospital . . . severe thoracic injuries . . . released November 18." She looked up from the sheet. "Now there's one woman who's lucky she wasn't wearing a seat belt. Otherwise she would have ended up like her husband."

"It didn't say anything about being a computer whiz on that nameplate," I said over my shoulder to Marie, who was smiling broadly. It was hard not to like these two efficient women, who would certainly be formidable enemies for anyone who broke the law in their town.

"She's my secret weapon," the Chief said.

"Did she run my plates, too?"

"It's coming up on the screen," Marie called back. "It took a little longer, because I had to set up an interface with the New York Motor Vehicle Bureau."

"Okay," the Chief said, as she examined her computer screen. "Let's see now. We've got a 1987 blue Honda Accord four cylinder sedan registered to Theophanes Nikonos." She paused, looked at me quizzically, and repeated my first name. "Theophanes?"

"You can call me Theo."

"Okay, Theo. Address on the registration is 4892 Avenue B, New York, New York. May I see your driver's license?"

I handed her the laminated plastic card and watched while she entered my Social Security number in the computer.

"I'm running it through NCIC," she said. "It'll take just a minute."

The NCIC was the National Crime Information Computer, the data bank originally set up by the FBI as a central clearing house for criminal records that could be accessed by Police Departments across the country.

I waited silently while the SEARCHING code blinked on and off under my name and number. Finally, the message NO DATA AVAILABLE appeared on the screen.

"So far, you're clean," she said. "The car is yours, it has no outstanding tickets, and you don't seem to have committed or been charged with any crimes."

"What's the error rate?" I asked.

"Negligible," the Chief said. "But I guess there's always a chance of error, depending on who inputs the database. Why? Was there a mistake in the data we just accessed?"

"Not my data," I said. "But it might be worth rechecking the data on Harrison Duquesne."

"Why?"

"His wife claims he's still alive."

The pleasant expression on Chief Greer's face froze.

"Where did you hear that?" she asked.

"From Laura Duquesne herself."

The Chief's eyebrows once again lifted in surprise.

"You actually talked to her?"

"Last night," I said. "Just before the Samoans showed up."

"Did you have permission to see her?"

"Let's just say I went in . . . unannounced."

"I see. And that's when the assault took place?"

"That's right," I said. "Apparently they didn't want anyone talking to her."

"Were there any witnesses to this assault, other than employees of the Walden Clinic?"

"Only one."

"Laura Duquesne?"

"Yes."

"You realize, of course, the Clinic would have grounds for a countercharge."

"Yes."

"Technically, you could be charged with breaking and entering," she said.

"Technically."

"At the minimum, it would be misdemeanor trespass."

"I know."

"Maybe you should talk to a lawyer before you say anything else."

"I don't want a lawyer. I want you to come with me to the Walden Clinic so that I can identify my attackers."

"Maybe I should warn you, this isn't just a small-town clinic you're dealing with," the Chief said. "It's part of a chain owned by the Zydecor Corporation. They've been buying up healthcare facilities all over the area. The nursing home in town is one of theirs, too."

"Zydecor?" The name sounded familiar. "There was a Doctor Zydek there last night."

"Doctor Zydek?" She sounded surprised. "He's the guy who owns it all. I wonder what he's doing in town?"

"It sounded to me like he was making sure I didn't talk to Laura Duquesne."

"You know, if you pursue this, you might end up in jail yourself."

"That's a risk I'm willing to take."

I watched while Chief Greer put on her pistol belt like any

other good cop would do, and then checked her face in the mirror like any woman would do.

"I've always wanted to get inside that place and take a look around," she said. "Let's go see your witness."

THIRTEEN

The Walden Clinic looked innocent enough in the daylight, a drab rectangular box of a building that gave no hint of any sinister activity inside. It was one of the larger buildings in Dickson, a three-story structure sheathed in faded yellow stucco. According to the Chief of Police, it had once been a rooming house for the Polish immigrants who came to work in the local coal mines. Now it was a combination residence and treatment center for individuals with addictive and other personality disorders.

The woman at the reception desk frowned when she saw me, obviously remembering my failed attempt to get past her on the previous afternoon. The fact that I was back with the police must have unnerved her. Even before we could speak, she was on the phone calling for help.

Almost immediately, a side door opened and Roland Metzger appeared. He came towards us with a welcoming smile.

"Can I help you?" he asked, his voice a lot more pleasant than it had been last night.

"He's one of them," I told the Chief.

"I beg your pardon?" Metzger asked. He did a good job of looking puzzled.

"He's the one who took my tape recorder," I said.

"What tape recorder?" he asked. "What are you talking about?"

"Oh, come on, you know damn well what happened."

"Don't raise your voice," Metzger said. "Loud conversations disturb our patients." He indicated a doorway across the hall from the receptionist. "We can talk in the conference room."

The room contained a circular white Formica table and four white director's chairs. A copy of one of Cézanne's Provençal landscapes hung in a cheap frame on the wall.

"I'm Roland Metzger," he said, extending his hand to the Chief. "I'm in charge of security. Now can you tell me what this is all about?"

The Chief introduced herself and shook his hand. She turned to me. "This gentleman is Theo Nikonos," she said. "He's an investigator from New York."

Metzger continued his act, which consisted of looking mildly curious and treating me like a total stranger. He extended his hand to me, and after a slight hesitation, I shook it. His thick fingers gave him a powerful grip, but there was nothing in his handshake to suggest he harbored any animosity towards me.

"Mr. Nikonos claims he was assaulted on the premises last night," Chief Greer said.

"Really?" Metzger's eyes widened. "Last night?"

"Around ten o'clock, according to Mr. Nikonos."

"But that's impossible," Metzger said in an innocent voice. "For security reasons, we lock the doors at nine o'clock. Nobody's allowed in or out between nine at night and six in the morning."

"Mr. Nikonos claims to have gained entrance through a window in back," the Chief said. "Which of course would have been illegal," she quickly added.

"No one reported any sign of a break-in last night."

"Quit the innocent act, Metzger," I interrupted. "You and those two Samoans found me, gave me a beating and left me in the alley."

"I don't know what he's talking about," Metzger said to the Chief. "I never saw this man before in my life."

"He admitted breaking and entering," the Chief said. "I could arrest him on a misdemeanor charge if any of your people could confirm they saw him on the premises last night."

"I can certainly check with the rest of the staff. But I was on duty last night. If anyone broke in, I would have known about it."

I didn't understand what Metzger was up to, but I wasn't going to allow his obfuscations to distract me from the real reason I came here.

"We can settle this all very easily," I said. "Laura can confirm that I was here last night."

"Who?" Metzger asked.

"Laura Duquesne," I said. "The woman you didn't want me to see."

Metzger gave me a disdainful smile and shook his head, as if my charge wasn't worthy of comment.

"Well?" Chief Greer asked. "What about it?"

"I don't see how Mrs. Duquesne would be of any help," Metzger said. "She was transferred out of here nearly a month ago."

"She was here last night," I insisted. "I saw her. I talked to her."

"That's ridiculous. I could prove she is gone by showing you our records, but of course, they're confidential."

"He's lying," I told the Chief. "They've got her strapped to a table in a room in the basement."

"We don't keep any patients down there," Metzger said. "This is an old building, and the basement rooms don't have proper ventilation or emergency access. They're not suitable for patients who need constant monitoring."

"She's down there," I insisted. "I saw her."

"We'd be in violation of state guidelines if we kept anyone down there," Metzger said.

"Well, there's one way to prove who's telling the truth," I said.

"I guess there wouldn't be any harm in taking a look," Chief Greer agreed.

"I know the way," I said, before Metzger could argue any further.

I led them down the back stairs, pointing out the window through which I had gained access. The basement was exactly as I remembered it, damp and poorly lit and smelling of mildew. I hurried ahead, proud of myself for having found a way to once again penetrate the Walden Clinic's defenses.

It was working out exactly as I planned. The Professor might not be happy that I got the local police involved. But it was the best way I knew to insure that Laura would be given more humane treatment. Maybe we'd be able to get her out of here and into a proper institution. Although I didn't fully realize it at the time, I was already unconsciously taking on the role of Laura's protector. Metzger couldn't stop me now, not with the Chief of Police beside me.

I threw open the door to the basement room. The room was too dark to see anything. But even before I could find the light switch, I sensed that something was terribly wrong.

FOURTEEN

Laura was gone.

So was the table to which she had been strapped.

What I remembered as a chamber of sepulchral isolation was now transformed into a crowded storage area, stacked with cardboard boxes, rusting paint cans and a metal filing cabinet with a large dent in one side. A thin film of dust covered everything, suggesting that the contents of the room had been undisturbed for months.

There was no sign that anyone had ever been kept in the small windowless room.

I stepped through the doorway.

"She was here last night," I insisted, searching the floor for some sign, some piece of evidence that would prove I was telling the truth.

But the only footprints on the dust-covered floor were my own.

Metzger and the Chief waited silently in the doorway.

"Maybe this is the wrong room," I said uncertainly.

Metzger didn't try to stop me as I searched the rest of the basement, going from room to room, opening doors and peering inside, and finally coming back to the place where I was convinced I had seen Laura the night before.

"Where is she?" I demanded. "What did you do with her?"

Metzger turned his back to me.

"I've seen this kind of behavior before," he said to the Chief. "It's typical delusional activity, imagining events that never happened. He probably needs professional help."

"You bastard," I muttered.

"You'd better get him out of here before he gets violent," Metzger said. "If he comes back again, I'll have him arrested." He turned to fix his eyes menacingly on me, "Or maybe I'll arrange to have him committed."

The Chief apologized to Metzger and hurried me out to her car.

"It seems like you've got a credibility problem, Theo," she said as we drove back to the police station.

"I told you the truth," I insisted. "I was there last night and his goons attacked me."

"He denied he ever saw you."

"He's lying."

"You weren't exactly honest with me, either," she said. "The only reason you filed charges was to get inside the clinic without getting beaten up again. That was the whole point of this little exercise, wasn't it? You wanted to see the Duquesne woman again."

"She was there last night," I said.

The Chief shook her head.

"Even if she was, that's no crime. The Walden Clinic is a licensed health-care facility. They have a legal right to keep patients on the premises."

"But why did he lie about Laura not being there?"

"Maybe he was protecting her privacy."

"She told me she was being held against her will."

"It's your word against his."

"You could get a search warrant."

"For what?"

"To look for Laura."

She let out a long, tired sigh.

"I'll be honest with you, Theo. I'd like nothing better than to find some evidence of illegal activity at that Clinic, so we could shut them down. It's nothing but a Medicaid mill. They bring in patients by the vanload . . . addicts, alcoholics, glue-sniffers, you name it. The rumor is that they keep them purposely strung out on drugs until they max out the benefits, but we have no way of proving that. As long as the State certifies them, there's nothing we can do, unless we find evidence of some crime on the premises." She shook her head in frustration. "I'd like to get a search warrant and see if I could find some kind of illegal activity in there. I really would."

"Then why don't you?"

"The judge will want probable cause—which so far I don't have. Unless there's somebody other than the apparently missing Duquesne woman who could confirm your story."

"You could talk to Professor DeBray. I told him everything I told you."

"No good. What we'd need is a witness to the alleged beating."

"I can show you the bruises."

"Bruises wouldn't prove anything except that you suffered a recent injury."

"I called the Professor from a gas station in Scranton. The attendant saw me. My clothing was torn and muddy. That would establish when the beating took place, wouldn't it?"

"It's pretty thin stuff," the Chief said.

"What about the tape recording?" I asked. "I still have the tape recording of the interview. I didn't send it to the Professor yet."

"Do you have Metzger's voice on the tape? His or any of the other guards?"

"I don't think so. I turned it off before they showed up.

"Then there's no proof the interview took place at the Walden Clinic. So far, all we have is your word that any of this happened."

"There's Laura," I reminded her.

The Chief showed her annoyance by refusing to talk for the rest of the drive. She pulled up at the Municipal Building, where she motioned me to follow her back to her office. She took a handful of phone messages from Marie, tossed her hat on the desk, took off her sunglasses, and checked her hair in the mirror that sat atop the filing cabinet.

"Let's assume for a moment that everything happened

exactly the way you claim it did," she said. "You broke into the clinic to talk to Mrs. Duquesne. The guards found you with her, they gave you a beating and dumped you in the alley. Can you give me a logical reason why they'd do such a thing? What's the motive?"

"Obviously, they're trying to hide her."

"But why would they do that?"

"I don't know."

"You see, that's the big problem with your story. With a Medicaid mill, the more patients they have, the more money they get paid by the State. Therefore, it doesn't make sense for them to hide a patient. That would only cut into their profits."

"Unless they're not getting paid for Laura's care. Maybe they're keeping her there for some other reason, something they don't want anyone to know about."

She opened the top drawer of the filing cabinet and pulled out a gallon jug of spring water, a one-pound can of Maxwell House coffee and a paper filter.

"You don't give up, do you?" she said.

"I don't turn my back on people who need help."

She poured two cups of water into the top of the coffee machine, spooned the appropriate amount of Maxwell House into the filter, and pressed the start button.

"I'd like to believe you, Theo. I really would."

"But . . ."

"But there are too many holes in your story."

"So you're not going to help me?"

The coffee machine hissed and started to sputter.

"I didn't say that."

"But you still don't believe me."

"I'm not sure." She sighed. "Let's just say you've aroused my curiosity."

"But you won't try to find Laura."

"Is there something I'm missing here?" she asked.

"Like what?"

"The real reason for your interest in Mrs. Duquesne," she said. "You're obviously on a first-name basis with her. Do the two of you have some sort of prior relationship?"

"Of course not."

"Because I get the feeling that you're kind of attracted to this woman."

"Intrigued would be a better word."

"Based on your actions, I'd say it's a lot more than that."

"I only met her once," I protested.

"She must have made a terrific first impression on you," the Chief said. She turned and gave me a smile that defied me to disagree. "You seem pretty desperate to see her again."

"I just want to be sure she's okay," I said.

"You were willing to confess to a crime just for the chance to get back inside the Walden Clinic. That's taking a hell of a risk simply to check up on someone you met only once."

"She asked for my help."

"What kind of help did she want?"

I chose not to answer. I kept my eyes averted, concentrating instead on the stream of coffee that was quickly filling the decanter, sending its rich smell throughout the office.

"Did she want you to help her get out of there?" the Chief asked.

She had a highly intuitive approach to questioning, and my non-response provided her with the answer she sought.

"You met her once and you were willing to help her escape?" She shook her head in disbelief. "Are you that easily influenced by a beautiful woman?"

Her questioning made me uncomfortable, perhaps because she insisted on ascribing so superficial a motive to my actions.

"It's not what you think," I protested.

"Then tell me what it is about her that intrigues you."

Unless otherwise requested by the subject, near-death interviews aren't bound by the same confidentiality standards applied to psychological or medical records. The only proscription against my divulging information was Professor DeBray's desire for secrecy to avoid being "scooped" by other NDE researchers.

The problem in this case, however, was the disappearance of the subject and all records of her death. No matter how much the tape-recording of the interview excited the Professor, we would be open to charges of fraud unless I could locate Laura.

Hoping to convince Chief Greer to help in the search, I decided to share the details of Laura's near-death experience with her.

While I talked, the Chief busied herself filling two styrofoam cups with coffee. She handed me one cup and sat down behind her desk, where she gently blew on her coffee until it was cool enough to sip. I told her everything I could remember about the interview, ending up with Laura's claims of being drugged and held prisoner against her will and her desperate pleas for help. The Chief listened quietly until I finished my account.

"Do you believe what Mrs. Duquesne told you, about her husband still being alive?" she asked.

"Not really," I had to admit.

"Then how can you believe anything else she told you?"

It was a good question.

Unfortunately, I didn't have a good answer.

FIFTEEN

During my fruitless encounter with the police, I purposely withheld certain information. One of the items I didn't disclose was the identity of our local informant, whom I now set out to find.

Usually we don't get much information from the people who respond to our ads. They'll send us a newspaper clipping or a short note describing a near-death experience they heard about. But in the Duquesne case, our informant's letter included a hand-drawn map of the Walden Clinic, locating all the nurses' stations, the deployment of the security guards, the fire exits, the closed-circuit TV cameras . . . all the information necessary for me to get into the building and make my way down to the basement room without being seen. The letter-writer apparently knew all about the security that surrounded Laura Duquesne.

It was time to find out what else she knew.

The return address on the informant's letter led me to a turn-of-the-century red sandstone structure topped with what appeared to be its original grey slate roof. It was one of those beautiful old school buildings whose history traced the decline of towns like Dickson. After the boom years of the Second World War, the factories and mines shut down, unemployment went up, and the population dwindled. Neighborhood schools like this one were closed in favor of large Consolidated School Districts that could serve a dozen neighboring communities more cost-efficiently, and the hell with the fact that the students didn't know where Madagascar was, or in which war General Rochambeau fought, or even who was President of the United States before John F. Kennedy.

The abandoned school buildings were converted at first into dress factories and furniture assembly shops. When those jobs followed the bottom line to the non-union South, the old buildings were left vacant, became warehouses, were demolished for parks, and in a few lucky cases were converted into nursing and retirement homes. Eldercare was a recession-proof industry, and would probably remain so as long as the government kept mailing out those Medicare and Social Security checks.

A faded wooden sign above the main entrance to this particular recycled school building identified it as the Valley View Manor. Smaller letters underneath explained that it was a Lifecare Residential Community by Zydecor.

What had once been the old school's playground now served as a parking lot. To save on energy costs, the current owners had bricked over the window spaces. The inside of the building was noisier than I thought it would be. Children who had once been sent here by their parents to study English and geography and civics were back in the building again. Unfortunately for them, they were now aged and enfeebled seventy and eighty-year-olds, sent back by their own children to await that final Graduation Day.

They probably hated the place more now than they ever did in childhood, I thought. Imprisoned here for the rest of their lives, the oldtimers had nothing left to do except squabble among themselves, complain about their ailments, and keep their TVs on loud enough for their aging ears to try to make sense out of what was happening in the outside world.

Just inside the front door, behind a steel desk on the right, an enormous black man was dozing over some official forms. Although he was the only attendant on duty, he didn't seem to appreciate me waking him up. When I gave him the name of the person I came to see, he nodded and rose, without asking the reason for my visit. As far as he was concerned, I was just someone who was willing to babysit one of the residents for a few hours, which meant less work for him. He didn't even ask my name. I could have been Jack the Ripper, here to eviscerate some eighty-year-old woman, and it probably wouldn't bother him one bit. Except maybe for the cleaning-up later on.

The black attendant's huge body rippled as he walked, and his white athletic shoes screamed in anguish under the burden they carried. He led me down the corridor and into what was once the school's Main Assembly Hall, but was now divided up into dozens of small drywalled rooms. Each had a cheap plywood door that opened to reveal just enough space for a small bed, a chair, a dresser with mirror, and a TV table.

The attendant led me to a room where a wizened little creature was watching "Matlock" reruns on TV.

"Visitor, Angie," the attendant announced. Turning to me before he left, he added, "Keep the door open."

Angelina Galarza was probably a beautiful woman fifty years ago, when her back was straight, her lips were full and her breasts were firm. But the years had sucked the flesh from her bones, leaving her a shriveled husk of the woman she had once been. Her body shook with the characteristic tremors of Parkinson's Disease, a nerve disorder relatively common among the elderly. As a final indignity, her back was bent beneath the weight of an osteoporitic hump, which forced her to twist her head at an uncomfortable angle to look up at me.

"I'm from the Institute for the Investigation of Anabiotic Phenomena," I told Angie.

Her old brain cells were working, trying to figure out what that meant, but she didn't seem to be making much progress.

"You wrote us a letter about a Mrs. Duquesne," I explained. After having my feelings toward Laura questioned by the Police Chief, I thought it circumspect not to use her first name.

Angie's bony little face lit up in sudden recognition. Her thin lips separated into what was left of her ability to smile. Small glittering eyes darted anxiously from my face to the hallway outside and back to my face. She waved a skeletal hand towards me, a silent gesture to close the door.

"I didn't think you'd come," she said in a gravelly voice. There wasn't much left of her vocal cords after all these years. "Did you bring the money?"

"Fifty dollars," I nodded. "Just like the ad says."

She raised a trembling finger to her lips, cautioning me to be quiet. She turned up the volume on "Matlock" to cover our conversation.

"They listen to everything that goes on around here," she lowered her voice to a rough whisper. "They find out I have money, they'll take it away from me."

She watched hungrily as I took a fifty-dollar bill from my wallet.

"They take our Social Security checks," Angie said. "Everything is signed over. We don't even get to see the checks ourselves."

The NDE finder's fee wasn't supposed to be paid out by the interviewer. All such disbursements were normally made by mail, after the case documentation was reviewed by Professor DeBray. But I was certain that when I explained the circumstances, he wouldn't object.

"I'll need a receipt," I said as I handed over the money.

Angie's hands shook as she stared at the portrait of General Ulysses S. Grant in his bow tie, turned the fifty over to examine the Treasury Department Building on the back, and then brought the bill up to her nose and inhaled deeply.

"My husband, may God rest his soul, used to say you could tell if money is genuine by the way it smells," she explained. "He was in the printing business, and he said the government uses special inks that have a different odor than ordinary ink. It's kind of a greasy odor. Here, you can smell it for yourself."

She offered the bill for my inspection, but I politely declined.

"Counterfeiters never think about the way the money smells," she continued. "No matter how good they copy the engravings, they never match the smell of the real thing."

I was amused by her suspicious nature. In some ways, she reminded me of the old ladies who argued with the grocers in the Greek section of Tarpon Springs, where I grew up.

"You think the Institute would be passing out phoney money?" I asked with a smile.

"It's always the people you trust the most who end up tricking you," Angie said. "I like to be careful, especially when it comes to money."

"Now that you have the money, can we talk about Mrs. Duquesne?"

Angie's eyes grew wary. Her trembling fingers closed tightly around the fifty-dollar bill, clutching it to the hollow of her chest.

"I thought all I had to do was send in the information," she protested. "That's all the ad said. I kept a copy of the ad just in case there was going to be a problem like this. I kept it right in the top drawer of my dresser."

She struggled to get to her feet, but I waved her back down.

"It's okay," I said. "The fifty is yours to keep. I just want to ask you a few questions about Mrs. Duquesne."

"Why? What happens if I don't answer your questions?"

"All I want is a little more background, Angie."

"How come you call me Angie, but you call her Mrs. Duquesne? What makes you think you should be on a first-name basis with me?"

"I didn't mean to insult you," I said. "I was just trying to be friendly."

"How do I know you're not trying to con me?" she asked.

I sat down on her bed, so she could study me without craning her neck. In spite of her pugnacious attitude, I was beginning to enjoy her company.

"It would be hard for anyone to con you," I said, trying to soften her up with a little flattery. "You're a suspicious woman, Mrs. Galarza. The way you examined the fifty to be sure it was real, tells me a lot about you. And what you said about being tricked by people. You must have had some bad experiences in your life."

I handed her the receipt for the money, and offered her a ball-point pen. The tremors made it hard for her to control the pen, but she pressed down hard on the paper to compensate and managed to give me an approximation of what her signature must once have been like.

"We're not here to talk about my life," she said.

"That's right. I came here to talk about Mrs. Duquesne."

"It's okay, you can call her Laura if that's what you want."

"All right . . . Laura. Let's talk about Laura."

"You already saw her, didn't you?" Angie said.

"Yes."

"Did you see those two Samoans?" she asked. "Big bastards, aren't they?"

I smiled. "Not much bigger than the attendant who brought me to you."

"Maybe not, but I hear they're a lot meaner."

"I believe you. Now can we talk about Laura?"

"She's a beauty, isn't she?"

"I guess so," I tried not to sound too impressed. "It was kind of dark."

"So what's the problem?"

"Did I say there was a problem?"

"You don't have to. I can see it in your eyes. You don't trust her, do you?"

"I'm a lot like you, Angie. I'm afraid I don't trust anybody any more."

"Not even a woman as good-looking as her?"

"Especially not a woman as good-looking as her."

"But you trust me, because I'm old and ugly, is that it?"

"I didn't say I trust you, either."

Angie let out a happy cackle. The empty flap of skin under her chin waggled when she laughed.

"I'd offer you some coffee," she said in her raspy voice. "But they don't let us have hotplates in here. The State Health Department says we can only eat what they serve in the cafeteria. All those years I cooked for a husband and six children, four boys and two girls, and now I'm eighty years old and they won't even let me have a little hotplate."

The attendant opened the door without knocking.

"I told you not to close the door," he growled at me. "You close it again, you're going to have to leave."

"They don't let us have any privacy, either," Angie said, staring angrily back at the attendant. "Might as well take the goddamned doors off the hinges."

The attendant shook his head wearily. "It's for your own protection, Angie," he said. "You know the rules."

"They won't even let us lock the doors at night," she said, keeping her angry glare fixed on the back of the departing attendant.

"The real reason they want the doors open is because they never know when one of us is going to die," she said when he left. "That way it's easier for them to check up on us. But it's still not right, depriving us of our privacy."

"It's a shame you have to stay here if you don't like it. They can't force you to stay, can they?"

"I never said I didn't like it. For an old woman like me, it's better than living with my kids. At least I've got all my friends here, the ones that are still alive. We keep ourselves entertained by complaining about the way they treat us, and gossiping about what's going on in town."

"Is that how you knew where to find Laura?" I asked, trying to draw her back to the reason for my visit. "From those directions you sent us, you must know a lot more about her than what was in the newspaper article."

"Of course I do. You put a bunch of nosy old women together for twenty-four hours a day, and you'll get to know every last secret anyone ever tried to keep in Dickson since the town was founded. We're like the CIA." Her beady eyes took on a playful sparkle. She lowered her voice to a whisper. "Plus, I've also got a secret source, who gave me inside information."

"That's why you were able to draw the map."

She gave a shrug. "I knew exactly where they were keeping her," she said.

"Apparently you know a lot about Laura's near-death experience."

"Every last detail," she said.

"Did you know that her medical records are missing?"

"It doesn't surprise me," she said.

"And the attending physician suddenly left town?"

"There are a lot of peculiar things surrounding that girl."

"What sort of peculiar things?"

"You already got your fifty dollars worth," she said. "You want more information from me, you'll have to pay me more money. That's what they do in the movies."

"This isn't the movies," I said. "I'm not authorized to pay more than fifty dollars."

"Those must be cheap people you work for."

"Let's not play games, Angie. I'm trying to find Laura."

"You said you already saw her."

"I did, last night. But when I went back there today with the police, she was gone. They're hiding her somewhere."

"Damn! I was afraid of that."

"I thought maybe you'd have some idea where they're keeping her. Do you think they have her in the same building? Maybe on another floor?"

"No. They're too smart for that."

"If I don't find her, I'm afraid of what they might do to her."

"Jesus Christ," Angie hissed. "Shut up and let me think, will you?"

She sat with her eyes closed and her fists tightly clenched. The trembling in her body increased, as if she was using all of her limited physical strength to force long-dormant brain cells back into action. Properly chastened, I waited in silence until she opened her eyes.

"First I want to know," Angie asked in a whisper. "Will you really try to help her?"

"Yes," I quickly responded.

"You're not doing this to take advantage of her, just to get her story, are you?"

"No." I could have said more, told Angie that my interest in finding Laura had already gone beyond being fascinated by the particulars of her near-death experience, but the old lady's eyes saw something in my expression that must have satisfied her.

"All right," she said. "I believe you."

And then, in a voice too quiet to be heard by anyone but me, she told me where she thought I would find Laura.

She gave me directions to the Gravendahl Funeral Home.

SIXTEEN

The frail octogenarian had come up with a theory worthy of the "Matlock" reruns she enjoyed. Her solution to Laura's disappearance was natural enough, considering the preoccupation with the mechanics of death exhibited by many people her age. According to Angie, the most efficient local processor of human remains was the Gravendahl Funeral Home. They offered an irresistible combination of low-bid services and kickbacks to managers of various health-care facilities in the area, including both Valley View Manor and the Walden Clinic. As a result, their hearses were such a common sight at those institutions that nearby residents paid little attention.

Her theory was that Laura Duquesne might have been removed from the clinic in one of those hearses, her body wrapped in a sheet like any ordinary corpse. Even if someone saw the pickup, it would have been impossible to identify the individual being transported.

Angie was unwilling to speculate whether Laura was still alive when she was wrapped in the undertaker's shroud. But the somber expression on her face indicated that she feared the worst.

Like most people, I have always felt uneasy about visiting funeral parlors. Psychology texts generally ascribe such feelings to the unconscious but ever-present fear of death that resides in all of us. In my case, however, an additional factor is at work. I have always considered the manipulation of human cadavers for public viewing to be a distasteful endeavor. While mourners are considering the cosmetically-altered remains of their loved one in the viewing room, they are unaware that another corpse is already being prepared in the room below, its blood being drained by special pumps which later infuse the arteries with formaldehyde-based formulas that not only preserve the flesh, but also restore its pink, life-like color.

That grim preparation room was where I intended to start my search for Laura.

The Gravendahl Funeral Home was a large two-story wooden frame structure that had apparently once been a private residence. A covered portico had been added on one side of the building to allow coffins to be loaded into the hearse without exposing the pallbearers to the elements. Beyond the portico, an asphalt parking lot occupied the site, left vacant by the demolition of the next-door neighbor's house.

I entered the Gravendahl Funeral Home at eight p.m. It was the middle of the evening visitation hours for the late Martin Johansen. The viewing room, the meditation room and the lounge were crowded with Martin's relatives and friends. I signed a phony name in the guest register and paid my respects to the widow, who occupied the customary seat near the open coffin. She mistook the fatigue that reddened my eyes for grief, and reached up to give me a comforting hug. The widow's seal of approval was greeted with sympathetic nods by the other mourners, which made it possible for me to work my way through the crowd without being questioned.

At the end of the hallway near the kitchen, I found the door I was seeking. It was too narrow to permit access to a standard medical gurney, so I assumed there was another entrance outside. But in a traditional residential floor plan, it would definitely be the door to the basement. Hoping nobody noticed, I slipped into the waiting darkness. My nose was immediately assaulted by the harsh smell of formaldehyde. I waited at the top of the stairs, listening for any sound that might break the stillness below. All the fears of my childhood swelled within me as I contemplated entering, for the first time in my life, the domain of the dead, the workrooms where the mortician's art is practiced.

Slowly, I descended the stairs. I was afraid to turn on the lights, fearing a glowing basement window might reveal my presence. The narrow beam of my Mag-lite provided the only illumination. It revealed rows of empty coffins in a panelled display room at the bottom of the staircase. Beyond the coffins was an insulated stainless steel door, the type commonly used for meat lockers and other cold-storage facilities.

Unable to resist the impulse that brought me here, I opened the door. Inside was a large, temperature-and-humidity controlled room. The air felt about ten degrees cooler than the rest of the basement, an obvious attempt to retard bacterial activity. The minty smell was stronger here, almost offensive.

My Mag-lite revealed a room about twenty feet square, with white Formica walls and a white ceramic tile floor that sloped to an oversized drain. The room had apparently been custom-built for its grim purpose. The stainless-steel wall sink was a hospital design with faucets that could be opened and closed by the nudge of an elbow. A sterilizing vat occupied the space beside the sink. Ominous-looking surgical equipment rested in an oversized glass cabinet. Thick shelving supported heavy containers of neatly-labelled chemicals.

In the center of the room were two stainless-steel tables, on each of which rested a human body. Both bodies were naked, except for small white privacy cloths that covered the faces and the pubic areas. One of the bodies, that of an overweight white male, had a plastic tube connected from an incision in the groin to a pumping unit on the floor, which had apparently already done its job of transferring blood from the corpse to an opaque plastic container.

The other body, that of a woman, was still untouched. Her skin had the pallor of the dead, ashen grey except for the brown nipples of her breasts. I felt embarrassed for her at the careless manner in which her body was exposed. Yet I wasn't able to avert my eyes from those naked breasts. It wasn't any necrophilic curiosity that drew my interest. They just didn't seem to fit the dimensions I had imagined on the first night I met Laura.

It took a few moments for me to build up enough courage for what I had to do next.

Gently, as if I was afraid I might disturb her eternal sleep, I lifted the thin white cloth that concealed her face.

SEVENTEEN

My Mag-lite revealed the features, devoid of makeup, of an attractive woman, probably in her late thirties. Her skin appeared to have been recently washed, perhaps by the mortician. An unmistakable odor of disinfectant rose from her body. I felt a surge of relief as I studied the dead woman's features. Her face was as unfamiliar to me as the profile of her breasts had seemed.

It wasn't Laura's corpse. Which meant there was still hope that she was alive.

Trembling with excitement, I replaced the white cloth over the woman's face and backed out of the preparation room.

I was able to rejoin the mourners upstairs without drawing attention to myself. Gradually, I made my way to a small visitor's lounge, which was located behind the stairway that led up to the second floor. I gulped down a cup of black coffee and immediately poured myself another, hoping to fight off the fatigue that was catching up with me. It had been a long, stressful day following a night without much sleep, but I had to stay alert.

When someone fainted in the visitation room, I took advantage of the distraction to disappear up the steps and continue my search.

There were four doors in the upstairs hallway. Although no lights were visible beneath any of them, I nevertheless opened each door as surreptitiously as possible. The first door, according to a bronze nameplate, was Howard Gravendahl's office.

From the size of the space, I assumed it had probably been the master bedroom before the building was converted to a funeral home. I checked the papers on his desk, but found nothing incriminating. Any documents concerning Laura, if they existed, would probably be locked away. I didn't have time for a thorough search, so I went on to the next room. The sign grandly identified it as the Finance Office. It was less than half the size of Gravendahl's office. In an earlier life, it had probably been a children's room. It seemed too small for the equipment jammed into it, which included a desk, a computer work station, three filing cabinets and a chair for visitors. The third door opened to a full bathroom in which the tub, toilet, shower curtain and all the ceramic work were coordinated in soothing shades of blue. The last room was where the weakening beam of my Mag-lite at last revealed what I had been seeking.

There was no mistake this time.

It was Laura, laid out as if on display, in a long white hospital-style gown on a bed that occupied the center of the room.

She seemed even more beautiful than I recalled.

Whatever frightening events she may have experienced, none of it showed in her expression. Her face was relaxed and serene. No frown lines marred her appearance.

I felt her wrist for a pulse. The flesh was warm, the pulse slow and weak, but nevertheless steady.

She was alive, thank God.

But there was a mark on the back of her hand, a blemish I hadn't noticed the night before. A little further up was another. Raising her sleeve revealed a series of similar scars moving up along the veins of her arm and ending finally in a spot where a catheter protruded from her skin. The progressive upward track of the catheter suggested long-term intravenous activity. It suggested that what she had told me about being kept unconscious was probably true: catheters were normally employed for medication and IV drips.

She gave no indication that she was aware of my presence. She didn't respond to my efforts to wake her. I tried lifting her to a sitting position. Her body was limp, her muscles slack. Her head rolled loosely against her shoulders. She exhibited the classic symptoms of heavy sedation, possibly even an overdose.

When I opened her eyelids, the pupils were severely dilated. Her breathing was shallow. It sounded as if she was taking in just enough oxygen to sustain life. She was gradually slipping away.

If she was to survive, I had to get her out of here. But how? There were more than fifty people at the wake downstairs, some of whom were probably the Gravendahl employees responsible for bringing Laura here. I couldn't just take her down the steps. There was no way I could safely lower her from a second-story window. And it was only a matter of time before someone would come upstairs to check on her.

I would have to improvise.

Carefully, I rearranged Laura's body on the bed, smoothing her hair and gown to eliminate any sign of my visit. The bedroom was small, but it had the obligatory closet, which served as a convenient hiding place. I left the door slightly ajar, enough so that I was able to watch both the bedroom entrance and Laura's motionless figure on the bed.

In the darkness, my fatigue quickly overwhelmed me. I must have dozed off, because the next thing I knew, the bedside lamp had been turned on. A tall, silver-haired man in a black suit was bending over Laura. From the photographs I had seen in his office, I recognized him as Howard Gravendahl. Another black-suited man, young enough to be Gravendahl's son, waited in the hallway by the open door, nervously checking his watch.

"What time are they going to pick her up?" the younger man asked.

Gravendahl checked Laura's pupils and felt her pulse, the same ritual I had earlier performed.

"They never gave me an exact time," Gravendahl responded. "All I know is that they're supposed to call us before they arrive."

Satisfied with his examination, Gravendahl straightened up. He looked around the room, his eyes finally settling on the closet. As he approached, I drew back into the shadows. I watched his hand reach out, no more than a dozen inches from where I waited. My situation appeared hopeless. Even if I were able to overpower Gravendahl, the younger man in the hallway would be able to call out for help before I could reach him. Fifty alarmed mourners downstairs would make it impossible to get out of the building. There was no possibility of escape, particularly since I was determined not to leave without Laura.

I watched helplessly as Gravendahl's hand found what it was looking for: a small styrofoam box that rested on a chair next to the closet door.

"Are you going to give her another shot?" asked the man in the hallway.

"They told me to keep her unconscious," Gravendahl said.

"Why? Are they afraid we might find out what they're up to?"

Gravendahl opened the box and removed a narrow plastic cylinder. "I don't ask questions," he said. "The less we know about what they're up to, the better off we'll be."

From the cylinder he withdrew what appeared to be a pre-filled, disposable syringe.

"I wish I knew what was going on," the young man said.

"It's none of our business," Gravendahl responded. "Now stop whining. You're making me nervous. Go on back downstairs and attend to the widow. She acts like she wants to stay here all night."

The young man muttered something and disappeared.

Gravendahl held the syringe up to the light, squeezing the plunger until a bead of fluid on the needle indicated all the air had been expelled.

It wasn't more than six feet from the closet to where he was standing. As he bent over Laura, preparing to insert the needle into the catheter, I crept from my hiding place and came up behind him. He was old and his reflexes were slow. He didn't sense my presence until I had both fists clenched and was bringing them down on the back of his neck. He collapsed on the floor. Worried about hurting the old man, at the last minute I had pulled back, reducing the force of the impact. Still, it was enough to knock him senseless for a few minutes.

I emptied the contents of the hypodermic into his buttocks, plunging the needle right through the seat of his trousers.

The label on the syringe identified the contents as Nembutal, which is a powerful barbiturate. Gravendahl would be unconscious until morning, consigned to the same drug-induced slumber that rendered Laura oblivious to this sudden flurry of violence. I left him on the floor where he had fallen. Hopefully, he would serve as a form of human bait to lure the younger man into a position where I could overpower him, too. After checking to see that Laura was still breathing, I loaded my pockets with the remaining syringes. Armed with my newfound chemical weaponry, I returned to the closet and resumed my vigil.

It seemed to take forever until the mourners began to leave. I listened to the front door open and close repeatedly. Car doors slammed in the parking lot, engines started and farewells were shouted in the night. The noise downstairs gradually diminished until at last it seemed the building must be empty.

That was when I heard the sound of footsteps on the stairway.

"Dad?"

The young man stopped in the hallway and peered into the bedroom. The bed blocked his view of his father on the floor. He retreated down the hallway. I listened as the door to Howard Gravendahl's office was opened, followed by the door to the Finance Office, the bathroom, and finally back to the starting point. Hoping desperately that he wouldn't open the closet door, I watched him enter the room.

"Dad?"

He walked around the bed. He stopped when he saw his father's body awkwardly sprawled on the floor. Being an undertaker, he perhaps assumed the old man was dead. He let out a low moan and sank to his knees beside his father's body.

I hit him in the neck with a fresh syringe of Nembutal. He collapsed almost instantly. He must have fainted from the shock of the attack, because the barbiturate wouldn't have had such an immediate effect. I waited until I heard his breathing slow down, an indication the drug was doing its work.

There were no sounds coming from downstairs. A quick check revealed the visitation room was empty, except for the late Mr. Johansen.

The stillness was shattered by the sound of a telephone ringing in Gravendahl's office.

I remembered what he told his son, about a telephone call before Laura was to be picked up.

There was no time to waste. I wrapped a bedsheet around Laura to protect her from the cold. She looked like a mummy when I was done, but at least she would be safe from the elements.

Gently, I lifted her from the bed. She was limp and surprisingly light in my arms. Carrying my precious bundle, I hurried out of the room. With luck, I could reach my car before anyone from Walden Clinic showed up.

I was halfway down the stairs when I saw a shadow move in the visitation room.

I froze.

Was I mistaken?

No. It moved again.

The entrance to the visitation room was halfway between the bottom of the stairs and the front door. Someone was moving into position to block our escape. I didn't know how many there were. With Laura in my arms, I couldn't move quickly enough to outrun anyone. And I was determined not to abandon her.

I would just have to take my chances, hoping that somehow I'd find a way to get past this final obstacle. After all, I did have the Nembutal syringes in my pocket.

Slowly, I continued my descent.

The shadow paused just inside the entrance to the visitation room, just out of sight.

As I came closer, I waited for someone to pounce. A floorboard creaked. Someone in black stepped in front of me.

I recognized the face immediately. It was the widow of the late Martin Johansen. She had been lingering in the funeral home until the last possible moment with the corpse of her dead husband. Her eyes bulged. Her mouth dropped open. She stared in horror at the bundle I was carrying.

It took a moment for me to understand why. Here I was in a funeral parlor carrying what was obviously a human body wrapped in a white sheet. The old woman probably thought I was the local ghoul, stealing a fresh corpse for some bizarre purpose.

As I headed for the front door, she let out a scream and fainted dead away.

EIGHTEEN

I had seen enough drug abuse among friends in college to recognize the seriousness of Laura's condition. Unaccustomed to ministering to the living, the mortician had apparently given her an overdose of the Nembutal. Since the syringes were pre-measured, he must have administered the injections more frequently than instructed.

If something wasn't done to revive her, she'd drift off into a coma that could easily become terminal. The near-death experience she described to me would have been merely a dress rehearsal for the real thing.

Unfortunately, I couldn't take her to a hospital. The Walden Clinic staff knew she was heavily drugged. When they discovered she was missing, they would start checking every healthcare facility in the area. It would be a simple matter to send out an ambulance with the proper documentation to pick her up.

But I couldn't allow that to happen. She had begged me to help her, and I was determined to try.

I headed east on Interstate 81, eager to distance us from Dickson City. Just outside of Scranton, I stopped off at a drug store to pick up some off-the-shelf supplies I would need during the days ahead. Twenty-five miles later, a few miles east of Mount Pocono, I turned off the Interstate and searched along a two-lane highway until I found what I thought would be a safe place to stop. During the tourist season, The Mountain Lake Motor Lodge probably did a good business. But around midnight, on an offseason night, it was the kind of place most people pass by without noticing. Tucked among the pines, it was a long, one-story building that extended back from the highway on a narrow lot. The office was up front, and the doors to the rooms faced a narrow driveway and parking lot. The place seemed ideal for my needs. The location was isolated. I doubted Metzger would ever trace us here. And only one of the twelve rooms had a car parked in front of it. Which meant I wouldn't have to worry about prying neighbors wondering what was going on in the room next door, particularly if I ran into problems with Laura.

When I checked in, I asked for the room on the end. I wanted to be as far back from the highway as possible. The sullen night clerk grunted, accepted my cash deposit, gave me the key to Room 112, and went back to his midnight snack without having spoken a word.

It was after midnight. There was no traffic on the highway in front and I couldn't be seen from the office. Nevertheless, I took extra precautions to be certain my moves were unobserved. I backed the car up to the doorway of Room 112, positioning it in a manner that blocked any view of the entrance from passing motorists. First I unloaded the supplies I had picked up on the way. Then, when I was certain no one was watching, I quickly carried my precious human cargo into the room. I placed her gently on the bed and unwrapped the protective bedsheet.

Once again, I found myself entranced by her beauty. Her golden blonde hair swirled on the pillow beneath her head. It framed the pale and flawless features of her face, imparting to them the almost angelic quality of a Renaissance painting. She looked utterly helpless and vulnerable and out of place on that motel bed. It reminded me of the moment when I first encountered her in that sequestered chamber beneath the Walden Clinic, modestly covered in white and bound to the table like some Aztec offering to the Gods.

Why were they trying so desperately to keep this delicate creature hidden away from the world, I wondered. I recalled the panic in those pale blue eyes when she begged me to help her.

What possible horror could evoke such visible fear in a woman who already knew death's deepest secrets?

They were questions for which I had no answers. All I knew was that Laura's life depended on what I did tonight. What I had in mind was risky, but keeping her safe from her former captors left me with no alternative. Fortunately, I had some experience in dealing with drug emergencies. A college roommate of mine had overdosed several times with narcotics, which resulted in my acquiring a rudimentary knowledge of drug-abuse treatment techniques. In addition, my Master's program required extensive course work on the use of drugs in the treatment of psychiatric disorders. I might not be an expert, but with the help of the items I picked up in the drugstore, I was ready to begin the dangerous process of detoxification.

The most important goal in any overdose situation is to simply keep the victim breathing. After making certain that Laura's air passage was unobstructed, I rolled her over on her stomach, turning her face to one side in the approved recovery position. Her vital signs were deteriorating. Her pulse seemed slower than it did at the funeral home. Her blood pressure was eighty over sixty, according to the home-use kit I had picked up at the drugstore. That was low, but not yet dangerous. She was breathing more slowly, too. So slowly, I was worried she might stop breathing altogether. It was the natural progression of symptoms in cases of barbiturate abuse. The depressive effect on nerve signals in the brain triggers depression of cardiac activity, blood pressure and respiratory rate which, if not reversed, inevitably results in collapse of the body's ability to survive. Along the way, the complications of shock, cardiac arrhythmia, and breathing difficulties can also prove fatal. All I could do was hope that none of these other problems would arise while I worked on her.

I wrote down Laura's blood pressure reading, pulse and breathing rate on the telephone pad for later reference. In a hospital, forced walking with close medical monitoring would keep her body functioning until the drug's effects wore off. In addition, they would give her a diuretic such as Mannitol to purge the barbiturates from her system, an IV drip of electrolyte replacement solution to help maintain proper cardiac activity, and possibly a central nervous system stimulant such as Coramine to reverse the sedative effects of the Nembutal.

I didn't have access to the appropriate pharmaceuticals, but I was able to pick up some workable substitutes on the way from Scranton. The functions of both the stimulant and the diuretic would be performed by the caffeine produced in some extra strong Maxwell House, which I could brew in a newly purchased coffee maker. I could stir in some bicarbonate of soda, which would alkalinize her urine and promote barbiturate excretion. As for the electrolyte replacement therapy, the best available substitute was eight quarts of Gatorade. Because her stomach wouldn't be able to hold down solid food for a while, I also stocked up on liquid protein drinks, and some easily digestible Hershey bars. It was alternative medicine, not approved by any doctor, but it was all I had to work with.

What I used to do with my roommate was start him off with a cold shower. The idea, a paramedic once explained to me, was to shock somnolent muscles awake by triggering the shivering reflex. This purely involuntary response to cold is produced by the rapidly alternating contraction and expansion of muscles, which tends to stimulate other bodily functions and thus begin to rouse the system.

I was afraid to try the cold-shower treatment on Laura, however. In her condition, she might slip from my grasp and injure herself. Instead, I turned the air conditioning down to its coldest setting, placed plastic bags of motel ice cubes on the backs of her shoulders, thighs and legs.

It didn't take long for the first response to appear. Tiny pimples became visible as the skin contracted around the fine hair on her arms. Her warm pink lips started fading to blue. The trembling started slowly at first, but soon her teeth were chattering and her entire body was vibrating, as if some unseen hand was shaking her.

I sat by the bed and watched, until I noticed that her fists were clenched. It was a natural reaction for someone who was cold. But it was also the first non-reflexive physical movement I had seen since finding her at the funeral home. It meant the initial treatment was working. I propped her up against the back of the bed, where I could hold her while I tried to force-feed her some coffee. The bicarbonate-laced coffee I made was the thickness of espresso. She gagged and coughed and sputtered, but I considered even that to be progress. Any kind of response was welcome at this point. I kept at it until I was able to get a small amount of coffee down her throat.

Before long, I was walking the floor with her, dragging her in the beginning like a limp doll, but then gradually noticing movement in her knees until finally she was taking her first tremulous steps.

I kept it up for hours, a bizarre marathon walk around the small room with most of her weight on my arms. I have to admit to a certain guilty pleasure in being able to hold her close and enjoy the warmth and musky female smell of her body. It was also exhausting. I was working without much sleep. My arms and legs ached. My ribs throbbed with pain from the previous night's beating. I desperately needed bed rest. But every time I thought I couldn't go a step further, the realization that Laura was totally dependent on me kept me moving.

Nembutal is a short-acting barbiturate, which means that the effects normally wear off in about four hours. Laura's overdose was adding a few hours to that schedule. But I knew the real problem still lay ahead. Short-acting barbiturates are notorious for producing physiological dependency. The marks and catheter in her arm suggested they had been sedating her for months. Daily injections of Nembutal, no matter how carefully administered, will turn the most unwilling subjects into hopeless addicts. And that was the problem I now faced with Laura. In rescuing her from the deceptive tranquility of an overdose, I was delivering her into the far more violent and frightening storms of withdrawal.

She would soon enjoy a brief respite in her symptoms, a period of lucidity and normal behavior as her body purged itself of the drug and reached a temporary level of chemical equilibrium. Unfortunately, it wouldn't last long. The violent, life-threatening reactions of withdrawal often start within hours after the last dose wears off.

What worried me most was that she might not have the strength to survive the horrors that lay ahead.

NINETEEN

Anybody who ever worked a crisis-intervention hotline knows how important it is to keep talking to the subject, no matter how one-sided the conversation may be. A continuing dialogue maintains a link with the world of reality for even the most disoriented individuals. It's the psychological equivalent of CPR, a life-support technique for use in emergency situations.

But Laura was unresponsive and unable to speak, so all the talking was up to me. I didn't know whether she could actually hear anything I said. All I could do was keep talking and hope some of my words would penetrate the chemical fog and help to save her life. I urged her to keep moving, to fight off the deadly drowsiness that threatened her. I pleaded and begged and scolded and appealed to her will to live. I used everything I ever learned about psychology. I knew what was going on inside her mind, why her brain was reluctant to emerge from its altered state of consciousness. Contrary to popular belief, a drug overdose is often an extremely pleasant experience for the addict, because it delivers an intensified version of the normal high. The cocaine user experiences a more powerful rush; the sedative user, a more blissful peace; the psychedelic user, more exotic visions. An overdose of the drug of choice produces fatally seductive pleasures from which most addicts are reluctant to emerge.

Which explains why Laura resisted my efforts to rouse her. Her brain was obviously content to remain suspended in the eerie calm of acute barbiturate intoxication. In that comatose state, she suffered no pain, experienced no fear. It was a place of blessed refuge that no outside threat could penetrate. Considering the traumas she had suffered in the last six months, I could understand her brain's reluctance to be roused from its torpor.

One of the basic techniques of crisis-intervention therapy is to identify a goal important enough to the subject to enhance the will to live. In Laura's case, however, her NDE interview had already given me the necessary insight into her psyche. I knew the one goal that was vital to her survival, the reason she'd want to live. It was the same reason she claimed she was sent back from her NDE: to find and help the husband everyone else thought was dead.

It was preposterous, I knew. The coroner had personally confirmed Harrison Duquesne's death. But I shamelessly pretended that I believed he had survived the car crash, and vowed I would do everything I could to help in finding him. I made up stories about how she and I would get the investigation officially reopened, the evidence reexamined, how we wouldn't give up until we located him, and how happy he'd be to see her again. Under the circumstances, I felt no guilt about lying. A few falsehoods were a small price to pay for Laura's survival.

As the night wore on, I grew more fatigued. Despite my efforts, Laura never said a word. I still didn't know whether she could hear me, much less comprehend what I was saying. After a few hours, the sound of my own voice was all that was keeping me awake. My psychological gimmicks and exhortations were starting to sound repetitive and useless, even to me. To break the monotony, I sang some of the few songs I know, and at one point I tried to liven up our marathon walk by changing it into a clumsy version of the two-step. Anyone watching would have thought I was drunk, the way I stumbled and swayed around the room and occasionally lost track of what I was saying. It was the cumulative effect of stress and fatigue and lack of sleep. My mind was slowing down. My endless one-sided conversation grew more reflective. I started to reminisce, quickly lapsing, like any drunk, into the story of my life. I was full of self-pity, particularly when I talked about how my career, my marriage and my life had all become part of a continuing process of aimlessness and failure from which I couldn't seem to escape. I told her of my fear that I, like Sisyphus, was doomed to repeat the same self-defeating pattern for the rest of my days.

In the lonely life I lived since the divorce, I had never shared this personal angst with anyone. It was the sort of intimate revelation that I feared would be considered a sign of character weakness. I don't know what possessed me to suddenly start discussing my innermost fears. Especially with someone who was going through a crisis of her own. But it felt good to talk about it, even if my audience was as damaged a soul as I was.

Our constant circling was interrupted only by my struggles to get alternating doses of coffee and Gatorade down her throat, and the inevitable trips to the bathroom when the diuretic effect kicked in. As the night progressed, we suffered no crises more serious than my own embarrassment at helping her on those bathroom trips.

By three in the morning, she was starting to come out of the first phase. She was still groggy, but her pulse and respiratory rate were beginning to show some improvement.

Sometime before dawn, Laura recovered enough to indicate with a motion of her arm that she wanted to stop. I helped her gently into a stiff-backed chair by the TV. She seemed relatively alert, and was able to sit up straight without my help.

I smiled and answered her unasked question.

"You're safe here," I said. "They don't know where you are."

I brewed up two more cups of fresh coffee. After a night without sleep, I needed the extra caffeine as much as she did.

"What happened?" she finally asked, her first words of the night.

"They gave you an overdose," I replied. "It was probably accidental."

She stared at me with tired eyes. The neurons in her brain were probably not yet firing at their normal speed, so it was taking extra time for her to understand what I was saying.

"How bad was it?" she asked.

"You were comatose. You could have died."

"But I didn't," she said softly.

"You were lucky."

"It wasn't luck. It was you."

Embarrassed by the gratitude in her eyes, I buried my face in the coffee cup.

"Maybe you shouldn't be talking," I said. "You should rest now, and save your strength."

"Why?"

"I'm afraid it's going to get worse. A lot worse."

"But I'm feeling better now."

"It's just a temporary phase." I unwrapped a Hershey bar and held it to her mouth. "Eat some chocolate. Build up your energy. You're going to need all the strength you have."

I fell back on the bed and closed my eyes in exhaustion.

My relief at having revived Laura from the overdose was tempered by my knowledge that what she had already endured was but a prelude to the agonies that still awaited her. By my calculation, it was at least twelve hours since the last injection of Nembutal entered her veins. That was well beyond the half-life of the short-acting category of barbiturates. I had spent most of the night helping purge her body of the drug, and she would soon be suffering the consequences.

Having redeemed her from the chemical equivalent of Purgatory, I was about to watch her descent into Hell.

TWENTY

Her torment started in the dim grey light of dawn.

Six months of barbiturate medication had worked its terrible alchemy on Laura's body. In such cases of long-term drug exposure, a gradual process of biological adaptation takes place. Mutations occur at the cellular level as the body adjusts to the constant presence of the offending drug in the bloodstream. Although an innocent participant in her own addiction, Laura was tissue-dependent on Nembutal, as thoroughly enslaved as the most hardened junkie.

Every cell in her body would soon be screaming in pain as it tried desperately to function without the barbiturates to which it had become so accustomed. Her system had already purged itself of that overdose. Now her body was entering the initial stages of withdrawal.

The sleeping beauty I rescued the night before was transformed into a desperate, thrashing creature, caught in the throes of a severe psychotic episode. Her eyes rolled wildly in their sockets. Her hair was drenched with sweat. Episodes of what appeared to be intense physical pain alternated with hysterical outbursts that could only hint at the monsters who roamed through her hallucinations.

Most of what she said made little sense. It was a strange gibberish of unconnected words and broken sentences that came out in a frenzied rush, interrupted with cries of pain and shouted warnings and pleas for help. She was experiencing the classic "rebound" effect of barbiturate withdrawal. The symptoms displayed in this phase are generally the exact opposite of the original effects of the drug. In Laura's case, it meant an unleashing of all the anxieties and fears and hysteria that had been masked for months by the sedative effects of the Nembutal.

I took her in my arms and tried to calm her, pulling her frail and trembling body into the protective shelter of my embrace. That innocent act of mine triggered a startling response from her. Caught in the dementia of the withdrawal syndrome, she imagined herself to be in the arms of her husband. Her fears were momentarily forgotten as her mind adjusted to this new illusion. She snuggled closer against my chest, suddenly romantic and whispering passionate pledges of everlasting love. I knew the words weren't meant for me, but I wanted to comfort her. I held her tighter and began to stroke her hair, enjoying an intimacy that rightfully belonged to Harrison Duquesne.

"Don't ever leave me again," she begged.

She was lost in a world of delusion, a place where she was finally reunited with her husband. She raised expectant lips to mine. Her pale blue eyes, unable to distinguish reality from illusion, gleamed with erotic promise. A rising fever added a blush of pink to her features far more beguiling than any makeup could ever achieve. Even the ravages of withdrawal were unable to erase her luminous beauty.

"I won't leave you," I found myself replying, using the words she would expect her husband to use. "I promise I won't."

"I love you, Harry," she whispered, her voice husky with passion.

For the briefest of moments, I argued with myself about the ethics of the situation. To deceive a woman in a moment of such vulnerability would normally be considered an immoral act. But after months of abusive treatment, she was in desperate need of compassion. It isn't unusual in such cases for the human mind to create an artificial reality as a survival technique. If she needed the illusion of a loving husband to help her through withdrawal, how could I refuse to play the role?

"I love you, too, Laura," I said, giving her the answer she seemed to be waiting for.

She offered her lips to me. I tried to hold back, hoping to keep it a polite and friendly kiss. But her lips burned with a passion that had been building within her during those months of isolation. My chivalry dissolved the instant her lips touched mine. I responded greedily, wanting as much of her as I could get, refusing to let go until we were both breathless.

"I'll always love you," I said when our lips finally parted.

Suddenly I wasn't sure whether I was speaking for Harrison Duquesne or for myself. She hungrily lifted her mouth to mine again.

"My darling," she moaned.

If only I'd had the strength to resist. Even now, I still can't account for my behavior. Maybe I was caught up in the excitement of breaking an ethical taboo. Maybe it was her total surrender, the unquestioning way she offered herself to me.

Or maybe, just maybe, it was the result of emotions I had been repressing since our first encounter.

In any event, I gave in to her hungry lips, losing myself in the moist heat of her mouth, forgetting entirely about Harrison Duquesne and the surrogate role I was supposed to be playing. All that mattered was the feverish coupling of our lips. I kissed her with a desire that surprised even me.

It wasn't enough.

Her lips sought mine again and again.

I tried to convince myself what I was doing was a form of therapy, but I knew better. I couldn't stop even if I wanted to. Her passion wasn't intended for me, but I didn't care. I was a victim of my own loneliness and emotional isolation, desperately feeding on the intimacy she offered.

We were two lost souls, searching in each other's arms for our own separate versions of love.

She didn't want to let go of her husband.

And I didn't want to let go of her.

TWENTY-ONE

Demons invisible to me soon regained control of Laura's mind.

Her cries of pain made it easy to imagine the horrifying phantasms attacking her, probably the usual litany of apparitions for women in her condition: cockroaches burrowing beneath her skin, snakes slithering between her thighs, cancerous growths eating away at her breasts. A lifetime of nightmares was exploding in her brain, each one more hideously intense than the last.

Driven by hysteria, she tried to escape from the protection of my arms. I had to struggle to subdue her, to protect her against herself.

Mental tumult gave way to physical agony as the very chemistry of her body underwent rapid and brutal changes. Nerve endings that had long been numbed came back to life with excruciating results. Muscles released from months of sedation strained involuntarily until they threatened to separate themselves from their attachments to bone. Innermost organs went through violent spasms of protest. Every tremor that wracked her body echoed through my own as I continued to hold her in my arms.

By late afternoon, she was screaming for an injection of Nembutal. My own eyes filled with tears as she pleaded with me to have mercy on her.

It would have been easy for me to relieve her torment. The drugs she so desperately wanted were close at hand, hidden from her in a plastic bag in the toilet tank. Without the supply of pre-filled ampules I pocketed at the funeral parlor, I never would have made this dangerous attempt at detoxification. A partial dose would suppress her symptoms if they became life-threatening. But until that threshold was reached, I had to deprive her of any relief. As agonizing as it might be, the only way to deal with her addiction was to allow the withdrawal process to run its course.

TWENTY-TWO

She suffered her first seizure in the late afternoon. It came without any warning. A powerful spasm rippled through her body. Her extremities grew rigid. Her muscles contracted. Her fingers dug into my arms. Her face became a tense mask, mouth open, teeth bared, eyes bulging.

For a single terrifying moment, she stopped breathing.

Instinctively, I pressed my lips against hers and breathed into her mouth.

No response.

I tried again, sucking in a great lungful of air before expelling it in a powerful burst deep into her lungs.

Again and again I tried, until at last I was rewarded with a shallow exhaust of sour-smelling air from her mouth.

That first seizure was my signal to intervene with a partial dose of Nembutal. To avoid possibly fatal consequences, I had to slow down the progress of her symptoms. I took an ampule from my hidden store and injected half the contents into the catheter in her arm. It would mildly reintoxicate her, and give both of us an opportunity to rest before the demons returned.

The effect was nearly instantaneous. Desperately hungry for barbiturate relief, her bloodstream immediately raced the drug to her central nervous system, which threw the internal switches that calmed her mental state and dulled her pain. Her muscles relaxed. Her eyelids closed. Her breathing slowed. The half-dose contained enough pacifying power to put her to sleep.

I took advantage of the respite to hurry out to the local mall. Guessing at her size, I bought some simple clothing for Laura: a loose sweatsuit, a hooded jacket, some undergarments and a pair of athletic shoes. After quick stops at a pharmacy and a convenience food store, I was back at the motel before she woke up.

Fully clothed, I lay down on the bed beside her, draping an arm over her shoulder to alert me when she awoke. We were more than twenty-four hours into the detoxification process. She had survived the initial phase of withdrawal symptoms, but the most dangerous part of the procedure was still to come.

People die in detox centers from a variety of causes. I knew that continued seizures could cause brain damage and fatal *status epilepticus*; rapid changes in blood pressure could trigger respiratory collapse; high fever and dehydration could induce irreversible coma.

To counter those threats, all I had was a stolen supply of Nembutal, the blood-pressure kit and my stock of basic medicine-cabinet items from the local pharmacy. I knew if I called Professor DeBray, he would advise me to rush her to the nearest hospital. But I couldn't risk exposing Laura to possible discovery by those who had chemically brutalized her.

When I spirited her away from her captors, I assumed a moral responsibility for her well-being. In spite of the potential hazards of my amateur detoxification treatment, I was convinced she would be safer with me.

The agonizing physical symptoms recurred through the night with renewed brutality. With each new hallucination, she tried harder to tear free from my grasp. But I wouldn't have let her go if a gun was placed against my head. I held on tight, determined to protect her from any possibility of self-destruction.

I was certain that when she recovered, she wouldn't remember anything about how I held her and kissed her and caressed her when she needed compassion most.

I was determined to do everything within my power to protect her from the demons of withdrawal, her captors, from the whole world, if necessary.

I was her champion, her defender, and it made me feel better about myself than I had in a long time.

TWENTY-THREE

When I started to remove Laura's nightgown, I felt I was engaging in a forbidden act.

My hands trembled as I exposed more of her naked flesh. Modesty should have been an early victim of the desperate circumstances in which we found ourselves. Yet the prospect of seeing her nude body had an unnerving effect on me. I worried once again whether I was taking advantage of the situation, invading a defenseless woman's privacy under the guise of helping her.

But I knew I had to do something to break her fever. It was the middle of the following night, and her temperature had been rising rapidly. The most recent reading was one hundred four degrees, a dangerous level for an adult.

A professional caregiver would feel no qualms about giving her an alcohol sponge bath. But for me, it was a more complex experience. The most intimate details of her body were exposed to me. I was visually trespassing, without her knowledge or permission. Yet I couldn't resist admiring the expanse of naked flesh before me. What I saw was a nubile sculpture whose graceful anatomy was the perfect complement to the loveliness of her face.

Marring all this beauty were two brutal red scars that formed a cross on her chest. The vertical part of the cross was a long scar that bisected her sternum; the horizontal line was a shorter scar that ran just beneath her breasts. The two incisions were designed to allow four flaps to be pulled back during the operation in which she died. Regularly-spaced, almost zipperlike red dots marked where the medical staples had been inserted to close the huge wounds.

What I found most puzzling were a dozen vivid red circles where the electric-shock paddles had been applied. They should have faded long ago, but for some reason they remained visible, ugly reminders of the resuscitation procedure. My eyes filled with tears at the savagery her delicate body must have endured. It made me more determined than ever to protect her from further harm.

I first ran the sponge gently across her forehead, cooling the hot skin. She let out a low groan, but remained motionless. I moved down her body, stroking her flesh with the cooling evaporative alcohol. Her arms were limp when I raised them, as were her legs. Embarrassed by my actions, I was glad she was unconscious. I felt uncomfortable about invading a woman's most private areas without permission. By the time I was done, her body no longer held any secrets from me.

The sponge bath was a ritual I was to perform every two hours until her fever broke the following morning. I tried feeding her solid food then, some white bread and cold cuts, but it wouldn't stay down. So I kept her on the liquid diet on which she had subsisted for the past thirty-six hours. It consisted of Ensure nutritional supplement protein drink, one of the liquid food products that keeps thousands of New York addicts from starving to death; plus copious amounts of Gatorade to restore fluid levels and the electrolyte balance in her body. Between the two, they probably approximated the nutritional contents of the tubal feeding regimen on which she must have been kept at the Walden Clinic.

With her temperature returning to normal, I was feeling more relaxed. We managed to get through the second day of withdrawal, and much to my relief, I was able to deal with her most serious physical reactions. I gave her the kind of constant, dedicated attention no hospital staff could ever provide. I bathed her, cleansed her, took her to the bathroom, helped her perform the most private rituals of a woman's life. Yet, perhaps mercifully for her, she seemed unaware that a near-stranger was ministering to her daily needs. She drifted in and out of various hallucinations, calling me at times by her husband's name, other times mistaking me for one of the Walden Clinic attendants, never once correctly recognizing me. There wasn't much I could do about her delusional state, but at least that part of her condition wasn't life-threatening.

The storms that raged within her body continued. Periods of relative peacefulness alternated with screaming and clawing frenzies, accompanied by frightening physical disorders. It was a textbook case of withdrawal syndrome, with the symptoms reaching a peak on the third day and then gradually diminishing.

By the fourth day, I had her completely weaned from even the partial doses of Nembutal. I removed the catheter.

On the fifth day, exhausted by the punishment her body had been inflicting upon itself, she fell into a deep, nearly comatose sleep.

I bathed her again, knowing it would be probably be the last time I would be allowed to touch her naked body. I combed her hair and dressed her in a fresh nightgown from the local mall. She looked as beautiful as the first time I saw her.

When she awoke, it would have been impossible to recognize that she had been through the ordeal of detoxification. Her eyes were clear. A healthy shade of pink colored her cheeks. All signs of physical tremors and mental anxiety had disappeared. I was proud of what I had done.

She glanced around the motel room, her weary mind trying to absorb the change in surroundings from the basement cell she had previously occupied.

"It's okay," I said, taking her hand in mine. "You're safe now."

"The guards...?" she asked in a weak voice.

"You won't have to worry about them any more. You're free now."

"But how . . . ?"

As I expected, she remembered almost nothing about the events of the previous days. Her last memory was the injection of Nembutal that put her to sleep before she was transferred from the Walden Clinic. Since that time, she had been mostly unconscious or delirious, her brain unable to properly register information for future recall. This was merciful for her but sad for me. The intimacy we had enjoyed during her recovery was gone, existing now only in my own memory. Whatever emotional bond had been growing between us was wiped out, a victim of her amnesia.

I explained briefly how I found her, brought her to the motel, and helped her through the initial overdose and the detoxification process that followed. To avoid embarrassing her, I was careful not to provide too many details, particularly about the passionate outbursts that punctuated her withdrawal. Perhaps because of self-guilt over the surrogate role I had played in those episodes, I decided the joy I found in her arms would remain a secret, known only to me.

When I was finished, she gave me a weak, but grateful smile.

"You came back for me," she said.

"I promised I would," I responded.

She squeezed my hand, and I wanted to take her in my arms and kiss those beautiful lips again, kissing her for myself this time, and not as a stand-in for Harrison Duquesne.

But she was awake now, fully conscious and unaware of the feelings she stirred within me.

"Will you help me find my husband?" she asked.

I have to admit feeling a sense of disappointment. Perhaps I was expecting a stronger expression of gratitude for saving her life. But it was apparent the spectre of her husband still remained between us.

"We've already been through this," I reminded her. "I'm sorry about what happened to your husband, but he's dead. You have to accept that fact and get on with your life."

"Harrison is still alive," she insisted. "He's alive, and I intend to find him."

I stared at her for a moment, trying to decide what to say, choosing my words carefully.

"You have to achieve closure," I said. "I know it's been hard for you. You didn't see your husband's body. You didn't attend a funeral. That's why you're in denial. It's not unusual. It happens to people when they're deprived of the chance to work through their grief. Maybe I should take you to Harrison's grave. That might help you accept the finality of it all."

"Harrison is not dead!" She sat up in bed, her eyes afire. "He's alive. How many times do I have to tell you, he's still alive."

"I'd like to believe you, Laura. I really would. But there just isn't any proof to back up your claim."

"You're an investigator. You could find the proof."

"I already talked to the coroner," I said. "He conducted a very thorough investigation at the time. There's no doubt in his mind about the identification."

"Somebody must be lying," she said. "I don't know why, but somebody's lying."

I didn't respond. Laura stared at me, her eyes widening as she understood the significance of my silence.

"You think I'm lying, don't you?" She withdrew her hand from mine. "You think I made it all up."

"I didn't say that."

"But it's what you're thinking. I can tell. You think I made it all up, all that business about dying and going to the other side, but I didn't make it up." Her voice took on a desperate edge. "You can check the medical records. You'll see I'm telling the truth."

"I tried to get copies of your records. But the hospital can't seem to find them."

"What about the doctor who treated me? Doctor Subdhani? You could talk to him."

"He's not so sure you were really dead. He thinks it was some sort of equipment malfunction. Anyway, he left town right after I talked to him. And his nurse can't find any of your records on his computer files."

"But it happened just the way I said it did. I'm telling you the truth." She started shaking her head and rocking back and forth for emphasis. "The tunnel, the light, the people on the other side, it all happened. But Harrison wasn't there. They told me he's still alive. That's why I came back, so I could find him and be with him again."

"And what if I investigate and it turns out you're wrong, that it was all some sort of hallucination, like the ones you had when you were going through withdrawal? What then?"

"Help me, Theo," she pleaded. "I know you don't believe me, but my husband is out there somewhere. Please help me find him. Please?"

There was no way I could refuse her. Although I was skeptical about her story, I knew she'd never be able to get on with her life until she accepted the truth about her husband's fate. And there were some troubling aspects about her medical treatment that deserved to be cleared up. Considering Professor DeBray's tremendous interest in this case, I was sure he'd agree I should investigate further.

"First I'll have to take you to New York," I said. "There's someone I want you to meet."

Her face brightened. "Does that mean you'll help me?" she asked.

"I don't really have much choice," I said. "I can't very well leave you here for those goons from the Walden Clinic to find."

"You're a terrific guy, Theo." She threw her arms around me and hugged me in gratitude. "I knew I could count on you."

"I can't promise you'll be happy with the results of my investigation," I cautioned her.

"I know everything will work out fine," she said.

But I wasn't so sure. One of the Professor's most basic rules was to avoid emotional involvement with interview subjects. I had already violated that rule. Now I was wondering whether I really wanted to find Harrison Duquesne. I wasn't sure I wanted to share Laura with anyone, even her husband.

"Just for argument's sake," I said. "What if it turns out that you're wrong? What if we find out that your husband really is dead?"

She stared at me for a long moment before answering.

"Well, in that case," she said softly, "I guess I'd want to be dead, too."

TWENTY-FOUR

Was she a fraud?

The question haunted me all the way back to New York.

Why was she hidden away from the world? Why did the guards react so violently at my intrusion? And what possible horror did she fear?

They were questions for which I had no answers, and which thus far she had refused to discuss.

The questions kept coming as I drove through the deepening gloom of that April evening. The dense fog of the high Poconos dissolved into drizzling rain that continued all the way across New Jersey. Laura sat silently beside me, unwilling to provide any clarification.

If she were a fraud, why would she concoct that incredible story about the survival of Harrison Duquesne, a story that she must have known would be easy to disprove?

What possible reason would she have to carry on so stubbornly with her fabrication, in spite of the coroner's findings?

And after all the emotional and financial pain I had already suffered as a result of my first wife's dishonesty, how could I allow myself to be so easily charmed by a woman whose credibility I questioned?

The backyard lights of suburban New Jersey gave way to the harsh yellow glare of the Lincoln Tunnel. Entering Manhattan, I headed down Ninth Avenue towards the Village. It was a warm, wet spring evening. The rain had cleaned the streets better than the Department of Sanitation ever did, transforming the plastic garbage bags that lined the sidewalks into glistening black sculptures. The moist air smelled of fast food restaurants and rotting vegetables from the Ninth Avenue *bodegas*. It felt good being back in the city.

The Professor's machine had been answering his phone for the last three days, so I didn't expect him to be home. Until I could get in touch with him and make other arrangements, Laura would have to stay with me. I made a left on 14th Street and headed for the studio apartment I was subleasing on Avenue B. It wasn't much of a place: a tiny single-room apartment with a worn convertible couch that doubled as a bed, a kitchenette built into one wall, some cheap bookshelves against the other, and a dining table in between. It certainly wasn't the lifestyle I envisioned for myself when I was studying for my PhD.

I apologized in advance for the shabbiness that awaited her inside. The building was slowly deteriorating. The lobby was poorly lit, because some of the tenants had the habit of stealing the light bulbs. Many of the black and white ceramic floor tiles were cracked or missing. Graffiti covered the walls. As usual, the elevator was out of order. When I pressed the button for the fifth floor, the best it could do was produce a sluggish shudder followed by a mild jolt.

Apologizing once again, I led Laura up the dimly-lit stairs. Most of the residents of the building seemed to come from places like Bangladesh and Senegal and Malaysia. Every day at suppertime and for hours after, the hallways were filled with the surprisingly pungent aromas produced when these homesick immigrants prepared their native foods. So I didn't pay too much attention to the mildly obnoxious odor that hung in the hallway on the fifth floor. It didn't seem any more offensive than usual.

If I had any idea of what awaited us inside my apartment that night, I never would have opened the door. The vomit still rises in my throat when I remember the stench that greeted us. It was the greasy odor of putrefaction, the sickly perfume of death.

My knees almost buckled. My stomach erupted in protest. Behind me, I heard Laura retching.

Covering my nose and mouth with a handkerchief, I bravely turned on the lights.

The source of the foul odors was lying on the floor beside my overturned couch. His mouth was open, his tongue swollen. My favorite necktie was wrapped tightly around his throat. Necrosis had already blackened his skin. Three days of waiting to be found had bloated his already plump body until it resembled a grotesquely over-inflated balloon figure, straining at the seams of the clothing that confined it.

Unlike the fortunate subjects of his NDE interviews, Professor Pierre DeBray would not be returning from the dead to discuss his experience.

TWENTY-FIVE

An eerie sense of calm came over me.

I felt strangely detached from my surroundings. I seemed to be observing myself from a distance, a silent spectator of events over which I had no control. I watched myself give Laura the car keys and listened to myself as I calmly instructed her to go downstairs, lock herself in the car, and wait there for me.

When she was gone, I watched my hands go through the motions of closing the door, latching the deadbolt and fastening the security chain, thus locking myself in the room with Professor DeBray's bloated corpse.

The man who had intervened in my life at a time when everyone else abandoned me was dead. It was impossible to describe how much I owed to him. His offer of employment had saved me from joining the ranks of the homeless. His friendship and respect had helped me through my worst moments of depression and despair. And most important for my self-confidence, he had treated me as an intellectual equal.

In my dissociative state, I was impervious to the foul odor that filled the room. But I was concerned about its effect on my neighbors, who might call the police to investigate. Traumatized by the ugliness of my mentor's death, my mind struggled to deal with the immediate issue of my own self-preservation. It was only a matter of time before the police showed up, found DeBray's body, and accused me of murder.

Worse yet, the real killer might return, at any moment. For all I knew, I was next on someone's hit list.

That thought helped to rouse me from my stupor.

What was important now was determining how to deal with the situation in which I found myself. Carefully side-stepping my way around the corpse, I opened both windows as wide as possible. I hoped the simple act of ventilating and cooling the room would delay the discovery of the body for a few more days, maybe as much as a week, before the police started looking for me.

The bloated fingers of the Professor's left hand were trapped between the necktie and his throat, where they had fought unsuccessfully to keep his breathing passage open. One of his Gucci loafers lay halfway across the room, kicked off in his death struggle.

It was obvious that a violent struggle had taken place before he was strangled. My small dining table was upended. One of the two chairs was broken, the other lay in a corner. My few dishes and glasses were lying in the sink. The toaster and clock-radio were smashed. My old psychology textbooks and Ph.D. workpapers were strewn over the floor. I could imagine DeBray struggling to free himself, knocking over furniture as he fought for those last few breaths.

But that wouldn't account for my closets and drawers being emptied of clothing.

Whoever killed the Professor had also gone through every possible hiding place in my small apartment, obviously searching for something.

But for what?

The bankruptcy left me with little of value except my books and clothing. Even the most desperate burglar would have seen at a glance that my apartment contained nothing worth stealing, and not wasted any time trashing the place.

I tried to make some sense out of what had happened. But the grotesque scene defied logic.

What was DeBray doing in my apartment? He had never been here before, never even expressed any interest in where I lived. My last contact with him was my telephone call reporting on the interview with Laura.

How soon after that conversation did he come to my place? And for what reason? Was he lured here by his killer? And if so, why?

And why, why, why kill DeBray?

TWENTY-SIX

One of the most universally reported after-effects of the NDE is an attitudinal change towards death. Almost without exception, the near-deathers I interviewed no longer exhibited the fear and foreboding with which the rest of us regard the end of life. Invariably, they consider the process of dying as a rather pleasant journey to which we should all look forward.

Laura's behavior fit the pattern. When I returned to the car, she seemed more concerned about my psychological well-being than her encounter with a dead body.

"Are you all right?" She greeted me with an anxious smile.

I muttered something about being okay, and started the car.

"Who was he?" She asked the question as calmly as if I had just rejoined her after talking to an old friend.

"He was the man I wanted you to meet. His name was Professor Pierre DeBray."

"You worked for him?"

I nodded grimly as I pulled away from the curb.

"You shouldn't feel sorry for him . . . ." she began to say.

I knew what was coming next. Like all the other near-deathers, she wanted to explain how wonderful it was to die, how those who pass away are really very happy on the other side, and how I shouldn't think of death as time for mourning. But in my current state of mind, I didn't want to hear it.

"And why shouldn't I feel sorry for him?" I asked, unable to hide my anger. "Did you see what they did to him?"

"I'm sure he's happy now," she said, putting a hand on my arm as if to comfort me.

"Spare me the platitudes," I told her. "We're talking about a man who was strangled to death. Nobody deserves to die like that. Nobody."

Still upset, I spun the wheel into a particularly sharp left turn on Fourteenth Street. The sudden change of direction threw Laura off-balance. Her hand slipped away from my arm. She was silent as we drove towards the Village. It wasn't until we turned south on Broadway that she finally spoke.

"Nobody deserved to die the way I did, either," she said. Her voice was gentle, but each word was clearly a slap at me.

I slowed down the car, and this time, when I made a right turn on Eighth Street, I was careful not to throw her off-balance again.

"I'm sorry," I told her. "I shouldn't have snapped at you like that."

"It's all right," she said.

"I know you're trying to make me feel better, and I appreciate it. But you don't understand how I felt about the Professor."

"I said it's all right," she repeated, but the tone of her voice said it wasn't.

I found a slightly-illegal parking spot on Henry Street and walked back two blocks to the building on Eighth Stree where DeBray and I had spent so much time discussing the NDE interviews.

His office was in a block of 19th-century rowhouses that had been beautifully rehabbed and sold off in sections as condos. The brickwork and masonry were freshly sandblasted and tuckpointed; the old narrow sash windows were replaced with double-width thermopane glass backed with black mini-blinds; the entry treatment consisted of an enameled black door with gleaming brass fixtures and leaded glass sidelights. With all the new wiring and plumbing and interior work, the narrow building was probably in better shape now than when it was first built.

The offices of the Institute for the Investigation of Anabiotic Phenomena were located in a cluttered five-room unit on the first floor that had also served as the Professor's living quarters.

Just last month, he had given me a spare key to the place, along with the four-digit code for disarming the security system. He never adequately explained why he wanted me to have access. At the time, I took it as an indication of his trust in me. Now I wondered if he had been motivated by some strange premonition of his own death.

The line between the Professor's work and his personal life had always been blurred. Stacks of files and printouts and scholarly books and computer equipment usually competed for space with furniture and bedding and cooking utensils. Now in death, the demarcation had totally disappeared. Everything he owned was dumped on the floor in a mindless mess of case files and bedding and books and upended drawers and cushions and clothing and videotapes and shoes and computer storage and software discs. His prized classical CD's glittered like ornaments atop the pile.

It resembled the detritus left behind after floodwaters recede.

Whoever trashed my apartment had performed the same ritual here, but on an obviously larger scale.

There might be something here that would reveal the identity of the killer. I wasn't a policeman, so I didn't have the procedural training that would have enabled me to patiently sift through the minutiae of DeBray's life in the hope of finding some clue to his murder.

But it didn't take any great investigative talent for me to conclude that a near-death interview in Pennsylvania could cause a murder in New York City.

TWENTY-SEVEN

If I was right, we were both in danger.

If the Professor's murder had something to do with Laura's near-death experience, then the killer might well have been searching for clues to her whereabouts. By helping her, I was probably putting myself at risk. It certainly wasn't a prospect I welcomed. While she might not be afraid of dying, it was a fate I was not yet ready to embrace.

She was asleep when I returned to the car. The sound of the engine coming to life awakened her.

"Did you find what you were looking for?" she asked in a drowsy voice.

"Pretty much," I replied, trying to sound as if I had found nothing amiss in DeBray's place.

She rolled her lovely blond head against the back of the seat and turned her face towards me.

"That was where your friend lived, wasn't it?"

"I wouldn't exactly categorize him as a friend," I said. "I never felt comfortable calling him by his first name."

"But you took his death so hard . . . I thought he must have been a close friend."

"We were close," I agreed. "But our relationship was a lot more complex than mere friendship. There were times when he was kind of a father-figure to me, somebody I could count on when I really needed help." I paused, thinking about how much DeBray had done for me, but not wanting to talk about the details of my downfall. "But most of the time, what we had was a teacher-student relationship. He had this particular field of expertise, and it seemed as if he wanted to teach me everything he knew about it. Whenever I'd bring back an interview that intrigued him, he'd go over it with me, analyzing it and discussing it in great detail." I found myself smiling at the memory. "Sometimes he made me feel I was back in college, taking a special course in near-death phenomena. The man was intense. He was very good to me. But all he really cared about were those theories of his."

"Do you think that might be the reason he was killed?" she asked. "Something to do with his work?"

The tone of her voice suggested she didn't take the question seriously, that she was simply making conversation.

"I doubt it," I quickly lied. "It was probably just another random act of violence. The kind of thing that happens every day in New York."

It bothered me not to be completely honest with Laura. But it would have been unfair to burden her with my fears. After all she had been through, her psyche was still in fragile condition. Any suggestion that she might have been even indirectly responsible for DeBray's murder could easily push her over the edge. My suspicions about his murder, along with the questions I had about her imprisonment in that basement chamber, would have to wait until she grew stronger.

"Where are we going now?" she asked.

We had passed St. Vincent's hospital, and gradually drifted north and east until we reached lower Park Avenue with its synchronized lights. Now I was heading uptown, without any specific destination in mind.

"I don't know," I said. "Find a place to sleep, I guess."

"Shouldn't we go to the police, or at least call them?"

"And tell them what? That the man I worked for was strangled in my apartment? Not a good idea. They'd arrest me and charge me with murder."

Rather than a careless act by a desperate person, leaving DeBray's body in my apartment was really a clever move by the killer to neutralize me. It meant I couldn't go to the police with my suspicions, nor could I seek their protection for Laura. All my actions were suddenly circumscribed by the fear of discovery. If I became too much of a threat to DeBray's killer, an anonymous phone call would lead the police to the corpse, and inevitably to a warrant for my arrest.

"But I could be your alibi," Laura said. "You were with me the whole time."

"They'd claim we were in it together."

"What about the manager at the motel? He could verify that we were in the Poconos all week."

"It's only a two-hour drive. There are people who make that commute every day."

She let out a slow sigh.

"So what are we now, fugitives?" she asked.

"Not yet. Not until the police find the body."

"How long before that happens?"

"A few days, maybe," I guessed. "A week at the most. I opened the windows, but the smell is pretty strong."

"That doesn't give us much time," she said.

"It's me they'll be after, not you."

"Then we'd better hurry, if we're going to find Harry."

I was incredulous.

"With everything that's happened, all you can think about is me looking for Harrison?"

"You promised," she reminded me.

"I told you before, I'm not a detective," I said. "And from everything I know, your husband is dead."

"Stop saying that!" she shouted. "He's not dead! He's still alive and we have to find him!"

Such single-minded devotion made me envious of Harrison. No one had ever cared for me that much. I softened my tone of voice and tried again.

"Okay, let's assume he's alive. I know I agreed to help you, but finding missing persons requires special skills. All I have is an advanced degree in Psychology. My training is in the behavioral sciences. If you're serious about finding Harrison, what you really need is a private detective, or someone with a law-enforcement background. Someone who knows how to track down people. I don't have that kind of expertise."

"You can do it, Theo. I know you can."

"I'm not so sure. I'm basically an academic type. I'm very good at research and theoretics. But I don't usually do well when it comes to real-world problems."

"Don't underestimate yourself, Theo. You risked your life to rescue me, and then you nursed me back to health. If you could do that, you could do anything. Besides," she added, "If you don't help me, who will?"

It was a question for which I had no answer. The only person I knew who took her story seriously was the Professor. I remembered how excited he was in our last conversation. He was convinced that finding Harrison Duquesne would provide scientific proof of his near-death theories. After years of scorn from his peers, the final victory would be his. He thought the Duquesne case could turn out to be the most important assignment he had ever given me. He had no way of knowing it would also be his last.

Never mind that I had my doubts about her story then, and I still did now. I really had no choice. I owed it to the Professor to follow through on this one last NDE investigation. If by some incredible miracle Harrison Duquesne turned up alive, it would give DeBray a posthumous victory over his critics.

I didn't expect that to happen, of course. But the search for Laura's husband, as fruitless as it might be, at least offered me the chance to spend a lot of time in her company.

"I don't want you to get your hopes up too high," I cautioned her. "But I said I'd help you, and I will. If your husband is out there anywhere, we'll find him."

She gave me the kind of grateful smile women usually reserve for men who bestow great gifts upon them, then threw her arms around me and kissed me on the cheek with those magnificent warm lips of hers.

"You're a wonderful human being, Theo. I knew I could count on you."

It wasn't exactly an expression of love, but it was close enough for the time being.

I drove on contentedly, marveling at how quickly she could change my mood from gloom to joy.

"Do you have any suggestions where we should start?" I asked.

"We're not too far from my place," she said. "Why don't we go there?"

"Your place?"

"My apartment," she explained. "Where Harrison and I live. It's just off Park Avenue on Sixty-Third Street."

There was a mention of a New York address in her file, but in all the excitement of the past week, I had forgotten about it.

"It's been six months," I pointed out. "Maybe somebody else lives there now."

"No. It's a condo unit. The monthly fees and all the bills were paid through automatic withdrawals from a special checking account at Chemical Bank. We always kept enough money in the account to cover a year's expenses."

"What about the key?"

"I'll get it from the doorman. We always left a duplicate key with him for emergencies."

"You don't have an ID."

"What's the matter with you, Theo? All I want to do is go home. Why are you making it sound so difficult?"

Maybe I was getting paranoid. It all sounded so easy. Yet it could just as easily be a trap. There had been plenty of time since DeBray was killed for the murderer to find a way to get into Laura's apartment. Or to set up some kind of surveillance outside.

In the end, it was probably my fatigue that decided the issue. The prospect of a comfortable bed, a hot bath and the chance to relax in comfortable surroundings overcame my sense of caution. For the time being, I would keep my fears to myself.

It was almost midnight when we arrived at her apartment building. The rain had stopped. The interiors of the cars parked on the block were obscured by fogged windshields, making it impossible to tell whether anyone was watching our arrival.

The night security in Laura's building consisted of an emaciated black man with false teeth who looked like he was at least a hundred years old. He wore a faded navy blue uniform with red trim on the lapels and hat. After a few minutes of questions about her health and the obligatory expressions of sorrow about Harrison Duquesne, the old man supplied her with a key.

As the elevator took us slowly up to the eighth floor, Laura grew visibly nervous. I could guess what was on her mind. If Harrison was alive, the logical place for him to be was at home. Like many grieving widows, she probably expected to open the door and find her husband watching TV or reading a book in bed or doing whatever he normally did at this time of night. I was beginning to wonder myself what awaited us inside the apartment.

After a bit of fumbling with the keys, we soon had our answer. The apartment was dark and quiet. The air inside smelled stale and musty. Laura went from room to room, turning on the lights, opening the closets, checking behind the doors. Her search proved futile, as I expected it would.

Disappointed, she disappeared into the bathroom.

"Make yourself comfortable," she called out. "There might be a beer in the refrigerator. I'll fix us something to eat when I'm done." Her last words were drowned out by the sound of the shower. She was retreating to that traditional refuge of women victimized by sexual or psychological trauma, where soap and hot water provide a symbolic cleansing of the stains that defile their souls.

The Duquesne apartment was what the New York Times Real Estate Section would offer to appeal to a double-income couple with no children: the living room was coldly modern, with stark white walls, a wooden parquet floor, a black leather couch and matching black leather Eames chair, a big-screen TV, and a huge red and brown abstract painting by Zalameda occupying most of one wall. There was little to identify the residents. Instead of photographs or collectibles atop the long black buffet, the only ornamentation was a sharply pointed obelisk, sculpted of Lucite. The windows looked out on Sixty-Third Street. There were two bedrooms, one of which was converted into a home-office/den, with a convertible couch to handle the occasional guest. The kitchen matched the white of the living room and dining alcove, except for the splashwall behind the sink and stove, which was protected with blue Portuguese ceramic tiles.

I found a single bottle of Killian's Red behind a six-pack of Diet Coke on the bottom shelf of the stark steel and glass refrigerator. The cool air inside the refrigerator smelled of long-spoiled milk and rancid meat, reminding me of the sickly odor of the Professor's corpse. I turned on the kitchen exhaust fan to get rid of the smell, and just to be on the safe side, washed the bottle of beer before I opened it. I'm not normally a beer drinker, but tonight I needed one.

If this were television, a private detective would take the opportunity to look around the apartment, opening drawers and closets, examining correspondence, doing whatever the scriptwriters imagined a detective should be doing. Given the same opportunity, I sat down on one of the black leather couches and turned on the TV to see if the "Late News" had anything I should worry about. There was some videotape of a fire in a Spanish dance club, a drug bust on the Lower East Side, a fatal traffic accident on the George Washington Bridge, but fortunately no mention of the police finding a man who had been strangled to death. At least they wouldn't be looking for me tonight.

The hot shower worked its revitalizing magic on Laura. She came out of the bathroom smiling, wearing a maroon terry robe with matching maroon slippers and a towel wrapped around her wet hair. She was in familiar surroundings now, and walked with an assurance that I had not seen before. Gone were the slump from her shoulders, the fear from her eyes, the caution from her step. The absence of her husband appeared to be temporarily forgotten. Her smile revealed two dimples which had been in hiding during the gloom of the past week. Coming home had restored her confidence in herself, and her body language reflected it.

I realized this new woman who stood before me was the real Laura Duquesne, perhaps not exactly as she was before her NDE, but probably fairly close. She was a creature too beautiful, too elegant for someone like me to do anything except fantasize about. She smelled of soap and clean wet hair and sweet femininity.

Seeing her in such almost intimate proximity, I felt more jealous than ever of Harrison Duquesne. How many times had she stood before him in this apartment, completely naked beneath her robe, ready to give herself to him? I tried to shake away the carnal thoughts. There was no point in torturing myself with images of her disrobing, with fantasies of her leading the way naked into the nearby bedroom where she had so often willingly surrendered her body.

The innocent expression on her face told me she harbored no such sensual thoughts about me. She was still the wife of Harrison Duquesne, married to his memory if not his corporeal reality, and in her mind was therefore off-limits to anyone else. I was here only because she wanted my help in finding him.

Did I really want to find Harrison?

After all, if I found him, I would lose her.

TWENTY-EIGHT

I was in love with a near-deather.

I couldn't take my eyes off her as she busied herself in the kitchen searching for something for us to eat. She quickly located a box of pasta and a bottle of four-cheese spaghetti sauce, and soon had the contents bubbling away on the stove, filling the air with the rich aroma of Italian cooking. While the pasta and sauce cooked, she wiped the dust off the table, cleaned the sink, and filled a garbage bag with spoiled food from the refrigerator, sending me down the hall to deposit it in the incinerator chute. When I returned, the table was set and she had even produced a bottle of red wine.

There we were, after midnight, sitting down to a lovely pasta dinner, forgetting for a moment the frightening events which had drawn us together. Laura was certainly a gracious hostess. This sudden burst of late-night activity, however, had less to do with hospitality than with her desperate need to reestablish the normal patterns and routine of her earlier life.

"I haven't had a meal like this, I mean solid food, in a long, long time," she said as she raised her glass of wine and touched it to mine in a toast.

The wine we were drinking was a Valpolicella, ruby-red and fragrant, the perfect choice for the pasta.

I wondered how many times Harrison Duquesne had come home to romantic meals just like this, with Laura smiling at the table across from him. Did he love her as much as she loved him? I was growing increasingly jealous of Harrison, whose hold on his wife evidently extended from beyond the grave.

We ate slowly, and she had only a small portion of pasta, so that her stomach could accustom itself to solid food again. My wine glass was soon emptied. When she attempted to refill it, I moved the glass away.

"You don't like the wine?" she asked.

"It's a delightful wine. But I had a beer, too. I think that's enough for tonight."

The combination of alcohol and fatigue was already beginning to have an effect on me. If I kept drinking, I was afraid I might blurt out my feelings for her in some sudden sophomoric outburst, and leave her confused and wary of my intentions.

"Not even half a glass?" she teased.

"No, thanks."

She refilled her own glass.

"I admire your self-control. It reminds me of my husband. He was a very self-disciplined man."

Christ, the last thing I wanted to hear about was Harrison Duquesne. But what could I say? She had invited me into her home because I was supposed to help her find her husband. It was inevitable that she would want to talk about him, and obligatory that I display some interest.

"You expected to find him here tonight, didn't you?" I asked in a gentle voice.

She stared down at her plate, where she was twirling some of the last few strands of pasta around her fork.

"You think that's silly of me, don't you?"

"No, no," I said. "It's a natural reaction for . . . someone in your situation." I almost said it was a natural reaction for a grieving widow, but caught myself in time.

"You're just being kind," she said. "You want to know what's really silly?"

"What?"

She kept twirling the pasta around, just toying with it.

"I get the feeling that someone's been here, in the apartment, while I was gone. Do you think maybe it was Harrison?"

"I think it's just your imagination."

"I knew you'd say that." She put down her fork and sat back. "But things have been moved. Not so you'd really notice, until you looked for something, like when I was looking for the spaghetti. Things were moved around in the cupboard. The same thing in the bedroom. Someone was here, Theo."

"Your memory is playing tricks on you," I suggested. "When you consider what you've been through, it's surprising your mind is as clear as it is."

"Well, maybe . . . ," she said in a dubious voice.

It was time to change the subject, get her off this line of thinking, even if it meant talking about the one person I'd prefer to forget.

"How long were you married to him?" I asked.

"Almost four years. We would have celebrated our fourth wedding anniversary in July."

I thought for a moment she was going to break into tears, but she bit her lower lip and managed to regain enough control to continue.

"Do you believe in love at first sight, Theo?"

"Yes, of course I do," I quickly responded.

There was a time when I didn't, when my studies in human behavior convinced me that such romantic notions were myths invented by sentimental teenagers and perpetuated by songwriters and romance novelists. But that was before I met Laura, I thought, as I stared into those luminous blue eyes of hers.

"Well, that's what happened to us," she explained. "Harrison said he fell in love with me the moment he saw me."

"And you? Was it love at first sight for you, too?"

"To be honest, it took me a little longer." She smiled shyly. "Maybe a week."

"When did you first meet each other?" I asked, growing more interested with each question.

"It was just two months before we were married," she said. "We had one of those quick courtships."

"So that would have been the month of May, four years ago?"

The timing had a depressing significance for me, because it was the same month I became acquainted with Elizabeth. Talk about parallel lives. Why couldn't I have met Laura instead?

"I remember it was a rainy Saturday afternoon when we first met," she continued. "It was at the Frick Museum. Have you ever been there?"

"At least a dozen times. It's one of my favorite museums in New York."

The Frick Museum is actually the opulent Fifth Avenue mansion that was once the home of Henry Clay Frick, a nineteenth century industrialist. The artwork he acquired during his lifetime remains on display exactly as it was when he lived in the mansion. What I particularly like about the Frick is that, in addition to its magnificent art collection, it affords a unique insight into the attitudes and lifestyle of an age we shall never see again.

"It's my favorite, too," she said. "I used to wander through the rooms and pretend I lived there, that all the visitors were my guests, and when they left, I'd be alone to enjoy my art and antiques." She smiled self-consciously, as if she was embarrassed by her revelation. "You probably think that's silly of me, don't you?"

"Not at all," I said. "It's easy to fantasize when you're confronted by such great beauty."

Which is exactly what I was doing now. On one level, I was carrying on a fairly normal conversation, while on another level I was fantasizing about holding Laura in my arms as I had done in the motel room, stroking her hair, feeling her smooth lips pressing against mine, perhaps my hand moving inside her blouse . . . .

"The museum is about eight blocks from the subway station," she went on. "The wind blew my umbrella inside out, and I was totally drenched by the time I got there. My raincoat turned out not to be waterproof, my hair was wet and my shoes were soaked. I still don't know what Harrison saw in me that day. I must have been an absolute mess."

What an impossible statement, I thought. Did Venus look any less beautiful when she rose, with glistening hair and lustrous skin, from the waters of the ocean? The same had to be true for Laura. I could imagine how she must have looked on that fateful Saturday. If anything, the rain would only enhance her beauty, like some sea nymph who emerges from her watery home, her lips moist, her cheeks pink, her face clean and fresh and sparkling with droplets of moisture.

"I was standing in front of a Whistler painting," she said. "It was a huge portrait of a woman in a pink and grey gown."

"The portrait of Valerie Meux," I commented. "In the rear quarter panel of the main dining room. It's beautiful, isn't it?"

"Yes." She paused, and for a moment, she stared at me with a curious gaze, as if she was really seeing me for the first time. The moment passed quickly, however. "Anyway, I was just standing there, shivering from the wet and the cold, and I heard this wonderful voice behind me saying that if Whistler had painted my portrait, the result would be his greatest masterpiece."

"That would have been Harrison," I muttered.

Laura's eyes went dreamy and a vague smile touched her mouth as she recalled the distant moment.

"It was a ridiculous thing for him to say," she continued. "I could never be an artist's model. Usually, I ignore men who try to start conversations with me, but there was something about his voice, a sincerity and . . . friendliness, I guess, that made me feel he was different."

I almost groaned aloud. It must have been so easy for Harrison, discovering this lovely creature standing alone in a room specifically designed by Henry Clay Frick to stir the emotions of his wealthy guests. How vulnerable she must have been, her mind transfixed by a romantic work of art, her body cold and wet and susceptible to a comforting touch. Why, oh why couldn't it have been me who came up behind her that day?

"After that, we were inseparable," she said. "We couldn't get enough of each other. He proposed to me just two weeks after we met."

"I'll need a picture of him," I said. "So I'll know whom I'm looking for."

What she produced was one of their wedding pictures. She was wearing a knee-length white lace dress and holding a modest bouquet of roses. She was looking up adoringly at her new husband, who was about three inches taller than her, a slender man in a dark suit who smiled at the camera with obvious pride in his conquest. I wanted to hate him, but all I could generate was envy for his singular place in her life.

"It was a civil wedding," she explained. "I wanted to get

married in church, but that would have taken longer to arrange and Harrison didn't want to wait."

"He was the impatient type?"

"I wouldn't call him impatient at all," she said, the dutiful wife defending her husband's reputation. "Harrison just didn't like to waste time. He was an MBA, you know. He was very good at analyzing situations and making quick decisions. That's what he did all day long at work. It carried over into his personal life, but that didn't bother me. I liked him to be so decisive."

"What sort of work did he do?"

"He was a management consultant for Merrill, Deloit and Paine, one of the major national accounting firms."

"He was certainly a handsome man," I was forced to admit as I studied the photograph.

Much better looking than me, I thought. It was easy to see why she was attracted to him. He had the sleek, polished look of a *GQ* man. His eyes were dark and deep-set, looking at the camera with an almost hypnotic intensity. His nose was so finely-chiseled, it made me think plastic surgery. Ditto the chin, with its too-neatly-placed cleft. He was smiling in the photograph, but the sensuous curl of his lips made it seem closer to a sneer. His thick, dark hair was combed straight back in the European style, covering part of his ears.

"Maybe you could find me a few more pictures tomorrow," I said. "Some close-ups, maybe, that show his face from different angles."

We probably could have gone on talking all night. She certainly seemed eager to continue sharing her memories of Harrison with me. I thoroughly enjoyed being so close to her. But I had built up a major sleep deficit over the last week, and my eyes were closing despite my efforts to stay awake.

Finally, when I was no longer able to keep my head from drooping, she led me into the guest room. The couch opened up into a convertible bed with fitted sheets and what, to my exhausted body, felt like the softest pillow I had ever set my head upon. I immediately slipped off a mental precipice into a black, dreamless sleep.

The interruption came after what seemed like only moments had passed, but was really hours later. It felt like I was swimming back up to the surface of reality. In the darkness, I could barely make out the shape of Laura's body hovering above me.

"He was here, Theo! He was here!"

"What?" I was still groggy. "What is it?"

"He was here, I tell you! He was here in the apartment!"

"Who are you talking about?"

"My husband! Harrison! He was here!"

TWENTY-NINE

Was she going delusional on me again?

I searched her face for some sign of madness, some telltale twitch or sudden mood swing that would suggest a psychotic episode. All I could see in that lovely face was pure joy.

"I told you he was alive," she said, struggling to control her excitement. "You didn't believe me, did you? Admit it. You didn't believe me."

"Take it easy, Laura. Why don't you take a deep breath and calm down, and then tell me what's going on?"

"He came back! Harry came back to the apartment! He really is alive!"

"We've already been through this, Laura. All that business about things being moved around, it's all in your mind."

"No. This is different. This really happened."

"Did you see him?"

"Of course I didn't see him. I wasn't here when he came back."

"Now I'm confused," I said. "If you didn't see him, how do you know he was here? Did he leave you a note?"

I was being only partially facetious. If I was expected to believe Harrison Duquesne was alive, I would need some hard evidence to substantiate the claim. That was what the Professor would have demanded, and I could accept nothing less.

"You're being difficult again," she said. "He was probably in too much of a hurry to leave a note. But I know he was here, and I can prove it. Come on, I'll show you."

She led me down a short hall to her bedroom. It was a spacious room, decorated in a softer and more feminine style than the severe black and white modernity that dominated the rest of the apartment. The walls were covered with paper, not paint; the pattern a traditional design of delicate blue flowers on a beige background. The furnishings were Queen Anne style, with its graceful curves and flowing lines. A ballet dancer curtsied in a gold-framed reproduction of a Degas pastel on the wall above the bed. The entire room was bathed in the soft glow of indirect lighting from frosted-glass wall sconces.

Apparently Harry allowed his wife to decorate the bedroom to her own taste. The result was an apartment that reflected the esthetic sensibilities of two totally different personalities: one of them cold and efficient, the other warm and romantic.

"Over here," she said, motioning me inside.

I felt an odd and slightly erotic excitement upon entering this room where the Duquesnes performed the most intimate acts of their marriage. There was a soft imprint on the mattress, indicating that even in his absence, she had been sleeping tonight on her own side of the bed.

"This is where Harry kept a lot of his important things," she said. "I don't know why I didn't think about it earlier, when you were asking all those questions."

She led me into a walk-in closet that was lined with aromatic cedar. The interior was illuminated by a bare light bulb. She pushed aside a rack of clothing and pointed to the back of the closet, where a section of the cedar paneling had been removed, revealing a small safe built into the wall. The door of the safe was open. Inside, I could see the blue cover of a U.S. passport, some white envelopes, what looked like a folded stock certificate, a key ring with a single key on it, and a stack of hundred-dollar bills, neatly bound in their original bank wrapper. According to the wrapper, I was staring at ten thousand dollars in cash.

"I woke up to get a drink of water and that's when I remembered the safe." She spoke in a conspiratorial tone. "I wasn't sure there'd be anything helpful inside. That's why I didn't bother you until after I opened it."

"I appreciate that," I said in a weary voice. "But I wish you would've waited until morning."

Although there was an element of vicarious pleasure in looking at someone else's money, what I really wanted to do was get back to bed. The sun wasn't up yet, which meant I had only had about three or four hours of sleep. My body was telling me I was going to need a lot more than that if I expected to function effectively.

"I'm too excited to go back to sleep," she said. "But you look like you're ready to collapse. Maybe I should make you some coffee."

"Coffee will only keep me awake," I said. "Let's clear up this business about Harrison first. You said he was here. That you found some kind of proof. What was it?"

"There was an envelope he always kept in the safe," she said. "A yellow envelope wrapped with grey duct tape."

"And . . . ?"

"Well, you can see for yourself. It's gone!"

"That's it?" I groaned. "That's your proof?"

"You don't understand." Her voice suddenly became defensive. "That envelope was the reason Harry had the safe installed. It was very, very important to him. He never would have risked taking it on a weekend trip to Pennsylvania. That means he must have come back for it. After our trip. Don't you see? He must have come back here after the accident. That's the kind of proof you wanted, isn't it?"

What she was doing was fairly common for people so heavily into denial. She was skillfully fabricating her own theories, weaving fact with wishful fantasy into a seemingly logical construct. Faced with such determination, the best approach I could take was to go along for the time being, to accept her statements as factual until they could be proven otherwise.

"What was in the envelope?" I asked.

"I don't know."

"Did you ever ask him?"

"I did, once," she said. "He told me it was something very personal, and that it would be useless to anybody else."

"You never asked him again?"

"I always respected his privacy."

"You never tried to see what was inside?"

"I'm not that kind of person," she said. "I believe a marriage is based on trust. If I started snooping around, I'd be breaking that trust."

"Apparently he didn't trust you enough to tell you what was in the envelope."

"Please, Theo. Don't talk like that. I love my husband. If he felt he had to keep something secret, it didn't bother me. It was probably something to do with his work. You don't have to make it all sound so . . . so sinister."

"I'm sorry," I said. But I really wasn't.

The more I found out about Harrison Duquesne, the less I liked him. I was beginning to get a picture of a one-sided relationship, and it bothered me.

"Maybe somebody else took the envelope," I said, trying a different argument. "Anybody could have been in here during the last six months."

"You mean a burglar?" she asked. "But the safe was hidden."

"Maybe not hidden well enough. An experienced thief could have found it."

"But the cedar paneling was in place, and the safe was locked, just like we always left it."

"Maybe the burglar didn't want anybody to know he was here. He could have gone through the whole apartment, and then tried to put everything back the way it was. Maybe that's why you thought some of your things had been moved around. He didn't get it all back exactly right."

"But what about the cash?" she asked. "Why would a burglar take the envelope and leave behind ten thousand dollars in cash?"

Why indeed, I wondered.

"What about a safety deposit box?" I asked, trying a different approach. "If the envelope was so important to Harry, maybe he decided to transfer it to a safety deposit box. That way, he wouldn't have to worry about burglaries."

"I doubt it," she said. "If he wanted it in the safety deposit box, he would have put it there long ago."

"Do you have a duplicate key to the safety deposit box?"

She nodded.

"Then we can check it out in the morning," I said. "Right now, I'd like to get back to sleep."

As is often the case, what I wanted most managed to elude me. Having been wakened from a deep sleep, I was unable to return to that restful state. In the fading hours of the night, I knew the NYPD would be faithfully performing its duties.

How long would it take them to find DeBray?

THIRTY

In most American cities, the discovery of a strangling victim would be a major news story. Not so in New York, where the overnight body counts can run into the double digits. Corpses are found in dumpsters, bathtubs, abandoned buildings, burned-out automobiles, penthouse apartments, airport parking lots and children's playgrounds; the victims having been shot, drowned, knifed, burned, crushed, suffocated, drugged or struck with the legendary blunt object; the remains are collected by policemen, firemen, paramedics, morgue attendants and scuba divers. The electronic media simply doesn't have enough air time to fully catalogue the nightly harvest of the dead.

And so, although there was nothing about it on the morning TV programs, I couldn't be sure DeBray's body hadn't already been discovered, and a warrant issued for my arrest.

Were the police already searching for me? Did I dare go outside? What if they found my car?

We were supposed to go to the bank to examine the contents of Harry's safety-deposit box. How far would I get before being arrested?

As a possible murder suspect, the best strategy for me was to stay off the street. Hiding out in Laura's apartment seemed like a good idea. As long as I kept out of sight, I'd be safe from the police.

But was that safety merely an illusion?

Whoever murdered the Professor would have no trouble finding Laura's apartment. If she was next on the hit list, all the killer had to do was look up her address in the telephone book, in which case, staying inside could turn out to be be more dangerous than confronting the police.

My options were all disagreeable. I never considered myself a brave person. Yet as much as I wanted to withdraw from this suddenly ominous world, I knew that inaction in the face of danger is the best guarantee of disaster. I could not allow myself to be immobilized by fear. By the time Laura finished dressing, I was ready to go, clean-shaven and relatively presentable in a blazer, white shirt and blue jeans I had rescued from my apartment the night before.

What should have been a pleasant nine-block walk to the ChemBank branch on Seventy-Second Street turned into an uneasy expedition through a seemingly hostile environment.

From the moment we stepped out the front door, I was convinced we were being watched. Every police car became a possible threat. Every passerby appeared suspicious, particularly those who approached too close. I tried to avoid eye contact with other pedestrians, preferring to study those around us by their reflections in store windows. For me, the simple act of walking down the street became a clandestine operation.

Laura, on the other hand, seemed unaffected by my grim demeanor. She was enjoying her new-found freedom, experiencing the warm touch of sunlight on her face for the first time since the accident. She looking stunning in an ankle-length black coat worn open to reveal a short red linen dress, with matching red pumps, a pink silk scarf at her throat and that soft, straw-blond hair catching the occasional breeze. Her happy voice bubbled on about the beautiful spring morning, the clear air, the pleasures of walking outdoors after months of being confined to a darkened room. She took my arm and smiled and told me of her gratitude for my help. But her cheerful mood did little to calm my anxieties.

In spite of my unspoken fears, we made it safely to the bank. I never owned enough valuables to need a safety-deposit box, so the entire procedure of gaining access to the vault was a new experience. Of particular interest to me was the signature card, which was time-stamped and dated every time the vault was entered. According to the card, the last time Harrison had signed in was eight months earlier, which was two months before the fatal accident. When I tried to point out the significance of the date to Laura, she simply shrugged it off. She wasn't interested in any details that didn't support her version of the truth.

When she opened the safety-deposit box, however, she was quick to point out the absence of Harrison's precious yellow envelope.

"You see?" she said. "I told you it wouldn't be here."

The box contained some legal documents, an insurance policy, and another stack of money, this one also consisting of hundred-dollar bills. The bank wrapper indicated there were fifty bills in the stack, amounting to five thousand dollars. Not as much as we had found in the apartment safe, but still more cash than I had earned in any month since my job was eliminated at Grumman.

"You were right," I agreed. "No surprises here."

"Except for the money," she said.

"Excuse me?"

"The money," she repeated, staring at the stack of fifties. "The money surprises me."

"You didn't know about it?"

"It doesn't seem like the kind of thing he'd do," she said, shaking her head slowly.

"The money in the closet safe," I said. "You didn't know about that either, did you?"

"I'm sure he wasn't trying to hide it from me, if that's what you're getting at," she said. "If he wanted to hide any money, he wouldn't keep it at home or here in the bank. He's too smart for that."

I noticed she kept slipping in and out of the present tense when she was talking about him. It was a verbal cue that, despite her protestations, she still had some inner conflicts about whether Harrison really was alive.

"I'm just a little surprised that he's keeping so much cash around," she said. "You know, not bearing interest. Harry didn't talk much about his work, but I know part of it had to do with moving his clients' money around. He used to do the same with our money, always looking for the best rates of return. Even our checking accounts pay interest. So, frankly, I'm puzzled at all this cash we're finding."

"Maybe you should look into those checking accounts," I suggested. "Make sure the money's still there."

"I'm sure it is," she said. "But even if it's not, Harry had as much right to spend the money as I did. Maybe more, because he had a bigger salary than me."

It sounded to me like Harry ran the couple's finances with very little input from his wife. Most marriage counselors would consider that a sign of an unhealthy relationship, using money as a means of exerting dominance. Yet, Laura's love for her husband seemed unshakeable. She had an explanation or excuse for every action of his that I questioned. She was convinced that, alive or dead, Harrison Duquesne could do no wrong.

With her permission, I went through the other documents in the box. One envelope contained the condo mortgage papers. I couldn't resist peeking at the dollar figures. Their two-bedroom unit required a mortgage three times the purchase price of the unit Elizabeth and I once owned.

Another envelope contained birth and baptismal certificates, from which I learned that Harry was six years older than Laura, that he was born in New York City. There was no father listed on his birth certificate. According to Laura, Harry's mother raised him by herself. The father provided no child support, and never visited little Harry. The identity of the father was a secret Harry's mother took to her grave.

It was the kind of life history that would certainly elicit sympathy from a woman like Laura. It helped explain why she felt so protective towards him. Unfortunately, it also helped explain why Harry might have developed some unfortunate character traits.

"At least he left you some insurance," I said.

It wasn't much of a policy for a supposedly successful executive like Harry. Fifty thousand dollars in term insurance, with a double-indemnity clause for accidental death. It wouldn't even cover the outstanding mortgage on the apartment. During my days at Capitol Casualty and Auto, I knew of sanitation workers who had better insurance coverage.

"With double-indemnity, you'll collect a hundred thousand dollars when you file your claim," I told her.

She stared at the policy as if it was covered with some evil writing.

"Put it back," she suddenly said.

"What do you mean?"

"I said put it back. I don't want to touch it."

"What's wrong?"

"Please, Theo. I don't want to have anything to do with it."

"We're talking about a hundred thousand dollars," I said. "Don't tell me you can't use that kind of money."

Her eyes suddenly filled with tears.

"Did I say something wrong?" I asked helplessly. I slid the insurance policy back into the metal box and closed the top. "What's wrong?"

She tried to hold it back, but her chin started to quiver and her shoulders started to tremble and I could see her tears getting ready to spill over.

"I don't want insurance money," she whimpered.

She started to sway. Instinctively, I reached out for her. She fell into my arms, where all the grief and anguish she had been suppressing came pouring out in huge, violent sobs. Her body shook uncontrollably. Her tears soaked through my collar. Her breath came in tortured gasps. I held her tight, afraid she might collapse.

"I don't want insurance," she said between sobs. Her voice was wet and barely audible. "I want my husband."

Against this outpouring of grief, I felt ashamed of the emotions I was experiencing. The sweet fragrance of her perfume blended maddeningly with the musky female scent of her body. Her flesh felt warm and soft against mine. Her breath was hot on my neck. I was locked together with the woman I desired more than I ever thought possible. She was helpless and vulnerable and I wanted to lift her chin and kiss her and wipe away her tears.

But those tears belonged to Harrison, not to me.

As much as my heart ached for her, I knew I had to resist. I was, after all, still performing the role of her therapist. I had to remind myself I assumed that responsibility when I rescued her. So far, I had been successful in guiding her back from a drug-induced madness to a state of relative mental equilibrium. Playing the role of her husband when she was delusional had been a legitimate form of therapy to help her through the agonies of withdrawal. But now she was a rational, thinking human being, grieving for a lost husband. A level of trust existed between us. For the sake of both of our futures, I dared not violate that trust.

Perhaps she sensed what I was feeling, too, because she pulled herself out of my arms. She turned her face away, as if ashamed to let me see the damage her tears had done to her mascara. I waited while she searched her purse, found a compact, and with a few expert strokes repaired her makeup.

No amount of cosmetics, however, could hide the sadness that remained in her eyes.

"Taking the insurance money would be admitting he's dead," she explained. "I can't do that."

"I understand."

"It would be fraud, wouldn't it? I mean legally? Especially now that I proved I was right?"

"You mean not finding the envelope?"

"Of course. It's proof, isn't it?"

The vagaries of human perception had led us to two radically different points of view about the contents of the safety-deposit box.

"I don't know what happened to the mystery envelope," I said. "But if you add the five thousand dollars in here to the money in the apartment safe, that's fifteen thousand dollars. That's an awful lot of cash, even for emergencies." I didn't remind her of the fact that she hadn't known about the money. "I don't know why he kept so much cash laying around. But it's been six months now and the money is still there. If Harry is alive, why doesn't he come back for the money?"

"I'm sure there's a reason," she said. "When we find him, you can ask him."

"Of course," I said. "And I'll also ask him why he turned his back on a beautiful woman like you."

"Now you're being sarcastic," she said, disregarding the compliment.

When we left the security of the bank, the paranoia returned. Once again I felt like a hunted man. I scanned the streets ahead, constantly searching for any threat. With my new-found fugitive mentality, I found myself walking close to the buildings, pausing before reaching each intersection so that we wouldn't have to stand exposed on a street corner, while waiting for a traffic light to change.

Laura thought I was overdoing it. Despite my imaginings, none of the threats I feared had materialized. The trip to the bank turned out to be spectacularly uneventful. But coward that I am, I kept scanning the streets, looking for someone who might be lying in wait.

When we turned the corner on Sixty-Third Street and were almost back to the safety of Laura's condo, I finally saw him.

THIRTY-ONE

He was sitting in a black Ford Taurus, waiting for us.

Somehow he had managed to find a metered parking space directly across the street from Laura's building, where he could watch everyone who entered or left the premises. Fortunately, we came up on his car from the rear. If it wasn't for my almost irrational scrutiny of every vehicle, moving or parked, we would have walked unaware into his field of view.

At first, I didn't see his face. All I could see was a partial silhouette of the man behind the steering wheel, but that was enough to send a shiver of fear through me. That military-style haircut, the ox-like neck, and those powerful shoulders were features that had been burned into my memory during the brutal beating outside the Walden Clinic.

His ominous presence suggested it wasn't paranoia that kept me on edge all morning. What must have really been working on my mind was an unconscious foreboding about the ease with which we could be found. We had, after all, behaved with incredible predictability since returning to New York. Like laboratory mice, when threatened with danger we retreated to the security of familiar surroundings. As someone well-schooled in such behavior, I should have known better. Whether through fatigue or just plain carelessness, I had succumbed to a primitive homing mechanism that made our discovery inevitable.

I pulled Laura into the nearest doorway, which turned out to be a women's shoe store. A young salesman looked up and smiled at us.

"What's wrong?" Laura asked.

"It's Metzger," I replied. "From the clinic."

I nodded towards the front windows. Metzger's car was parked less than thirty feet from where we stood. From this angle, his profile was more clearly visible.

"Oh, my God," Laura gasped. She shrank back behind me in an attempt to get out of sight. "Did he see us?"

"I hope not."

The salesman started towards us.

"Are you looking for anything in particular?" he asked.

Laura mumbled something about wanting another pair of red shoes, using it as an excuse to retreat to the back of the store.

I pretended to browse near the entrance, watching Metzger from behind the reflective safety of the plate glass windows. He was talking to someone on his cellular phone. Probably reporting that he had arrived on station. A cup of coffee sat on the dashboard in front of him. A bag of Dunkin' Donuts rested on the seat beside him. When he finished the phone call, he took a sip of coffee and slumped down into a more comfortable position. He was settling in for a long day. How many days he had already been waiting for us, I had no way of knowing.

"What do we do now?" Laura whispered. She held up a pair of red patent leather pumps for my inspection, trying to make it appear that she was asking my opinion about the style. The salesman had retreated behind the counter, where he busied himself entering data into the computerized cash register.

"We have to try to get out of here without being seen," I whispered.

She placed the red shoes back on their display stand and thanked the clerk, a remarkable display of etiquette for a moment of such high anxiety.

Metzger was too intent on watching the apartment building to notice what was happening behind him. Laura went out first, heading back in the direction from which we came. When I saw no reaction from Metzger, I followed her.

We met around the corner and walked quickly to the end of the block, where we watched to be certain we weren't followed.

"Now what?" she asked.

"I'm not sure."

"How are we going to get back into the apartment?"

"We can't go back," I said. "We'd never be able to get past Metzger."

"But all my clothes are up there."

"Forget your clothing," I said. "It's not worth the risk."

"We were able to get in last night without being seen."

"Maybe he was asleep at the time. It was pretty late when we showed up."

"What about this morning? Why didn't he see us this morning?"

"For God's sake, I don't know. Maybe he was having breakfast."

"You don't have to get upset," she said. "I'm just asking questions."

"I'm sorry. But I don't have the answers. I'm as confused about all this as you are." We walked slowly down Park Avenue, while I tried to think it through out loud. "If Metzger is watching the place alone, he obviously can't stay there twenty-four hours a day. He has to eat and sleep and go to the bathroom. He might even spend the night in a hotel room nearby. Remember, we were only in the apartment for what, eight hours maybe? We showed up after midnight and left before nine a.m. The timing probably coincided with some sort of break in his routine."

"Then why don't we wait for tonight? We could be in and out again while he's on his break. Just like we did last night."

"Last night was pure luck," I said. "What if he changes his routine? What if he stays later, or comes back at night and sees the lights on?"

"You think he knows which apartment is mine?"

The idea seemed to frighten her.

"I'm sure they know everything about you," I said.

She blushed suddenly, my thoughtless remark probably stirring up memories she hadn't yet shared with me about her confinement at the Walden Clinic.

"I was in the insurance business for a while," I explained. "I know the kind of information that's available to health-care providers. In a case like yours, they can get access to everything the police turn up, as well as everything available through the Insurance Clearing House. They not only know your apartment number, they know your credit history, what kind of TV you bought last year, what stores you shopped at, where you went on vacation, and what the results were on your last Pap smear. It's all available in your health insurance and credit card files."

"But that information is supposed to be confidential, isn't it?"

"Health-care providers get a lot of leeway. Everyone assumes they're working in the best interests of the patient. Even if they're caught doing something unethical, the authorities usually give them the benefit of the doubt. That's why it was so easy for them to keep you locked up for so long. And now that they have access to your records, you'll never get away from them. They can follow you wherever you go by tracking your credit card purchases."

"That won't be a problem," she said. "I don't have my credit cards. Everything was in my purse, and I don't know what happened to it." She hesitated for a moment, suddenly remembering. "The last I saw it was in the car. It was on the seat, right between . . . between Harry and me. Maybe the fire . . ."

Her voice trembling, she couldn't find the words to finish the sentence. I put my arm around her shoulder.

"I didn't mean to upset you," I said gently.

She shook her head.

"No, it's okay," she said. "You're . . . you're probably right. We can't go back to the apartment. But where else can we go?"

"The safest thing would be to leave the city."

"I agree."

"Unfortunately we won't get very far," I said. "I've got just about enough gas to get over the George Washington Bridge. And I went through most of my money when we were in the Poconos. All I have left is maybe twenty-three or twenty-four dollars, if I count all the change I keep in the ash tray."

"Can they track your credit card purchases, too?"

"I don't have any credit cards," I said, feeling embarrassed by my admission. "No money, no plastic, I guess I'm not much of a help, am I?"

"Don't talk like that, Theo. You've already done so much for me, I could never repay you."

She wrapped her arm around mine and held it tight.

We walked silently for a while, looking probably more like lovers than two lost souls. If it weren't for our dire situation, I would have been content to walk like that for hours, reveling in the scent of her perfume and the warmth of her body beside me.

Suddenly she stopped.

"Wait a minute, Theo." A smile spread across her face. "I forgot about the money," she said.

Slowly she removed a thick white envelope from her coat pocket. She snapped off the rubber band that held it closed. Inside was the stack of hundred-dollar bills Harry had left behind in the apartment safe.

"I was going to put it in the bank," she explained. "But in all the excitement, I forgot. Here, take it."

My hands trembled as I held the envelope.

"That's ten thousand dollars!"

"It's yours. Consider it a partial payment for everything you've done for me."

For a moment, I was overwhelmed. To me, ten thousand dollars represented a small fortune. It was enough to pay off the rest of the money I owed the bankruptcy court and still leave me almost two thousand dollars to get out of New York with Laura.

"No. I can't accept it," I said, reluctantly handing the envelope back to her.

"You've more than earned it, Theo." She tried to press the envelope once again into my hands.

"I can't take money from you," I insisted.

"Why not? You've earned every cent of it."

"I'm not doing this for the money," I told her.

"Don't be foolish. You barely have enough money for a tankful of gas."

"You shouldn't be waving all that cash around out here. It's too dangerous. You might get mugged."

"Don't change the subject," she said. "It takes money to get out of the city, and you said you were broke. At least take the money for expenses."

"Well, maybe just for expenses," I grudgingly agreed. "But I won't need all of it."

I took the envelope, counted out fifty hundred-dollar bills, and returned the rest to her.

"It's just for expenses, though. When this is all over, I'll account for every penny. Whatever is left over, I'll give back to you."

"You don't have to make such a big deal out of it."

"I have my own reasons for helping you," I said. "They have nothing to do with money."

"It's because of the Professor, isn't it? Well, I guess that's as good a reason as any. The important thing is that you're helping me look for Harry."

My heart ached to tell her the truth, to tell her how much I loved her and how desperately I wanted to help her move beyond the denial stage of the grieving process so that she could accept and hopefully embrace my love. Unfortunately, everything I knew about human psychology told me that moment of truth would have to wait until I could convincingly prove to her that her husband was unquestionably, irrevocably, indisputably dead.

"You'll find him," she smiled. "I know you will."

THIRTY-TWO

Five thousand dollars might not seem like a lot of money to some people, but for me it was a sword, a means of doing battle with those who threatened us. This suddenly aggressive attitude of mine would be no surprise to a behavioral scientist, whose compatriots long ago established the fact that money is a mind-altering substance, affecting us in much the same way cocaine does. It produces a feeling of euphoria, stimulates the nervous system, increases the heart rate, creates the illusion of power and control, and causes dramatic changes in behavior.

Which is exactly what was happening to me.

My mind seemed to be working more clearly than ever, able to analyze the dangers we faced and devise appropriate countermeasures. I could see that running from Metzger would serve no useful purpose. What I had to do was neutralize him, keep him from coming after us for as long as possible. To accomplish that task, I headed downtown, where I used some of Laura's money for a distinctly illegal purpose.

Fourteenth Street is as close as New York gets to the legendary soukhs of Marakesh or the night markets of Hong Kong. An international assemblage of hawkers and retailers fills block after block with a bewildering variety of merchandise spilling out of the stores onto tables that compete with customers for space on the crowded sidewalks. In this frenzied atmosphere, the most profitable items for the dealers are often those which remain hidden in cases under the counters, waiting for a knowledgeable buyer.

The New York TV stations had done a special report on cellular phones a few years ago, with a reporter using a hand-held electronic scanner to listen in on supposedly private conversations. Shortly after that report the FCC cracked down, outlawing the manufacture and sale of scanners that could pick up the cellular phone signals.

It took me only three stops before we found an electronics store willing to sell me one of those outlawed scanners for two hundred dollars more than the legal models. Since I'm not much of a technological buff, the vendor had to give me a short course in how to turn the unit on and off, and how to tune in to the specific megahertz bandwidths reserved for cellular phones as well as those for police communications.

Armed with my electronic eavesdropping equipment, I returned with confidence to Sixty-Third Street. Metzger was still in his car, watching for us. All I needed now was for Laura to call the building doorman and ask him for a small favor.

After searching for two blocks for a pay telephone that wasn't out of order, we found one on the corner of Sixty-Second and Madison. From there, Laura made her telephone call. I listened carefully to the conversation. The doorman had already heard from the night security guard that Laura had returned home. He was glad that she was fully recovered, and sorry about Mr. Duquesne. Yes, the duplicate key to her apartment was at the front desk, where she had left it this morning. He could certainly understand that the apartment needed airing out. After all, it had been closed up for almost six months. Of course the smell of spoiled food and stale air would be disturbing to her. He wasn't supposed to leave his post downstairs, but as a special favor to her, just this once he'd be willing to go up to her apartment to open up the windows. But if it rained, of course, he couldn't be held responsible for any damage to the furnishings. It was a pleasure talking to her again, and he looked forward to seeing her later.

When she hung up, we hurried back to Sixty-Third Street. Metzger was still in his car, watching the entrance to her building. The doorman was nowhere in sight. We found a vantage point behind the stone stairway of a rehabbed townhouse, where we could see both Metzger and the windows of her apartment. Neither of them moved. What seemed like interminably long minutes went by. Ever the fatalist, I wondered what was wrong. Had Metzger worked out some previous arrangement with the doorman? Did he know we were watching him? Was this some sort of trap?

Metzger suddenly stirred in his seat. Something had caught his attention. Laura poked me.

"There it is," she said.

Up on the eighth floor, the second window from the far end of the building was being raised. It was impossible to tell from down here who was opening the window. We knew it was the doorman, following Laura's instructions. But Metzger had no way of knowing. As far as he was concerned, it had to be Laura who had opened one window, and was now opening the second.

As I anticipated, Metzger picked up his cellular phone. I immediately switched on the scanner. I put it in automatic mode to search the cellular bandwidth for the call. According to the salesman, the closest signals would automatically cut in, and I could isolate the one I wanted.

The technology performed exactly as the vendor said it would. There was an initial squawk, a flutter of static, and I soon heard the word that Watson unknowingly immortalized when he first responded to Alexander Graham Bell.

"Hello?"

"It's me." I recognized Metzger's voice. "We've got some activity in the apartment."

"Good."

"Somebody just opened the windows."

"Was it the woman?"

"I can't tell," Metzger said. "The windows are eight stories up and the angle is bad."

"What about the man?" Although he didn't identify himself on the phone, I recognized the second voice. It was Doctor Zydek, the shadowy figure who questioned me that night at the Walden Clinic. "Is he there, too?"

"All I can tell you for certain is that somebody opened the windows in the apartment," Metzger said.

"You were supposed to be watching the entrance. You weren't supposed to let them get past you."

"I told you this was a job for two or three people. You can't expect me to run a twenty-four surveillance all by myself."

From where we stood with the scanner, I could see Metzger sipping his coffee while they talked.

"All right, all right," Zydek said. "I'll send the Samoans to help you out."

"Make sure they bring the ambulance. Just in case somebody calls the police. I don't want any trouble with the New York cops."

"No problem. They'll be in clinic uniforms and have all the necessary legal documents, in case you run into any problems."

"It'll take a couple of hours before they get here," Metzger said.

"A few more hours shouldn't make much difference."

"What do you want me to do when the Samoans show up?"

"For the time being, nothing. Just keep watching the entrance. Now that you've located the woman, the important thing is not to lose her again."

"We could go up there and grab her," Metzger said. "We could get into the apartment and grab her without any trouble. Then we could wait in the apartment and see how that works out."

"And what about that Greek, Theophanes? He's probably up there with her."

"I'll kill him," Metzger said in a voice that sounded as calm as if he was talking about the donut he was eating. "Eventually, we're going to have to get rid of him anyway."

"There'll be plenty of time for that later. Right now, it's more important that you keep watching the entrance. You know who we're looking for."

"You really think he's going to show up?"

"Just remember, I don't want him hurt."

A sudden chatter of static signalled that the connection was broken. I switched off the scanner while it was still mindlessly searching the cellular bandwidth for other calls.

I guess I should have been frightened by the casual manner in which Metzger talked about killing me. But I was momentarily

175

beguiled by my own brilliance. My first attempt at electronic eavesdropping had worked beautifully. It enabled me to listen in as Metzger fell victim to the simple deceptive maneuver of opening two windows in an empty apartment. The CIA couldn't have planned a better operation. Not only would Metzger be isolated here in New York watching an empty apartment for at least another day, the Samoans would soon be joining him. With the three of them safely out of the way, I was ready to go back to Pennsylvania, to look further into the fate of Laura's husband.

THIRTY-THREE

I sometimes wonder what would have happened to us if, rather than continuing my investigation, I fled instead with Laura to some safe haven in Florida or Texas or even Mexico. Given the murderous intentions of our pursuers, it would certainly have been the prudent thing to do.

What I decided instead was to return with her to the hill country of northeastern Pennsylvania, to the dismal town where she had so recently been held captive. A few days earlier, I would have thought it inconceivable to be returning to those dangerous environs. As an academic, I was far more comfortable with cerebral activities than those which placed me in physical danger. Yet it was precisely my inherent academic curiosity that kept drawing me deeper into this unwelcome drama. To the best of my knowledge, all previous investigations into the mysteries of the near-death experience had produced rather routine, although occasionally intriguing, results. Yet for some unknown reason, this particular case had become a tragic aberration. The attempts to thwart my inquiry had escalated ominously. What appeared at first to be a misguided attempt to keep Laura from any public contact had spun out of control. There was now a major cover-up in progress, involving missing hospital records, a disappearing doctor, the purposeful alteration of the room where Laura had been held incommunicado, and false statements made to the Dickson Police Chief. What was far more frightening was the way Laura had been turned into a drug addict, Metzger's pursuit of us to New York, the death threat made against me, and of course the murder of Professor DeBray.

I calculated my window of opportunity to save us to be no more than forty-eight hours. The NYPD would surely find the Professor's body by then, and issue the inevitable warrant for my arrest. And it wouldn't take Metzger much longer to discover that he had been deceived, and begin his search for us with renewed fury.

My best alternative, therefore, was to return to Pennsylvania, to seek the answers that had so far eluded me. The logical starting point was the scene of the original accident, the place where Harrison Duquesne went over the cliff in his car.

We arrived at the site late in the afternoon.

Route 380 is a divided highway, the main artery from the Poconos into Scranton. From its highest point, where it connects with Interstate 80 near the ski areas at Mount Pocono, the roadway meanders gradually downward until it curves around the rocky outcrop of Bald Mountain, where it begins the suddenly precipitous final descent into the Lackawanna Valley.

Anyone who reads the tourist information sign at the nearest rest stop knows that massive glaciers covered the area during the Great Ice Age. The glacial action shaved away entire mountainsides, exposing, as in this instance, huge vertical expanses of bedrock that were unable to sustain vegetation. Bald Mountain was the obvious name for a treeless slope of stone that rose eight hundred feet from the stream bed below to its barren top. What the tourist information sign didn't explain was why some nameless highway engineer decided to cut Route 380 into the side of the rock cliff at about the three-hundred foot level.

Driving around the Bald Mountain Curve is a spectacular way to approach Scranton. As Laura had already discovered, it's also probably the most hazardous stretch of the entire highway, the logical place for an accident. The westbound lanes heading downhill towards Scranton hug the cliff face around the inner curve. The uphill eastbound lanes run along the outer edge of the precipice, affording a stunning view of Roaring Brook Canyon hundreds of feet below.

It wasn't very difficult finding the exact place where the accident occurred. According to the original newspaper article Angie had sent us, the car left the roadway about a hundred feet above the curve. The vehicle left the downhill lanes, crossed the grassy divider, miraculously managed to get across the uphill lanes without being struck by oncoming traffic, and slammed through the protective steel guardrails. It went airborne for most of the drop, although when it hit the loose rock far below, it rolled end over end for another fifty yards before erupting in a fireball.

I pulled off the road about a quarter of a mile above the curve. Even from across the highway, I could clearly see where repair work had been done on the guardrail. The new stretch of replacement metal gleamed in the sunlight, not yet having weathered enough to match the dull grey finish of the undamaged portion.

The scanner's silence indicated no presence of police activity in the area. Nevertheless, I took the precaution of hiding my car out of sight along a service road used by the locals for dumping old appliances.

"I don't know what you expect to find here," Laura said as we walked back to the highway. "It's been over six months since the accident."

She seemed only mildly curious, as if the tragedy that occurred here had happened to someone else. Her apparent lack of emotional distress was to be expected, given her insistence that Harrison had somehow survived the accident.

"When I was doing insurance claims work, it was company policy to have our people visit the accident scenes," I explained. "The idea was to reconstruct everything that happened, talk to any witnesses, talk to the police. Sometimes in our follow-up interviews, the police would tell us things they didn't put in their official reports, suspicions they couldn't prove. Those on-site investigations helped us weed out the fraudulent claims. Incidentally, what company handled your auto insurance?"

"I'm not sure. Harrison took care of all that."

"You should look into it. At the minimum, you should get compensated for the loss of the car, and probably most of your medical bills, too."

We stood at the roadside, waiting for the traffic to thin out. The speed limit around the curve was 55, but as usual, everyone ignored it. A heavy semi-trailer thundered past. Its turbulent windstream almost knocked Laura off-balance.

"So you've done this sort of work before," she said. "I'm impressed."

"I never did any of the field work," I admitted. "But I used to read at least twenty or thirty on-site reports every week, so I have an idea about what to look for. You're probably the only witness, so we should start with you telling me exactly what happened."

"We already went over this once."

"I know. But I'd like to walk through it, just the way it happened."

"Like I told you before, I was sleeping at the time. I don't remember very much."

"Whatever you remember will help." Another semi roared past. "Where were the two of you going?"

"No place in particular. The leaves were changing and Harry suggested it would be nice to spend the weekend in the Poconos, just driving around and seeing the fall colors."

While she was talking, I was examining the roadway. The only skid marks I could see were the short straight variety, indicating drivers braking as they went into the turn too fast. I didn't see any skid marks that would be compatible with a car leaving the road at an angle. But then, a car that drifted off the road wouldn't make any skid marks.

"When did you leave the city?" I asked.

"About three o'clock on Friday afternoon. We thought we'd beat the weekend rush, but it turned out everybody else had the same idea. We got stuck right in the middle of it. The traffic was bumper-to-bumper almost all the way to the Delaware Water Gap. What should have been an hour-and-a-half drive to Stroudsburg turned into a four-hour trip."

I wondered if this was all a waste of time. Maybe it just posturing on my part, an effort to impress Laura. Reading all those accident reports didn't necessarily make me an expert on the dynamics of such events.

"You spent the night in the Poconos?"

"At the Split Rock Resort. We had a delightful supper, although I think Harry drank a little too much, which was unusual for him."

"Not much of a drinker, was he?"

"No. But he seemed to be in such a good mood, with the long weekend and all, that I didn't mind." She gave a little shudder. "I've thought about it a lot, you know. That's probably what caused the accident. All that drinking the night before interfered with his sleep. He tossed and turned and kept waking up all night. And then driving around all the next day, no wonder he dozed off."

"But Scranton is a little out of the way, isn't it? I mean it's on the other side of the Poconos. Why were you heading in this direction?"

"There were some places he wanted to see, not in Scranton, but on the other side of the valley. Factoryville, where the baseball player Christy Mathewson was born, and the remains of Asylum, where exiles from the French Revolution bought land and started to build a home for Marie Antoinette."

"Sounds interesting. Was Harry a history buff?"

"Not really. They were just places to see. Frankly, I was a little surprised when he first suggested the trip. He was so wrapped up in his work, he hardly ever took any time off."

Still not completely sure what I should be looking for, I studied the grade of the road, the way it curved around the sheer rock face. Sometimes the accident investigators found hazards in the road design itself, which helped the insurance company limit its liability. To my unpracticed eye, however, the roadway seemed perfectly ordinary. Both the downhill and uphill lanes were wide, with adequate shoulders. They curved gracefully around the sheer rock outcropping, sloping inward through the curve, in accordance with Federal roadway standards that have been adopted by all the states.

"So you spent the whole day Saturday just driving around the Poconos, looking at the fall foliage?"

"We had the perfect weather for it," she said. "It was a lovely October day, cool and crisp and sunny. We drove up along the Delaware River, stopped at Winona Falls. We had lunch in a little restaurant near Milford called the Stendahl House. I could tell you what we ate, if you want to know. It's strange, I seem to remember every little detail of what we did, as if it all happened yesterday."

"It's a very common reaction for trauma victims," I said, slipping into my psych-major mode. "One theory is that a sudden shock can intensify the chemical and electrical exchanges between the brain synapses that store our memories. They say that's why everyone remembers exactly what they were doing when they heard the news that Kennedy was shot. The shock intensified the memory."

"You're really something, Theo." She smiled. "You can explain almost anything, can't you?"

The compliment was as welcome as it was unexpected. It struck an Oedipal chord within me, echoing almost verbatim the praises my mother used to shower upon me. Like a little boy, I couldn't resist showing off my knowledge.

"Of course, there are other theorists who claim it's simply a matter of mnemonics," I babbled on, basking in her admiration. "Everything we ever learn or experience is stored somewhere in our brains. The real trick is to find the key that helps recall a particular memory. The mnemonic theorists will say that the Kennedy shooting is simply the memory key that helps us recall what we were doing at the time." I looked at her and worried that I was getting too esoteric, so I gave it up with a smile. "Let's just say that it's very natural for you to remember that last day with Harrison very clearly. So what did you do after lunch?"

"We drove around Lake Wallenpaupack, went up to Lackawaxen to see the Roebling Bridge, visited Horace Greely's house in Hawley and went to Zane Grey's studio."

"You were typical tourists."

"There's a lot to see up here. I was surprised."

"Harry knew his way around?"

"I guess he had been up here before. His business took him all over New Jersey, Pennsylvania, New York and Connecticut."

"That's pretty much my territory, too. I've just never been to Scranton before."

"To be honest, I don't know whether he was ever here before, either. He might have been, because he seemed to know so much about the area. But he never talked much about his business trips."

"So that takes you to suppertime," I probed.

"We had supper at a small restaurant in Matamoras, one of those places where the waitresses all dress up in Colonial costumes and the beer is served in big tankards. Penn's Landing, that was the name of it."

"Did Harry drink much at supper?"

"All he had was some white wine. But we didn't get out of there until about seven-thirty. Why are you so interested in what we did that day?"

I didn't want to admit that I was floundering. Asking questions was really a way of stalling, while hoping that something significant would occur to me.

"That's the way investigators conduct these interviews," I said. "So you left the restaurant at about seven-thirty, and the accident happened, according to the newspaper article, at nine-thirty. What happened in between?"

"I don't really remember. I was sleeping the whole time. I dozed off almost as soon as I got in the car. Maybe it was all that fresh mountain air. Maybe that's why Harry got sleepy, too."

"You don't remember stopping for gas or asking directions?"

"No," she shrugged. "I was sound asleep. I don't remember anything until the car was bouncing across the road, headed for the guardrail. When it hit the rail, my door popped open and I fell out."

"What about the air bags? Didn't they inflate?"

"It was an older BMW. A pre-airbag model."

"Lucky for you. If the car had had air bags, you would have been trapped inside. You would have died in the crash."

"It couldn't be any worse than dying in a hospital," she murmured.

THIRTY-FOUR

Unlike the constant flow of vehicles on the heavily-traveled roads around New York City, the traffic patterns on Route 380 were sporadic. The semi-trailers seemed to travel in clusters, the smaller trucks and passenger cars raced each other in their own "wolf-packs," and solitary RVs struggled along in the rear. The gaps in the traffic allowed us to safely cross to the divider island. After a winter's thaw-and-freeze cycle, I didn't expect to find any tire tracks left behind in the hardpacked dirt by the out-of-control BMW. What I did find was a webwork of old ruts that could have been made by the police and rescue vehicles.

"Let's say the car crossed here." I had to shout to be heard above the traffic that roared past on both sides of us. "Were you awake at this point?"

She squinted her eyes, as if trying to look back into the past.

"I . . . think so." She nodded. "I remember seeing the guardrail. We were going right at it."

"The car didn't approach at an angle?"

"No. I think we hit it head-on." She stared at the shiny replacement railing. "Is that the place where we hit it?"

"Probably. But don't think about that. Think about what was happening inside the car."

"It's hard to remember. It all happened so fast. I felt the car bumping and I woke up and suddenly we were bouncing over the divider and headed across the other lanes."

"Was Harrison trying to get control of the car?"

"No. He was slumped over. His head was resting against the window."

"He wasn't turning the steering wheel?"

"I already told you, no!" A gap in the traffic noise made her words seem harsher than she intended, and almost immediately, she apologized. "I'm sorry. I know you're trying to help and you want to make double-sure of the facts. But it was dark in the car. I couldn't see much. The best I can remember, Harry was slumped over. He was either asleep, or unconscious. Frankly, I was kind of in a state of shock, seeing us headed towards the guardrail."

"Okay, now let's go over there and take a look."

We crossed the uphill lanes during another lull in the traffic. The shoulder on the far side of the highway was about twelve feet wide. The surface was hard-packed gravel. The guardrail was anchored in cement pilings, with two feet of looser gravel on the other side. For further protection, a row of rough-hewn, hip-high boulders lined the edge of the precipice. I was hesitant about going too close to the edge. The gravel around some of the boulders had eroded during the spring rains, making the footing dangerously soft.

"The car hits the guardrail," I prodded. "What then?"

"At that point . . . I thought we were going to be okay. I thought the guardrail would save us. That's what they're for, isn't it? To keep cars from going over the edge?"

"It depends on the speed of the vehicle and the angle of approach," I said.

"Well, we went right at it. When we hit the guardrail the front of the car seemed to collapse, just like you see in those TV commercials. I was thrown up against the dashboard."

"No seatbelt," I said.

"I always use the seatbelt."

"The police report said you weren't using the seatbelt that night."

"I'm sure I had my seatbelt on," she insisted. "I always do. It's a habit."

"Maybe you didn't buckle it properly. You wouldn't have been thrown from the car if you were using the seatbelt."

She hesitated, searching her memory.

"I don't know. Maybe you're right. I was pretty sleepy when I got to the car."

"You're a very lucky woman. Air bags or a seatbelt would have trapped you in the car."

"Hitting that dashboard is what did most of the damage to my chest, according to the doctors. I remember bouncing off the dashboard and then I don't remember much of anything else until I was in the ambulance and I wasn't able to breathe."

"You don't remember being thrown from the car?"

"The police told me the door must have popped open on impact, and I was thrown free. I don't remember it at all. Frankly, I didn't even know the car went over the edge until they told me. I thought at first the guard rail stopped us."

It seemed like a fairly straightforward recounting, much like the verbatims I used to review at Capitol Casualty and Auto. There didn't seem to be anything helpful in what she had told me so far, or if there was, I hadn't recognized it.

Gingerly, I approached the edge of the escarpment. I have always been afraid of heights, and all those fears welled up in me as I looked out over the edge. Knowing Laura was watching me, I tried to keep my demons under control. The fear of heights is actually a fear of falling, or worse yet, a fear of being unable to resist the impulse to jump. I reminded myself that the barrier of large rocks lining the edge offered more than sufficient protection. Yet the rational part of my mind noticed how precariously those rocks were perched on the lip of the precipice, and I drew back slightly.

Far below us, forming an immense slope at the base of the cliff, was the accumulation of thousands of years of erosion and dozens of years of roadway construction. From this distance, the rusted remains of Harrison Duquesne's BMW resembled some oversized turtle sunning itself on the rocks below.

Laura came up behind me.

"It's still there!" she gasped. She held onto my left arm for support.

"You recognize it?"

"Well . . . I guess I do. There's not much left, is there?"

Part of the vehicle was buried in the debris that had rained down the face of the mountain in the most recent landslides. The hood was missing, two of the doors were bent open at grotesque angles, and the battered metal carcass had been left to rust through the winter months after the fire had done its work.

"What it tells us is that the police considered the accident fairly straightforward, so they didn't need the chassis for their investigation." I was showing off again, flaunting my limited knowledge of accident investigative work to impress her. Standing alone with Laura following my every word, with the warmth of her body pressing against my arm and her blue eyes turned up at me, I felt a sophomoric yearning for her approval. "It wouldn't be easy pulling the wreckage out of there. Fortunately the fire would have eliminated any environmental hazards, such as oil or gasoline leaking into the creekbed. My guess is they'll leave it there to be buried by the rocks, unless somebody complains."

"Are we going down there?" she asked.

"Not if you don't want to."

She stared uncertainly down the rocky slope. This was the first time she had actually seen any physical evidence of Harrison's death. A close-up look at the car in which he died might help her accept the fact of his death. But it had to be her decision, not mine.

"Do you think we'll find anything?" she asked.

"I doubt it. The police mechanics would have checked out the vehicle for any obvious mechanical problems. They know a lot more about that sort of thing than I do."

I studied her face for some clue to what was going on in her mind. Did she see the twisted metal for what the police claimed it was: the automotive crematorium in which her husband perished? Or did she see it as the vehicle from whose ashes, like the legendary Phoenix, Harrison Duquesne had somehow risen? From her impassive expression, it was impossible for me to tell.

"I think we should go down," she finally said.

We found a pathway a few hundred yards up the road. It was probably the same one the police had used, since it seemed fairly well-traveled. The track wound down the side shoulder of the slope, avoiding the steep and unstable front face. Some low scrub brush provided occasional handholds. It was still a long way down. I wasn't very enthusiastic about making the descent, but Laura's determination urged me on. Somehow, she managed to negotiate the narrow path despite the handicaps imposed by her high heels and long coat. This woman who had looked so elegant and feminine on the streets of New York was demonstrating a tenacity I didn't realize she possessed.

The path took us down to the dry stream bed, which after a short hike, led us to a point just below where the BMW was lodged.

Even to my unpracticed eye, the slope appeared unstable. Signs of rockslides were everywhere. Half-ton boulders rested patiently in the loose stone, waiting for their chance to break free once again and continue their interrupted plunge to the canyon floor.

We had to pick our way up through the rocks to reach the wreckage of the BMW. It was a more treacherous task than coming down the steep pathway. Loose stones slid away underfoot. Large boulders were too easily dislodged. Thousands of tons of delicately-balanced sandstone and granite were poised above us. Each step we took had to be carefully placed to avoid destabilizing the precarious equilibrium of the entire slope. Faced with the prospect of being buried in a rockslide, examining the BMW was looking less and less like a good idea to me. Once committed, however, my ego wouldn't permit me to turn back.

There wasn't much of the BMW left to see. A car's identity is created by body design and trim, paint and chrome, exterior and interior details working together in aesthetic harmony. All of those elements had been stripped away or destroyed by the elemental forces of fire and rock. The rusted hulk that remained revealed as little about the luxury vehicle it had once been as a broken skeleton would reveal about the beauty of the woman whose flesh once adorned it.

Laura let out a long sigh.

"It's hard to tell if this is really the car," she said.

I pointed to the blue-and-white ceramic hood emblem, which was cracked and burned, but still recognizable.

"I told you there wouldn't be much to see," I said.

It looked as if the car was slowly sinking into the loose rock. The wheel assemblies were already out of sight, and the trunk was partially obscured by a large chunk of stone. The constant flow of debris from above was gradually devouring the vehicle. By next winter, it would probably be totally out of sight.

Laura touched the roof of the car, her fingers gentle and lingering, the way a person might touch a tombstone.

Was it my imagination, or did the rusted chassis seem to tremble at her touch?

I stared at it, fascinated by the trick my mind was playing on me.

She quickly removed her hand, but the chassis continued to vibrate.

A loose rock fell into the engine compartment.

I felt the ground begin to tremble beneath me. A nearby boulder broke loose and rolled a short distance before stopping again. From far up the slope, I heard a rushing sound, like high surf during a winter storm.

When I looked up, the entire rock slope seemed to have given way. Something had triggered an avalanche. It was roaring down on us, a massive frontal wave of boulders and stones, throwing clouds of dust hundreds of feet into the air.

Desperately, I looked around for an escape route. But it had been a long and difficult climb to reach this point. There was no way we could hope to outrun an avalanche.

I put my arms around Laura, as if my puny body could protect her from the onslaught.

For the first time in years, I began to pray.

THIRTY-FIVE

Without even thinking what I was doing, I replicated the survival techniques my primitive ancestors had once taught their children. I crawled into the nearest available hole, which happened to be the wrecked chassis of Harrison's BMW. I pulled Laura in behind me, and covered her body with my own.

We were just in time. Almost immediately, the avalanche roared down on us. Boulders thundered on the roof. The car shook violently. The rusted metal hulk shuddered under the violent pounding. The weakened roof started to collapse.

I waited helplessly for a single direct hit by a boulder to crush the roof. Or for the chassis to be torn from its resting place by the avalanche and thrown down the slope.

The cataract increased in fury. Thousands of tons of loose rock and dirt, moving with monstrous violence and speed, engulfed us. The noise and vibration and darkness had a disorienting effect. Soon I could no longer tell whether the chassis was stationary or moving downhill. Debris poured in through the window and door openings. I held on to Laura with all my strength, praying that the wreckage would hold together. As fragile as our shelter might seem, it represented our only hope.

If we lost its protection, we would be exposed to forces so elemental, they could grind up a human body in seconds.

The flood of dirt and stone rose above my ankles to my knees and then to my hips, immobilizing me. The air filled with foul-tasting dust, making it almost impossible to breathe.

Instead of saving our lives, I feared the chassis was merely delaying our dying.

And then, with what I would swear was an enormous sigh, the tidal wave of rock subsided.

A few stray boulders clattered through the doorway.

I waited, testing the silence to be certain I could trust it. Beneath me, Laura let out a cough. Raising myself to allow her to breathe was difficult, because much of my body was encased in dirt. The chassis let out an occasional groan. But the roof had held.

We had both survived, but when the dust settled, I could see how close we had come to death. Two large boulders were trapped in the rear window well. They had undoubtedly served as a protective shield against the violent shower of stones, any of which could easily have crushed our skulls. The roof, although it was bent precariously inward, was another life-saver. And the loose dirt pouring in the doors had stopped well short of suffocating us.

But the most glorious sight of all was sunlight streaming in through tiny openings among the rocks. It was a sign that we were near the surface.

The only way out was to somehow tunnel up through the shallow layer of stone. The risk, of course, was that any effort to free ourselves might start another rockslide, this time with fatal consequences. That meant we had to move each rock with painstaking care, testing first to determine whether its removal would create disastrous results. We started at the front windshield, where the rocks were smaller and the surface seemed closer. One by one, we removed stones and boulders from the windshield space, piling them up where the back seat had once been. When the interior of the car was filled with rock, we crawled out onto the hood, into the space we had created. From there we began working our way up to the surface using the same wormlike process. Occasionally, our tunnel would threaten to collapse in a shower of rocks and dirt. Each time it happened, Laura and I froze, terrified of being buried alive.

Although I had inherited a healthy physique, I've never performed much heavy physical labor. But that afternoon, I'm convinced I moved as much rock as any miner who once dug coal in the nearby anthracite fields.

It was nearly sunset when I finally pulled Laura to the surface. The air was fresh and sweet and free of dust. The rocky slope around us looked deceptively serene. In geologic terms, what we had experienced would probably be considered a relatively minor event, a mere rearranging of the slope into a more stable pattern. Traffic on the highway above continued unimpeded. As long as the integrity of the roadway remained undamaged, even the state police would pay little attention to a rockslide.

When I considered how narrowly we had avoided death, my hands began to shake. It was only by an accident of angles and elevation that the chassis remained close enough to the surface for us to dig our way out. If the vehicle had been located closer to the canyon bottom, where the slope leveled out, we would have been buried under twenty or thirty feet of rock.

Our deaths would have gone unnoticed. Our bodies would never be found.

While I sat there, numbed by our ordeal, Laura seemed more concerned about her appearance than how close we came to losing our lives. She still exhibited the casual indifference to death so characteristic of NDE survivors.

"We can't go anywhere looking like this," she complained.

To someone who didn't know her, it might seem like vanity. To me, it was merely a signal that she was eager to put this experience behind her and press on.

"I'll need some new clothing," she said.

"We can stop at a mall," I said, the words coming out mechanically, without really thinking what I was saying.

"And a long, hot bath."

"We've got money for a nice hotel."

"And maybe even a dinner in a fancy restaurant?"

"If that's what you want."

"What I want is a chance to feel civilized again. I want to go to a nice restaurant, order food from a real menu, have a glass of wine, and enjoy the kind of dinner that normal people eat. Do you think we could do that, Theo?"

"I'm sure we can find a suitable place."

Laura was standing shoeless on the rocky slope, her pantyhose shredded, her clothing and face filthy, running her fingers through her hair to remove the matted dirt . . . and she was discussing this evening's menu possibilities as if it was the most natural thing in the world.

There was something wonderfully therapeutic about that moment. It encapsulated what I consider one of Laura's most intriguing gifts: her ability to transcend adversity in a way that affected those around her.

Like many near-deathers, she seemed to inhabit a more serene world, one in which she remained untouched by the traumas that affect ordinary mortals. While we sat on the rocky slope, she somehow managed to draw me, if only momentarily, into the serenity of her world. I felt my anxieties begin to dissipate. My hands stopped shaking. My breathing came easier.

Looking back, I am still amazed at how rapidly my anxieties were dissipated. I don't know whether this was some talent she acquired as a result of her NDE. All I know is that she was able to accomplish in a few moments a task which might have been beyond the reach of many veteran psychologists. Instead of focusing on our brush with death, I was already looking forward to what promised to be a pleasant evening.

But first, we had to get back up to my car.

The pathway seemed steeper than I recalled. Fatigue made us clumsy. Twice I slipped, once nearly going off the edge into the void below. Laura saved me both times. The pain of making the climb in her bare feet was offset by the sure-footedness it provided her.

By the time we reached the top, it was twilight. Traffic on the highway was a lot heavier as the evening rush hour approached. The more careful drivers already had their headlights on. Some of them flicked their high beams, warning us away from the side of the road. If anyone thought it unusual for two people to be walking along the road at that hour, no one stopped to offer help. It was too dangerous for drivers to slow down for us as they came around the curve. And our torn and dirty clothing probably caused us to be dismissed as homeless, or worse yet, mentally ill, the kind of troubled people to be avoided as darkness approached.

We made our way slowly along the side of the road, waiting for a break in traffic to allow us to cross.

Soon we were back where we started, at the place where the BMW had broken through the guardrail and gone over the cliff.

Something about it was different.

Something had changed.

I paused by the section of guardrail that had been replaced. I stared at the huge boulders that sat beyond the rail, protecting the edge of the cliff.

If we hadn't examined the site earlier, I probably wouldn't have noticed anything different.

"What is it?" Laura asked. "Is something wrong?"

I pointed to the edge of the cliff.

One of the boulders was missing.

"It must have broken loose," she said, although her tone of voice indicated she didn't believe her own words.

I stepped over the guardrail.

The dirt shoulder at the edge of the cliff had collapsed. But even in the dimming light, I could see that the boulder had been pushed from its original position. A depression in the ground indicated where the heavy stone had been resting until a short time ago. Scuff marks between that indentation and the guard rail showed where someone had slipped and strained to roll the boulder to the edge of the cliff.

This was no casual prank. Each of the boulders must have weighed at least five hundred pounds. It would take all the strength a good-sized man possessed to dislodge it from its resting place and roll it the short distance to the edge of the cliff.

The vertical drop from that point was more than two hundred feet to the top of the rocky slope, where the point of impact was clearly visible; and the resulting rockslide covered another hundred feet to where the BMW wreckage was now buried. The offending boulder itself was nowhere to be seen. It was swallowed up in the rubble of the avalanche which it had triggered.

I shuddered as I peered into the abyss, but not because of my fear of heights. It was something more ominous.

"Theo? What's wrong?"

"The avalanche," I said. "It wasn't an accident."

"I don't understand."

"Someone tried to kill us. That missing boulder was pushed over the edge on purpose. That's what triggered the avalanche."

"Are you sure it wasn't an accident?"

I pointed to the fresh marks in the dirt.

"It took a lot of effort to move a rock that big," I said. "It was a very deliberate attempt to kill us."

She seemed more surprised than frightened.

"Do you think it was Metzger?" she asked.

"I don't know. I thought we left him in New York."

"Maybe he followed us."

"I was watching for his car in the rearview mirror. If he followed us, I'm sure I would have seen him somewhere along the way."

"Then it must have been one of the others."

"One of the Samoans? They're supposed to be on their way to New York."

"Maybe they saw us. Maybe they recognized your car."

"They don't know my car."

"We stopped for gas in New Jersey. Maybe they stopped there at the same time. That's where they could have seen us."

"I guess it's possible," I said. "It would be an almost unbelievable coincidence, but I guess it could have happened that way."

"Don't you believe in coincidences?"

"I believe in the predictable patterns of human behavior. Sometimes those patterns lead to confluences of events that appear to be coincidental. But not in this case. What happened here doesn't fit the previous behavior pattern of anyone at the Walden Clinic."

"Why not?"

"Consider what happened."

"You said someone tried to kill us."

"Exactly. I could understand if someone from the Clinic wanted to kill me. I certainly wouldn't like it, but on an intellectual level, I'd understand it. Especially after they killed the Professor. The problem I'm having is the attempt to kill you, too. It doesn't compute. They could have killed you any time during the last six months, but they didn't."

"They kept me drugged most of the time."

"Yes, but they kept you alive."

"If you could call it that."

"They kept you alive," I repeated, more firmly. "That's the important point to remember, they kept you alive. Which means you apparently have some value to them. That's why they want you back in their custody. You heard Metzger's instructions on the scanner. They were very specific about getting you back unharmed. They were even sending out an ambulance for you. Given that mind-set, I'm sure it wasn't one of the clinic people who rolled that boulder over the cliff."

"Then who . . . ?"

"You tell me."

"I . . . I have no idea."

"No enemies? Other than the people at the Walden Clinic?"

She shook her head, her eyes so innocent that I felt silly asking the question. It was hard to believe that anyone would want to kill this lovely creature.

"What about your friends? Any of them ever act strange, show any sign of mental problems?"

"Not that I know of. Harry and I didn't have a wide circle of friends." She quickly changed the subject. "Can we talk about this later, Theo? My feet hurt and it's getting dark. I think we should get out of here."

"You're right, I'm sorry. We shouldn't be standing out in the open like this."

We found an opening in the traffic and dashed across the highway. As we approached the car, I half-expected to find someone lurking in the bushes or hiding in the back seat. Fortunately, neither of those threats materialized. Laura sank gratefully into the front seat. She massaged her bare feet and reminded me we'd have to find a place to buy her some shoes.

I checked the car carefully, looking for any signs of sabotage. I could find nothing amiss. When I turned the ignition key, the motor responded instantly. The headlights revealed no suspicious figures darting out of sight. The brakes appeared to be working properly. Only when I was satisfied no one had tampered with the car, did I proceed cautiously down the road to the shoulder of the highway.

I was hoping for one last view of the accident site. The darkness deprived me of that opportunity. All that was visible now were the lights of the traffic flowing in both directions around the fatal curve.

I entered the flow of traffic a few hundred feet from the place where Harry's car drifted off the road. It was an eerie feeling retracing his route.

The road banked gently as it headed downhill around the Bald Mountain Curve. I shuddered as my headlights illuminated the repaired guardrail on the far side of the eastbound lanes. For a fleeting instant, something registered in my mind, an evanescent perception, an image so vague it remained beyond the reach of my conscious thought process, yet it continued to trouble me as I drove.

The car straightened out as we came out of the turn and the road started to level out.

Before us lay the city of Scranton, its lights spread across the floor of the Lackawanna Valley. The lights of a few smaller towns were scattered partway up the mountains on the other side of the valley. It was a deceptively pretty scene. As far as I was concerned, it was enemy territory. For that reason, I was glad we were entering the valley under the protective cover of darkness.

THIRTY-SIX

Our search for a safe place to spend the night led us to a building that had barely survived its own encounter with death.

It was an old marble-columned structure that previously served the city of Scranton as a railroad station. The trains that once stopped there, according to the brochures at the registration desk, took passengers to every major city in the United States. When the glory days of the American railroad came to an end, the station was abandoned. The doors were locked and the old building remained vacant for decades. All signs of life disappeared from its hallways.

Like any other octogenarian, its vital systems began to deteriorate. The heating system broke down in the first winter. The water supply went next, its pipes bursting in the cold. The electrical wiring was sold for scrap. The once-proud Lackawanna Station was a dead building, a concrete corpse destined to be dismembered and then buried in some local landfill.

But in what can only be described as the real estate version of a near-death experience, the old building was resuscitated by the last-minute intervention of local preservationists.

In a miracle of marketing, Lackawanna Station was brought back to life as a hotel. The mosaic-tiled waiting room was reborn as an elegant French restaurant. The wall of ticket windows was transformed into a railroad memorabilia bar. The offices upstairs were converted into comfortable hotel rooms with high ceilings and six-foot windows. On the tracks behind the station, a collection of vintage steam locomotives sat hissing, part of the historic Steamtown U.S.A. exhibit funded by the National Park Service.

Railroad buffs and hobbyists now came from all over the country to stay at Lackawanna Station, where they could pay homage to the era of steam travel and mingle with others who shared their passion for the past.

I'm not particularly interested in railroad nostalgia. But a hotel where many of the guests wore engineer's hats and talked incessantly about locomotives would probably be the last place anyone would expect to find us. It seemed like the ideal hideout. Any search for us would most likely be concentrated among the low-priced chain motels on the fringes of town. In an effort to further avoid detection, I parked the car a half-mile away, out of sight between two old buildings near the University of Scranton.

Our torn and dirty clothing had already been discarded in the changing rooms at the first shopping mall we found. I was wearing a brand-new blazer and tan slacks with cheap loafers. Laura had opted for a pink-and-white nylon warmup suit and white cross-trainers. She also picked out a few inexpensive dresses and some cosmetics. Except for their souvenir engineer caps, most of the guests in the hotel's lobby wore clothing that looked like it was purchased at similar stores.

Paying cash in advance allowed us to register under false names. With the money in hand, the desk clerk didn't require any identification. I asked for two adjoining rooms facing the front of the hotel. It was apparently an unusual request. The desk clerk explained that most guests preferred the rooms facing the back of the hotel, which offered the best views of the old locomotives. When I didn't take him up on his suggestion, he shrugged his shoulders and produced keys for two rooms on the third floor. They turned out to be exactly what I was looking for. The windows provided great views of the driveway and parking lot, as well as anyone approaching the hotel entrance on foot. A week earlier, I would have dismissed such precautions as symptoms of incipient paranoia. Now I embraced them as prudent measures necessary for our survival, further indication of how dramatically my life had changed since I met Laura.

I continued to marvel at how unaffected she seemed to be by the dangers we faced. It was more than just the usual near-deather's indifference to mortal threats. With some jealousy, I realized it was probably also a result of her fixation on finding Harrison. Her devotion to him was so strong, it had become the central purpose of her existence, overpowering any fear for her own safety.

Was it a bond that would prove impossible to break? Was I foolishly committing myself to a relationship that existed exclusively in my mind?

Did she see me only as a good samaritan trying to reunite her with her husband?

It was too late for such questions, I thought as I stared out the window.

Whatever the future might hold for us, I had no choice but to continue on the path I had chosen. My life had already been forever altered by my involvement with her. In many ways, I was no longer the same man I once was.

Feeling temporarily secure in the protective darkness of my room, I sat by the window watching the street below. A yellow taxi pulled up to the hotel entrance, discharging an overweight man and a slender, grey-haired woman. They were both laughing, both a little unsteady on their feet. The man dropped what looked like a dollar bill while he was attempting to pay the cabdriver. No one noticed it but me. The cab pulled away. The people disappeared into the hotel. The dollar bill remained in the driveway.

I watched other guests enter and leave the hotel. None of them noticed the money. It was an interesting problem in perception, I thought. An object clearly visible from my third floor window was seemingly invisible to people passing within a few feet of it.

As a security measure, Laura and I had agreed to leave the door between our rooms partially open. The glow from the connecting doorway provided the only light in my room. I could hear the sound of running water filling a tub, where she was enjoying her much-anticipated hot bath.

Down below, someone finally noticed the dollar bill. It was one of the hotel employees, possibly someone whose job it was to keep the area around the entrance free of debris. A man trained to look for pieces of paper on the ground will inevitably find more of them than those accustomed to looking straight ahead.

This might explain why my first attempt at being an accident investigator had met with so little success. Reading field reports in the comfort of an office in New York was a lot different from looking for old skid marks on a mountain highway. I had gone to Bald Mountain unsure of what to look for and uncertain of how to look for it. Worse yet, I didn't even know how to properly evaluate what little I had seen. There was a lot more to being an accident investigator than I had assumed.

I thought back to the night of the accident, reconstructing how it must have happened. There was no question about the basic facts. Everything the original newspaper articles reported was corroborated by Laura's account. The path of the car was easy to retrace. The replacement guardrail provided testimony to the force of the impact. The location of the burned-out wreckage indicated a minimum two-hundred foot drop before the vehicle hit the slope and tumbled the rest of the way down to its final resting place. The way it happened all seemed so clear to me. I played it over and over in my mind, like a mental videotape I could speed up or slow down at will. I broke it apart, moment by moment, freeze-framing and zooming in, looking for a clue, an anomaly, a single detail that didn't fit the equation.

I was sure there was something I had seen, which, if I were properly trained, would have been as obvious to me as the paper money was to the doorman downstairs.

There had been one fraction of an instant on Bald Mountain when I had the uncanny feeling that I caught a glimpse of what could be an important clue, but it happened so quickly, my mind was unable to process the information.

Whatever it was that I thought I had seen up on the dark highway continued to tantalize me, staying just out of reach of my ability to recall it.

My classes in perceptual theory taught me that even a stimulus too slight to be consciously recognized can trigger extensive perceptual processing on a subliminal, non-directed level. The way the brain is wired, many problem-solving functions also operate on an unconscious level. Which explains why, after struggling unsuccessfully to solve some mind-bending problem, the answer often comes when we least expect it, for reasons we don't understand.

If there was any significance to what I thought I saw on the mountain, I was confident it would eventually rise to the surface of my consciousness, where it would be revealed in stunning clarity. Unfortunately, I had no way of knowing when, or even if, that magical moment of sudden insight would occur.

With our lives in mortal danger, it might be too late to make any difference.

THIRTY-SEVEN

My seemingly endless ruminations were interrupted by a sudden flood of light filling the room.

It came from the connecting doorway, where, framed in the open passage and silhouetted from behind by the glow from her own room, stood Laura.

She was wearing one of the two dresses she had bought at Wal-Mart. It was a pale blue garment of inexpensive Indian silk, a knee-length design with long sleeves, softly padded shoulders, and a low neckline. The strong backlighting from her room showed through the thin silk, revealing the silhouette of her nude body beneath it.

She seemed totally unaware of the intimate view she was providing. I did the gentlemanly thing, which was to avert my eyes from those seductive contours. After sponging her naked and fevered flesh during those terrible days of withdrawal in the Poconos, her body could no longer claim any secrets from me. But this was an unintended display of her figure that I was certain she would now rather keep private. Until she knowingly invited me to gaze upon her, I was determined not to give in to any voyeuristic tendencies.

I rose and turned on the lights in my room and invited her inside.

"You're beautiful," I murmured.

"You haven't even washed," she said.

"I was looking out the window," I tried to explain.

"All this time?"

"I was watching the entrance to the hotel," I said. "I wanted to see if anybody showed up who might be looking for us."

"Like the police?"

"Or Metzger. Or anybody else I might recognize."

"And?"

"And nothing. I mean nobody."

"Then I assume it's safe for us to go downstairs to eat."

"Well . . ." I hesitated.

"Oh come on, Theo," she pouted. "It's been over six months since I've had a restaurant meal. We can find a seat in a corner if you're worried about us being seen."

There it was again, I thought. That nonchalant attitude of hers that I found so troubling. She seemed so . . . so normal.

But why should her very normality bother me? Did I expect her to be more emotional, more unstable simply because she was a woman? Did I secretly want her to be more dependent on me? Or was the problem far more complex? She was demonstrating a well-established ego-defense mechanism. It might be based on self-deception. But it was nevertheless successful in helping her to remain calm despite the perils we faced. Perhaps what was really troubling me was a subconscious envy of how well she was able to cope. After all, my own more rational approach to our situation had only produced mounting anxiety and confusion on my part.

"Okay," I said. "Maybe I'm over-reacting. We'll probably be safe downstairs."

"Wonderful!"

"But we'll have to sit where we can see everyone who comes through the lobby doors."

I started to turn out the lights, but she stopped me.

"Wait a minute, Theo. You're not going downstairs looking like that, are you?"

"Do you think I need a tie?"

"Have you looked at yourself in the mirror? You might want to clean up a little."

It didn't take a mirror to see that she was right. Although my clothing was new and clean, my hands were still covered with grime from the episode on the mountainside. When I touched my cheek, I could actually feel the dirt on my face.

"I'm sorry," I murmured. "I guess I was preoccupied."

She waited patiently while I took what must have been the world's fastest shower, used the complimentary shaving kit, brushed my teeth, gargled, and even tried out the free shoe-shine cloth.

I was rewarded for my efforts with the kind of smile I hadn't seen from a woman since I made the mistake of asking Elizabeth to marry me.

She slipped her arm through mine and we went down to dinner looking like a typical twenty-something couple out on a date.

The French restaurant downstairs was crowded with late diners. But maitre d's have an affinity for beautiful women, so we were seated quickly, at a prime table where both of us could see everyone who entered or left the hotel. The waiter also fawned over Laura, and I was aware that many of the other diners were casting covetous glances in her direction. After months of being deprived of human contact, she must have been delighted by the attention she drew. I asked her to order for both of us, watching as she enjoyed her reentry into some semblance of normal activity. When she was finished with the waiter, she was mine once again, her smile reserved for me alone.

What little effort it took for her to fill me with pleasure. I would have been content simply staring at her across the table, like some art student who, upon seeing La Gioconda for the first time, forgets all about theories of color and composition and loses himself in the strange beauty of the image before him.

She was wearing light makeup: a bluish-grey eyeshadow to complement her eyes, a bit of blush to add color to her cheeks, a moist red lipstick to make her mouth more inviting. As far as I was concerned, the artificial enhancements, although attractive, were not really necessary. Anyone staring into those liquid blue eyes would never notice the cosmetics which framed them. The promise of her mouth was not in the kiss-proof red coloring created by some anonymous biochemical engineer, but in the ripe lips that begged to be crushed by a lover.

Looking at Laura, it was impossible to imagine anyone wanting to confine her in what amounted to a dungeon. The dress she wore, although an inexpensive type of silk, looked exquisite on her. The neckline was just low enough to reveal the smooth upper slopes of her breasts accented by the double strand of pearls she had been wearing since morning.

"Theo, you're staring," she said.

"I'm sorry," I replied, feeling my face reddening. "I was just looking at your pearls."

"Really?" She smiled to indicate her disbelief.

"Really," I answered, too embarrassed to admit the truth. "I've always thought pearls are the most feminine of all the gems a woman can wear."

"And why is that?" she asked, still smiling, playing along with me. "Are you going to give me some valuable psychological insight into choosing jewelry?"

The waiter brought the wine, a pleasant Cote d'Luberon, offering the cork for my approval. Since this was Laura's evening, I yielded the ritual to her. She performed the prescribed sniffing, and when she nodded her head, the waiter filled our glasses.

"Actually, there really is a psychology to why people wear particular types of jewelry, but that's an entirely different topic," I explained, eager to demonstrate that there were reasons other than sexual for me to have been staring at her bosom. "What I meant about being feminine is the nature of the pearls themselves. Diamonds and rubies and other gems are cold and hard. They're nothing but polished rocks."

"Very valuable polished rocks," she reminded me.

"That's true. But they're still rocks. A pearl, on the other hand, is the only gem created by a living organism. You could compare the process to the growth of a child in a mother's womb. It starts with a tiny irritant that's actually called a seed, entering the body of the oyster. Once the seed is inside, the oyster nurtures it and helps it to grow, just as any mother with her unborn child. The oyster sacrifices part of the lining of its own body to cover the growing pearl with layers of nacre. That's why the nacre is called mother-of-pearl."

She looked at me over the top of her wine glass, those blue

eyes now in shadow, thinking, studying me as I had earlier studied her.

"I've never met anyone quite like you," she finally said.

"Nor I you."

"I mean the way you talk," she explained. "I never met anyone who talks like you do."

"Sometimes I talk too much," I said, thinking back to the criticisms of my ex-wife.

"No, not all," Laura said. "I enjoy listening to you. You look at things and see meanings and connections other people don't. I find it fascinating."

It was the closest she had yet come to expressing an interest in me. Was I finally making some progress with her?

"And I find you fascinating, too," I said.

I reached across the table for her hand. Her skin was warm, and as soft and smooth as I remembered. How I longed to hold her in my arms again, caressing her the way I had done during her hallucinatory episodes at the motel.

She stared at me for a long moment, her face offering no hint of what she was thinking.

"I owe you a lot, Theo," she finally said. She spoke slowly. She seemed to be weighing each word carefully before giving voice to it. "I owe you my life," she said. "And I like you. I really do. You're a wonderful person, and I enjoy your company." She paused, whether for emphasis or as a sign of her ambivalence, I don't know. "But you have to remember, I'm a married woman. I have a husband."

She pulled her hand away, slowly, as if she didn't really want to.

"But you don't . . ." I started to say.

She raised a finger to her lips.

"If you feel anything for me, you won't say it, Theo."

"All I meant was . . ."

She cut me off again.

"We've already been over this before," she said. "When I was dead, they told me I had to come back to save the man I love. I was told that Harry is still alive, and that belief is the only thing that keeps me going. If I didn't believe with all my heart that somehow I'd find him, I never would have survived what they did to me at the Walden Clinic."

The waiter brought our appetizers, two small plates with six escargots in butter and garlic on each. Laura waited until he was gone before she continued.

"You were the answer to my prayers, Theo. You promised to help me find Harry, and you've shown you're willing to risk your life to do so. I have to do my part by keeping the faith. I can't, for one moment, feel any doubt that Harry's alive, otherwise I'm afraid of what might happen. I have to be faithful to him, Theo. Can you understand that?"

What else could I do but agree?

Disappointed by her rebuff, I turned my attention to the food in front of me, using the act of eating as a temporary refuge from an uncomfortable situation. The escargots were cooked with a little too much garlic for my taste, but the meaty flesh inside was exactly the right consistency. The waiter seemed to hover at our table, whisking away the dishes as soon as we finished. We were soon alone again, and I still had one question that was troubling me.

"You never told me exactly what they did to you at the Walden Clinic," I said.

She took a long sip of wine before responding.

"Does it matter?" she asked.

"It would help if I knew their motivation, why they're so desperate to get you back."

She took another sip of wine.

"It's something I don't want to discuss," she said.

There was something cold and hard and final in her tone of voice, warning me not to pursue the question.

I couldn't help wondering what she was hiding.

THIRTY-EIGHT

Perhaps I should have questioned Laura further about what happened to her at the Walden Clinic.

But at the time, I thought such an approach would be inappropriate, if not actually harmful. The mental scars left by those months of confinement were obviously still too raw and tender to probe. After all she had been through, I couldn't bring myself to cause her any additional pain.

The waiter brought our entrees. Laura had ordered *canard aux cerises*, a Breton specialty of duck cooked in a sweet cherry sauce, served with golden saffron rice and sprigs of fresh coriander. For me, she had ordered a basic *Boeuf Bourguinon*, a favorite of French farmers. Our waiter ladled the dark stew into a deep dish, which had been pre-heated. The wine-scented aroma reminded me how long it had been since I was last able to afford a meal in a French restaurant.

I thanked Laura for her selection, which was just what I needed to restore my energy. She had avoided ordering any seafood, she explained, because she wasn't certain how fresh it would be so far from the New York and Philadelphia fish markets. I marveled at her remarkable powers of recuperation. After all those months of tubal feeding at the Walden Clinic, it was amazing to see her eat solid food so quickly, and with such enthusiasm. She laughed it off by explaining that she had a lot of time to work up an appetite, but I could sense that the memory made her uncomfortable.

By unspoken agreement, we avoided any further mention of sensitive topics for the rest of the meal. We talked about the food, the hotel, the weather; about movies, mystery novels, and basketball; about where we grew up and what our childhood dreams had been.

We sipped our wine and talked and ate and generally acted in as conventional a manner as any of the other young couples in the restaurant.

And yet as I listened to us talking, I began to understand the real significance of what we were doing. Her insistence on eating out "like normal people do" was actually an unconscious defense mechanism, an inborn form of ego reinforcement to keep her vulnerable psyche from crashing.

Instinctively, she had created a therapeutic environment into which we could both retreat. It all seemed so civilized: a pleasant evening in an elegant restaurant, enjoying the local version of *haute cuisine* and the ministrations of an attentive waiter. The horrors of what had certainly been the most traumatic few weeks of my life seemed so far away, I felt myself being slowly drawn into the protective aura of normality that surrounded her. It was a comforting feeling.

For dessert, Laura had ordered creme brulée for both of us. It came in the small white ceramic bowls in which it was baked, each topped with a brittle golden crust of caramelized sugar. The lightest touch of a spoon cracked the thin coating to reveal the soft creme anglaise hiding beneath.

"You were right," I said at last.

"About what?"

"About wanting to eat in a nice restaurant. I feel absolutely regenerated, as if I've been going through some wonderful new kind of therapy."

"You were just hungry," she said with a smile.

"No, it was more than that. You were right about wanting to act like a normal person again. I'm glad we did this."

We lingered over coffee. Most of the other diners were gone. The waiters were starting to set up the tables for the next morning's breakfast buffet.

By the time we finished our coffee, we were the last customers in the restaurant. The lights were dimmed and our waiter was eyeing us with a surly expression, smiling only when we finally paid our bill. It was after midnight. The hotel lobby was deserted. Scranton was apparently a town that went to bed early.

Normally a good meal and a bottle of wine serves as a wonderful sleep inducer. It certainly worked that way with Laura. After performing her nightly ablutions, she quickly slipped into the arms of Morpheus. For me, however, it wasn't that easy. I was unable to enter even the *hypnogogic* period, that drowsy cycle which precedes the first stage of sleep. I lay in bed with my eyes closed but my mind wide awake, my senses alert. In spite of my body's need for rest, my brain continued firing millions of electrical and chemical impulses through the synaptic network in a vain attempt to retrieve an elusive memory from wherever it was stored. I found myself drawn to the window, where I sat as before, staring out at the empty streets, hoping to see in the darkness some shadow that might trigger a flash of recognition.

The answer was out there, I knew. The only way to find it was to go out into the night and search for it.

I never would have left Laura alone if I thought she wouldn't be safe. But neither did I want to expose her to any unnecessary mental distress.

Before leaving, I slipped into her room to check that her door was securely locked. The light from her bathroom provided the only illumination, casting a dim glow on her lovely features. My beautiful near-deather was curled up in the sleep of the innocent. Her hands were pressed childlike beneath her cheek. Her mouth was slightly open. Her breathing was deep and regular. Her brow was untroubled, suggesting pleasant dreams. I would have been perfectly happy to sit beside her all night and watch her while she slept.

But something had registered in my subconscious on Bald Mountain, and I was determined to retrieve it from that subliminal level, if I had to spend the rest of the night retracing the route of the death car.

The streets in Scranton were deserted at that hour of the night. I didn't encounter any traffic until I reached Route 380.

Most of the vehicles on the highway seemed to be long-haul truckers using the cover of night to make better time.

As the road climbed towards the Bald Mountain Curve, I could see nothing off the right shoulder but the metal guardrail and a yawning blackness. Ahead of me a heavily-loaded semi crawled slowly up the hill. The angle of the road changed, pitching slightly inward. It held that angle around the curve, until the road straightened out again. About two miles up the road, I was able to make a U-turn and head back downhill, retracing the path of Harrison Duquesne's doomed BMW.

The traffic moved a lot faster in the downhill lanes. I was doing 10 miles over the legal 55, and trucks were blowing past me as if my car were standing still. I marveled at their recklessness, considering the dangers of the curve ahead. Anyone going off the road on the right shoulder would slam into the solid rock face of the mountain. The left shoulder led across the grassy divider into the uphill lanes, and from there, over the edge of the cliff. I found myself clutching the steering wheel tightly as the road banked to the right, indicating the proximity of the approaching curve. I had no desire to repeat Harrison's mistake. After safely navigating the passage, I realized I had been too intent on my driving to notice anything else. I continued downhill for another mile until I found a place where I could make a U-turn and perform the exercise all over again.

I was attempting to do a form of memory retrieval reintegration used in psychoanalysis when long-forgotten childhood experiences or repressed events must be recalled. The triggering mechanism is the exposure to a psychological souvenir, or cue factor, which must be systematically searched out by the analyst. Unlike conscious memories, for which the triggering mechanism can be quite simple, the cue factors for unconscious memories are usually unpredictable and are often arrived at accidentally.

Like a psychoanalyst methodically guiding a patient over the same familiar ground time after time in hopes of breaking through a psychic barrier, I drove again and again around the Bald Mountain Curve, searching for an elusive cue.

It was a peculiar quest on which I found myself. I didn't actually know what I was searching for. All I had to go on was the vague feeling that something had registered on my mind while I was driving around the curve earlier in the evening. I knew that perception can occur even though the stimulus input is presented so briefly or at such low intensity as to be below the threshold of conscious awareness. Finding something that close to invisibility was a difficult, if not impossible, assignment. But I had to try.

Each time I made the circuit, the driving became easier. My hands relaxed on the wheel. My foot no longer hovered over the brake pedal. Soon I was keeping up with the speeding truckers. The stretch of highway that had seemed so dangerous at first no longer frightened me.

Something about the way the car was handling intrigued me. I couldn't quite put my finger on it, but I knew it was related to the accident, so I kept concentrating, trying to visualize exactly how the tragedy occurred. I shuddered at the thought of the BMW drifting across the divider, across the uphill lanes, and over the edge. I made the U-turn and headed downhill again and again. I felt completely at ease. I had the road memorized. I knew exactly where the roadway banked before entering the curve; where I needed less pressure on the steering wheel; where the road straightened out; and how far it was to the next U-turn.

As I drove, I had the feeling the road was trying to talk to me. As if it wanted to tell me something about what had happened that night. At first, I ascribed it to fatigue, and warned myself to be careful lest I meet Harrison's fate.

But then, as I was approaching the curve for what must have been the twentieth time, the road finally surrendered its secret.

It wasn't at all what I expected.

There were no signs or arrows pointing to it. Many hundreds of drivers passed by every day without paying any attention to it. Yet like all such discoveries, it seemed almost ridiculously obvious. I wondered how I could have overlooked it all this time.

I turned the car around and made the circuit once again, eager to take another, more careful look at it. I wanted to be certain I wasn't experiencing the hallucinatory effects of sleep deprivation.

I drove more slowly this time, ignoring the semis roaring by in the passing lanes.

Sure enough, as I approached the curve, there it was again.

And then, with frightening clarity, for my brain had been subconsciously working on the problem for hours, I knew exactly what must have happened on that tragic night. I went through the curve, and made the U-turn again, to return to the place where I first had the astonishing insight.

Heart pounding, I slowed down and pulled off the road on the inside shoulder, about a quarter of a mile above the curve. It was just about the place where Laura and I had crossed the highway earlier, tracking the route of the BMW.

I wanted to be wrong.

Oh, God, how I wanted to be wrong.

I sat there, staring at the road and trying to cast doubt on the validity of my own assumptions. Was my judgement impaired by my lack of sleep? Did the darkness and unfamiliarity of the terrain cause a perceptual distortion? Could I be misinterpreting the physical data and arriving at a terribly erroneous conclusion?

Did I really believe my experience with Capitol Casualty and Auto qualified me as an expert in on-site accident investigations?

On an emotional level, I wished I were mistaken. On an intellectual level, I was convinced I was right. I could see the evidence in the beam of my headlights.

At first I felt stupid for not seeing it before. But then I realized the local police hadn't seen it, either. And they were supposedly the experts.

My mind was racing ahead as I analyzed the implications.

No one would believe me, of course. I wasn't really sure I believed it myself. Before anyone would take my theory seriously, I knew I'd have to find some way to get independent confirmation of what appeared to be the facts.

But if I was right, the implications were enormous. It went to the very heart of Laura's claims about her near-death experience.

And it would change forever my relationship with her.

THIRTY-NINE

Did I dare tell Laura what I had discovered?

The question troubled me all the way back to the hotel.

I found her still asleep, blissfully unaware of my absence. She didn't seem to have moved in all the time I was gone. Such total lack of nocturnal movement is usually an indicator of prolonged REM sleep, the deepest and most paralytic form of slumber. It is named for the rapid eye movements that paradoxically accompany what appears to be complete physical immobilization. Normally REM sleep occurs in fifteen-minute cycles throughout the night. What Laura was experiencing was the extended REM cycle typical of patients who survive drug overdoses, withdrawal syndrome and other brain insults.

During REM sleep, large and continuous movements of the eyeballs beneath the closed lids indicate that highly active and emotional dreams, often nightmares, are in progress. Small and sparse movements suggest tranquil and fairly passive dreams. Fortunately, Laura's eye movements were of the latter variety, indicating to me that she was enjoying peaceful dreams and a restful sleep.

I certainly didn't want to disturb her at that moment.

In the morning, I felt even less inclined to do so. I decided against telling her about my late-night visit to the accident scene, or the discovery I made on the highway.

Was it an act of perfidy on my part to withhold the information? I think not. My secrecy was motivated by love, not selfishness; by caution, not deceit. The conclusion I had reached, if it proved correct, could utterly destroy the protective shell she had so carefully constructed around her fragile psyche. Therefore, I had to be absolutely certain of the factual basis of my theory before I said a word about it to her. Even then, I wasn't at all certain I had it within my heart to cause her such pain.

There was no point in going to the local police for the independent confirmation of fact that I needed. They had already reached their own conclusions about the accident, as mistaken as they might turn out to be. As a result, they would be loath to cooperate. Even if they did cooperate, their data was probably not adequate enough to prove my theory. If such data were available locally, it would probably be difficult to retrieve in a format that would be usable. In addition, I was afraid Laura might guess what I was after.

For all those reasons, I decided instead to use my contacts at the Auto Insurance Information Clearing House in New York, an organization that I had used routinely when I had worked for Capitol Casualty and Auto.

In an effort to help prevent insurance fraud, the AIICH maintains a massive computerized national database of auto accidents. The database allows insurance investigators to cross-check the specific details of any questionable claim against almost thirty years of carefully compiled information on U.S. auto accidents. The purpose is to uncover any patterns, similarities or anomalies that would suggest an intent to defraud.

Access to the AIICH files is supposed to be legally available only to the participating insurance companies and, under certain circumstances, law-enforcement agencies. My name would have been removed from the approved list when I was fired from Capitol Auto Insurance. As with most such organizations, however, AIICH's information was always available to anyone who was willing to pay the going rate.

The man to call was Worthington Lewis. He didn't actually work for the Clearing House, but his cousin Florence did. The scheme was originally Florence's idea. She used her cousin as a security screen. Worthington took the requests on his own home phone and passed them along to Florence at meetings in the local Dunkin' Donuts. That way, the duo circumvented the automatic taping mechanism that recorded all calls coming in on AIICH lines. After years as the main contact person, Worthington knew exactly what information was available, how long it would take to retrieve, and how much it would be worth.

I left Laura in the room and made a telephone call from a phone booth across the street. At first, I was just going to order some customized historical and topographical accident tracking data. But then I remembered something Chief Greer had said, and ordered some financial information as well.

"Two thousand dollars," Worthington said after I explained what I wanted.

"That's pretty expensive," I responded. "I thought accident reports went for around two hundred fifty dollars."

"For basic reports, yes. That sort of thing is pretty straightforward. But what you're asking for is some specialized work. Like that positional plotting analysis you want. We've never had that kind of request before."

"But you can do it, can't you?"

"Of course we can. If the data's there, we can retrieve it and repackage it any want you want. I assume you'd like to have visual plotting of the information. It'll make it easier to understand than just a page of numbers."

"I guess so," I said.

"And you'd probably want to go back farther than just five years. Once we set up the program, we can go back as far as the files go."

"That's even better."

"And you understand that the underlying topographic data has to come from the Pennsylvania Department of Transportation."

"Of course."

"And that financial disclosure information, that's not something we usually request. We'll have to access Commonwealth of Pennsylvania data banks for that, too."

"I assumed you would."

"Well, there you go. We're talking a custom order here. We can't just punch a button and get a printout. We're going to need to create a special retrieval program. That means more time and more risk."

"But this is all readily available information, isn't it?" I asked. "Especially those topos. They should be easy to get. All you have to do is ask for them."

"That's true. But the AIICH mainframe computer automatically records any request for data submitted by outside agencies. It records the date of the request, date of receipt, identity of the individual making the request, that sort of thing."

"I'm sure you have a way of dealing with that."

"Of course we do. But it takes time, Mr. Nikonos. And it exposes us to extra risk. That's why this package costs what it does. You have to understand, we don't just pull our prices out of thin air. What we charge is based on a calculation of the time involved and the degree of risk. For what you want, two thousand dollars is a very fair price."

"All right," I grudgingly agreed, knowing that I had no alternative. "How long will it take?"

"The basic accident report we can get today. If Pennsylvania DOT is on the ball, we can get the topos faxed to us by late tomorrow. The location analysis and the financials will probably be an overnight job. So we're talking end of day Thursday, maybe Friday on the outside."

"I need it faster than that. Can't you get it today?"

"That would be difficult. Very, very difficult."

"Come on, Worthington. It's all computerized. It shouldn't take more than a few minutes to access those data banks."

"That's true, but there are safeguards built into the system. Taking shortcuts can be risky."

"I'll give you an extra thousand dollars if you can do it today."

"That makes three thousand?"

"If you can do it today."

"The best I can promise is by the end of the business day."

"Agreed."

"Do you have a fax number where we can send the material?"

"No. I'm on the road, traveling."

"We can do FedEx Red Priority. Fastest delivery known to man."

"No, I'll be moving around."

That was true, but also I didn't want to give out an address where I could be traced.

"Well then, where do you want me to send the stuff?" Worthington asked, sounding impatient. "It's too risky for me to hold onto these reports. I like to get rid of them as fast as I can."

For obvious reasons, I couldn't have the material sent to my apartment. Likewise with Professor DeBray's place. It was unnerving to realize how isolated a life I had been living. I had lost touch with most of my old college friends, who were probably scattered all over the country by now.

The only person I could think of was my ex-wife, Elizabeth. I didn't want to get involved with her again, even in the most peripheral manner. But I didn't have much choice. I'd have to call her, of course, and grovel a little before she'd agree to accept the delivery. It would be the first favor I asked of her since the divorce. She'd probably open the package when it arrived, but the material inside would be meaningless to her. After some hesitation, I gave Worthington her address in New York.

"When can I expect the money?" he asked.

"I'll send it to you as soon as I get the report."

"You don't understand," he said. "Until we get the money, we don't start the work."

We ended the conversation with me promising to send three thousand dollars by Western Union so he could have the cash in hand before lunch. Laura's money was disappearing a lot faster than I had anticipated.

When I returned to the hotel, Laura, anxiously awaiting my return, was awake and freshly showered.

"You shouldn't have left me alone," she said.

"I didn't want to disturb you," I responded. "You were sleeping so peacefully."

"Your note said you had to make a telephone call. Why didn't you make the call from here?"

"Because the number I called would be automatically entered on the hotel's room billing records. If anyone finds out we stayed here, I don't want them to know who I called."

"I thought maybe it was a call you didn't want me to hear."

"Of course not," I said. "I was just being cautious. The man I called has access to information that might be helpful. But it'll take him a while to pull it all together."

"What kind of information?"

"It's technical stuff about the accident." I tried to play it down. "It might turn out to be nothing."

A knock on the door and a voice from the hallway announced the arrival of room service, which Laura apparently had ordered in my absence. Under polished silver-plated warming covers were dishes heaped with scrambled eggs, bacon and hashbrowns, accompanied by a stack of rye toast, a pitcher of orange juice and a pot of coffee.

"You should have awakened me," she said as she poured herself a glass of juice. "I would have gone with you."

"You need your rest," I said.

"So do you," she said.

She sipped on her juice and watched as I attacked my breakfast. I was almost done when she spoke again.

"I was frightened when I couldn't find you," she said. "I was afraid you left me."

"I'm sorry. I didn't mean to upset you. I should have waited until you woke up."

"Please don't leave me alone again, Theo. Promise me you won't."

The intensity of her plea startled me. I looked up, but she had already lowered her eyes, as if she was embarrassed by the words.

Maybe I was reading too much into her request. It was, after all, quite natural for a woman in her situation to fear being left alone. Taken on that level, it was simply a plea for protection. And yet, her body language suggested there was a deeper, more emotional subtext to her words. Was it wishful thinking on my part?

"You don't have to worry," I said, my voice dropping to a hoarse whisper. "I promise I won't leave you alone again. Not ever."

It was a vow easily made in the highly-charged atmosphere of that moment. But what would happen to that promise if, as I was now beginning to suspect, I discovered that Harrison Duquesne might still be alive?

FORTY

By mid-morning, we were entering the lair of the enemy, the small town where our frightening adventure had begun. It was probably the single most dangerous place for us to be. I tried not to think about what might happen if anyone from the Walden Clinic learned of our presence. Instead, I tried to concentrate on the questions I had to ask, and the person I was hoping would have the answers.

I fiddled around with the police scanner until I found the wave-band used by the Dickson City Police Department. I wanted to find out whether the local police had been alerted by the NYPD to look for me.

Most of the dialogue on the scanner was in cop-talk, that peculiar law-enforcement jargon which uses numeric codes as a bureaucratic shorthand for describing everything from going to the bathroom to investigating a multiple homicide.

The long gaps of static between the dispatcher's messages indicated it was a quiet day in the small town. According to the numeric-code translator in my Scanner Handbook, one of the town's two patrol cars was investigating a minor fender-bender in the 1300 block of Dundaff Avenue, and the other was providing back-up for the crossing guard at the Montessori School. There was nothing on the scanner about the police looking for a blue Honda driven by a fugitive named Theophanes Nikonos, which suggested I wasn't facing imminent arrest. Nevertheless, I still felt uneasy about being back in Dickson.

Unlike the anonymous streets of New York, driving through the small Pennsylvania town offered none of the protective camouflage of crowds. Traffic was light enough and the speed limit slow enough for everyone on Main Street to get a good look at us. If there was any doubt that we were outsiders, it was dispelled by our out-of-state license plates. Every person we passed had to be considered a potential adversary, who although unknown to me, might be working for Doctor Zydek.

I wasn't worried so much for myself as for Laura, who was growing increasingly uneasy as we drove through town. We were heading to the Valley View Manor, I explained to her, which was owned by the same corporation that owned the Walden Clinic. I tried to calm her down by telling her we had the advantage of surprise. That no one would be expecting us to show up there . . . that whoever tried to kill us on Bald Mountain probably thought they had succeeded . . . .

Laura wasn't totally convinced by such flimsy logic. And frankly, neither was I. The larger mystery in which we were entangled was made up of a series of smaller mysteries, the most intriguing of which was the identity of the person who wrote the original letter to Professor DeBray. It was that letter and the accompanying map which first led me to Laura. I was convinced now that the old woman whose name was on the letter couldn't have written it. Angelina Galarza had lied to me. And somehow, when I met her, I managed to overlook the physical evidence that proved she was lying. It was time to see if I could prod the old woman into telling me the truth.

Cautious as ever, I parked the Honda two blocks away from the front entrance of Valley View Manor. Laura stayed in the car to monitor the scanner messages while I went in to see what I could learn from Angie.

The interior of the former schoolhouse was as noisy as I remembered. The cacophony of dozens of TV sets tuned to different channels poured from open doorways into the hall. From somewhere in the building came the loud voice of a woman leading an octogenarian exercise class. An old man in a bathrobe was walking slowly down the hallway towards me, his nose attached by a clear plastic tube to the oxygen tank he was pushing before himself.

The obese male attendant who had been sleeping at his station on my previous visit was no longer there. In his place was a muscular woman in a white pantsuit. She was lazily leafing through a copy of *U. S. News & World Report.* When I drew closer, I could smell the odor of stale cigarette smoke hovering about her. The name tag on her breast pocket identified her as Ms. Louise Murtha.

"Can I help you?" she asked. Her voice had a surly tone that suggested she didn't enjoy having her reading interrupted.

"I'd like to see Angelina Galarza," I said.

"Angie's not with us anymore," she replied, not looking up from her magazine. "Are you a relative?"

"I'm a friend. Can you tell me where she is?"

"They took her to the Gravendahl Funeral Home, but she's probably buried by now."

"You're telling me she's dead?" I asked, unable to hide the disappointment from my voice.

"We prefer not to use that word around here."

"But I saw her a little over a week ago," I protested. "She looked to be in good health, except for the Parkinson's."

"She was eighty-four years old. When they're that age, you've got to expect it."

"How did it happen?" I asked, thinking of the spry little creature who, despite her age, seemed an unlikely candidate to succumb willingly to the entreaties of the Angel of Death. Whatever questions I had for Angie were now doomed to remain unanswered. The identity of the letter-writer would remain a mystery.

"It was the day before yesterday. I wasn't on duty then. But Joey said it was peaceful, if that's what you want to know."

"Joey?"

"The big black man who used to work here. He's the one who tried to wake her up in the morning. She must have passed away during the night."

"What was the cause of death?"

"Old age, I guess," she said with a shrug.

"Is that what it says on the death certificate?"

"Look, it's not complicated." She finally looked up from her magazine. "These old people, after a while, they just stop breathing, that's all. The doctor will probably put it down as respiratory failure, unless there was a history of some other medical problem."

"Wait a minute," I interrupted. "Are you saying there's no death certificate?"

"I didn't say that." Her voice suddenly took on a guarded tone.

"Did a doctor inspect the body?"

"I don't know. I wasn't on duty that morning."

"You're not supposed to release a body to the mortuary until a physician officially certifies the death. That's standard procedure in every health-care facility."

"I told you I wasn't on duty that morning."

"But you should have a record in your files. Can I see the Galarza file?"

"Our files are all confidential," she said. She looked at me with growing suspicion. "Why are you asking all these questions? Are you a cop?"

In the past, my old insurance company business cards often gained me access to restricted files. But I was already certain from Ms. Murtha's defensive attitude that Angie's body had been removed without the benefit of any medical authorization. I decided to back off and try a different approach.

"I'm just an old friend of the family," I lied, in as sincere a tone of voice as I could generate. "I'd like to pay my last respects. Did you say they took her to the Gravendahl Funeral Home?"

"That's right, but like I told you, she might be buried already. They don't usually have a viewing unless the deceased's family pays for it. Most of the time the families can't even be located."

"So you haven't contacted any of her relatives?"

"We don't know where they are," she said, and quickly added, "Do you?"

"I've been out of touch," I murmured. "Didn't any of them ever write to her?"

"Not even a Christmas card."

"That's too bad," I said. An address of a family member probably wouldn't have turned up any useful information, but I hated to see another avenue of inquiry closed off.

"It's not unusual in this business," Ms. Murtha explained. "A lot of times, if there's any surviving relatives, they don't want to be bothered."

"What do you normally do with the personal effects when you can't locate the family? Do you hold everything for safekeeping?"

She shook her head at the naivete of the question. "You've got to be kidding," she said. "We're not talking about rich people. These are all Social Security and welfare cases. The stuff they leave behind, you can't even sell it at a flea market."

"What about Angie's things? Could I take a look?"

"Are you really a friend of the family?"

I pulled a fifty-dollar bill from my wallet.

"You must be a really good friend," she said in a surprised voice.

She put her magazine down, took the fifty-dollar bill and led me down the hallway. As we passed Angie's room, another old woman in a bathrobe was already sitting on what had been Angie's bed. She was watching "Oprah" on TV.

"You've already got a new tenant," I commented. "You don't waste much time."

"We try to be efficient," Ms. Murtha said. "We've got forty-three people on the waiting list for admission. It wouldn't be fair to keep them waiting any longer than necessary."

At the end of the hallway was a utility storage closet. Inside it were mop buckets, floor wax, cartons of generic soap and toilet paper and a rug-steaming machine. Permeating everything was the powerful odor of Pine-Sol disinfectant.

Ms. Murtha pointed to two black plastic garbage bags jammed into one corner of the closet.

"That's Angie's stuff," she said. "If somebody doesn't claim it by the end of the week, it goes to the Salvation Army."

"She didn't have very much," I murmured.

"We don't encourage our residents to bring in a lot of personal items. All we recommend is a few comfortable pieces of clothing and maybe some things with sentimental value that they want to hold onto. We provide everything else they need."

It was the time-honored approach to control of institutional populations, a procedure with its roots in Orwellian theory.

Stripping the residents of the outward signs of their former individuality is the first step in a process of depersonalization, which, when completed, creates the kind of social environment most group homes prefer: a docile community of residents who seldom challenge the administrators. If that doesn't work, of course, chemical manipulation can be used to achieve the same goal. The success of the program at Valley View Manor was evident in the way residents tended to stay in their rooms, spending their final days in pajamas and bathrobes, and staring blankly at their TV screens.

Yet somehow Angie had seemed to successfully resist those efforts, maintaining not only her personal dignity, but her mental acuity and sense of humor. I could imagine the staff being irritated by her failure to be subjugated by their methods of behavior modification, and possibly even relieved when the stubborn little woman finally died. But that was no reason to ship her off to the mortuary without a doctor's signature.

As superficial as that medical formality might be, it was nevertheless a legal requirement. The more I thought about that fact, the more suspicious I became. One of the first lessons I learned in insurance claims administration was that missing medical paperwork and procedural shortcuts are usually good indicators of criminal fraud.

With the knowledge that each resident's stay will inevitably end in death, why would Valley View Manor not have set in place an efficient, routine procedure for the medical certification of death? And if such a procedure was in place, why was it circumvented in the case of Angelina Galarza?

The questions made me wonder whether Angie's passing was as peaceful and natural as Ms. Murtha suggested.

"That's Angie's stuff," she repeated, bringing me back from my reverie.

"It's really not much," I said. "A woman lives for over eighty years and all that's left of her life doesn't even fill two garbage bags."

"Like I said, we don't encourage them to bring much when they move in."

And whatever was left when she died was probably picked over by the staff to make sure the Salvation Army didn't get anything valuable, I thought. Still, there might be something useful, a scrap of paper with an address or a note or some other item that might answer some of my questions.

"Do you have a place where I could look through this stuff?" I asked.

"You're really a friend of the family?"

"I was a good friend of Angie's," I said, posthumously elevating our relationship.

"Oh, what the hell, you can keep it," she said. "We were going to get rid of it, anyway."

After her initial gruffness, I hadn't expected the sudden burst of generosity. The surprise must have shown in my face, because she quickly tried to explain herself.

"I liked the old girl," she said. "She didn't take any crap from anyone, including me."

I reached for my wallet.

"You don't have to do that," she protested, but after looking around to make sure no one was watching, happily accepted another fifty-dollar bill. "Thanks. Anything else I can do for you?"

"You can promise to forget I was here," I said as I picked up the two garbage bags.

"No problem," she responded. "No problem at all."

I wasn't really prepared just yet to go pawing through Angie's garments in search of unknown clues. I put the two bags in the trunk and tried to remember the way back to the Gravendahl Funeral Home.

I wanted to see if I could get in to examine Angie's corpse.

FORTY-ONE

We arrived at the Gravendahl Funeral Home in time to see a bronze-toned casket being loaded into a hearse. I knew it couldn't be Angie's casket, because the preparations were too elaborate for someone whose relatives didn't even send her Christmas cards.

I parked halfway up the block, where Laura and I could watch the proceedings. Judging by the number and quality of the vehicles in the parking lot, the funeral was probably that of some local VIP. I watched Howard Gravendahl talk for a few moments with a woman I assumed to be the widow. He reminded me of a kindly old grandfather, stoop-shouldered and sympathetic as he escorted the widow to the car immediately behind the hearse. He seemed to have fully recovered from the blow I delivered to his head.

When he was satisfied that everything was in order, Gravendahl took his place in the passenger seat of the hearse. Howard Junior was doing the driving. They waited patiently while one of their black-suited employees locked the side door of the funeral parlor and another darted out into the street to halt any oncoming traffic. A third employee was moving through the parking lot, attaching purple funeral flags to the vehicles, and reminding the drivers to turn on their headlights. When all was ready, the hearse moved slowly out into the street, followed at a respectable distance by the widow's car. The traffic jam in the parking lot gradually unwound itself into a slow-moving line that proceeded through the nearby intersection without stopping. The final car in the cortege was occupied by the three black-suited attendants.

Whoever it was in the casket had done us a big favor. With his death leading to interment at this particular hour, the deceased had made it easier for us to get into the funeral home. With the Gravendahls safely on their way to the cemetery rites, Laura and I had no reason to fear entering the building.

The front door was unlocked. From inside came the sound of a vacuum cleaner. We followed the sound to the visitation room, which had already been stripped of the mournful trappings that had surrounded the corpse. The flowers were gone, taken to the cemetery along with the casket. The kneelers and guest book and the memorial photographs of the deceased had been removed. The chairs were folded and stacked against the wall.

The woman running the vacuum cleaner had a tired face and hair that was too black to be anything but dyed. She was wearing a printed blouse, blue jeans and white athletic shoes.

When she saw us, she shut off the vacuum.

"They just left for the cemetery," she said.

The simple artifice of donning sunglasses and sad faces seemed to label us in her mind as mourners.

"You can probably catch up with them because they usually drive slow, especially through town," she added.

"I don't understand," I said, trying my best to look confused.

"The Crowell funeral. They left here not more than five minutes ago."

"We're not here for the Crowell funeral," I said, trying to sound despondent. As we had planned, Laura fumbled in her purse until she found a packet of tissue. Playing the role of a bereaved couple had seemed like the most discreet way to find out whether Angie's corpse was still on the premises.

"But there's no other funeral scheduled today . . . ." she said, then stopped, her mind searching for and finding the only other logical reason for our presence there.

"Oh. Oh, I'm sorry," she said when she saw Laura raise the tissue to wipe an imaginary tear away from one of her eyes. "I really am sorry," she repeated. "You're here to make funeral arrangements, aren't you?"

I nodded, giving her a gloomy smile. The most obvious fictions are always the most easily accepted.

"We have an appointment with Mr. Gravendahl," I lied.

"You just missed him. He won't be back for at least an hour, maybe an hour and a half."

"But I called him earlier this morning," I lied again. "I was very specific about what time we'd be here. He said he'd be available to meet with us."

"There must be some sort of mistake. Mr. Gravendahl always makes it a point to be at the cemetery for the interment. And especially for a funeral like Mr. Crowell's."

"What about his assistant? Does he have somebody to handle things when he's not here?" Of course I knew everybody was gone. Laura and I had watched them all leave.

"His son is driving the hearse," the cleaning lady said. "Even Mrs. Gravendahl went with them. She usually doesn't join the cortege, but she knew Mr. Crowell. Did you know him?"

"You mean there's nobody here to help us?"

"They're all gone to the cemetery. I'm just the cleaning lady."

"How could he do this to us?" I tried to sound indignant.

Playing the grief-stricken wife, Laura sobbed and dabbed at her eyes once again with the handkerchief. I hoped she wasn't overdoing it. It didn't seem to really take much to convince the cleaning lady of our sincerity.

"Maybe you'd like to sit down for a while," she said to Laura. "There's some coffee in the lounge, maybe some donuts, too."

She led us to a small room which she hadn't yet had time to clean. A narrow side table was cluttered with empty coffee cups, a few of which had served as makeshift ashtrays. The coffee machine was still plugged in. Only two sugar donuts remained on the large tray next to the coffee machine.

Laura sat down on a black leather couch while I filled two paper cups with stale-smelling coffee.

"It's her father," I whispered to the cleaning lady. "He passed away last night at Evangelical Hospital."

"Oh, we get a lot of funerals from there," the cleaning lady said.

"The point is, we have to get back to New York this afternoon," I lied. "Mr. Gravendahl assured us we could finalize the funeral arrangements before lunchtime. Now you say he won't be back for an hour and a half? I'm really disappointed with him."

"I wish I could help you, but all I do is the cleaning."

"That's okay, it's not your fault," I said. "But if I can't rely on Mr. Gravendahl to keep his word, it makes me wonder if perhaps I selected the wrong funeral home."

I handed one of the coffee cups to Laura, who continued with her pretense of sniffling into a tissue.

"Oh, no, sir, you made the right choice," the cleaning lady loyally responded. "Mr. Gravendahl is one of the most respected funeral directors you'll find, and not just in Dickson, but in the whole Lackawanna County. He gets business from all the local nursing homes, and you know they wouldn't keep coming back if they weren't happy with his work."

"Well, I'm glad to hear that," I said. "But I hate to sit around here and waste time. It's really difficult, especially for my wife."

"I'm really sorry," the cleaning lady apologized again. "Maybe I can get you something to read, or maybe you'd like to go in the kitchen; there's a TV in there."

"One of the matters we were supposed to attend to was the selection of a casket," I said. "I was told there's a display room downstairs." I lowered my voice. "My wife is very particular. She wants the finest casket available for her father. Strictly the top-of-the-line, no matter how much it costs."

"I'm sure Mr. Gravendahl can supply what you want," the cleaning lady said. "If he doesn't have it downstairs, he can order it for next-day delivery."

"That's good to know," I said. I filled another cup with coffee and handed it to her. "I really appreciate your taking the time to help us. I know you've got a lot of other work to do."

She dipped one of the leftover donuts into her coffee before taking a bite. "It's all right, I'm almost done with the vacuuming," she assured me. "I know Mr. Gravendahl would want me to be helpful."

"And we'll be sure to tell him," I said. I took a sip of the awful coffee. "You know, maybe we could save a little time and look at the caskets while we're waiting."

The cleaning lady looked uncertain. "I don't think I could do that," she said. "I don't know the prices."

"Oh, for goodness sake, we don't care about the prices. We're only interested in getting the best casket available. And the sooner we make that decision, the sooner we can get back to New York. I'm really not prepared to sit around here for an hour and half doing nothing, particularly with my wife so upset."

I glanced at my watch, trying to act impatient. "Perhaps I should look for another Funeral home, one that would be more responsive to our needs," I added.

I could see the indecision in her eyes. She obviously didn't want to get involved in her employer's business affairs. But I was representing myself as a customer for one of Gravendahl's highest-profit caskets, and by implication, an expensive funeral. If I knew anything about psychology, I knew she was thinking she might be blamed for the loss of business if I walked out.

She didn't seem happy about doing it, but she finally agreed to take us downstairs to the salesroom.

I had been down there before, of course, on the night I had been searching for Laura. But this time I had to pretend to be interested in the caskets. There were about a dozen of them on display, arranged in angled tiers around the walls, with two additional caskets forming an island in the center of the room. The selection available included a miniature white casket with golden handles for children, a plain grey casket with simple satin interiors that looked like the economy model, and a series of increasingly ornate caskets that led up to an imposing heavy-gauge bronze model with genuine silk interior, sculptured brass corners and carrying bars, and guaranteed weatherproof seals.

"This would be the top of the line," the cleaning lady said. "But I don't know the prices."

I nodded approvingly and ran my hand over the polished bronze. After closely examining it, we moved on to the display of optional interior treatments available for use with any of the caskets. After that was a display describing concrete burial vaults which, according to the accompanying brochure, were now required by most cemeteries as additional protection against ground collapse. This last display consisted of miniaturized units to show the various constructions, from a plain slab-top box to a version with elaborate tongue-and-groove construction, featuring a 100-year plastic gasket.

Laura and I engaged in role-playing, studying the displays, carefully considering and discussing the merits of each offering, purposely stalling until the cleaning lady finally remembered that she had work to do upstairs.

With a brief apology, she left us downstairs while she went back to her cleaning. I waited until I heard the sound of the vacuum cleaner before I turned my attention to the real object of our visit.

At the rear of the display area was the door I had entered on my previous visit. It was one of two entrances to the preparation room, where the mortician's art was practiced. The door opened with a sigh as the insulating seals released their grip. I felt a rush of cool air against my face. From out of the darkness came the unpleasant odor of embalming fluid. I felt along the wall until I found the light switch.

The fluorescent lights flickered in protest, as if reluctant to reveal the room's secrets. In the center of the room were the two stainless-steel embalming tables I had seen on my last visit. Only one of them was occupied. Lying in the cold metal trough was a small, shriveled figure. With its wrinkled skin and diminutive size, the motionless mass seemed more like a museum exhibit than a human being.

It was, in fact, the earthly remains of the late Angelina Galarza.

FORTY-TWO

Once again, I found myself in the presence of death. Unlike Laura, whose own thanatopic experience gave her an easy acceptance of the situation, I felt uncomfortable approaching the cadaver.

Angie's corpse was a shrunken version of the woman I remembered. What little flesh and muscle had clung to her bones in life had released their grip. In death, her face had lost its personality. Flaccid skin sagged against the underlying bone, emphasizing the skeletal appearance of the corpse. Her hands, freed by death from the tremors of Parkinson's, lay blessedly still at her sides.

"Do you recognize her?" I asked.

"No." Laura shook her head as we moved closer. "I never saw her before."

Although she had been dead for two days, Angie's corpse was still a work in progress.

"Her name was Angelina Galarza," I said. "She pretended to be the person who wrote to us about your NDE."

"I don't understand."

"Someone wrote a letter to Professor DeBray, describing your case, and telling us where to find you," I said. "Whoever it was even drew a map showing how to reach the room where you were being held. I should have known Angie didn't write the letter. I should have realized it as soon as I met her."

"How could you possibly know?"

"She had Parkinson's disease, which made her hands tremble uncontrollably. The day I met her, the tremors were so bad, she could barely sign the receipt for the money I gave her. I didn't think much of it at the time, because it's not an unusual ailment among the elderly. And frankly, at the time, I was more concerned about where Metzger had taken you. It wasn't until a few days later that I realized the significance of those tremors. It would have been physically impossible for someone with Parkinson's to have written the letter, much less drawn the map."

"If she didn't write the letter, then who did?"

"Obviously, it was somebody who knew you were being held incommunicado. Someone who wanted you to be found, but for some reason wanted to keep his or her own identity secret. It would be helpful to know who that person was. That's what I wanted to talk to Angie about."

"It was dangerous coming back to Dickson," Laura said. "Now I understand why you did it."

"I thought it was worth the risk. I thought maybe if I confronted her with the facts, she might tell me who she was protecting."

Since no public viewing of the old woman's corpse was scheduled, there was certainly no rush for the Gravendahls to finish their work. As long as the body had been pumped full of formaldehyde, they probably felt it could wait until after the Crowell funeral. Yet it offended me that they would leave Angie's naked corpse exposed in this manner while they dealt with other, more important clients.

"Why do you think she went along with it?" Laura asked. "I mean, an older woman like her, you wouldn't expect her to get involved in something like that."

"They might have given her some money," I said. "The way Valley View operated, the patients apparently had to sign over everything they had, including their Social Security checks."

"You think someone bribed her?" Laura shook her head. "Sorry, Theo. That sounds too complicated. I can't believe anybody would actually pay bribe money because of me. I'm not that important."

"You never know," I said. "But you could be right. Maybe I'm overthinking it. From what I know of Angie, she might have gone along with it for the excitement. She was pretty bored with her life at the nursing home."

"Or maybe she did it because she wanted to help me," Laura said, her voice growing soft and gentle. "She looks like the kind of woman who's helped a lot of people in her lifetime."

The pathetic reminders of an old woman's vanity decorated Angie's skull: dead hair wrapped tightly around pink plastic curlers, put up during the last conscious moments of her life. A few of the curlers had come loose in the process of moving the body.

"I was sure no one would ever find me," Laura continued. "Whatever her motives might been, that letter told you where I was. I'm grateful to her for whatever she did."

Considering the circumstances, this was as close to a eulogy as Angie was ever likely to get. She deserved better than this, I thought.

"She helped me to find you twice," I said. "The second time was when they moved you out of the Walden Clinic."

"I don't remember any of that."

"You were heavily sedated when they moved you. I had no idea where to look for you, until Angie decided they must have brought you here."

"This is where they brought me? To a funeral home?"

"I never would have thought of it, but as Angie pointed out to me, funeral directors regularly remove bodies from nursing homes and health care facilities. It was the perfect cover for getting you out of the Walden Clinic. And sure enough, I found you unconscious in a room upstairs. Benevolent old Mr. Gravendahl had given you enough Nembutol to kill you."

"But why would he do that?"

"I think it was an accidental overdose. Morticians aren't accustomed to working on living bodies. I assume he wanted to keep you quiet because he had a funeral going on downstairs. But if it wasn't for Angie, I never would have found you in time. Gravendahl would have been scheduling you for his next funeral. Angie might not have been totally honest about the letter, but she more than made up for it by figuring out where they were hiding you."

"She saved my life," Laura murmured. "Not just once, but twice. A woman I never met . . . a total stranger."

A chill went through me as I watched her bend over the corpse to kiss Angie on the forehead. She lifted the dead woman's right hand and rubbed it lovingly against her cheek. Her lips moved, but I couldn't hear the words. I didn't know whether she was simply praying for the repose of Angie's soul, or attempting somehow to communicate with the dead woman. NDE literature is filled with reports of heightened psychic powers and the ability to talk to the dead. I'd swear the lights flickered for an instant, although it could have been my imagination or perhaps a power surge caused by the vacuum upstairs.

When Laura was done, she gently arranged Angie's arms in the traditional death's cross.

"What was that all about?" I asked.

"I was just trying to thank her," Laura said. "I hope she heard me. I know she's not suffering any more, but I'm so sorry she's dead."

"I'm sorry, too," I said. "And also suspicious."

"What do you mean?"

"Well, you have to admit, the timing of her death is more than a little coincidental."

"She was an old woman, Theo. Old people die. That's the way it works."

"She didn't look like she was dying the last time I saw her. Sure, she had Parkinson's, but not the advanced stages. Her mind was still sharp, her eyes were clear, and she seemed bright and alert to me."

"Are you suggesting she was murdered?"

"I'm thinking it's a possibility. After all, someone murdered the Professor. And someone tried to kill us yesterday on Bald Mountain."

"But why kill an old woman? A patient in nursing home?"

The thought seemed to appall her.

"Maybe to keep her quiet," I said. "Remember, someone was using her to keep their own identity secret."

"You mean the person who wrote the letter?"

"Well, you have to admit it has a certain logical symmetry," I said. "But we don't really know for sure that Angie was murdered. I might be wrong."

"I hope you are." She shook her head sadly. "But how can we tell? There don't seem to be any wounds on her body."

"We have to look more closely."

"What are we supposed to be looking for?"

"I'm not sure," I said. "Anything out of the ordinary, I guess."

Like most people would be, I felt ill at ease and strangely embarrassed in the presence of a naked corpse. But Laura, with her acceptance of death, seemed totally comfortable handling the dead flesh. Soon she was undoing the pink curlers and combing out Angie's hair.

"I don't think you should be doing that," I warned.

"She'd want me to," Laura said. "No woman likes to be seen with her hair in rollers. Not even by her undertaker."

"They'll know somebody was messing around with the corpse."

"At this point, what does it matter? We're in enough trouble already."

The logic was irrefutable. I left her to work on Angie's hairdo while I examined the old woman's flesh.

After reading hundreds of medical reports related to auto insurance investigations and the extensive documentation required for my NDE work, I had a good theoretical knowledge of what doctors look for to determine cause of death. In actual practice, however, I was limited to a superficial surface examination. Although the Gravendahls had scalpels and other medical utensils at hand, I had neither the desire nor the training to begin poking around inside Angie's body.

The fact that no cosmetic work had yet been done on the corpse was fortuitous. It meant that no suspicious marks on the body would have been concealed by makeup. The problem was the loose and wrinkled skin that covered the old woman's cadaver. A needle mark might suggest death by lethal injection, for example. But that tiny pinprick could easily be hiding between the folds of skin on her arms or legs or even between her toes. It required a meticulous inspection of the corpse, a procedure which was distasteful for someone with my sensitivities. Although the body had been washed, I was nervous about touching it. The wrinkled skin felt cold and rubbery. It moved loosely over the underlying flesh. Wherever I touched Angie, the depressions of my fingermarks remained behind. Pervading it all was the strong minty odor of formaldehyde, which was beginning to nauseate me.

"Theo?"

"Yes?"

"You said to look for anything unusual?"

"Did you find something?"

"There are strange little purple dots on her eyelids."

If I hadn't been so squeamish about looking at the old woman's frozen facial features, I probably would have noticed the telltale markings earlier.

They were tiny round dots, no larger than pinpricks. They were arranged in no discernible pattern. A more careful examination of Angie's face revealed similar purplish dots around her mouth.

"What are they?" Laura asked.

"The medical term is *petechiae*," I answered. "I've read about them in medical reports and autopsies. One of the near-deathers I interviewed last year had them."

I curled back Angie's eyelids and found, just as I expected, more dots inside. The soft tissue inside her mouth exhibited the same condition.

"Are they the sort of thing you were looking for?" she asked.

"Definitely," I assured her. "We're lucky we got here before the cosmetologist. It wouldn't take much makeup to hide them. They're actually tiny hemorrhages. They're caused when a sudden increase in blood pressure ruptures minute capillaries near the surface of the skin."

"You mean she had high blood pressure?"

"Well, not exactly. The increased pressure usually comes from an outside source. In the case of the near-deather I mentioned, the source of the pressure was a rope around the neck."

"Are you saying she was . . . strangled?"

"Sometimes *petechiae* are indications of renal failure, but she didn't exhibit any of those symptoms when I talked to her."

I examined Angie's throat. "I don't see any obvious signs of strangulation, either. Usually heavy bruising and discoloration would be visible on a strangling victim, but she's got loose, wrinkled skin, and that makes it hard to see any bruising. Most likely, someone just put a pillow over her and pressed down hard."

"The man we found in your apartment . . . Laura said. "The professor . . . he was strangled."

"That's right," I said.

"Do you think the same person killed them both?"

"It's a possibility."

Upstairs, the vacuum cleaner continued to drone. It was getting close to an hour since the cortege had left for the cemetery. The Gravendahls would be coming back soon. I turned out the lights and closed the door to the preparation room. It was time for us to withdraw from the melancholy environs of death.

If I didn't report what I found to the police, the evidence of possible homicide would be buried with Angie's body, where even minimal decomposition would soon erase the tiny, telltale *petechiae*.

Chief Greer had already demonstrated her willingness to investigate any report of criminal wrongdoing by the Zydecor enterprises. But the last time I went to see the Dickson police, they ran my plates and checked for outstanding New York warrants. Such efficiency made me nervous. If they flagged my name on the initial inquiry, which was simply a matter of a few keystrokes on the computer, the Dickson police would be automatically notified of any subsequent NYPD warrant on me as soon as it was issued. So I did the cautious thing and called in my suspicions from a pay phone just outside the city limits.

When she found out it was me on the phone, the dispatcher's voice dropped into a carefully guarded tone. Marie Krislaski might be a wizard with the computer, but she was an amateur when it came to concealing her intentions. She asked me to please hold on, there'd be a short delay while my call was patched through to Chief Greer, who was out of the office. When the chief finally came on the phone, she sounded a lot friendlier than the situation warranted, asking me when I got back to town and how long I was staying.

It didn't take a degree in psychology to understand what was going on. I assumed she was already in a patrol car, talking to me on a cellular unit while she was heading for my location. With Caller ID, the dispatcher could instantly pinpoint where I was calling from and inform the chief. I calculated I had a maximum of two minutes before I could expect the police car to show up. That didn't give me much time to explain about the *petechiae* and the missing death certificate. Particularly when the chief kept trying to interrupt and ask questions that I knew were designed only to stall me and keep me on the phone longer.

The only virtue in being wanted for murder was knowing that anything I said about another homicide would be taken seriously by the police. The downside, of course, was that I could end up with a second murder charge against me.

I hurried through my suspicions and hung up and got out of there as quickly as I could. As we sped away, I kept the scanner tuned to the frequency used by the Dickson police. I listened carefully for the numeric codes normally used for pursuit of a fleeing suspect. I didn't hear any transmissions that mentioned a blue Honda with New York plates. I also didn't hear any transmissions alerting the state police or other local law enforcement agencies. My guess was that Chief Greer didn't want to share any credit for my capture. If she wanted to play the lone wolf, that was fine with me. Nevertheless, I avoided the more heavily-patrolled routes into Scranton. I drove through the tree-lined residential streets of the Green Ridge section, past imposing stone mansions built by the mining barons of a bygone era and now occupied by the more prosperous of the area's thirty-somethings.

All I could hope was that Chief Greer wouldn't guess where I was headed next.

"Why is this happening, Theo?" Laura's voice was filled with anguish. "Is it because of me? Are those people dead because of me?"

"You shouldn't blame yourself . . . ."

"But it is my fault," she insisted. "If I was still at the Walden Clinic, if you never found me, do you think your professor would be dead? Do you think that poor old woman would be dead?"

I didn't have an answer that I liked, so I let her keep talking.

"I can accept death, Theo. It's not anything I'm afraid of, because I know what it's really like. That's why it didn't bother me when I saw Professor DeBray's corpse, or when I saw Angie's."

She paused, and I sensed she was trying desperately to keep from crying. "But now I realize it might be my fault they're dead. I'm not sure I can handle that."

"Laura . . ."

"Don't you see, Theo? It's all because you helped me escape from the clinic. They want me back." Her voice trembled and she started to sob. "They're killing the people who helped you to find me. I'm afraid they'll kill you, too."

I reached out and, wrapping my arm protectively around her shoulders, pulled her close to me. She lowered her head against my chest. I could feel the warmth of her tears soaking through my shirt.

"I don't want them to kill you, Theo," she sobbed. "But I don't want to go back there. What they'll do to me . . . oh, God . . . ."

She broke down at last, crying openly with no attempt to conceal her violent sobbing. I held her tighter, but it didn't seem to do much good. She was going through an emotional crisis. I let it play out until, fatigued, she fell asleep.

Whatever they did to her at the Walden Clinic was obviously an extremely traumatic experience, one that she wanted to block from her conscious mind, but she was unfortunately, painfully, unable to do so.

At some point, I knew, all would be revealed.

Meanwhile, I was left to ponder the paradox that troubled me ever since the attempt on our lives at Bald Mountain. If they wanted Laura back badly enough to kill those who had helped her escape, why were they now trying to kill her, too?

Or was it possible, and this was just the faint beginnings of a thought in the back of my mind . . . was it possible that someone else was involved?

Someone who wanted Laura dead?

FORTY-THREE

How far had I traveled from the person I once was?

There was a time when I had lived in fear of strangers on late-night streets, when I had double-locked, bolted and chained my door to deter intruders who never arrived, when I had avoided subway cars that were occupied by ominous-looking groups of teenagers. Now I was shrugging off attempts on my life, examining the corpses of murder victims, and easily eluding the police and other pursuers while in the company of a woman I had rescued from her captors.

I wasn't really a superhero, although I have to admit there were moments when Laura's admiring glances made me feel like one. It would also be foolishly sentimental to conclude that I was somehow transformed by love, although I was beginning to feel a kinship with those cinematic heroes who regularly fight incredible odds for the opportunity to press their lips against those of Hollywood's leading ladies. From a psychological standpoint, my conduct had more to do with Tolman's behavioral experiments with rats than with Ovid's theories of love. I was simply trying to find a way out of a frightening maze in which I had somehow become trapped. Just as Tolman looked on while his rats darted down blind alleys, my actions had apparently been carefully monitored, even anticipated. How else to explain the missing medical records, Doctor Subdhani's disappearance, Professor DeBray's murder, the avalanche that nearly killed us, and finally the murder of Angelina Galarza?

And yet, like the rat in the maze, I was doomed to continue turning corners, confronting new obstacles and backtracking in the hopes of finding a way out. This is what led me inevitably back to Scranton Evangelical Hospital. Laura accompanied me inside. We took the elevator down one floor to the Records Department. Behind the counter was the same grandmotherly volunteer in the pink jacket who was on duty during my previous visit. She greeted me with a smile that faded as soon as she recognized me.

"You're back again," she said with a sigh.

"I'm still trying to locate those medical records," I said.

"I can't release any records without the proper authorization."

"That's why I brought along Mrs. Duquesne," I explained. "The records I'm looking for are hers. She can sign any necessary request forms."

The volunteer didn't seem to welcome this information. As she did the last time, she retreated behind a request for identification. Laura produced her passport. The volunteer put on her red-rimmed reading glasses. She scrutinized the passport picture; too carefully, I thought.

"I'll be right back," she said, walking off with Laura's passport. When she returned from the back room, she was followed by the familiar slender figure of Mrs. Hillier, the records supervisor. Mrs. Hiller was wearing a bright yellow dress that seemed a little too broad-shouldered for her slim physique. She didn't look happy to see me, either.

"The last time I was here, there seemed to be a problem finding Mrs. Duquesne's medical records," I said, trying to sound reasonable and easy to deal with. "Hopefully, we can get a copy today."

Mrs. Hillier ignored me. She was busy comparing Laura's features with those of the passport photo. I wouldn't have been surprised if she asked for a handwriting specimen.

"One moment, please," she said, and turned away to make a brief phone call, the contents of which she shielded from our ears.

So far, no one had asked for the date of Laura's hospital stay or any of the standard questions about her confinement that would normally be used to locate patient records. I took this as a bad sign.

Sure enough, the next person we saw was Clarence Renshaw, the hospital's pint-sized chief administrative officer. He was dressed for success in a chalk-stripe charcoal grey suit, accented with a bright red silk necktie and matching red silk foulard artfully stuffed in his lapel pocket. If I wasn't mistaken, a few more hair implants had been added since our last meeting. He wore his best official smile, but it couldn't hide the worry in his eyes. I had a feeling this was going to turn out to be another dead end.

I repeated Laura's introduction and restated the reason for our return visit. Renshaw gave her a gentle handshake, told her how well she looked and how pleased he was that she had fully recovered from her accident. As for the records, he gave a helpless shrug.

"We're still having a problem retrieving those particular records," he told her. "As I already explained to Mr. Nikonos, we've been changing over to a new computer system and it's resulted in a few unanticipated problems."

I was surprised he remembered my name.

"It's been a week," I pointed out. "You said you'd have it all worked out in a day or two."

"I know, I know, and I'm terribly sorry. But we've tried everything. We know the information was entered, because of the gap in the coding sequence. But there's some sort of glitch in the system. We can't retrieve any of the data on Mrs. Duquesne's confinement. Fortunately for us, the problem appears to be limited to that one particular file. But we can't seem to find any trace of it."

"Maybe it was erased."

Renshaw threw back his shoulders as if he was insulted by the suggestion.

"Impossible," was his haughty response. "There are too many safeguards in place for that sort of accident to happen."

"Maybe it wasn't an accident," I persisted.

"Don't be ridiculous. Why would anyone choose to erase Mrs. Duquesne's medical records? I don't want to minimize the seriousness of her loss, but what possible reason could anyone have for doing such a thing?"

"Maybe there's information in the file someone doesn't want us to see."

"Such as?" Renshaw sounded unconvinced.

"I don't know. Maybe something incriminating."

"Incriminating?" The tone of Renshaw's voice suggested he didn't like the sound of that word. "Just what are you getting at, Mr. Nikonos? A malpractice suit? Are you threatening to take us to court?"

It wasn't at all what I had in mind, but if it worried him, it wouldn't hurt to let him think so. I responded with a shrug.

"If we were facing a malpractice suit, erasing the file would be self-defeating," Renshaw hurried to explain. "The very fact that the records are missing would probably be viewed by a jury as an attempt by the hospital to cover up its mistakes."

"What about backup files?" I asked. "Don't you keep duplicate copies of all your computer records?"

"Of course we do. But I'm afraid the duplicate was made before anybody discovered the problem with the original. There's no data on the backup, either."

"What about microfiche?"

"We stopped using microfiche years ago. We get much faster access with the computers."

"What about the original paperwork? Don't you keep that anymore?"

"The problem is storage space. A hospital generates huge amounts of paperwork every day. We simply don't have the room to store it all. Once the data is loaded into our computers, the original paperwork is shipped off to a storage facility in Utah. We've initiated a trace for the documents in question, but the retrieval process normally takes a few weeks."

"We don't have that much time," I said.

"Well, I'm sorry, but it's the best we can do. Perhaps you should check with the attending physician. He was the one responsible for the treatment Mrs. Duquesne received. He should have his own copies of her medical records."

There was no point in pressing him any further. The damage had already been done. Somebody had obviously gone in and erased Laura's records. Renshaw was either an exquisite liar, or he really had no knowledge of what happened to the files.

"Why are you so interested in my medical records?" Laura asked as we rode the elevator back up to the lobby.

"Because they're missing," I said.

Call it paranoia, but when we left the hospital, I kept looking back to make certain we weren't being followed.

"Do you really think they were erased?"

"Definitely."

"But why?"

"Obviously, somebody doesn't want us to see them."

Laura had to hurry to keep up with me. I had parked the car three blocks from the hospital, behind a low-income housing project where I thought it would go unnoticed by passing police patrols.

"It could be a mistake," she argued. "Hospitals make mistakes all the time."

"Not in this case," I said as I unlocked the car. "I'm pretty sure your file was erased on purpose."

"But couldn't it have happened just like they said? Some kind of glitch in the system?"

I circled the neighborhood a few times, checking the rearview mirror to see if anyone was making the same turns behind us.

"One thing the Professor taught me was to look for patterns," I explained. "If those missing records were an isolated event, I might accept Renshaw's glitch-in-the-computer theory. But you have to consider the disappearing records in context with everything else that's happened. What they did to you. What happened to DeBray and Angie. There's a pattern that emerges. And it all seems to have started with your near-death experience."

I knew she was in a fragile emotional state. Worried about the impact my words might have on her, I put an arm around Laura's shoulder and drew her close to comfort her.

"It's not your fault," I said. "So don't blame yourself."

She relaxed against me, her warm body melting into the security of my embrace.

"We're dealing with someone who must feel terribly threatened by your near-death experience," I explained. "The question we have to ask is why it would lead to murder."

I already had some suspicions, of course. But it would have been premature to share them with her. Like any reputable researcher, I wanted further verification before I went public.

But I was running out of places to look for that verification. I didn't really expect to find Doctor Subdhani in his office, but I thought it would be worth a try. I parked the car two blocks away from his office, shielding it from view among the garbage dumpsters behind a strip shopping mall.

Subdhani's waiting room was empty. His hard-looking blonde receptionist was at her post behind the sliding glass panels. Her thin lips parted in an unfriendly smile. The way my luck was going, I expected her to tell me Subdhani was still out of town on his unannounced vacation. The receptionist surprised me by ushering us directly into the doctor's private office.

"Make yourself comfortable," she said. "The doctor'll be here in a few minutes."

It might seem unusual to be waiting in a doctor's private office rather than out front. I thought nothing of it, however. After all, I had been here before. I assumed she was simply being considerate, probably because of Laura's presence at my side.

We waited for nearly twenty minutes before I heard any activity out front. A door opened. A hushed conversation took place. The sound of a door again. A long silence.

Until then, I had been waiting patiently. But the silence made me uneasy. I strained my ears to the limits of their capacity, but I could detect no other sounds. Five minutes went by, and then ten.

Finally, just when I was ready to give it all up, I heard footsteps in the outer office, followed by a muffled exchange of words. Slowly, the office door opened.

Instead of Doctor Subdhani, the man who entered the room was Roland Metzger.

I guess I shouldn't have been surprised. I certainly was aware of the risks involved in coming back here.

Metzger smiled at us, savoring his moment of triumph.

The two Samoans quickly entered the room, cutting off all hope of escape.

Metzger reached inside his jacket and withdrew a pistol. I don't know much about guns, but this one was big and menacing, one of those black military-style automatics favored by the stars of action movies.

Instinctively, I rose and placed myself in front of Laura, as if I could protect her from this threat with a simple movement of my body.

"It's all over now," Metzger said with a grin.

He pulled back the slide at the top of the barrel. I was close enough to see the coppery glint of the cartridge being chambered. All I could do was watch helplessly as he raised the pistol to my head.

FORTY-FOUR

The prospect of imminent death affects people in fairly predictable ways. According to the best available research on the subject, during their final moments of mortality individuals invariably act out the roles for which their lives prepared them. The religious person will normally utter a final prayer. An aggressive personality might put up a desperate fight. The loving mother will think of her children. Others may cry or beg for mercy or exhibit stoic acceptance of the inevitable, depending on their personalities.

My response, although it might at first seem atypical and perhaps even bizarre, was actually quite normal for someone with my particular background and training. I found myself looking inward, studying myself as if in a mirror, observing my own reactions, or lack thereof, in the face of imminent death. I like to think it was the same sort of analysis and observation to which Freud and Adler subjected themselves during their final moments.

In my case, I was fascinated by my almost total lack of anxiety. I experienced none of the physical symptoms normally associated with such life-threatening situations. I could detect no sign of the famous "fight or flight" response, with its accompanying rush of adrenalin. Nor did I feel the corollary shortness of breath, rapid heartbeat or dry mouth.

This was the first time in my life anyone had ever aimed a gun at me, and yet I felt totally calm, even detached.

Near-deathers have often described similar feelings to me. Yet I wasn't quite ready to accept a metaphysical explanation for my passivity. There might be a more scientific answer in the research done by Frankenhaeuser, who postulated that the "fight or flight response" may be diminished when the individual feels helpless to act.

That was certainly true in my case. I knew any resistance was futile. There was nothing I could do but stare at the barrel of the gun that appeared to be aimed directly at my forehead.

If there was one emotion I felt, it was shame. I was embarrassed by the incredible hubris I had displayed in bringing Laura back to Pennsylvania, the intellectual arrogance that led me to think I could somehow evade her pursuers on their home ground. For all my good intentions, I had delivered Laura back into the hands of her captors. Now we would both face the consequences of my bumbling.

I was certain they were going to kill us.

The only question was the timing.

Never having owned a handgun, I was surprised at the small diameter of the opening through which a fatal slug of lead could be fired. It seemed unfair that an aperture of so narrow a gauge had within it the power to extinguish my life. Yet a bullet in the brain would be a much speedier and more humane way to die than the agonizing struggle for breath that consumed the final moments of both Angie and the Professor.

While I contemplated the merits of various forms of execution, Metzger's assistants went to work with silent efficiency. They bound our wrists with white plastic restraining strips, the type used to control patients in the violent wards. After being immobilized, we were checked for hidden weapons and hustled out a side door to a waiting ambulance.

What turned out to be my final ride to the Walden Clinic took less than ten minutes. We were led up a flight of stairs to the clinic's medical facilities. Laura tried to resist entering the room, screaming and kicking and trying to brace her feet against the doorway. When that didn't work, she tried using the old passive protest trick of going limp and collapsing. None of her delaying tactics worked. The attendants picked her up and carried her through the swinging doors.

Every drug and alcohol detox center has a medical facility like the one to which we were taken. It serves as a miniature hospital where patients can receive more sophisticated medical intervention than can be administered in their rooms, including, when necessary, emergency resuscitation and even life-support. The Walden Clinic's medical facility consisted of three interconnected rooms, each containing progressively more sophisticated equipment. The first room contained supply cabinets, some basic monitoring devices, and two gurneys.

Laura was lifted onto one of the wheeled gurneys. While one attendant removed the plastic restraining bonds, the other secured her with leather straps around her arms, her waist and her legs. She continued to moan and struggle, her eyes wild with fear and begging me to help.

There was nothing I could do.

Once she was secured, it was my turn. They didn't even bother to take off my blazer. Two stiff leather straps went around each arm, one at the wrist and one at the elbow. My legs were bound similarly at the ankles and just above the knees. Another heavier strap went around my waist, and one around my chest. All were buckled tightly, making it impossible to move anything except my fingers and my head.

After checking the straps, Metzger nodded his approval. He unfolded his cellular phone and punched in a pre-dialed number. "They're ready," he said in a voice that was barely above a whisper.

I didn't understand what was happening. From the moment they picked us up, every action seemed to have been pre-planned.

What were they going to do to us? Surely we didn't have to be strapped down if they planned to kill us. I turned to look at Laura, whose frightened eyes continued to beg me for help. I wanted to apologize to her for my impotence. I wanted to tell her how sorry I was to have taken her on this futile adventure that in the end had proven fruitless. We had come full circle from the point at which I first met her. As on that first night, she was once again strapped to a table, the subject of some still unexplained endeavor. The difference now was that our relationship was no longer that of researcher and subject. I would gladly have sacrificed my own life to save hers.

And yet, of course, I knew that was impossible. It was Laura they really wanted, not me. I was simply a peripheral irritation, a temporary impediment. Having seen two corpses already, I harbored no illusions about my ultimate fate.

The only question was what they wanted with Laura. Even now, faced with death, I couldn't restrain my curiosity. It was a question that had puzzled me ever since I first found her in that dismal basement chamber. Time and again, she had refused to enlighten me about what had been done to her, about why she so desperately feared going back. Whatever the secret, it had already claimed two lives. Perhaps now I might finally discover what she had been hiding from me.

Someone entered the room.

I felt a shadow over my face. Looking up, I saw a gaunt man staring down at me, examining me with the intensity usually reserved for laboratory specimens. He had a neatly-trimmed beard which slowly parted into a smile, revealing a set of cigarette-yellowed teeth. He smelled of stale tobacco smoke and expensive deodorant.

"You've caused us a lot of trouble, Mr. Nikonos," he admonished me. His voice was gentle, but the words were filled with menace. "We should have dealt with you properly when we had the chance."

I recognized the voice and the beard as that of Doctor Zydek, who had preferred to remain in the shadows during our first encounter.

"It was a mistake letting you go," he said. "But I can assure you we won't repeat that mistake."

Not feeling any braver than usual, I didn't say anything.

As if he read my thoughts, he chuckled softly. "You have good reason to be afraid," he said. He turned to Metzger. "Is the equipment ready?"

"Yes, Doctor."

Laura's whimpering grew louder. Zydek ignored her.

"Has she told you anything about us?" he asked me.

I shook my head, unable to form any verbal response.

"I didn't think so," he said. "She's a very loyal woman, you know. She would rather die than betray the man she loves."

He paused and smiled again. "Have you ever seen a woman die, Mr. Nikonos?"

Behind him, Laura let out a scream. Metzger put his hand over her mouth.

"It's all right," the doctor said. "People expect screams in a place like this. How about it, Mr. Nikonos? Are you ready to see this woman die?"

"No," I gasped, finding my voice at last. "No. Please don't hurt her."

"I'm afraid I have no choice. I need her to die."

He nodded to Metzger, who rolled Laura's gurney into the next room.

"You'll be able to watch from here," Zydek said.

"Don't!" I shouted. "Let her go. I'll take her place. Kill me instead."

"A very noble sentiment. But what's the point?" He smiled ominously. "We're going to kill you, too."

I could see Laura looking back at me from the other room. Tears were streaming from her eyes. I screamed and thrashed against my bonds.

"Don't! Don't! My God, why are you doing this? Let her go!"

One of the Samoans stunned me with a punch. When I recovered, they already had a clear plastic mask covering Laura's mouth. It was attached with thick elastic bands around her head. A flexible tube connected the mask to a green oxygen tank. She seemed to be breathing normally. Metzger stepped out of my field of view momentarily. He reappeared wheeling an EKG machine with its tangle of monitoring leads. While he separated the wire leads, the doctor moistened the small circular contact pads with conducting jelly and attached them to Laura's flesh. There were twelve contact pads. Two were attached to her head, at the temples. Two were attached to her arms, at the joints inside the elbows, where the blood ran closest to the surface. Four were attached to her legs: two inside her thighs to monitor the femoral arteries and two at the ankles to check circulation at the extremities. The other six leads were attached to her chest in an arc that ran from her sternum, underneath her left breast and along her rib cage. As a final indignity, her breasts were left exposed to view.

"Let's run a test," the doctor said.

He flipped a toggle switch to start the EKG monitor. A narrow strip of paper started rolling out of the unit. The doctor examined the strip, comparing it with another that Metzger handed to him.

"There's no change from her previous reading," Zydek said. "Cardiac activity is perfectly normal. I don't think we should have any complications." Over his shoulder, he called out to me. "Are you watching, Mr. Nikonos?"

In fact, I couldn't take my eyes off Laura. She in turn was staring intently at me, as if she was determined that her last image of this world would be my face, rather than the faces of her killers. As much as I didn't want to witness her death, I couldn't turn away. It would have been tantamount to abandoning her. All I could do for her was to maintain our visual embrace, smile at her, and mouth the words, "I love you."

The oxygen mask prevented me from seeing her response.

"Cut off the oxygen," the doctor ordered.

Metzger quickly spun the handle on the oxygen tank.

Laura reacted with a sudden spasm. Her head lifted up. I could see her chest heaving as she struggled to suck oxygen into her lungs from what had now become a deadly vacuum. The mask drew tighter around her mouth. Her eyes bulged with agonal effort. Her fingers opened and closed, apparently involuntarily. She went into convulsions. I could swear I heard her bones snapping as the tremendous stress of her death throes flexed the muscles and joints with her last remaining bits of strength, surging and straining against the leather bonds.

For one brief moment, I thought she was going to break free.

And then, suddenly, all movement stopped.

Her body relaxed and sagged back onto the gurney.

Her eyes remained open.

Even before I heard the doctor's pronouncement, I knew Laura was dead.

FORTY-FIVE

Nothing in my life had prepared me for the absolute despair that engulfed me at that moment. I had seen so many of my dreams die in recent years, there were times I thought of myself as a latter-day version of Job. I seemed to have been singled out to endure one after another of those peculiarly modern tribulations which God reserves for upwardly-mobile Americans in the latter part of the twentieth century.

Like my Biblical predecessor, I was stripped of everything I ever owned, including my self-respect. Dreams of wealth, prestige and a happy marriage had dissolved into long-term unemployment, divorce, and personal bankruptcy. Instead of a Ph.D., my years of academic work left me with a burden of tens of thousands of dollars in unpaid student loans, on which the interest continued to compound. In a few short years, I had been reduced to an existence of lonely penury.

But it all faded into insignificance when I saw Laura die.

Until then, no calamity that befell me seemed irreversible. No misfortune could completely eradicate what little hope I held for my future. I could rationalize the loss of all the dreams I once had for my future.

Except for Laura. I realized now that she had been the most precious dream of all. With her death, I lost my own desire to live.

Like Othello after the slaying of his beloved Desdemona, I felt a despair of suicidal proportions. If I could have taken my own life, I would eagerly have done so, in the notion that my death would somehow reunite us.

"Thirty seconds and counting," came a voice from the other room. It sounded like one of the Samoans, his voice thick and deceptively lazy.

The murderous quartet still hovered around Laura. What sort of ghouls were they? Wasn't it enough that they had killed the woman I loved? Why did they have to stand there and stare at her corpse? Were they satisfying some sort of necrophiliac urge?

"Forty-five seconds and counting."

The brutal manner in which they chose to end her life made no sense to me. If they wanted to get rid of her, there were easier ways to do it. They could have killed her at any time during the six months they held her captive. Why now? Why here? And with all the sophisticated medical equipment at their disposal, why did they resort to this particularly brutal form of suffocation?

"One minute and counting."

I couldn't wait for them to turn their attention to me, to extinguish my life so that I could join Laura. They would have to eliminate me, I was certain, since I was the only witness to the terrible crime they had committed.

"One minute fifteen seconds."

"All right," Doctor Zydek said. "Intubate her."

There was a sudden flurry of activity around Laura's corpse. One of the Samoans held her mouth open while Metzger slipped a curved plastic tube down her windpipe. When the breathing tube was in place, the mouthpiece was quickly attached to a hose leading to an artificial respirator, whose bellows was already in operation. Zydek raised two round paddles above Laura's breasts, waiting for the Samoan to strip away the remnants of her blouse.

"We'll start with one hundred joules," Zydek said.

Thick black cables connected the paddles to a unit at whose controls Metzger was stationed. He turned a dial. I heard a low electrical hum.

"Charging," Metzger said.

"One minute thirty seconds," the timekeeper intoned.

They worked with the well-rehearsed efficiency of a trained medical team. That part didn't surprise me. This was, after all, a detox clinic, where sudden and often violent death is not an unusual occurrence. What did surprise me was seeing the way they went to work on Laura.

It was hard to believe, but it appeared they were actually going to attempt to revive her. First they murdered her, and now they were trying to bring her back from the dead? It seemed such incredibly insane behavior. All I could do was hope that they succeeded.

While I didn't understand their motives, I knew what they were doing. It was a procedure I had read about in dozens of NDE medical reports. They were following the standard emergency protocol for resuscitating a clinically-dead patient. The paddles held aloft by Zydek were cardiac defibrillators. They were designed to deliver short but powerful electric shocks to the heart, in the hope of restoring its normal activity. One hundred joules was the standard initial voltage.

"One minute forty-five seconds."

A high-pitched electronic beep announced that the defibrillator had reached full charging capacity.

"Clear!" Zydek ordered, warning them to avoid physical contact with the corpse or any metal object through which the electric current might be conducted. Any shock that was strong enough to restart a heart was by definition also strong enough to stop one. The others stood back as he prepared to place the electric paddles against Laura's naked flesh.

I heard the snap of electricity as the paddles made contact with naked flesh.

The electric current surged through Laura's corpse, stimulating her dead muscles and sending them into a convulsive spasm. It was a macabre spectacle. Her limbs thrashed violently against the leather restraining straps for a few brief seconds, mimicking a living body. When the charge ran its course, her body fell back, as lifeless as before.

Doctor Zydek removed the paddles, leaving behind two red marks on her skin.

"No cardiac response," Metzger said. He was watching the EKG readout. "She's still asystolic."

"Two minutes and counting," said the Samoan timekeeper.

The electronic beep again announced the machine's readiness.

"Clear!" Zydek ordered.

The procedure was repeated.

The electric shock once again surged through Laura's corpse, setting off another mindless spasm.

"No cardiac response."

"Two minutes fifteen seconds."

"Give her the Lidocaine," Zydek said. "And hurry."

There was an urgency in his voice. The time constraint against which he was fighting was the point at which brain damage occurs, normally around four minutes after the flow of blood to the brain has been interrupted.

Metzger shoved a long hypodermic needle into Laura's chest, just below her left breast. He quickly emptied the contents into her heart.

"Clear!" Zydek barked.

Once again Laura's corpse gave a violent bounce, shuddered against the restraining straps as if trying to break free, and then fell back inert.

"Still no cardiac."

"Two minutes thirty."

"Give me three hundred joules," the Doctor ordered.

"Three hundred," Metzger repeated as he turned the dial.

The electronic beep sounded.

"Clear!"

Contact.

Spasm.

"No response."

"Two minutes forty five."

Electronic beep.

"Again! Clear!"

Contact.

Spasm.

"No response."

Electronic beep.

"Clear!"

Contact.

Spasm.

"No response."

"Three minutes."

Electronic beep.
"Clear!"
Contact.
Spasm.
"No response."

Their best efforts appeared to be futile. Even if she did start to respond, the procedure was getting dangerously close to the time limit for brain damage. Her flesh was already turning a lifeless grey as the blood ebbed away from the upper surfaces of her body.

"Give me four hundred joules."

"Four hundred," Metzger repeated.

That was the maximum, I knew. If she didn't respond now, she never would.

"Three minutes fifteen seconds."

The electronic beep sounded.

"Clear!"

Contact.

Spasm.

"No response."

"Goddammit! We're losing her!"

"Three minutes thirty seconds."

Electronic beep.

"Again! Clear!"

"Again—"

"Wait!" Metzger shouted.

Silence.

No one moved.

"I think she's coming back," Metzger said. "I'm getting a systolic."

Laura's naked chest heaved. She started to gag. Zydek quickly pulled the respirator tube from her mouth. She coughed and sputtered and gagged some more, but blessedly, she was moving and reacting and breathing on her own again.

She was alive!

Although I was a near-death researcher, I had never witnessed the actual event. Even Professor DeBray, recognized as the leading international authority on the subject, had never been present during an NDE. It was left to me, a skeptic when it came to the deeper significance of these phenomena, to view the unfolding of the entire sequence. I had personally witnessed a human being die, listened to a countdown of three and a half minutes without any vital signs, and watched as she was brought back to life before my very eyes.

But any professional considerations were overwhelmed by my joy at having Laura restored to life. The color quickly returned to her face. She was still gasping and coughing, her throat probably rubbed raw by the ventilator tube. Some spittle and pink foam dribbled out of the side of her mouth. But she was breathing on her own, and that was all that mattered.

"Laura!" I called out. "Laura, I'm here."

My face was the last image she had seen before she died. And I wanted my face to be the first image she saw on her return to life. I gave her as brave a smile as I could produce. At first she didn't seem to recognize me. I had a fleeting moment of panic in which I worried whether she had been out too long, whether any brain damage had occurred. But slowly, weakly, yet nevertheless radiantly, her lips formed a smile.

I had no idea what further gruesome experiments our captors had in mind. Our situation seemed hopeless. We were strapped to tables, as immobilized and vulnerable as laboratory mice awaiting unknown and painful futures. But incredibly, I began to feel the first faint stirrings of hope. After seeing Laura return from the dead, I had to concede that no predicament, no matter how desperate it might appear, could be considered completely hopeless.

Her smile had an effect on me more powerful than the electric current they used to bring her back to life. It flowed over me like sunlight, dissipating the paralyzing fog of despair. My mind began to focus on strategies of survival rather than submission. I saw the figures hovering over us as obstacles to be overcome rather than executioners who would soon be carrying out their mission.

I had made the emotional journey from suicidal depression to euphoria in less than five minutes. The romantics among us might consider such highs and lows to be part of the price of being in love. In the world of clinical psychology, however, such extreme mood swings are warning signs of an incipient manic-depressive condition. Looking back, I wonder whether the stress of those extraordinary times pushed me to the brink of madness. Even now, I'm not really sure. Certainly many of my actions at the time had a manic quality. I had been acting entirely out of character. I barely recognized the person I had become, I was rushing from one crisis to another, more excited than frightened, thriving with very little sleep. Like most manics, I had an inflated sense of my mental ability, and a grandiose idea that I could solve every problem that confronted me. I had never been modest about my intellectual ability, but I was suddenly infected with a sense of infallibility.

The great paradox, of course, was that any chance Laura and I had for survival depended entirely on those aspects of my behavior which might have been altered by a psychological disorder. If a retrospective analysis indicates I was truly suffering from a temporary bipolar disorder at the time, I can only say it was a fortunate aberration.

After all, what "normal" person would have the arrogance to even consider the possibility of escape from the circumstances in which I found myself?

The very concept was insane.

FORTY-SIX

"Are you ready to speak to us, Laura?" Doctor Zydek asked.

His voice was as pleasant and friendly as that of a family practitioner addressing a hospital patient on his morning rounds.

Laura groaned in response.

"Your throat probably hurts from the trauma," he went on, still sounding sympathetic. "Do you want some anaesthetic spray?"

She nodded eagerly. Metzger handed Zydek a small aerosol can. Laura opened her mouth to accept the soothing spray.

"Is that better?" he asked.

She nodded.

"Now let's talk about what you saw when you were dead. Did you see your husband?"

She shook her head.

"I'd prefer a spoken answer," Zydek said, his voice turning harsher as he repeated the question. "Did you see your husband when you were dead?"

"No." Laura's voice was a hoarse whisper. I had to strain to hear her.

"That's better. Did you see other people that you knew?"

"Yes."

"You saw your parents and grandparents and other relatives who were dead?"

"Yes."

Laura started to cough. Zydek gave her another blast of the aerosol spray.

"But you didn't see your husband?"

"No."

"Did you ask about him?"

"Yes," Laura whispered.

"And what did they tell you?"

"They said he's still alive."

Up to that point, it was the same story Laura had told me. It seemed like a fairly straightforward NDE interview, except for the fact that Laura had just been deliberately asphyxiated and then restored to life by the very man who was interviewing her.

"Where is your husband now?" Zydek continued.

"I don't know."

"You were supposed to ask."

"I did. I did. But they wouldn't tell me."

"Laura, we've been over this before. I need an answer. I'm going to have to send you back."

He reached for the oxygen mask.

"No! Please, please don't!" Laura whimpered, her voice still weak from the ordeal her lungs had suffered. "I asked them. I really did. But they wouldn't tell me where he is."

"Why won't they tell you?"

"I don't know. But I asked, just like you wanted."

"Did you ask your dear dead mother about him?"

"Yes."

"And your dear dead father?"

"Yes."

"Did you tell them how painful it is to struggle for your last dying breath?"

"Yes, yes, I did!"

"But they refused to help you?" Zydek persisted. "Your own mother and father refused to help you?"

He was taunting her now, trying to anger her into revealing whatever it was he thought she was hiding. I know I should have screamed out and begged him to stop, to leave her alone. It would have been a futile gesture, but it would at least have let her know I shared her pain.

Instead, for reasons I'm ashamed to admit, I remained silent. Zydek was probing an area that went to the very core of the near-death experience. I was too fascinated to do anything to interrupt.

"It . . . it wasn't like that," she said.

"Then tell me what it was like. Was your mother happy to see you again?"

Laura didn't respond.

"Maybe she doesn't love you anymore. Maybe that's why she won't tell you where your husband is."

"She knows what you're doing," Laura said. "They all know."

"If they know what I'm doing," Zydek said, "then surely they know where Harrison is."

"Maybe they have a reason for not telling me."

"I'm running out of patience, Laura. What will it take to get them to answer my question?"

"If they won't tell me, there's nothing you can do to force them."

"Oh, I think there is," he said, placing the plastic mask on her naked chest. "As you already know, asphyxiation is an agonizing way to die. It gets worse each time, because of the cumulative damage to your throat and lungs. We can repeat the procedure for as long as it takes. If your parents have any love for you, I'm sure they'll want to end your suffering."

With horrifying clarity, I finally understood why Laura had been so desperate to escape from the Walden Clinic. Legitimate NDE research is a normally benign attempt to penetrate the veil that separates our world from the continuum beyond. What Zydek was doing was a grotesque perversion of that work. He was using homicide as a research technique. By snuffing out Laura's life, he was sending her to walk among the dead, with the mission of bringing back information from the other side.

"I need to find your husband," Zydek said. "I'm going to have to keep sending you back until you get the information I want."

"Oh, please, please, please don't," Laura whimpered.

I remembered the fear in her eyes that first night when the Samoans led me from her room. I remember thinking how unusual it was for a near-deather to be so frightened, and wondering what could possibly scare someone who had already experienced the ultimate horror of death.

Now I knew.

It wasn't death itself that she feared. It was the agonizing manner in which her life was slowly extinguished, struggling and gasping for air until her lungs and throat had no breath left with which to scream. And then, having passed beyond pain into the peace of death, she was brought forcibly back to life only to have the dreadful process repeated again. Dear God, how many times had it been repeated during the six months they held her captive? From the profusion of defibrillator burn marks I had seen on her chest, I guessed that it must have been dozens of times.

That explained why she had done so impossibly well on the N-DERP scale. The NDE account that was so perfect that I suspected fraud, was actually a synthesis of multiple NDE's. There might have been variations in individual experiences, but eventually they all blurred together in her memory and she recounted them all, constructing one archetypal experience.

Were there instances when she struggled not to return, to stay on the other side for peaceful eternity? How awful it must have been each time she was called back by the electric shocks, knowing that what awaited her was merely a period of recovery before being sent back on the awful journey.

Laura let out a scream and shook her head from side to side as Metzger struggled to place the mask over her face again. One of the Samoans grabbed her by the hair. He twisted those beautiful blonde strands around his huge fist and clamped his other hand over her forehead, holding her painfully still. Metzger cupped the mask over her mouth and tightened the straps. Any further struggling by Laura was useless.

The homicidal proceedings began again.

I tried to close my ears to the awful sounds of Laura being put to death. The thrashing of her body as she struggled to breathe seemed to go on longer than I thought possible. The average person can go without oxygen for more than two minutes before losing consciousness. In his depravity, Zydek must have extended the agonizing interval by supplying minute amounts of oxygen, a deliberate effort to inflict the greatest amount of torture possible.

That was when I decided I would kill Zydek.

It was the first time in my life I had ever been angry enough to consider taking the life of another human being. My rage was so intense, I wanted not only to kill him, but to extract retribution in the Biblical sense, imposing my vengeance upon him with the same instruments of horror he was using on Laura.

But first I had to get free.

While they were engrossed with the mechanics of death, I struggled with the gurney. I began to rock my body, moving my weight back and forth. If anyone saw me, they would think I was fighting vainly against my bonds. In fact, what I was doing was setting up an undulating wave pattern which, when maintained in a steady frequency, transferred my movements down the legs of the gurney to the rubber wheels. Soon I could feel the entire assembly rocking synchronously with me, struggling against the friction brake that held the wheels in place. Fortunately, the noises I made were camouflaged by the sounds of Laura's death struggle.

The friction brake holding the wheels finally gave way. The gurney began to move. I found I could roughly control its path by changing the direction in which I rocked my body. The Samoan had left the gurney little more than eighteen inches from the nearest counter. But that counter sat atop a cabinet which contained a series of shallow, inch-high drawers. The configuration suggested the drawers contained medical instruments. I continued the wave pattern. The gurney moved slowly, lurching in the direction of the counter a few millimeters at a time. I tried not to think about what the Samoans would do if they saw what I was up to. I tried to block everything out of my mind except my body movements and how close I was getting to the counter.

After what seemed much longer than the minute or two I'm sure it really took, the tubular frame of the gurney touched the counter. My hands were bound at the wrists, which didn't give me much movement. But I found that I could twist my right wrist and thereby extend my fingertips enough to reach out a little more than six inches. That limited range of movement put only one drawer, the top one, within reach.

I pulled the drawer open the few inches I could and reached inside it to feel . . . to feel . . . nothing!

I could see the tips of instruments in the drawer, but they were too far inside for me to reach. All I could feel was a thin cloth that lined the bottom. In the other room, I could hear Laura struggling for her last breath. My fingertips pressed down on the cloth, pulling it forward, drawing the instruments with it. The cloth quickly bunched up under my fingers. I watched the instruments draw closer. I could see . . . a pair of long surgical scissors, angled at the neck and totally useless to me . . . a small rubber-tipped hammer for testing reflexes . . . and suddenly, there it was: a flat piece of surgical steel about six inches long, gracefully curved at the tip.

A scalpel!

I pulled it closer, my fingers grasping at the cold metal, turning it carefully to avoid contact with the cutting edge. I lifted it from the drawer and placed it on the gurney, where I could hide it from view with the palm of my hand.

From the other room, I heard Metzger's voice announce that all vital signs had ceased.

The death watch began.

In the silence that followed, any further noise I made would be easily overheard. But I couldn't stay where I was. At any moment, one of them might turn around. If they saw me by the instrument drawer, they'd know immediately what I was doing.

"Thirty seconds and counting," said one of the Samoans.

Slowly, as quietly as I could, I closed the drawer. I had to get back to where they left me. There was no way to do it without attracting attention. I had to take the risk.

"Forty five seconds and counting."

Bracing my hand against the counter, I pulled myself as close to it as I could, and then with all the strength I could muster, pushed myself off. The wheels squealed as the gurney shot back to the center of the small room.

"Let her go, you bastards!" I shouted in an effort to cover the noise.

"What the hell?" Metzger jumped up.

Zydek turned around.

The Samoans stared placidly.

"Let her go!" I shouted again, struggling briefly against the restraining straps, and then falling back, feigning exhaustion.

"One minute and counting."

"You want me to dope him up?" one of the Samoans asked in a bored voice.

"Plenty of time for that later," Zydek said, turning back to Laura. "Just check to make sure he's still tied down. And fix the brake on that damn thing."

The Samoan grunted and came towards me, his ponderous body rippling as he walked. His lazy eyes looked me over. I was sweating from my efforts to reach the drawer, but he probably attributed it to my angry outburst. He tested each restraining strap to satisfy himself that they hadn't been tampered with. As a further precaution, he pulled at my arms to be certain they were still firmly secured. When he was satisfied, he kicked at the foot brake, locking it into place. Then he waddled back to Laura's corpse. He had been too preoccupied with the straps to notice the scalpel hidden beneath my hand.

"One minute fifteen seconds."

As soon as he left, I started working to free myself. I wasn't sure how much time I had. I didn't know how I could possibly hope to overcome the four of them. But now that I possessed the instrument of my deliverance, I knew I had to work fast. The scalpel's exquisite cutting edge was designed to slice through the toughest tendons and muscles. Once I got it positioned properly, it easily cut through the restraining strap. My left wrist was free!

"One minute thirty seconds."

A cell phone started ringing. Metzger answered the phone and quickly handed it to Zydek.

As I cut away at my bonds, I listened to Zydek questioning the caller in an anxious voice.

"When?" he asked. "Are they sure? Who was she? How soon?"

The call clearly upset him.

"That was Gravendahl," he told Metzger after handing back the phone. "The police showed up at the funeral home with the county coroner. They're taking away the body of some woman named Galarza. Apparently she was one of our nursing home patients. You know anything about it?"

"She died a couple of days ago," Metzger said. "I'm surprised she wasn't buried already. What's the problem?"

"They think she was murdered."

"For Christ's sake, that's ridiculous. The woman died of old age."

"There wasn't any death certificate."

"It's that goddamn Subdhani. He's still out of town. I can get one of our other contract doctors to back-date a certificate."

"It's too late for that now," Zydek said. "And too risky. We're going to have enough problems without back-dating documents."

"Just because there's no death certificate doesn't mean she was murdered," Metzger argued.

"The coroner found evidence that points to suffocation."

"Son of a bitch!" Metzger muttered.

"You know anything about it?" Zydek asked again.

"All I know is what I told you. She must have been about ninety years old."

"The coroner took custody of the body. The police are already on the way to the nursing home. They'll probably come here next. That's all we need now, the police accusing us of murder. Next thing you know, the state will be investigating all of our facilities."

"But how can they tell what happened to the old woman?" Metzger asked. "I mean without an autopsy?"

"They found little purple dots around the eyes and mouth, just like the ones you see on our patient here." He pointed to Laura's face. "Those dots are caused by pressure hemorrhages from the small capillaries, which is a very common indicator of death by asphyxiation."

"Gravendahl should have buried the woman two days ago," Metzger complained. "Then we wouldn't be having this problem. All the money he makes with us, you'd think he'd take our business more seriously."

"We can deal with Gravendahl later," Zydek said. "You'd better get over to the nursing home and stall the police. I don't want them showing up here until we get rid of these two. I'm going to need the ambulance brought around the back and two body bags to hide them."

When Metzger and the Samoans were gone, Doctor Zydek began the task of bringing Laura back to life once again.

He was too intent on his work to notice me. Freed from my bonds, I sat up on the gurney. I watched in silence as he jolted Laura's body with the electric shock paddles. I waited patiently until I heard the tortured gasps that signalled Laura's revival.

That was when I stepped forward to kill him.

The only question in my mind was whether I should sink the scalpel into his back, allowing him to die without knowing the hand that took his life, or whether I should invite him to turn, so that he could look into the eyes of his executioner.

I decided on the latter course, reasoning that a punishment so extreme demanded that the victim understand the reason for his death.

I whispered Zydek's name, wanting to see the horror in his eyes as I plunged the scalpel into his chest.

I still shudder when I think of the blood lust I felt at that moment. And how totally unprepared I was for what happened next.

FORTY-SEVEN

Zydek spun around, the fully-charged electrodes still in his hands. I felt a tingling as one of the paddles brushed past my head. The second paddle glanced off my right wrist. Although it was only a momentary contact, the shock jolted me. The muscles in my right arm went into an involuntary spasm. My fingers opened. The scalpel dropped from my grip.

Suddenly unarmed, I backed away from Zydek, trying to stay out of reach of the electric paddles. There was a lethal amount of current flowing through them. I had seen the effects on Laura, the way her lifeless body had jumped and strained against the straps as the electricity surged through her muscles.

Zydek cut me off from the exit, using the outstretched paddles as a barrier which I dared not cross. With surprising ease, he maneuvered me into a corner.

I was trapped. There was no way to get past the menacing electrodes. Zydek advanced slowly, smiling as he moved in on me, relishing the moment of his victory.

I had nothing with which to fight him off except my bare hands. But bare flesh is no defense against 300 joules of electricity. Whether the electrodes made contact with my chest or the open palms of my hands, the effect would be the same.

I stared at the paddles, trying to brace myself for the powerful shock.

I might be facing death, but I was determined that whatever agony I endured, Zydek would have to share.

In one last, desperate move, just as the paddles were about to touch me, I grabbed one of his wrists with my hands.

The electricity hit me with explosive force, knocking me off my feet and throwing me against the wall. My body shook violently. I heard my muscles snapping and my joints popping. The current buzzed and rang in my ears. My chest ached. My eyes burned. Everything in the room seemed to turn a brilliant gold color and then faded into black. I heard a loud scream, and felt myself slowly sagging to the floor.

The last thing I remember before losing consciousness was the surprise in Zydek's eyes as the charge of three hundred joules surged through him. My sweaty hands on his bare flesh had served as a perfect ground, allowing the electric current to flow freely from my body to his.

In electrocuting me, he had electrocuted himself.

How long I remained unconscious, I don't know. When I awoke I was still gripping Zydek's now-limp wrist. My fingers were stiff. It took a few seconds before I was able to pry them loose. I sat up and took a deep breath. Zydek didn't move.

Although we had both been exposed to the same amount of electricity, the differences in physiology favored me. I was younger and stronger than he. My heart was better able to withstand the powerful shock, my lungs able to recover faster.

Zydek remained motionless on the floor beside me, his skin color an ominous shade of grey. His jaw hung open, and his breathing was shallow. His pulse was weak, almost imperceptible.

He was alive, but just barely.

I could easily have picked up the paddles and finished him off, but the blood lust that had raged in me a short time earlier had subsided.

"Is he . . . dead?" Laura asked.

"Not quite," I replied, rising unsteadily to my feet.

Too much time had elapsed since the Samoans went to get the ambulance. They'd be coming back at any moment. I had to get Laura out of there before they returned. I found the scalpel and cut through her restraining straps. When I tried to get her to sit up, she nearly fainted. It was obvious that she didn't have the strength to walk.

Behind me, Zydek began to stir. I was running out of options. There wasn't any time to think things through; it was time to just get the hell out of there. I picked up Laura, ran out into the hallway, and went into the first unlocked door I found. Inside the room was a recovering middle-aged alcoholic suffering from a bad case of *delirium tremens*. He was more frightened by the imaginary horrors he saw crawling on the walls than by our sudden presence.

The problem now was how to get Laura out of the building. She was starting to tremble, and I was afraid it was a sign that she might be slipping into shock. Whatever I did would have to be done quickly.

My mind raced through the possibilities. An ambulance was supposed to be brought around to the back entrance. I had to find a way to reach that ambulance without being intercepted by the Samoans or the security guards downstairs.

Our alcoholic roommate was jittery and wide-eyed, his delirium more powerful than the medication he had been given. Although he didn't seem upset at our presence thus far, that could change at any moment. There was no way of telling what unseen storms raged in his mind, or what sudden stimulus could trigger a psychotic episode. The instability of the patient populations in rehab and detox centers was notorious. That was, after all, one of the reasons for the employment of "enforcers" like the Samoans.

But an enforcer could handle only one or two patients at a time. And we were trapped in a building with three floors of drug addicts and alcoholics in various stages of recovery. Some might be ready for release. Others would be immobilized by medication. A small percentage would certainly have violent tendencies. And many would be suffering some degree of disorientation, unable to focus on the reality around them.

If I could find a way to send them all flowing into the hallways at the same time, the sheer numbers would overwhelm the guards and guarantee chaos. It was ironic that a psychologist would seek refuge among the dysfunctional.

Was my plan ethical? I doubt it. Would it work? I hoped so.

All I needed was a panic-generating stimulus. I found it right outside the door. In a small metal box on the wall was the main fire alarm.

Clutching Laura more tightly with my left arm, I raised my knee to support her weight as I strained to reach the alarm box with my right hand. I pulled down the handle, and immediately the building was filled with the ear-shattering clamor of electronic alarm bells.

In a normal environment, the sounding of a fire alarm would produce an immediate response. In this institution, the cacophonic alarm seemed to go unnoticed.

I stood alone in the hallway, wondering if the patients were all drugged to a stupor. Maybe the alarm bells would do nothing but alert the Samoans to my attempted escape.

But gradually at first, and then in a sudden, panicky rush, the patients came out of their rooms. Some were crying. One or two were screaming. Most seemed confused, as if they didn't understand what the noise was. At the far end of the hallway, one of the Samoans appeared. When I turned, Doctor Zydek was staggering out of the medical facility. He spotted me and started to shout, but the alarm bells drowned out his voice.

The Samoan was coming closer. He hadn't yet seen me in the crowded hallway, but he was sure to see Zydek gesturing. I needed to create more chaos. Above the fire alarm was a glass window housing the fire hose required by state law. I smashed the window to get at the hose. I handed the nozzle to one of the more coherent-looking patients and motioned for him to help me. He dutifully pulled out the hose, while I spun the red valve to turn on the water. The last semblance of sanity quickly disappeared from the hallway when the high-pressure stream of water snapped the hose out of his hands, sending it dancing wildly in the midst of the patients, the waterjet powerful enough to knock some of the more unfortunate ones off their feet.

It was pure pandemonium. The hallway was quickly flooded. The screams of panicked patients rose above the sound of the fire alarm. One woman was crawling naked on all fours, her hospital gown torn from her body by the force of the water. Others splashed through the flooded corridor in search of the fire escapes. I saw two men giggling and enjoying the spectacle, as if it was some strange sort of entertainment. Others were apparently so heavily medicated they could do little but stand in the rushing water and try to comprehend what was happening around them.

I picked up Laura and joined the crowd of soggy patients scrambling down the nearest fire exit. Chaos had already spread, along with the water, to the floors below. I kept watching for Metzger and the other Samoan, in case they were back from their mission to the nursing home. If either of them were on the premises, I hoped they were upstairs, trying to make their way to Doctor Zydek. All that mattered now was that I was able to follow the flow of patients down to the ground floor and out the back without being stopped by any guards.

The ambulance was waiting right where it was supposed to be. The keys were in the ignition. The motor was running. No one was inside.

I slipped Laura into the passenger seat.

The first fire engines were arriving.

As I pulled out, a uniformed guard spotted me. He ran alongside the ambulance, shouting at me and banging on the door, but it was too late.

We were free!

But for how long?

I raced the ambulance down the midnight streets, eager to get out of Dickson as quickly as I could. Conditioned by events of the past few days, my thought processes were those of a fugitive. I drove in fear that I might be apprehended at any moment. An ambulance, after all, is not the vehicle of choice for anyone trying to evade the police or other pursuers.

I headed down the valley to Scranton, to Doctor Subdhani's office, where, fortunately, my car had not been stolen from its earlier parking spot. There were tickets on the windshield for some infraction. Fortunately, my spare key was still wired underneath the front bumper.

I quickly transferred Laura from the ambulance. In a well-intentioned but probably futile effort to protect the ambulance's supply of drugs from theft by the local addicts, I carefully locked up the vehicle before leaving it behind.

Being back in my own car felt good. Familiar objects usually tend to reinforce feelings of security. But what made me feel even more secure was the fact that I was leaving Scranton behind. As the car climbed up into the Poconos, I switched on the police scanner. Driving through the mountains, I listened to reports of a four-car accident on Interstate 80, an attempted robbery at a 7-11 in Daleville, a stolen RV in Tobyhanna, and a half-dozen other police calls, but no mention of two fugitives driving eastbound in a blue Honda with New York plates.

Exhausted by her ordeal, Laura was asleep when we crossed the Delaware River Bridge connecting Pennsylvania and New Jersey. But even in sleep, she wasn't able to escape the horrors that had been inflicted upon her. Freud described dreams as fragments of the day's events, and if that's what they truly were, then I could imagine the nightmares that tormented Laura. Reliving those events would explain the tortured gasps that interrupted her breathing; the low, haunting moans that escaped from her lips; the tremors that shook her body. Her pulse, when I felt it, was racing, and her skin was wet with perspiration.

I wanted to awaken her, to release her from the dreadful images, but she needed rest, and I knew that the dreams, as awful as they might be, were part of the vital REM phase of the sleep cycle.

I pulled her close and tried to comfort her as I drove. After a while, she drifted off into the deeper, calmer phase of Delta-sleep.

Meanwhile, I was having my own nightmares. My mind was unable to free itself from the horror of what I had witnessed. The gruesome spectacle of Laura's asphyxiation and resuscitation played over and over in my mind, etching itself deeper into my memory with each replay.

As extreme as Zydek's methods might be, the proceedings were nothing less than a carefully-controlled interrogation of a terrified subject.

What he had done was the intellectual equivalent of parting a curtain, inadvertently revealing some of the terrible machinations that had been so skillfully hidden from me.

It helped me to finally understand the monstrous nature of my real adversary.

FORTY-EIGHT

My academic background had trained me to be skeptical, to look for flaws and weaknesses before accepting any theory as fact. But I realized now I had not been faithful to those principles. As a result, I had made a grievous miscalculation.

There is a linear component to analytical thinking by which any value judgement, once made, exerts a bias on all subsequent observations. Those aspects of data that support the judgement will be perceived more vividly, perhaps even subtly skewed to fit the existing mindset. Data that doesn't conform is downplayed or dismissed. In colloquial terms, we see what we want to see, hear what we want to hear. As a result, any assumption reached too early runs the risk of becoming a self-proving hypothesis. Psychiatrists call it premature closure.

And that is precisely the trap into which I had fallen.

My attitude towards Doctor Zydek and his associates was formed by the brutal beating they had administered to me, and was reinforced by their devious efforts at hiding Laura.

I had rushed to an early judgement, and everything I had seen since then was colored by that initial opinion. Now I found myself questioning the validity of the resulting conclusions.

Was the beating I suffered that first night related to the murder of Professor DeBray? I was beginning to think not.

Did Metzger's stakeout of Laura's apartment have anything to do with the rockslide on Bald Mountain? I no longer thought so.

Had Zydek ordered the murder of Angelina Galarza to keep her from revealing any further secrets? I was now certain he didn't.

Doctor Zydek was a brutal man who had proven he was capable of the most unspeakable evil deeds. But that didn't make him automatically guilty of that litany of crimes. Yet how easily those events had all been tied together in my mind, so that they seemed to result from one as-yet-unknown motive.

It wasn't until Metzger confronted us at gunpoint that I first began to question my earlier suppositions.

Whoever triggered the avalanche on Bald Mountain had left Laura and myself behind for dead. But Metzger didn't display any surprise when we turned up alive at Doctor Subdhani's office. He asked no questions about how we could have survived. Indeed, he had apparently made arrangements with Subdhani's receptionist to be notified of our arrival. Certainly those weren't the actions of anyone who had witnessed our entombment under tons of rock.

Later at the Walden Clinic, when Doctor Zydek took the phone call informing him that the police were investigating Angie's death as a homicide, he seemed genuinely shocked. As a psychologist, I pride myself on being able to detect when someone is lying or role-playing. Zydek was guilty of neither. And Metzger seemed as confused by the phone call as Zydek. Their words and reactions convinced me they had no prior knowledge of, or complicity in, Angie's murder.

And through it all, never once did I hear either of them mention Professor DeBray's name. Not even when they were threatening to kill me.

Despite the revulsion I felt about their treatment of Laura, I had to admit my earlier assumptions about the two of them apparently were wrong.

But if Zydek and Metzger were not the murderers of my friends, then who was to blame?

I was left to ponder the famous dictum of Sir Arthur Conan Doyle: "Having eliminated the impossible, whatever remains, however improbable, must be the truth."

And thus it was with great trepidation that I headed back to New York, where the truth awaited me.

FORTY-NINE

We crossed the George Washington Bridge at 2 a.m. By that time, I was pretty much on automatic pilot, slowing down whenever I saw a police car, and trying to keep out of the way of the occasional drunken driver or carload of teenagers using the empty expressways as drag strips.

I was driving without a license, the Samoans having taken my wallet when they searched me. It might seem a ludicrously minor offense when compared to the murder charge I faced, but the reality of it was that the lack of a driver's license guaranteed a trip to jail, where my fugitive status would quickly be determined. The wallet also contained what was left of Laura's money. Fortunately, there was enough gas in the tank to get us to New York, and enough loose change in the ash tray to pay the bridge toll.

The elegant Victorian brownstone where my ex-wife lived with her lawyer husband was on East Eighty-Third, just off York Avenue. The fuel gauge was hovering around empty when I got there.

The doorbell was mounted in an ornate polished brass plate that also contained an intercom speaker and the small round lens of a closed-circuit TV. Before pressing the bell, I smoothed back my hair and adjusted my collar. This would be my first encounter with Elizabeth since the divorce. I wasn't sure how I would handle seeing her again.

It took ten minutes of pressing the doorbell before Elizabeth's voice finally came over the intercom.

"Who is it?" she asked.

With me staring at the closed-circuit TV camera, she knew damn well who it was.

"It's me. Theo."

"Who?"

"It's Theo. We used to be married, remember?"

I could imagine her shooting worried glances at her husband Milton, who was probably standing right next to her. These were the two people I held responsible for the downward spiral in my life. Elizabeth, with her voluptuous body and soft voice, had seduced me into turning away from my doctoral dissertation and the bright academic career that was sure to follow. And together with Milton, she had betrayed me sexually, divorced me, and left me with huge financial obligations and a broken ego. I had promised myself I would never place myself at their mercy again, and now here I was, a supplicant at their front door.

"Oh God, what the hell do you want?" she asked.

"Did someone leave a package for me?"

"I don't want to see you. Go away."

The intercom went dead. I continued to press the doorbell until her voice came over the intercom again.

"If you don't leave, I'll call 911," she threatened.

"I need that package, Elizabeth."

"Go to hell. I don't want to have anything to do with you."

The intercom went dead again.

I kept pressing the doorbell until another voice came over the intercom. This time it was Milton. His voice was calmer than Elizabeth's.

"The police were already here," he said. "They warned us you'd probably show up."

"You didn't give them the package, did you?"

"I wouldn't be a very good lawyer if I did."

I thought I heard a chuckle.

"I'm in serious trouble, Milton."

"I know."

"I need a good lawyer."

"I know."

"Can I come in?"

"Do you realize what time it is?"

"I don't have anyplace else to go."

"Liz is pretty upset about all this."

I thought he was going to send me away, and doom Laura, whom he had yet to see, but surprisingly, the buzzer sounded, unlocking the front door.

Milton Goldman was waiting just inside. He had gained some weight and lost some hair since the last time I saw him. Dressed in a maroon paisley-print bathrobe, he looked more like Al Capone than a successful lawyer. He greeted us with the same cherubic smile that he used on juries.

"Who's your lovely companion?" Milton asked, obviously more interested in Laura than in me.

Behind him, at the bottom of the stairs, stood Elizabeth. She was wearing a red silk robe. Her hair was as dark as ever, probably with a little help from the drugstore. A few age lines were beginning to show around her eyes and her mouth. Her arms were folded across her ample chest, and her lips were drawn in a grim line. Her eyes locked on mine, and any notion that this first encounter since the divorce would be friendly was dispelled by the cold fury in those eyes. It was a look that would have once withered me, but this time it seemed to have lost its power. I was surprised to find that I considered her attitude rather infantile, the reaction of a spoiled child.

When I introduced Laura, Elizabeth drew further back, refusing to shake her hand.

Milton, however, gladly took Laura's outstretched hand, holding it a little longer than necessary. Ignoring Elizabeth's hostility, he led us through a set of double doors into the front room. Rather than being renovated and brought up to date, the interior of the old building had been carefully restored to its original state. A hundred years of varnish and scuff marks had been sanded away from the floor, revealing the natural grain of the blond oak. The living room was narrow, as most of the spaces in such buildings are, but the twelve-foot ceiling and the huge windows overlooking the street gave it a spacious feel. The focal point of the room was an ornate pink marble fireplace whose mantelpiece carried the obligatory antique Ingersoll clock and a gathering of intricately framed photographs. Above the mantelpiece was what looked like an original Alfred Bierstadt painting of a thunderstorm over the Rocky Mountains. It was a comfortable period room, with floral wallpaper, an overstuffed down couch covered in damask, matching wing chairs, and a maplewood secretary. In a room like this, a TV or stereo would have created historical dissonance, and there were none visible.

Milton motioned us to the couch while he lit the gas burner in the fireplace.

"Would you like some coffee?" he asked. "Maybe a little something to eat?"

Without waiting for an answer, he turned to Elizabeth, who was still standing, arms folded, in the doorway. "Why don't you whip up some coffee and sandwiches, Liz?"

She started to say something, but apparently thought better of it when she saw the look in Milton's eyes. She stomped off to the kitchen, where we soon heard the angrily overdone clatter of pots and pans.

"Maybe I should go help her," Laura said.

"I don't think that would be a good idea," Milton replied. "When she gets in one of her moods, the best thing to do is to ignore her."

"It's my fault," I said. "I didn't mean to cause any trouble for you. If you give me the package, we'll be on our way."

"Nonsense," Milton said. "I'm glad you came. After what we read in the newspapers, I was curious to hear your side of the story."

"But Elizabeth is really upset."

"Don't worry about Liz." Milton dismissed the idea with a wave of his hand. "I can handle her. Now why don't you tell me what's going on. All this business about murder, it's totally unlike you, Theo."

The aroma of fresh coffee soon drifted into the room. The noise level in the kitchen had diminished. I remembered that I hadn't had anything to eat since lunchtime. It must have showed on my face, because Milton called out for Elizabeth to hurry up with the food.

"All right, all right," she shouted back in an angry voice. "I'm doing the best I can."

Milton let out a long, despairing sigh.

"I'm sure you're familiar with her moods," he said. Turning his attention back to the reason I was there, he leaned forward. "Now tell me what's been going on with you, Theo."

He seemed genuinely interested, and knowing that I would probably soon be needing a lawyer, I decided to tell him everything. I started at the beginning. Not with finding Professor's DeBray's body, but with an explanation of the NDE research work I was doing for DeBray.

I could see from Milton's face that he was amused by my involvement in such an unorthodox endeavor. Although he didn't voice his opinion, I found myself reacting defensively, assuring him of my own original skepticism about the Professor's work.

His expression turned serious when I described my initial encounter with Laura in the basement room where she was held incommunicado. Milton didn't interrupt with any questions, allowing me to tell the story at my own pace, although he occasionally glanced at Laura, as if seeking verification of my account.

Elizabeth soon returned with a tray of hot coffee and ham sandwiches. She had put on fresh lipstick and combed her hair, and was looking as beautiful as she ever did. But her beauty paled in comparison to Laura, and I think she realized it. She made a point of showing no interest in my narrative. She put the tray down and immediately left the room.

Listening to myself talk, I was surprised by the ease with which I described the extraordinary events in which I was involved: my rescue of Laura and how I helped her through the agony of drug withdrawal; our discovery of DeBray's corpse and later that of the informant, Angie; the missing medical records and Doctor Subdhani's disappearance; the various attempts on our lives and how we had managed, at least thus far, to stay ahead of our pursuers.

There were moments during my account when I myself didn't quite believe all this could actually have happened to me. Or even more incredibly, that I was able to respond the way I did. I'm sure Milton felt the same way. But there was no disputing the fact that Professor DeBray was dead. And Laura, although struggling to stay awake, was at my side to confirm everything I said.

The mystery that had confounded me for so long gradually exerted its power over Milton. He turned his attention from me to Laura, who was, after all, the central figure in the drama. She was asleep, having succumbed again to the after-effects of her ordeal earlier. Her head was cradled by the arm of the couch, exposing her long and graceful neck. She was sleeping peacefully, unaware of Milton's scrutiny.

"I was expecting an alibi," he said when I was finished. "Some rational explanation for why you weren't guilty of murder. And you come up with this strange story of after-death visions."

"Technically, they're called near-death visions," I corrected him.

"It sounds like an episode of *Tales from the Crypt*," he said with a grin.

"It's not a joking matter, Milton. You wouldn't be smiling if you saw Professor DeBray's body. Or that poor old woman who was murdered in Pennsylvania."

"Of course. You're right. I'm sorry. But you have to admit, there are some parts of your story that seem to defy belief."

"What I told you is the truth. Every word of it."

All this time, he had been staring at Laura. The soft glow of the fireplace gave her features a pastel quality. She looked serene and untroubled, a sleeping princess who found in her dreams a refuge from the terrors of the past week.

"Incredible," Milton murmured. "Absolutely incredible."

"I swear it's all true," I insisted.

"I'm talking about your mystery lady," he said. "She's one of the most beautiful women I've ever seen. Absolutely incredible."

"She is, isn't she?"

"But do you really believe everything she's told you?"

"I didn't at first," I answered truthfully. "But I do now."

"Why? Because you're in love with her?"

I started to protest, but he quickly cut me off.

"Don't try to deny it," he said. "It's so damn obvious, the way you look at her. And I don't blame you, Theo. She's a beautiful woman. But you've been taking some terrible risks, and it's all based on what your mystery woman claims to have seen when she was . . . well, dead. What makes you so sure she's telling you the truth?"

"I'm hoping the answer is in the package that was left here for me," I said. "I have a theory about what's going on, and the information in that package might help me prove it."

Milton produced a key and unlocked the front of the cherrywood secretary. The "package" he handed to me was actually an oversized white shipping envelope, sealed with tape, and thick enough to suggest a heavy stack of documents inside. Elizabeth's name was printed in big block letters on the front of the envelope with the legend "Hold for Theo Nikonos" immediately below.

"You should have had my name put on it, instead of Liz's," Milton said. "That way, if the police searched the place, I could claim the information inside was protected by the rules of lawyer-client confidentiality."

Milton held up a crystal decanter of whiskey, politely offering me a drink before he poured one for himself. I declined.

"I didn't use your name because I didn't know you'd be this friendly," I confessed.

Milton went to the kitchen for ice cubes while I struggled to open the envelope. It was made of the same plastic-impregnated material used by commercial delivery companies, the kind that's impossible to rip open. To further insure no unauthorized access to the contents, Worthington Lewis had triple-wrapped the seams with fiber-reinforced strapping tape. After bending Milton's letter opener in a futile attempt to open the envelope, I followed him into the kitchen. A sharp steak knife finally did the trick.

Inside the envelope were three separate folders. The first one contained a facsimile copy of a topographic map, with computerized notations marking specific points on the roadway around Bald Mountain.

"Do you know why Liz is so pissed off?" Milton asked.

He leaned against the kitchen counter and watched while I unfolded the map.

"It's your mystery lady," he said, without waiting for an answer. "Liz didn't like the idea of you showing up in the middle of the night with a genuine goddess on your arm. That's why she didn't want to let you in. Just plain old female jealousy. She thought you were trying to show off a new girl friend."

The notations on the map corresponded to a thick stack of accident reports in the second folder. Almost all of the accidents on the map were clustered in two areas.

"But me, when I saw that woman on the monitor, I had a different reaction," Milton said with a smile. "You might find it surprising, Theo, but I was happy for you. That's why I let you in. I wanted to make peace with you." He swirled the ice cubes in his glass before taking a long, slow drink. "You know, I always felt guilty about what I did to you . . . I mean with Liz and the divorce and everything."

"It's okay," I murmured, trying to concentrate on the papers in front of me.

The notations on the map indicated that all the accidents in the uphill lanes were clustered just above the Bald Mountain Curve. The accidents in the downhill lanes, however, were all clustered below the curve, which was exactly as I had suspected.

Milton finished his drink and poured himself another. When he spoke again, his voice was so quiet, it couldn't have been heard more than a few feet away. He kept glancing over his shoulder, probably checking to be sure Elizabeth wasn't listening in at the doorway.

"It wasn't all my fault," he whispered. "She was the one who came on to me. Maybe it was the money thing that attracted her at first. But I didn't care. I'm an older man, and I was flattered by her attention."

There was a time when his comments would have infuriated me. But I was far more interested in what the accident reports and the topographic data revealed. What I saw in the data confirmed what I experienced myself on the night I had studied the curve. The angle of the roadway around Bald Mountain Curve appeared to play a major role in determining exactly where vehicles were most likely to go out of control.

"I'm not apologizing for what I did," Milton went on. "Liz treats me well. She seems happy, and I think we have a good marriage. If I had to do it all over again, I'd probably do the same thing."

He paused, as if he expected some sort of outraged response from me. But I found myself devoid of any emotion. Elizabeth was now part of a different life, one that I left behind when I entered that basement room and found Laura.

"I don't blame you for being angry with me," he said. "I know a lot of things went wrong in your life after the divorce."

Milton kept talking into my silence, his words punctuated by the clinking of ice cubes each time he raised the glass to his lips.

"We should put the past behind us," he said. "Just to show you my heart's in the right place, I'm willing to help you with this trouble you're in."

By the time I finished with the second folder, I knew exactly what must have happened on the highway that fateful night. There was still one more folder to go.

"Of course, you being a psychologist, you'd probably say I'm just doing it to make myself feel better," Milton continued. "What's the phrase for it, 'expiation of guilt'?"

The third folder contained a thick stack of computer printouts from various governmental and private data banks. It was a comment Chief Greer made about Zydecor that caused me to order this information. Although not readily available to the general public, the data was easily accessed by insurance industry representatives. It was the standard corporate disclosure information required for licensing and accreditation of health care providers, without which no governmental agency or insurance company would make payments. I was surprised by the amount of data Worthington Lewis provided in response to my request. It revealed a complicated web of interlocking corporations, all providing similar services.

By itself, that wasn't unusual. I had run across a number of similar corporate structures when I worked as a claims adjuster. Some businesses purposely divide themselves into a series of separate corporate entities, as part of a strategy to limit liability exposure. The idea is that the subsidiary corporation can shield the parent company's profits and assets from class-action lawsuits and excessive damage awards.

There are other, even darker, reasons for such corporate contortions, but I was too busy searching the long and often redundant lists of names to speculate any further.

I found what I was looking for on the bottom of page three. It was the name of the person responsible for what I now was convinced was a breathtakingly elaborate fraud.

FIFTY

The appearance of that particular name on the disclosure documents could, of course, be considered a coincidence. By itself, it proved nothing. In a court of law, it might not even rise to the level of evidence. But taken in context with the data in the other two folders, it was enough to satisfy me that I had indeed solved the mystery surrounding Laura's near-death experience.

"What is it, Theo?" I heard Milton asking. "Did you find what you were looking for?"

The title attached to that name confirmed for me the unwitting role I had been called upon to play. For someone with my knowledge of psychology, it was surprising how easily I had been manipulated.

"Theo?"

Everything was suddenly clear. Any lingering doubts I had were gone. Perhaps what I should have done then was to awaken Laura and tell her what I had discovered, thus putting an end to an extraordinary deception. But I was worried about the effect it might have on her. I couldn't risk breaking the heart of the woman I loved.

"Are you okay?" Milton asked.

I decided it would be best to remain silent about what I had learned, at least until the scenario played itself out a little further. In retrospect, of course, that was exactly the wrong thing to do.

"What's going on, Theo?" Milton asked. "Is that some kind of evidence you've got there?"

If I wasn't going to say anything to Laura, I certainly couldn't reveal anything to Milton, either.

"No," I lied, trying to sound casual. "It's just a computer printout of some not-very-helpful accident reports. I thought there might be something in them, but I guess I was wrong."

I wanted to get the documents out of sight before he grew more curious. But when I tried to stuff them back into the envelope, my fingers were making a mess of it.

"Take it easy, Theo," Milton said in a suddenly gentle voice. He put aside his glass. "Christ, you're trembling. What's wrong?"

"It must be the fatigue," I lied again. "I think it's catching up with me."

I finally managed to get the documents back into the envelope and rewrapped it all with the still-sticky tape.

Milton finished off his second drink, shaking the final unmelted pieces of ice into his mouth, chewing on them noisily while he poured himself another drink.

"What you need is a good night's sleep," he said. "I'd offer the guest bedroom to you, but I don't think Liz would approve."

Where once I would have been offended by so casual a rebuff, such actions no longer had the power to hurt me. I felt no anger, no emotion except a desire to get away from there and once again be alone with my beloved Laura.

"It's okay," I said. "Thanks anyway."

I stared at the open doorway beyond which I hoped Laura was still sleeping. Perhaps when we were alone, perhaps when she was well-rested, perhaps then I could tell her I knew the truth about the lie she was living.

The Ingersoll clock sounded its delicate brass chimes to announce the arrival of 4 a.m.

"So, what are you planning to do now?" Milton asked. "What's your next move?"

I sat down and slumped back in my chair.

"I'm not sure. Try to stay alive, I guess. That would certainly be the first priority."

"What about the police?" he asked. "Have you considered going to the police?"

"You're suggesting I turn myself in?"

"As a lawyer, that would be my advice."

"That's not a very attractive option," I said.

"Maybe not. But surrendering voluntarily would be a way to start working things out. The case against you might not be as strong as you think."

"That wouldn't solve anything," I said. "I'd end up in jail and the real killer would still be free."

"That's exactly the point," Milton said. "You might be safer in jail for the time being. You don't want to end up the same way Professor DeBray did, do you?"

"And what about Laura? Who's going to protect her if I'm in jail?"

"I could probably work something out with the police. After all, she is a material witness. She was with you when you found DeBray."

"Can you guarantee around-the-clock protection for her?"

"You know I can't give you that kind of guarantee. The police make those decisions on a case-by-case basis."

"Then I'm sorry, Milton, but I won't turn myself in."

"I think you're making a big mistake."

"Maybe so, but I'm not going to leave Laura on her own. I made a promise to her, and I intend to keep it."

"You could end up dead yourself."

"I know," I said. "But she needs me. Right now, I'm the only person in the world she can depend on. I'm not going to let her down."

Milton stared at me with the puzzled expression lawyers usually reserve for witnesses who render unexpected testimony under oath.

He poured himself some more Jack Daniels, a double this time, and added a handful of fresh ice cubes. He dipped his index finger into the glass, using it as a stirrer to swirl the ice cubes around before taking a sip. I wondered how long it would be before the quick succession of drinks started having an effect on him.

"You've changed, Theo," he finally said. "You're different from the way I remember you."

"Everybody changes."

"No. This is different," he said, circling back around the bar counter. "The things you're doing for this woman, the risks you're taking . . . you never would have done that for Liz."

I wasn't sure how to respond, so I remained silent.

"Do you remember what you were like when Liz said she wanted a divorce?" he asked. "You seemed so uninvolved, as if it was happening to someone else. You didn't put up a fight. You didn't argue. You just gave in to everything."

"At the time, I felt there wasn't anything much I could do," I said with a shrug. "You know Elizabeth when she makes up her mind."

"The point is, you didn't even try." The alcohol was finally starting to do its work. He was beginning to talk more slowly, not slurring his words yet, but drawing them out in the overly precise speech pattern consistent with the early stages of intoxication. "That was always your problem, Theo. You never really cared much about anything. You were one of those typical ivory-tower intellectuals: all theory and no action. You treated life like some kind of term paper, something you'd rather study and analyze from a distance, without getting personally involved."

"Four drinks and you're a psychiatrist," I said with a touch of sarcasm.

"Hey, I'm a criminal lawyer. Give me a little credit for knowing something about human behavior."

"Okay, I'm sorry I interrupted. You can proceed with your analysis."

He rested his elbows on the counter and pointed at me with the same hand that held his drink. "You're a smart guy, Theo. Even Liz, as much as she hates to admit it, still thinks you're the smartest person she ever met. But it's all book-learning. The way I see it, you were so hung up with your studies and your academic work, you never learned how to cope with real life. When Liz dumped you, that was probably the first time in your life you ever confronted failure. You couldn't deal with it. That's why your life went to hell."

"Now you sound like Oprah," I said.

He took another drink before continuing, a long drink that almost drained the glass.

"Okay, maybe it's pop psychology," he said. "But a year ago, I couldn't talk to you like this. You couldn't handle the criticism. And look at you now, you're smiling at me, like you think I'm a jerk. That's what I'm trying to say, Theo. You've changed. You're a different person now. You don't have that aimless quality about you anymore. You're more confident of yourself. You've got an edge to you now. Even your body language is different."

It was the alcohol talking, I knew: a chemically-induced lowering of inhibitions that allowed him to express opinions he would have otherwise kept to himself. But I listened carefully, because I recognized there was an essential truth in his crude attempt at analysis.

"You've been through a transforming experience, Theo."

He was beginning to get unsteady on his feet. When he tried to stand erect, he started to sway a little. He had to hold onto the counter for support.

"And you know what I think it was?" he asked. "I think it was your involvement with this near-death lady. She's the one who changed you."

"I'm doing my best to help her."

"No, it's the other way around. She's the one who's helping you."

His eyes were drooping and he seemed to be fighting off the inevitable. For someone who was slipping into an alcoholic stupor, his mind was amazingly lucid. I guess that's what made him such a good lawyer.

"I'm not sure I understand," I said.

"Of course you don't. They say a lawyer who represents himself has a fool for a client. And I think the same theory holds true for psychologists. Something died in you a long time ago, Theo, and you never even noticed it. I don't know what caused it, and I won't even try to guess. But I do know that this woman is something really special. What she did for you, Theo, was to bring you back to life."

FIFTY-ONE

There was a mixture of embarrassment and anger on Elizabeth's face when she returned to find Milton asleep in the wing chair, where I had guided him before he succumbed to the inevitable. Apparently this wasn't an unusual occurrence. She made some feeble excuse about Milton being exhausted and under a lot of pressure, trying to cover up for him and hide her anger at the same time. I wouldn't classify Milton as an alcoholic. But he was obviously a man who occasionally liked to have one drink too many. I felt a surge of sympathy for both of them, a little embarrassed myself at having been a witness to this marital secret.

It didn't take long for Elizabeth to revert to form. Just as Milton had warned, she didn't want us spending the night under their roof. Her excuse was that she didn't want the police to find me there. I knew that wasn't the real reason, but there was no point in arguing. I gently shook Laura until she awoke, and led her out of the house without any explanation. It was a measure of her confidence in me that she didn't even question why we were leaving.

I remember feeling a sense of relief when Elizabeth shut the door behind us and slid the dead-bolt into place. The symbolism of that simple action seemed to provide the closure that a divorce decree from the State of New York was never able to accomplish.

I was finally free.

I might be wanted by the police, hunted by Zydek's thugs, and caught up in a deadly intrigue, but the door had finally been closed on the most traumatic time of my life. I had made my peace with Milton, far more easily than I ever imagined possible. And in spite of the hostility she directed at me, I no longer felt anything but sympathy for Elizabeth. I could face the future, as difficult and threatening as it might be, without being haunted by the past.

I tried starting the Honda, but the battery was dead. While I'm not mechanically inclined, I knew enough about cars to trace the problem to a broken alternator belt.

Our options were dwindling.

We set off on foot for Laura's apartment, twenty blocks away, the only alternative left to us. I desperately needed some rest, and the apartment was well-stocked with food. We could hole up there while we tried to figure out what to do.

"Aren't you worried about the police?" Laura asked.

"They're after me, not you," I reminded her. "There's no reason for them to be watching your place."

Heads down against the cold, we walked quickly through the pre-dawn darkness. The only activity on the street was a Sanitation Department truck collecting garbage. We crossed the street to avoid the smell.

"What about Metzger?" Laura asked. "He'll come after us, won't he? And he knows where I live."

"That's true. But he won't show up for a while. He'll have to deal with the Dickson police first. That should delay him until morning. When he gets here, he'll probably do what he did before, stake out the building and wait for us outside. He won't want to risk any run-ins with the NYPD."

"But what will we do when he shows up?"

"I don't know," I shrugged. "Right now, I'm too tired to think about it."

"I know you'll come up with something," she said, a little more cheerfully than our circumstances seemed to warrant. "You're good at that."

And for the first time since we met, she slipped her hand into mine and held tightly as we walked.

We had no problem getting into the condo. We were greeted at the door by the same ancient security guard who let us in two nights before. I'm sure he disapproved of our disheveled condition, but he was a member of that vanishing generation of lobby attendants who mask their feelings with polite smiles. He pretended not to notice Laura's torn blouse when he handed her the spare key.

"Has anybody been asking about me?" she asked the security guard.

"Nope. Not a soul, Mrs. Duquesne."

"Well, if anyone does ask about me, would you please tell them I'm not in?"

"Sure thing. I'll tell the day guard, too."

"Thank you, Willis. I appreciate it."

She was still holding my arm. I was intensely aware of the soft warmth of her left breast pressing against my bicep. I could feel the guard's eyes on my back as we walked to the elevator.

"That was good thinking," I said. "You're getting to be more cautious."

"I'm learning from you," she smiled.

I entered the apartment first, switching on all the lights and checking the rooms and closets before allowing her to enter.

"It's good to be home," she sighed, kicking off her shoes and heading for the bathroom.

I slumped down in the leather easy chair and closed my eyes. Sleep must have come instantly: a deep, almost comatose slumber totally devoid of dreams.

When I opened my eyes, I was covered with a light blanket and the afternoon sun was streaming through the windows. Laura was sitting on the couch, staring at me.

Even in my half-awake state, she looked absolutely radiant to me. While I was asleep, she had bathed, shampooed, set her hair, put on some makeup and otherwise restored the exquisite femininity that had been so horribly abused at the Walden Clinic. She was wearing loose-fitting clothing; black slacks and a red long-sleeved blouse with a wide collar. The only visible sign of the torment she had endured was the edge of a red burn mark from the defibrillator pads that was not quite covered by the top button of her blouse.

There was something peculiar about the way she was looking at me.

"What is it?" I asked.

"Nothing." She shook her head. "I was just watching you sleep."

Her expression didn't change. She seemed to be studying me intently, as if looking for an answer to something in my eyes.

"Did I say anything in my sleep?" I asked, suddenly concerned that I might have revealed the secret I was withholding from her.

"No. You were too busy snoring."

Her scrutiny was making me feel uncomfortable. What was bothering her?

"Are you okay?" I asked.

"I've been worse."

I shielded my eyes from the sun.

"I didn't want to close the drapes," she explained. "Just in case anybody was downstairs watching the window."

"Good thinking. Did Metzger or his friends show up?"

"I don't know. I was afraid to look."

I leaned forward, groaning and trying to shake off the stiffness. I got up slowly and made my way to the window, where I stood in the protective shadow of the drapes while I studied the scene eight stories below us. It was a warm and sunny spring day. People were out in the street in light jackets. A young woman was walking two large white dogs, a brown delivery truck was double-parked while the driver made a delivery, two old men were arguing about something, a young man in a European-style trenchcoat checked his watch as he hurried along, and a beautiful black woman was wearing one of the shortest skirts I've ever seen. Traffic was backed up behind the delivery truck. One of the drivers was leaning on his horn, as if that would make any difference.

"Do you see any of the bad guys out there?" Laura asked.

She came up behind me and I was suddenly aware of the perfume she was wearing. It was a floral scent so light that it blended with the smell of her hair and her body to create a new, more sensual aroma far more seductive than the original fragrance.

"Not yet," I said. "But I'm sure they're down there somewhere."

I wanted her to stay where she was, close behind me, so that I could inhale her essence, taking it deep into my lungs and making it part of me. For one electric moment, I felt her breath on the back of my neck. And then she was gone, moving into the kitchen, opening the refrigerator, asking me if I was ready to eat. Apparently she had telephoned an order for groceries from the neighborhood market while I was asleep.

My appetite disappeared when I spotted Metzger. He pulled up in a light grey minivan with the driver-side window rolled down, the inevitable cellular phone in his hand. Stepping out of the van to stretch his legs was one of the Samoans. From eight stories up, I couldn't tell which one it was.

"They're here," I murmured.

Laura hurried back to the window.

"Down there," I pointed. "The grey minivan."

"Oh God," she sighed.

"The other Samoan is probably somewhere around the side of the building, where he can watch the service entrance."

"What do we do now?"

"For the time being, nothing. They don't know we're here, not for sure, anyway. I'd say we rest up, eat, get our energy back, and then decide what to do."

"You seem so calm."

"I always get calm when I'm desperate," I joked.

And suddenly she was in my arms, holding me tight and pressing her head against my chest. I could feel her body trembling.

"I'm frightened, Theo," she moaned. "I'm so confused I don't know what I'm supposed to do."

I wrapped my arms around her and tried to comfort her and just as suddenly as she had come to me, she pulled away.

"I'm . . . I'm sorry," she said, head down, avoiding my eyes. "I shouldn't have done that."

I took a step forward, but she retreated from me.

"Take it easy, Laura," I tried to reassure her. "Everything is going to turn out fine."

"Do you really think so?" she asked. Her voice sounded plaintive and almost childlike. "I hope you're right, Theo. Dear God, how I hope you're right. It all seemed so simple at first. But now I'm confused." Her voice wavered. "I don't know what to think anymore."

When she finally looked at me, her eyes were glistening with tears.

"What's wrong, Laura?"

"I . . . I don't want to talk about it."

"You're hiding something," I said. "After all we've been through, don't you think you can be honest with me?"

"I wish I could," she sobbed. "When you woke up before, I wanted to tell you how I . . . oh, Theo, I can't. It's wrong."

She ran to the bathroom and closed the door, turning on the faucet to cover the sound of her sobbing. I was left there to try to make some sense out of what she had said. I stared down at the street, where the Samoan had reentered the minivan. Had I made a terrible mistake about Laura's role in this affair? It was a possibility I refused to accept.

The rest of the afternoon, Laura seemed unusually quiet. Whatever was troubling her, it was obvious she wasn't yet prepared to share it with me.

We ordered a Domino's pizza for supper. She found enough spare change in a drawer to pay the delivery boy, although he didn't seem happy with his tip.

Over dinner, I reminded her of my background in psychology. "One way to solve problems is to talk them through," I suggested. "I'm a good listener."

"I know you are," she smiled.

I waited for her to unburden herself, but she concentrated on her pizza instead.

"I know something's bothering you," I said. "And I don't think it's those men waiting for us downstairs."

"You're right," she said, without elaboration.

"Talk to me about it," I urged her. "I'm here to help you."

"You've already done so much for me, Theo. I'll never be able to repay you."

"All I want is for you to be happy."

I thought it was a nice thing to say, but it drew a strange response from her. She pushed away her pizza and stared at me.

"But why?" she asked in a wary voice. "Why do you care so much what happens to me? Why are you going to all this trouble to help me?"

The real reason, of course, was that I was in love with her. But I didn't dare admit it. Confessing my true feelings would have to wait until I confronted her with the truth about her near-death experience.

"You asked for my help," I said. "Remember that first night?"

"Yes," she said slowly. "I remember. But there has to be more to it than that."

"I promised you I'd help. I'm trying to keep that promise."

"Other people have made promises to me. Nobody was ever as serious about keeping their promises as you."

"Then I guess I'm different."

"You certainly are," she said. She covered my hand with hers and gave it a gentle squeeze. "You're the only person who ever risked his life for me. That makes you really special to me."

It was the sort of ambiguous phrasing often used by women when they want to disguise their true feelings. For someone as unskilled with women as me, it was impossible to tell whether she was simply being polite or suggesting some deeper emotion.

"Are you ready to talk about what's bothering you?"

"I'm sorry, Theo." She pulled her hand back. "It's just too . . . personal. It's something I'm going to have to work out myself."

For a psychologist, I certainly wasn't doing a good job of drawing her out. We finished the rest of our pizza in silence.

A few times during the evening, she seemed on the verge of opening up. But each time she held back, retreating into innocuous small talk. Given the circumstances, it didn't seem appropriate to tell her what I had learned about her NDE. It wasn't a case of me wanting to withhold the information from her. I simply didn't want to add to whatever burden was already weighing on her mind.

Forsaking the chair, I settled down for the night on the black leather couch. It was long enough and comfortable enough for sleeping. But I had too much on my mind to doze off. In my intellectual arrogance, I had been relentlessly pursuing the truth about Laura's NDE without considering the consequences. Now, having finally discovered what I believed was the truth, I couldn't decide what to do.

If I revealed what I had learned, it would mean losing the

woman I loved. But if I maintained my silence, I risked exposing her to even greater danger than she faced before.

Laura left her bedroom door open, and I could hear her restless movements in bed. She didn't seem to be having any more success in sleeping than I did. I wondered what was behind the strange conversation we had over pizza. Until tonight, she had seemed so absolutely certain of everything. Now she claimed to be confused and unsure.

What was troubling her? Why didn't she want to share it with me? Did it have any link to what I knew about her NDE?

They were questions for which I had no answers, part of the larger puzzle that kept me awake long after I should have drifted off to sleep.

At some point, I began to think the wildly impossible thought that her hesitancy to speak might have something to do with a sea change in her feelings towards me. It was a stunning thought. But the more I turned it over in my mind, the more possible it seemed.

It could be something as simple as what psychiatrists call *displacement*, the unconscious transfer of feelings from an unattainable object or person to a convenient substitute.

What I preferred to think, and what made just as much sense, was that she was responding in a normal manner to the commitment I had already shown. We had been living together in enforced intimacy, accumulating shared experiences of a nature so terrifying and profound, few couples ever live through them. I had offered to lay down my life for her, which in Biblical terms is the greatest expression of love one person can show another. She knew how I felt about her. And if I knew anything about psychology, I knew she must be struggling with the same thoughts I was. All that was keeping us apart was her loyalty to Harrison. And as much as I thought that loyalty was misplaced, I had to admire her for it.

I must have been lying there thinking for two or three hours, before I heard a key slide into the lock of the apartment door.

It didn't make very much noise. If I had been asleep, even a light sleep, I never would have heard it. Yet the slight metallic rasping triggered a rush of adrenaline through my nervous system. Someone was trying to get into the apartment! I could feel my heart pounding and pulse rate accelerating. My breathing became short and shallow. I stared at the thin strip of hallway light that illuminated the opening between the floor and the bottom of the door. Moving shadows in that strip of light provided further evidence of an intruder's presence. Thinking immediately of Laura's safety, I rose from the couch and moved as silently as I could to her bedroom, where I positioned myself protectively between her and the doorway.

I strained my ears to hear the key slowly turning in the lock, the deadbolt squealing slightly as it was drawn back from the frame. The deadbolt finally snapped into the unlocked position, and I watched, mesmerized, as the entrance door began to open. The narrow angle of light from the hallway grew wider. A cool rush of air entered the room.

In the dim light, I could make out the silhouette of a tall, well-built man, wearing a raincoat with its collar turned up to shield part of his face.

He slipped into the room and closed the door.

For a moment, the only thing that penetrated the darkness was the sound of his breathing and the rustle of his raincoat. I could imagine the intruder flattened against the wall, one hand still on the doorknob, waiting cautiously to see whether any unseen enemy might launch an attack. I remained silent, waiting for his next move. Unable to detect any apparent threat, he finally switched on the light. The brightness blinded both of us for an instant, but I had the advantage of being partially hidden behind Laura's door.

I recognized him immediately from his photograph.

He was a tall man, probably three or four inches taller than me, with a sculptured, health-club physique. I recognized the dark, deep-set eyes and the finely-chiseled nose. They were features I had once attributed to plastic surgery. His lips bore the same sneering downturn that I remembered from the photograph. Although he had bleached his dark hair to a pale blonde color, he still wore it combed straight back in the European style.

I heard a rustling sound behind me.

"Harry!" Laura screamed.

She rushed past me and threw her arms around him before I could stop her.

"Harry! Oh, Harry, is it really you?"

Harrison Duquesne stumbled backwards, overwhelmed by the force of her greeting. He seemed to hesitate before wrapping his own arms around her.

"Laura," he murmured, as he began to stroke her hair. "I thought you were dead."

FIFTY-TWO

Harrison Duquesne was dead.

The fact that he died in the flaming wreckage of his BMW was a matter of legal record, certified and sworn to by the law enforcement and medical authorities who investigated the incident. Their records indicated, and Laura herself had told me, that she had last seen her husband in the death car before it went off the cliff.

Although the body was burned beyond recognition, the Lackawanna County coroner had identified the remains through blood typing, skeletal measurements and dental records.

The forensic evidence I had seen was incontrovertible.

Yet now, six months after a charred corpse was buried, the man who bore its name was standing before me.

It was a dizzying moment.

In revealing himself to us, however inadvertently, Harrison had validated the central and most controversial element of Laura's near-death experience.

His furtive reappearance also confirmed my worst fears.

I wasn't sure how he had managed to get past Metzger and the Samoans without being seen, but it didn't surprise me. He had already demonstrated an almost preternatural ability to come and go without being detected.

"I knew we'd find you," Laura squealed with delight.

She was absolutely ecstatic about being reunited with her husband, hugging him and kissing him and pressing her head against his chest and kissing him again. I could see tears of joy rolling down her cheeks.

Yet it was a moment that filled me with dread.

"Get away from him, Laura," I warned her, trying to keep the fear out of my voice.

Harrison's appearance here, where I least expected him to show up, could have only ominous consequences.

"Laura!" I called out again.

She turned to me. Her face was so filled with happiness, I despised myself for what I knew I had to do.

"You see, Theo, he's alive," she said. "All this time we've been looking for him, and now we've finally found him. Isn't it wonderful? We found him, and I have you to thank for it."

"Get away from him," I said.

"What?" The smile left her face. "What's wrong? What's going on?"

"Get away from him," I repeated. I backed away, looking around the room for something I could use as a weapon.

"But . . . but this is my husband."

"I know who he is."

Harrison Duquesne followed me with his eyes. He tightened his grip on Laura's arm, pulling her closer to himself, positioning her between the two of us. Slowly, and very deliberately, he moved to the narrow entrance hallway, thus blocking the only possible escape route. Laura seemed unaware of the defensive nature of his actions.

"Why are you so upset, Theo?" she asked. "I thought you'd be happy for me. Harry's alive, just like I've been saying. It was all the truth, what they told me on the other side."

"I already knew that," I said.

Harrison remained silent. Behind his deceptively calm eyes, I was sure his mind was working furiously, trying to evaluate how much of a threat I represented.

"You knew?" Laura seemed bewildered. "You knew he was alive?"

"Yes."

Her voice turned accusatory. "Then why didn't you tell me?"

"I wasn't really sure until last night," I tried to explain. I didn't dare admit my real reason for not telling her: the fear that I might lose the woman I loved. "Until last night, all I had were suspicions. I didn't want to say anything to you until I was absolutely certain."

"Then you should have told me last night," she insisted.

"I'm sorry, Laura," I said. "I didn't want to hurt you."

"Hurt me? What hurts is that you knew Harrison was alive and you didn't tell me. I'm really disappointed in you, Theo."

"There's more to this than you think," I said.

I saw only one object in the sparsely-furnished room that could serve as a weapon. It was the clear Lucite obelisk that decorated the far end of the buffet. I might be able to use it as a club or a missile, but first I had to get close enough to it without arousing Harrison's suspicion.

"There's more?" she asked. "You mean more secrets you've been hiding from me?" She withdrew further into Harrison's embrace. "I don't want to hear it. I have my husband back, and that's all I care about."

"He deceived you, Laura. He's not the man you think he is."

"I think you should leave, Theo. Before you say something we both regret."

"Harrison won't let me leave," I said. "He doesn't want anybody to know he's alive."

"Harrison?" she glanced up at her husband.

He stared impassively at me, his face devoid of emotion.

He made no attempt to move away from the door.

"Harrison?" she repeated, puzzled by his lack of response.

"He can't let me go, because I know what really happened that night on Bald Mountain."

It might seem foolhardy, taunting him with my knowledge of his activities. But I was already certain he wouldn't permit either of us to leave the room alive. What I was doing was trying to initiate a dialogue. As any hostage negotiator knows, the distraction of even the most apparently ordinary of conversations can often change the dynamics of a high-stress event. The longer such communication can be maintained, the greater the possibility for a peaceful resolution of the situation. The one subject I assumed

Harrison would be most interested in was whether his elaborate plan had been compromised.

"I know what happened that night on Bald Mountain," I repeated.

So far, he hadn't responded.

"I know why you're hiding, Harrison."

Still no response.

"Come on, Harrison," I prodded him. "If I can put it together, so can the police. It's only a matter of time before they figure it out."

He stared at me, turning it over in his mind before at last asking the one question I knew his fugitive mind would be unable to resist.

"How did you find out?" he finally asked.

"If there was one thing I learned when I worked as a claims adjuster," I said, "it was how easily an auto accident can be faked."

Again Laura started to challenge me, but Harrison shook her into silence.

"I want to hear this," he said. "It's important to me."

His only interest, of course, was in finding out how much I actually knew and how I had figured it out, so that he could determine what errors he might have made in his plan.

Now that I had him hooked, I turned my attention to Laura. I was far more interested in regaining her respect than in helping her murderous husband.

"Remember the night when I left you at the hotel in Scranton?" I asked her. "Remember when you woke up and I wasn't there?"

She nodded, and I wondered if she also remembered how glad she was when I returned, and how she had made me promise never to leave her alone again. I wondered, sadly, if that earlier desire for my companionship could ever again be rekindled.

"I couldn't sleep that night," I explained. "Something was bothering me about the accident, something that just didn't feel right. So I drove up to the Bald Mountain Curve. I thought if I retraced the route the BMW took I might get a better idea of what happened."

"It was six months since the accident," Harrison said. "There shouldn't have been anything left to find."

"Well, there's the wreckage, of course, but you already know we looked at that, don't you?"

Harrison didn't answer. His face remained passive.

"There weren't any skid marks, either," I said. "That's why the police thought you must have fallen asleep and drifted off the highway."

"That's exactly what happened," Laura interrupted. "I saw him before the car went off the cliff. I'm sure he was asleep."

"I'm sure that's what you think you saw," I told her. "But obviously you were wrong. After all, he's still alive, isn't he?"

She looked up at her husband, as if she was expecting him to enlighten her. Since no explanation was forthcoming from Harrison, I slipped into one of those academic dissertations to which I am prone. And which, I remembered ruefully, had once elicited a compliment from Laura.

"To make sense out of what we see, the mind mixes visual input with assumptions based on experience. For a brief instant, you saw a figure slumped in the driver's seat. You assumed it was Harrison, because he was supposed to be driving the car. You assumed he was asleep, because he was slumped over. It was a simple error of cognition."

She kept looking from me to Harrison, and back again, trying to puzzle it all through. Harrison wasn't saying anything, so I continued my discourse.

"Sometimes sensory input is too fast or too faint for us to be consciously aware of it," I went on. "But it can trigger associative functions, and initiate perceptual processing of the sensory cues on a subconscious level. That's what happened to me earlier in the day."

"What the hell is this?" Harrison demanded. "You're trying to show us how smart you are?"

"It's always been one of my failings," I said. "I tend to get lost in theory. But that's how I ended up figuring out how the car really went off the cliff. I'll stop, if you're getting bored."

"Yes, I'm bored," Harrison said. "But go ahead. Get on with it."

I smiled at Laura, whose face by now was a study in confusion.

"When we were driving around Bald Mountain Curve earlier in the day, I sensed something. It was just a hint, and I wasn't sure what it was, but I knew it had to be some sort of subliminal perceptual input. As hard as I tried, I couldn't elevate it to the level of conscious thought. So I went back up to Bald Mountain that night to try to duplicate the conditions under which I received the original cues. It's a psychological technique that can sometimes trigger a stronger, more conscious response."

Harrison sneered at me with the supercilious smirk I had seen in his wedding photograph. He had erected an elaborate structure of deceit, and his ego was convinced no one could see behind its facade. But I was about to prove him wrong.

"I drove around the curve over and over again," I said. "It seemed like a wasted effort, and I was getting ready to give up. But after a while, I noticed something about the way my car was handling. And that was the perceptual trigger I was searching for. Earlier in the day I must have absorbed subliminal cues about the angle of the road and the way my car went around the curve. Without me being consciously aware of it, my mind processed the information and connected it with other data stored in my long-term memory banks. When I recognized one of those perceptual cues, everything bubbled to the surface as a coherent whole. It was a perfect example of the *Poincare effect*. I suddenly understood what must have happened on the night of your so-called accident."

"Get to the point," Harrison said. "You don't have to go through the whole damn thought process."

"It's complicated," I said. In truth, I was purposely dragging it out, enjoying the opportunity to demonstrate how I had solved his elaborate fraud through nothing less than sheer intellectual ability. And, I have to admit, I was probably showing off a bit for Laura's benefit.

"What it deals with is the correlation between the physics of a moving vehicle and the angle at which the highway engineers had purposely banked the roadway around that curve," I said.

"When I was a claims adjuster, we were involved in a complicated lawsuit that required extensive testimony from a highway engineer. The engineer explained some of the principles of highway roadbed design. Newton's first law of motion dictates that a car moving downhill will travel in a straight line. To help downhill vehicles go around curves without drifting across the median into oncoming traffic, the engineers often bank the roads, just like they do with auto racing tracks. The frictional force that's created automatically helps guide even relatively uncontrolled vehicles around curves."

While I was talking, Harrison reached behind himself to lock the deadbolt and attach the security chain to the entry door.

"I tested it myself that night," I continued. "I took my hands off the steering wheel to see if I was right. I did it three times, and each time the results were the same. The road was straight going into the curve. Just as Newton's Law dictated, the car kept going straight. When it reached the banked portion of the curve, the effects of friction and gravity caused it to drift to the inside of the road rather the outside. I think the engineers overcompensated, maybe because of the dangers of going off the cliff."

"What's the point?" Harrison impatiently asked.

With the door securely locked, he felt confident enough to move over to the window, where he could check the activity in the street below. I used the distraction to take a step closer to the obelisk.

"The point is," I said. "Even if you fell asleep at the wheel, like the police thought, your car wouldn't have gone off the cliff *before* entering the curve. That would have violated the laws of physics. Which meant the BMW must have been purposely driven off the cliff."

"It's just a theory," Harrison said, dismissively. "You're trying to make it sound more convincing with all that talk about physics and banked roads, but it's just a theory you made up."

He was testing me, I thought, wanting to know whether the explanation I gave him was logical enough to occur to someone else, like the police.

"That's why I said I wasn't really sure," I told him. "Not until last night, when I was able to review a historical printout of every auto accident on Bald Mountain Curve during the last twenty years. The only cars that ever went off the cliff above the curve were those cars traveling in the uphill lanes, which for them would have been the far side of the curve. In twenty years, not a single downhill car went off the road *above* the curve, except yours."

"You're saying it wasn't an accident?" Laura asked. Her voice was softer now, unsure of itself.

"He faked his own death, Laura," I said. "I suspected it for a while, and now I have the documents to prove it."

Harrison seemed strangely relaxed for a man whose fraudulent death had been unmasked.

"You went to a lot of work for nothing," he said.

He reached into his pocket with his free hand, and in a movement that was shielded by Laura's body, removed a small revolver. He held it behind his right hip, out of her sight, but ready for use.

I could guess what he had in mind. Laura and I were the only two witnesses who could ever testify that he was still alive.

He could eliminate us easily, and return to being legally dead, that most exquisite of hiding places, the sanctuary from which no mortal court could ever extradite him, where he could remain forever beyond the legal reach of those who would seek him out.

FIFTY-THREE

Harrison might have the gun, but I was not entirely defenseless.

Years of studying human behavior had given me certain skills at playing mental games. I was certain Harrison wouldn't kill me until he knew exactly how much of his elaborate scheme I had figured out. If I was able to penetrate the obfuscations he had so carefully arranged, others could, too. Letting me talk was the best way for him to determine the weaknesses in his plan, and what new protective steps he might be required to take. And I, without any apparent means of escape, could do nothing but comply. Which meant I had to keep talking, even though the tension was making my throat painfully dry. It was the only way I could extend my life, and hopefully, Laura's as well.

"I found something else in the documents," I said.

"And what was that?" he asked.

"A motive," I said with a smile.

"You're a regular Mr. Know-It-All, aren't you?"

"I'm very good at research," I said.

"A motive for what?" Laura interrupted.

"A motive for a double murder," I said.

"I'm not sure I want to hear any more of this," she murmured.

Her unenthusiastic response brought a thin smile to Harrison's lips. How much of what he had done was she willing to forgive? If her love for him was so great that it brought her back from the dead, was it strong enough for her to forgive even murder?

"I'm sorry, Laura," I said. "You won't like what you're going to hear, but it's time you learned the truth about the man you're married to."

"What truth?" she responded, still loyal to her spouse. "I think it's like Harry said. You're making it all up."

"I didn't make up the car crash, Laura. It happened. You were there. And the car went off the road *above* the curve, just like I said."

"It was an accident," she insisted.

"But Harrison survived."

"Of course he survived," she said. "He's here, isn't he?"

As frustrated as I was by her attitude, I tried to keep my tone of voice calm and reasonable.

"All this time, you've been claiming that he was alive." I said. "But haven't you ever wondered who died in his place? They found a body in the front seat of the wreckage. We know it wasn't Harrison's body. So whose body was it? And how did it end up in the driver's seat?"

The questions, as obvious as they were to me, seemed to catch her by surprise.

She had no answer. It was clearly something she had never considered before. So blinded was she by her conviction that her husband was alive, so passionate was she in her desire to see him again, she had overlooked the terrible questions that his survival raised.

"The body was identified from dental records, skeletal measurements and blood typing," I continued. "Obviously the dental records were switched. Those things can be arranged. But the records switch would have had to have been done in advance of the car crash. And the victim also had to be carefully selected for his height and weight, so that measurements of the remains would match up with the information the coroner would request from Harrison's doctor. The blood type had to match, too. All of which means the death of the man who was found in the BMW must have been carefully planned long before it happened. And the only person who could have planned it was the man who survived: the real Harrison Duquesne."

"But . . . but why?"

"Your husband wanted to fake his own death," I said. "But for his plan to work, he needed a body. He needed someone else to die in the crash. When that car went off the cliff, it wasn't an accidental death. It was murder."

It was a terrible thing I was doing to the woman I loved: accusing her husband of murder, trying to turn her against him, and doing it all at what should have been a time of joyful reunion. I remember thinking: if I were her, I would have hated me for such behavior. A lesser woman would have exploded with fury. But in a move that only reinforced my admiration for her, Laura remained in control of her emotions and faithfully attempted to deflect my accusations by searching for alternate explanations.

"He wouldn't have done that," she said quietly. "At least, not on purpose. It must have been an accident."

"It was no accident," I said. "It was murder, carefully premeditated and planned well in advance."

I could see she was having trouble accepting the enormity of my accusation.

"I can understand why you don't want to believe me, Laura. But think for a moment. How else can you explain the presence of the other man in the car?"

"I . . . I don't know. I fell asleep. I told you that."

"No," I said. "You were drugged. That's what really happened. When you had that nice, long supper in Milford, Harrison put a fast-acting sedative in your food or in your drink. He wanted you unconscious when he arranged the phony accident."

"That's pure speculation," Harrison said. "You have no proof."

"It's the only logical explanation for the disappearance of Laura's medical records," I told Harrison. "You knew the blood tests would show the presence of powerful sedatives in Laura's system prior to the crash. That finding wouldn't have mattered if she was dead. But when you learned that she survived, you couldn't take the chance that the police would question her about the sedatives. It might lead to a more thorough investigation, which was the last thing you wanted. So you bribed somebody, maybe a computer hacker or someone on the hospital staff to get rid of those records."

Harrison watched me with cold, unemotional eyes. I found myself wondering how so warm and loving a human being as Laura could ever have given herself to him.

"It must have been a massive dose," I went on. "Because Laura told me she fell asleep right after supper, almost as soon as she sat down in the car. By itself, that didn't seem unusual. What made me suspicious was the time frame. Laura said you left the restaurant around seven-thirty. The car went off the highway at nine-thirty, which was two hours later. But it's less than an hour's drive from Milford to Scranton. That leaves an hour unaccounted for."

"I drove around the Poconos for a while," Harrison said, wasting no time in coming up with an alternative explanation. "I picked up a hitchhiker. That's who they found in the car. Just somebody who needed a ride."

But if that was the best alibi he could come up with, it wouldn't work.

"You picked up a hitchhiker after dark?" I asked. "With your wife asleep in the front seat? And the hitchhiker turned out to be someone whose dental records just happened to be misfiled under your name? I doubt it. What I think really happened is that you went to pick up your intended victim at some pre-arranged place. I don't know how you recruited the man who took your place, or what phony story you gave him, but it was all set up in advance. He never suspected you planned to kill him, not even when you pulled off the road above the Bald Mountain Curve. You must have pulled off at the same place we did, where the frontage road goes uphill into the woods."

"You have a very fertile imagination," Harrison said.

"Not half as good as yours," I replied. "You're the one who dreamed up this plan in the first place. All I've been doing is following in your footsteps. When I parked my car on the frontage road, I noticed it lined up perfectly with the place where your BMW went through the guardrail."

"A coincidence," Harrison countered.

"That's where you parked the BMW, knocked out your victim and then put him behind the steering wheel. The rest of it was easy. You probably held the car in place with the emergency brake while you jammed his foot on the accelerator. Then all you had to do was release the parking brake and the car shot across the highway and over the edge. Maybe with a little extra gasoline sprinkled inside to make sure the wreckage burned."

"Do you really expect anybody to buy that story?" Harrison scoffed. "No one would ever be able to prove any of it, much less believe it."

"When I start with the fact that the dead man wasn't you, then it's the only sequence of events that makes sense," I pointed out.

"I did smell gasoline," Laura admitted. "I remember that."

Except for a troubled frown, Laura's face gave little indication of how much a toll the accumulation of incriminating details was beginning to take on her faith in her husband.

"I thought you were supposed to be a psychologist," Harrison said to me. "Now you're pretending to be Sherlock Holmes."

"Deductive reasoning is just another form of logic. And logic was always one of my best subjects."

"You might have logic on your side, but you don't have proof. Where's the proof?"

"You keep saying that, Harrison, but what you don't realize is that you're the proof. The fact that you're alive is all the proof I need."

"But even Laura doesn't believe your ridiculous story." He looked down at her and squeezed her arm. "Do you, darling?"

"I don't believe . . . I don't want to believe any of this," she said, her voice dropping to an anguished whisper.

"There, you see?" he smiled. "If she doesn't believe you, why should anyone else?"

"But she hasn't heard the rest of the story," I said. "Shall I continue?"

"I wish you wouldn't," Laura said.

"What about you, Harrison?" I asked, knowing the answer even before I finished asking the question. "Do you want to hear what else I figured out?"

"I'm willing to listen," he said with a sneer. Of course he was, I thought.

As much as I loathed Harrison Duquesne and wanted to displace him in Laura's heart, I didn't relish the pain I was about to inflict upon her. My revelations would destroy the very dream that brought her back from the dead, the goal that kept her alive through six months of physical and mental agony. If I could have been assured that Harrison wouldn't harm her, I would have gladly agreed to reveal nothing further. But Harrison's cruel smile goaded me on.

FIFTY-FOUR

I was methodically stripping away the elaborate layers of deception beneath which Harrison had concealed his activities. Working with the patience of an archeologist, I was sifting through a history of horrors, revealing one fragment at a time, holding it up to the clear light of reason, where its significance could be carefully considered. Inevitably, each fragment led to another, and when I was done, I hoped to have reconstructed the entire evil mosaic.

Harrison seemed fascinated by the process, since it offered him a view of what other investigators might learn if they tried. He expressed only mild demurrals as I continued.

"There was someone else who was supposed to die that night, Laura," I said.

"No." She shook her head violently. "No. I don't want to hear this, Theo."

"You know it's true," I said. "There's no point in denying it."

"Please, Theo, please stop. What good is all this doing?"

Perhaps she was right, I thought. My effort to exchange information for a few more minutes of life was certainly working. But was I deluding myself? Was I responding to that most primitive and powerful motivator of all: the human survival instinct? Or was I merely engaged in some intellectual ego trip: one final, futile, self-glorifying demonstration of my analytic capability?

Considering that my lifetime had already lasted twenty-eight years, what value could possibly be placed on an extra ten or fifteen minutes of life?

Having embarked on this path, however, I felt impelled to go on.

"He tried to kill you that night, too, Laura."

"No! You're wrong! You must be mistaken!"

She looked up at Harrison, desperate for reassurance, but his face remained an unresponsive mask.

"It must have been an accident," she said, reverting to the same rationalization she had used earlier.

"The only accident is that you survived," I said. "He wanted you dead."

"No! I don't believe you!"

"He drugged you, Laura."

"You can't be sure of that," she argued. "You said yourself the hospital records were missing."

"You smelled the gasoline," I said.

"Maybe I was mistaken."

"And you told me you remembered buckling your seat belt," I said. "But the seat belt wasn't buckled when the car hit the guardrail. That means Harrison must have unbuckled it, to make sure you didn't survive the crash. Ironic, isn't it? He never anticipated that act would save your life."

"But . . . but he had no reason to kill me."

"You were an important part of his cover-up. Like the dental records and blood type and physical measurements of his victim, your death was intended to add credibility to the fake accident, and cut short any further investigation. It was supposed to look like another unfortunate case of a husband and wife dying together in a car crash."

At last she had run out of rebuttals.

But I could see from the agony in her eyes that she was still fighting the idea that she was indeed the target of so fatal a form of rejection. She bit her lip with such intensity, I thought her teeth would puncture the skin. She seemed afraid to look up at Harrison again, afraid that he might confirm everything I said.

"It gets worse, Laura," I told her.

"How could anything possibly be worse?" she asked in a weak voice.

"That wasn't the only time he tried to kill you. When we climbed down the cliff to examine the wreckage of the car, it was Harrison who rolled that rock off the edge and started the avalanche."

"Couldn't it have been Metzger?" she asked, her confidence in her husband beginning to weaken. "Or the Samoans?"

"Metzger's assignment was to bring you back to Zydek alive and unharmed. He wouldn't have done anything to endanger you. And if you remember, when Metzger found us at Doctor Subdhani's office, he didn't seem at all surprised to see us alive."

Behind her, Harrison's face still gave no clue as to whether my theories were correct. He remained surprisingly blasé as my list of accusations grew longer.

"When Harrison saw you tonight, Laura, what was the first thing he said to you?"

"He . . . he said he thought I was . . . dead."

"Because he thought he had finally gotten rid of you. He wanted you dead, and he thought he had accomplished it."

No artist, not even Goya in his moments of greatest despair, could ever have managed to capture the heartbreaking vulnerability of Laura's face at the moment she realized her love had been so horribly betrayed. The physical manifestations are easy enough to describe. Her blue eyes struggled to see through a film of wetness. Her lower lip began to tremble. Her flesh turned ashen. Doubt etched its lines across her brow. Her shoulders sagged under some unseen weight. Somewhere deep inside, at the central core of her being, the warm glow that had animated her *persona* was extinguished, deadening her emotions.

"But why?" she asked, having abandoned the last vestiges of denial. "Why would he try to kill me a second time?"

"He was afraid of you."

"I don't understand."

"It was because of what you found out during your near-death experience. You came back claiming Harrison was still alive. It must have shocked him when he first heard about it. After all those elaborate plans to fake his own death, there you were telling everyone who would listen that your husband had somehow, inconceivably, survived. And that you came back from the dead to find him. He was afraid you might ruin his plans, maybe even get the police to reinvestigate."

"Why would I worry about that?" Harrison muttered. "Nobody really believes those near-death stories. It's like UFO's and crop circles, just a lot of tabloid nonsense."

"The important thing is that *you* knew her story was true, Harrison. After all, you really were alive, just like Laura was saying. And when she was transferred from the hospital to Doctor Zydek's care, you were afraid he believed her, too. Suddenly, your plan to drop out of sight was coming unglued. You must have been worried about what else she learned on the other side. Did she know where you were hiding out? Did she know where you were planning to go? I'll bet you did a lot of research on NDE's, trying to figure out what might be going on. That's how you found out about the Institute for the Investigation of Anabiotic Phenomena."

"But I didn't know where Harry was," Laura interrupted. "When I was on the other side, they never told me anything about where he was. All they told me was that he was still alive. And that I had to go back to save . . . to save the man I loved." She shook her head at the thought. "Oh, God," she groaned. "How could he ever be the man I came back to save?"

I should have been delighted that her love for him had died, but my heart ached for the pain I was causing her. If we were both soon to die, what useful purpose was I serving by destroying a love she once treasured?

"I did read a lot about the near-death experience," Harrison admitted. "Enough to convince me it's nothing more than an illusion. All that stuff about the tunnel and the light is laughable. There's nobody waiting on the other side. There *isn't* any other side. It's all wishful thinking."

"But you weren't sure, were you?" I prodded him. "You couldn't take the chance that she might know something more. Somehow, you had to find out what else she might be telling Zydek. And that's where you had a real problem, Harrison. Since you went to all that trouble to convince everyone you were dead, you couldn't possibly try to go see her yourself. You needed someone else to question her. Someone you could trust. That someone turned out to be me."

Laura stared at me in disbelief.

"Oh, he didn't do it directly," I quickly assured her. "He was too clever for that. He read all he could about Professor DeBray's work with near-deathers. It must have seemed like the perfect solution. He knew if DeBray found out about your NDE, he'd send someone up to interview you. Then all Harrison had to do was get a copy of the interview tape. That way he'd find out everything you learned on the other side."

Laura stared at me in disbelief.

"Harry wrote the letter?" she asked.

I nodded.

"Your husband set the whole thing in motion. He wrote the letter describing your near-death experience, and he drew the map that showed exactly where you were being held. But he knew he couldn't sign his own name, and he was afraid DeBray might not follow up on an *anonymous letter*. So he hid behind an old woman, using her as a go-between to protect his own identity."

"That's a pretty far-fetched theory," Harrison said.

"Oh, come on, why deny it any longer?" I asked. "You made a mistake when you picked Angelina Galarza to hide behind. Angie had Parkinson's disease. She could never have written that letter or drawn the map, not the way her hands trembled."

The revelation about Angie's physical problem seemed to take Harrison by surprise. How could he not have noticed it? Perhaps, like me on my first visit to the nursing home, he didn't make the connection between her tremors and their effects on the use of a pen. Unlike me, when I asked her to sign my receipt, he probably hadn't even bothered asking her to sign her own name to the letter and map he had prepared in advance, perhaps thinking the writing wouldn't match. More likely, I thought, he might not have even risked visiting her in person, preferring to conduct his business with her on the telephone. It was a minor slip on his part, to be sure, but I felt a momentary surge of pride at having poked another hole in his plan.

"Just because she didn't write the letter doesn't mean I did," Harrison said. "And even if I did, what could possibly be wrong with writing a letter for an old woman who couldn't write it herself?"

"There was nothing wrong with writing the letter," I conceded. "The problem is that you went back and killed her so that she couldn't tell anyone about you."

Laura gasped, and for a moment I thought she was going to faint. Only Harrison's firm grasp kept her from plummeting to the floor.

"Once again, you have no proof," he challenged me, which was his way of asking for any evidentiary details I might have come across.

Of course, I had no physical proof, no hard evidence of the kind prosecutors prefer before bringing criminal charges against an individual. The handwriting on the original letter was undoubtedly disguised. Only two people had direct knowledge of exactly what happened. One of those was dead, and the other was her killer.

But the lack of physical proof never stopped Einstein or Hawking or Hubble from advancing some of their most important theories, and I didn't see why it should stop me. Although I don't pretend to be an abstract thinker of the first magnitude, I was quite pleased with the intellectual framework I had developed to explain the strange confluence of events in which I was entangled.

"The police already know she was murdered," I said. "I'm sure an investigation would uncover some link to you. Maybe she was a relative, or someone you knew from the past."

"Just because I was related to the woman isn't evidence of anything, and you know it."

It was as close to an admission as I was going to get from him.

"That's also why you killed DeBray, wasn't it?" I asked. "Because of the damned interview tape."

"From what I read in the New York newspapers, the police think you killed him," Harrison taunted me. "They found the body in your apartment. That's evidence against you, not me."

"We both know what happened, don't we? You originally planned to steal the tape from me. But after the Samoans beat me up, I went into hiding. So you went to New York, hoping to get the tape from the Professor. But you didn't count on his reaction when he found out you were alive."

"DeBray was a fool."

"Even at gunpoint, he must have been excited. The Professor spent twenty years searching for proof that the near-death experience really was a visit to the afterlife. Finding a living, breathing Harrison Duquesne must have been like finding the Holy Grail for him. It would have confirmed Laura's story, making her NDE the first confirmable case of someone coming back from the dead with information no one else could possibly have. But DeBray didn't have the tape, because I hadn't sent it yet. After you searched his place, you forced him to take you to my apartment. But the tape wasn't there, either. Not only did you not have the tape, but you knew the Professor couldn't wait to tell the world you were alive. So you strangled him and left him in my apartment."

Her eyes brimming with tears, Laura finally looked up at her husband.

"Is it true?" she asked.

He didn't answer. His eyes remained fixed on me.

"Tell her, Harrison," I goaded him, taking another tiny step towards the obelisk. "Tell her how you've been killing everyone who was in your way."

"Is it true?" she repeated the question, more plaintively this time.

His silence was all the answer she needed. She tried to pull away, twisting her arm against his grip, but he held her tight. And now, for the first time, she saw the gun. It was a brutal confirmation of everything I had charged.

"Are you going to kill us, too?" she asked.

Unlike me, she didn't seem unduly concerned by the prospect. This was, after all a woman who claimed to have no fear of death, the result of her having already made so many journeys to the other side.

"I don't have any choice," Harrison said with a shrug.

FIFTY-FIVE

Instant analysis is normally the domain of pop psychologists and talk-show hosts. A diligent psychologist needs more than fifteen minutes of personal contact before attempting an evaluation. In Harrison's case, however, my first face-to-face encounter with him was preceded by the kind of background investigation few psychologists ever perform. I had spent more than a week searching for the man, in the company of a woman who was privy to the most intimate details of his life. I knew about his marriage, his personality, his lifestyle. I had examined his safety-deposit box, slept in his apartment, and fallen in love with his wife. I had walked more than the Biblical mile in his shoes, and I was shocked by where the trail led. Seeing him close-up at last, able to observe his reactions and behavioral affects, I finally understood the true nature of the man with whom I was dealing.

Harrison's response to my litany of charges continued to be curiously passive. His expression remained blank, his face completely devoid of emotion. Except for his constant reminders that I had no proof, he seemed totally untroubled by the enormity of the crimes of which I accused him. Even the prospect of killing two more people didn't seem to distress him.

And therein lay the key to his psyche. He belonged to that most infamous fraternity of social deviants, those suffering from Antisocial Personality Disorder (ASPD), whose membership ranges from serial murderers and rapists to the less destructive but equally pathological activities of con men and scam artists. The one distinguishing characteristic that unites them all is their apparent total lack of conscience.

To apply the common, descriptive, label, Harrison Duquesne was a psychopath. Given that diagnosis, many things suddenly seemed clearer to me. That Laura had not seen this evil side of her husband was understandable. ASPDs can be exceptionally difficult to diagnose, even for trained professionals. In his classic work on the disorder, Cleckley warned that even the most severely and obviously disabled psychopath presents a technical appearance of sanity, often one of high intellectual capacities, and not infrequently succeeds in business or professional activities. Like others of his type, Harrison had managed to hide behind this mask of sanity, succeeding so well that until moments ago, his own wife had refused to believe how dangerous he was.

I could also understand why Laura was spellbound by his words when they first met on that rainy afternoon at the Frick Museum, and why she remained enthralled by him all this time. The literature describes the typical psychopath as a glib and even charming individual, exhibiting a seemingly carefree spirit and a strong, often grandiose sense of self-worth. Many of them have the uncanny ability to look directly into another person's eyes and lie so convincingly the other person never doubts them again.

What Laura didn't see, what most of the victims of psychopaths don't discover until too late, is the terribly deformed personality lurking beneath this thin veneer of normality. Therapists who deal with ASPDs describe them as arrogant, manipulative, and cunning pathological liars. They appear to be devoid of any sense of responsibility to society, lacking remorse or guilt for their actions, and unable to develop an emotional link to other human beings.

Those factors helped explain why Harrison, like so many others of his kind, could so readily employ multiple murder as a problem-solving device.

The only element that puzzled me was how, despite the emotional limitations of his personality disorder, he had once felt within himself a desire to enter into marriage with Laura. I have no illusions that he ever actually loved her. Perhaps it was a temporary yearning, an aberration caused by the same hormonal tides that flow through those of us who are considered normal. Whatever the reason for marrying Laura, it had obviously run its course long ago. And in the manner so common in disordered relationships, when Harrison appeared to withdraw emotionally, Laura had automatically overcompensated, filling the void between them with so much of her own love and affection that in the end she was unable to recognize the one-sided nature of the marriage.

From a clinical standpoint, I felt satisfied with my diagnosis. It explained the otherwise incomprehensible extremes of behavior displayed by Harrison. It helped me understand how a seemingly conventional man could develop and execute so diabolical a plan of deception and murder.

And it assured me that Harrison Duquesne would send a bullet into my skull without the slightest remorse.

FIFTY-SIX

My desperate game was nearing its end.

The only thing keeping Harrison from pulling the trigger had been his need to know how far his plan might have been compromised. But I was running out of information. And he was growing impatient.

"Are you finished with your pathetic little theories?" He asked. "Because I'd like to get this over with."

For the briefest of moments, I considered withholding the one last piece of information I had. It was the single most incriminating discovery I had made, the one that suggested a motive for his crimes. But in the end, I decided to trade even this for a few more moments of life, hoping those few moments might yet produce deliverance.

"I found the link, Harrison," I said at last. "I know why you faked your own death."

I watched for a reaction, but he disguised his feelings too well.

"At last we get to the interesting part of the story," he said.

"There had to be a lot of money involved," I said. "How much was it, Harrison?"

"You tell me, if you're so smart."

"Two million, four million, what difference does it make?" I said. "You saw your chance and you took it. But you didn't want anyone to come after you, and that's why you faked your death.

You thought it would close the book on everything, put you beyond the reach not only of your partners, but of the law. And it almost worked. You would have gotten away with it, if only Laura had stayed dead."

"What money?" Laura asked, bewildered. "What are you talking about?"

"You're very good," Harrison said. "How did you find out about the money?"

We were getting down to the final moments. This was the final bit of information with which I could bargain. Once I revealed the last of what I knew, he would be free to use the gun on me, and then turn it on Laura.

The obelisk remained tantalizingly, excruciatingly out of reach. I had no illusion that a weapon as crude as the obelisk was a match for Harrison's revolver. But even a futile attack with the heavy sculpture might cause enough of a distraction to at least allow Laura to escape.

"It was basic research," I said. "I was looking for a link, something that would explain Doctor Zydek's interest in you. It was the police chief in Dickson who gave me a clue, when she told me the Walden Clinic was part of a bigger chain. She said Zydek was buying up other health-care facilities. That meant there might be big money at stake. I wondered if that had something to do with why he wanted to find you."

Harrison remained silent.

"It was just intuition, but I decided to follow through on it. I was able to get copies of the financial disclosure documents all health care providers are required to file with the Pennsylvania State Attorney General's Office. According to the documents, Doctor Zydek owns all the stock in Zydecor, which in turn owns twenty-two different health-care facilities in small towns in Pennsylvania, New Jersey and New York. That includes nursing homes, rehab units, and halfway houses. None of them are very large, but put them all together, and the profit potential is enormous. Interestingly enough, each of them is set up as a separate stock corporation, with Zydecor owning all the stock."

"You've done your homework."

"It's all in the financial disclosure documents," I said. "It's all a matter of public record. And that's what you have to worry about, Harrison. Anyone who looks at those records could make the same connection I did."

"And what connection is that?"

"Your name is listed on those documents as an independent financial advisor, responsible for mergers and acquisitions."

"That's it?" Harrison laughed. "That's all the evidence you came up with? My name on a stupid form?"

"It's enough to connect you to Zydek," I said. "If I could make that link, so could the police."

I was in front of the buffet now. Trying to appear casual, I leaned against the top edge. The obelisk was directly behind me, easy enough to reach with either hand.

"You're not as smart as you think you are," Harrison said. "Even if the police make the link, Zydek won't admit to anything. He's in this as deep as I am. They could put him in jail for a long time if they find out what he's been doing."

"But Zydek didn't have anything to do with the murders, Harrison."

"It was his fault the old lady and the professor were killed. I wouldn't have had to do it if he hadn't kept Laura locked up."

"The police will question Zydek about Angie's death," I said. "But there's nothing to link him to it. What you should be worrying about is whether he tells the police about you and the health-care fraud the two of you cooked up."

"But I'm supposed to be dead, remember? What's he going to do, accuse a dead man of committing murder? They won't believe him."

"It doesn't matter what they think about the murder. Health-care fraud is a federal crime. The FBI will start tracing the money. That's the kind of thing the FBI does best. And sooner or later, the money trail will lead them to you. Stealing from Zydek is one thing. But stealing from the government was a big mistake."

"The government has nobody to blame but themselves," Harrison said, lapsing once again into a distorted rationalization. "They make it too easy. When somebody says, here take this money, just sign this piece of paper . . . weii you can't really call that stealing, can you?"

He glanced out the window again.

"Let me see," I started doing some quick mental calculations. "Zydek has twenty-two health-care facilities. Assume he's doing false billing, faked visits by doctors, kickbacks from pharmacists and funeral homes, and what else?"

"You tell me, if you're so smart."

"Well, I remember Angie telling me about her Social Security checks being signed over," I said. "To do that, Zydek's lawyers had to go to court and arrange for her to be declared mentally incompetent. As the primary caregiver, Doctor Zydek would automatically be appointed her legal guardian. Not only would he get her Social Security checks, he'd get control of all her assets, including bank accounts, stock holdings, and property."

"It's perfectly legal," Harrison pointed out. "It's called being probated."

"Except when the patients aren't really incompetent, and the reason for getting the declaration is to sell the assets and keep the proceeds. I suspect he did it to a lot of his nursing home patients. And that could add up to a lot of money. Maybe I should revise my figure upward. Ten million dollars?"

"You're getting warmer," Harrison smiled.

"So you stripped Zydek's accounts."

"I was only doing to him what he was doing to his patients."

"You took all of Zydek's money, transferred it to a dummy account, and then faked your own death to cover your tracks."

"It wasn't really Zydek's money," Harrison said. "If anybody had a right to that money, it was me. Until I came along, he was strictly a small-time operator, running a single nursing home in Dickson. I was the one who convinced him to expand. I was the one who told him which facilities to buy. I was the one who showed him how to work the loopholes in the health-care system. I taught him everything he knows."

"And then you left him broke. You took every cent you could lay your hands on."

"Consider it the cost of his tuition. With what I taught him, he could make that money back and a lot more."

"According to the financial reports I saw, he's on the verge of filing for bankruptcy. He's about to lose everything he owns. That's why he's so desperate to find you."

"Maybe I should have killed him," Harrison said with a shrug. "Then he wouldn't be causing me all this trouble."

"Too late for that," I said. "You might be able to elude Zydek's people, but sooner or later, some federal investigator is going to trace that money to you."

"I doubt it," he chuckled, turning away from me to look out the window again.

It was then that I made my move.

Grabbing the obelisk, I lunged towards him.

I shouted at Laura to run.

I knew I was doomed when Harrison turned back to me with a smile, as if he had been anticipating my attack, teasing me into exactly this foolhardy action by deliberately turning away.

He raised the pistol and aimed it at my chest.

The prospect of imminent death often has a distorting effect on temporal perceptions. People who have experienced this phenomena report that time seems to slow down, while thought processes speed up. The strange effect, known as *desynchronization*, is often described by those who experience it as being caught in a slow-motion film. Behavioral scientists theorize it is a psychological defense mechanism, designed to help an individual make split-second decisions in times of mortal danger.

It was an effect I had never experienced before.

Although I was less than ten steps away from Harrison, my feet seemed to be moving with incredible sluggishness. The distance felt insurmountable, even allowing for the apparent suspension of time.

My memory of those terrible moments is more like a series of still photographs than the more commonly described slow-motion film. Every action seemed to be broken into its most basic components.

I watched Harrison's index finger tighten on the trigger. The cylinder began to rotate, moving a cartridge into firing position. The hammer moved backwards, hesitated, and then fell forward. The sharp point of the firing pin struck the cartridge primer with a distinct click, igniting the explosive charge of gunpowder.

A yellow flash burst from the gun barrel.

I could swear I actually saw the slug coming out, a small dark cylinder emerging from the center of the muzzle blast.

I held up my left arm in a foolish attempt to defend myself.

The slug tore through the palm of my hand, and continued on until it slammed into my chest. For such a small piece of lead, it had a surprisingly hard wallop. The impact threw me backward against the wall, where I rested for a moment before sinking to the floor. I can recall the wall behind me feeling wet as I slid down to a sitting position.

Suddenly I was having a difficult time breathing. My left hand fell uselessly at my side. Inexplicably, my right hand still gripped the obelisk. I couldn't stand up. I could barely move my head. Unable to speak, I stared dumbly at Harrison, waiting for him to administer the final and definitive shot.

For some reason, Laura was pounding on Harrison's chest, screaming something that was unintelligible to my gunshot-deafened ears. He slapped her hard, sending her flying across the room. She landed beside me. A trickle of blood came out of her mouth.

"I'm sorry, Theo," she moaned. "I made a terrible mistake."

I didn't have a voice left with which to answer. All I could do was watch as she rose unsteadily to her feet.

"I was supposed to save the man I loved," she said, her battered mouth slurring the words. "All this time, I thought it was Harrison. But I was wrong. It's you I love, Theo, not him."

Harrison was standing in front of the window, his face silhouetted by the morning sunlight.

"Very touching," he said. "But she's not saving anybody."

He aimed the gun at me again, but before he could pull the trigger, Laura was halfway across the room.

She threw herself in front of the gun, screaming out in despair.

"I came back to save Theo, not you."

Another gunshot exploded. I watched in silent horror as Laura's body absorbed the bullet that was intended for me.

Despite her wound, she managed to stumble forward and collapse against Harrison. The momentum of her body knocked him off-balance, sending him crashing against the window. As he broke through the glass, he grabbed wildly for something, anything to hold onto. But all his hands could find was Laura, whose limp body offered him no support.

Locked together in a fatal embrace, they disappeared from sight.

I waited, straining my ears until I heard the awful impact of their bodies, eight stories below.

It was all over.

Laura was dead. Finally and irrevocably dead.

And I was ready to follow.

My mind, which had been struggling with the agony of surviving my wounds, suddenly seemed to break free of its corporeal distractions. The pain in my chest and my hand disappeared. A sense of calm and well-being enveloped me. I felt lucid and alert, and able to think more clearly than I ever believed possible.

This was the strange "moment of peace" which I had heard so many near-deathers describe. It was as if the dying are given one final respite in which, relieved of their pain, they are allowed to contemplate the arrival of death.

These were sacred moments, and I was determined to use them wisely. The teachings of most religions suggest the dying offer up prayers, forgive others, and contemplate or confess their own sins. Perhaps selfishly, I chose to follow the advice of the *Bhagavad Gita*. In those Hindu scriptures, it is written that whatever a man thinks of during his final moments, that alone will he attain in the next life.

There was a time when I would have approached the threshold of death with the scientific curiosity of William James, eager to learn the secrets of the other world.

But there was only one thing I wanted to find on the other side. I concentrated my final thoughts on Laura, and how much I loved her, and how dearly I wanted to be with her throughout eternity.

With her image fixed firmly in my mind, and remembering the taste of her blessed lips on mine, I calmly awaited the end.

It came more easily than I thought.

My last breath came out in a long sigh.

And then I died.

FIFTY-SEVEN

The actual moment of death, that sublime instant when the soul separates itself from the body, is an event seldom recognized at the time it occurs. Invariably, near-deathers report a period of confusion, often describing themselves as staring down at their own bodies. Unaware of their disembodied state, they often attempt in vain to communicate with medical professionals, relatives, or anyone else nearby.

For me, there would be no such confusion. With my background in NDE research, I was far better prepared for the final journey than most people. I was able to approach my own death with the dispassionate curiosity of a researcher, treating it as an opportunity to either vindicate or to disprove Professor DeBray's theories of the afterlife. Knowing what to watch for made it easier to recognize the significance of what was happening to me.

Near-deathers have described the signal the moment the soul leaves the body as a noise—a loud click, a buzzing, or a whirring sound. In my case, it sounded more like a strong wind howling past an open portal. Almost immediately, I felt myself being drawn out of my body, through the traditional gateway of the head. Many cultures, from the Hopis to the Hindus, consider it the only favorable way for the spirit to leave the physical self. The precise point of departure is through a region at the top of the skull called the *fontanelle*. Metaphysical works describe this as the *Brahmanic aperture*.

When I left my body, I felt like a butterfly leaving its cocoon. I drifted slowly upwards, hovering weightlessly near the ceiling. This was the period of *liminality,* the earliest stage of death, in which the spirit stays close to the flesh and is most easily recalled. Some societies, particularly those in East Asia and the South Pacific, believe the spirit may hover near the body for as long as forty-nine days. Except for the absence of the connecting *astral cord,* this stage of death closely resembled the out-of-body experiences first described by the Old Testament prophet Elisha, and documented more recently by the research of Calloway and Monroe.

The self-viewing or autoscopic aspects of the out-of-body experiences have led skeptics in the psychological community to dismiss it as an episode of *transient depersonalization.* But my own experience convinced me those skeptics were wrong. I suffered from none of the underlying conditions which normally trigger *depersonalization,* such as epilepsy or schizophrenia. In addition, my self-viewing took place from a distance of more than six feet.

Unlike typical autoscopic episodes, which involve viewing only a torso, I was able to see my complete figure, from head to toe. I also had the ability to move freely and independently, functioning far beyond the capabilities of a mirror-image reflection of my inert body. I was lucid and alert, with none of the depression or disjointed thoughts associated with *depersonalization.*

In fact, I felt quite happy, even elated. I joked with myself that I was literally "floating on air."

Below me, the body I once occupied had collapsed on its side, its mouth hanging open, one eye staring at the floor, a large red stain spreading from its chest, and the left arm twisted awkwardly behind. It was an unpleasant sight. I found it hard to believe that I had once occupied that limp mass of flesh.

I wondered what happened to Laura, and almost as soon as I thought of her, I was outside the building, looking down at the scene in the street below. I seemed able to go wherever I wanted, instantly, simply by thinking about it. Just as the Mahayana tradition teaches, the limitations of time and space and physical barriers all seemed to dissolve in this intermediate state of being.

The first body I saw was Laura's. She had landed on a red car parked in front of the building. The roof of the car caved in from the force of the impact, forming a nest of metal that cradled her broken and lifeless form. Her head was twisted at an odd angle. Both legs appeared to be broken. During the descent, the wind had pulled her skirt up around her waist, exposing the lower part of her figure. Blood oozed from all of her orifices, collecting in the metallic depression around her. The grisly scene didn't particularly upset me, because I knew Laura was no longer there. The figure on the car was merely her earthly cocoon, from which, like me, she had already departed.

Harrison Duquesne had landed on the sidewalk, with much more hideous results. He must have hit feet first, because part of his body had collapsed upon itself, driving one of his legs up into his stomach. His clothing was ripped open by the explosive flattening of his torso. His head was cracked open, allowing part of his brain to spill out on the dirty concrete.

Interestingly, the gun never made it down to the street. I could see where it came to rest, in a crevice in the concrete arch just above the building entrance.

A black policewoman was already on the scene, speaking into her two-way radio. Sirens blaring, two squad cars approached from opposite directions on Sixty-Third Street, in spite of its one-way configuration. More sirens in the distance announced the imminent arrival of the paramedics.

A curious crowd was already gathering. The policewoman managed to hold them back until the officers from the squad cars cordoned-off the area with yellow crime scene tape.

The EMS vehicle pulled up, but it was obvious to everyone their services wouldn't be needed. I saw Metzger and the Samoans standing behind the tape, watching the activity. When the paramedics placed white plastic privacy sheets over the two corpses, Metzger shook his head and left.

The policewoman was looking up, pointing to the broken eighth floor window. Suddenly the other policemen and one of the paramedics raced into the building. With my new-found ability to penetrate solid walls, I could easily have followed them. But I was bored with watching, and curious to get on with my journey into the afterlife.

It seemed that as soon as I formed that thought, I heard the return of the windy noise that had accompanied my death.

Something seemed to be opening above me.

I felt myself being drawn upward again.

I was moving faster and faster, until the street below, the building, the city itself was out of sight, and I was moving through space with such astonishing speed that the thought occurred to me that Einstein himself would never have been able to calculate the velocity.

I realized I had entered the fabled passageway to The Light, recalled in one form or another by virtually everyone who ever came back from a near-death experience, and celebrated in the prayers of most religions as the "ascension into heaven."

Whether there truly was a heaven, I was about to find out.

At first, I wasn't sure I was actually in The Tunnel, the most common form of ascent, documented in thousands of firsthand reports. I was all alone in an immense black void, hurtling towards what seemed like infinity, with none of the accompanying angels or spirit guides reported by others who made the journey. Unlike my initial out-of-body experience, I no longer had control over what was happening to me. I couldn't change direction or speed, even if I wanted to. As my speed increased, the black void appeared to close in around me until it took on the shape of a perfect cylinder.

In the fifteenth century, the Flemish painter Hieronymous Bosch portrayed The Tunnel as a vast, airy passage, large enough for otherworld travelers to walk upright with their spirit guides beside them. I found my own personal Tunnel to be much narrower than Bosch's, a shaft barely wide enough for my spirit body to make the transit safely. The interior was totally black, and I was being sucked through the vacuum at such incredible speed, I was worried what might happen if I brushed against the walls.

At the end of The Tunnel, as far away from me as the stars are from the earth, glowed the incredible beauty of The Light.

How can I explain the way that wonderful luminescence made me feel?

In all the NDE interviews I ever conducted, the one place where words invariably seemed to fail my subjects was in their attempts to describe The Light.

There was something in its glow that attracted me, that made me feel I wanted to become part of it. It had a warmth that seemed to reach down into The Tunnel, drawing me closer so that I could enter its loving embrace.

Semanticists might question my use of the word "loving" in this context. They would probably prefer a neutral modifier that was more descriptive of the physical properties of The Light, such as "yellow," or "white," or "bright," or "intense." Certainly I could say it was the most brilliant light I ever saw, that it was brighter than a thousand high-intensity carbon-arc searchlights, and that would definitely be true. But it wouldn't come near to approximating the unique nature of The Light. In spite of its intensity, it didn't hurt my eyes. Instead, I found it soothing, calming, welcoming, and to once again use the word that describes it best: loving.

I make no excuses for using so emotional a word.

Everyone who has ever seen and later tried to describe The Light has used similar language. It is the one central feature of all near-death experiences, a mystical illumination whose existence is documented in the written and oral traditions of all cultures and religions.

As usual, modern medical reductionists have a theory to explain away The Light. They attempt to dismiss it as a symptom of *cerebral hypoxia*, a final burst of light that occurs in the brain when the supply of oxygen is cut off. The comparison is made to a light bulb that gives off one last brilliant flash before it burns out, or the final dot of light on a TV screen when the power goes off. But if that were true, The Light would have been extinguished when I reached the end of The Tunnel. If the reductionists were correct, all awareness should have ceased. Everything should have gone black.

But the reductionists were wrong.

The Light didn't disappear. It grew larger and brighter, taking on a hypnotic quality that seemed to fill my mind. Like those who made the journey before me, I felt I was being drawn to the Source of All Love, and all that mattered to me was reaching it, to be in its presence and bask in its glory. I wanted, in Betty Eadie's famous words, to be "embraced by The Light."

Before I could hope to reach that mystic moment, however, I knew I would have to journey much deeper into the afterlife.

The path I had to follow was a well-documented one. Like the ancient explorers whose journeys into the unknown inspired the first crude maps of the world, previous voyagers to the other side brought back descriptions of the route to be traveled and the sights along the way. What I saw when I emerged from The Tunnel confirmed the accuracy of those accounts.

I found myself on a hillside, overlooking a landscape of dazzling incandescence. There was no sun in the sky, but everything I saw was bathed in the same strange and beautiful light that drew me through The Tunnel. Below me was spread a valley of incredible beauty, lined with golden meadows and flowering slopes. Through the center of the valley flowed a clear, sparkling river, whose banks were bordered with lush stands of trees. In the eighth century, Venerable Bede described this region as "the antechamber to heaven." The Ancient Greeks labeled it the Elysian Fields. The Tibetans call it the World of Clear Light. The near-deathers I interviewed had no name for it but considered it the most beautiful place they had ever seen.

The artists and poets of the Renaissance, more than those of any other era, concentrated their genius on this part of the afterworld. As magnificent as their works once seemed to me, I could see now what dismal failures they actually were, what pale imitations they produced. They were, after all, doomed by palettes of earthly colors and vocabularies of mortal words.

With such limitations, how could anyone accurately portray the wonders of Paradise?

Perhaps the most remarkable aspect of the landscape was the rich saturation of color with which every object was imbued. I had the impression that some sort of filter had been removed from in front of my eyes, allowing me to see hues and tints that never existed in the world I left behind. These were the true colors of Utopia, radiant hues that resembled gemstones in their lustre and brilliance. Leafs and flowers and individual blades of grass sparkled and gleamed, reflecting the intensity of The Light in a way no earthly vegetation could. It helped me understand the source of the strange imagery in Moslem accounts of the Pure Land of Amitahbe, where plants were described as flowering with precious stones.

One of the key elements of the death journey is the guide, a spiritual companion who leads the newly-deceased towards The Being of Light. Although medieval testimony invariably portrayed the guide as the Angel Gabriel, modern near-deathers are usually escorted by the spirit of a deceased friend or relative.

In my case, I felt the most appropriate guide would have been my former mentor, Professor DeBray. His presence would have made for a dramatic reunion, and I know he would have enjoyed explaining the mysteries of death to me.

But any reunion with DeBray would have to wait.

The guide with whom I had been provided was all the proof I needed that, this day, I truly was in Paradise.

FIFTY-EIGHT

She came to me from across the golden meadow, clothed in a long gown of an ethereal white material which floated weightlessly in the breeze. Her movements were slow and graceful. The grass seemed to part before her feet, as if it had the ability to anticipate her every step.

I stood transfixed.

This radiant being, this seraphic entity sent to guide me through the afterlife, was none other than my beloved Laura.

It was my first encounter with anyone in the noncorporeal state, that part of us which survives bodily death, and whose true nature has been consistently misrepresented in the popular culture. Centuries of folklore, fiction and fraud have portrayed the spirit world as a bizarre collection of restless ghosts, floating strands of ectoplasm, transparent figures, foul odors, shifting shapes of mist and fog, disembodied voices and dozens of other often frightening inventions.

As Laura came nearer, I could clearly see how mistaken such superstitious speculations were.

She was a phantasm, of course, but one which generally conformed to that mystical ideal to which all the world's major religions subscribe. Theologians express the concept as *Somatomorphism:* the soul imitating the body. But in Laura's case, that shape of air and light was more than a perfect reproduction; it represented the true glory of the human soul, undiminished by any labefactions of the flesh.

She appeared younger and happier than I remembered, and, if I dare use the word in this context: healthier. It was an idealized version of the Laura I knew who stood before me. This wasn't the frightened and disillusioned young woman who, in one last heroic act, sacrificed her own life in a futile effort to save mine. No. This was a more innocent, even virginal Laura, the way she must have looked before she was first despoiled by Harrison Duquesne.

Gazing upon her luminous face, I realized that the love I felt for her had not only survived death itself, but had actually grown stronger. Without saying a word, somehow she managed to communicate to me that she felt the same way, that now, released by death from her marital vows, she was finally free to love me, too.

It was all I could ever want from Heaven: to spend eternity with the woman I loved.

She beckoned for me to follow, and I knew instantly where we were going.

She was taking me deeper into the afterlife, where I was to confront the greatest mystery of all.

I followed eagerly.

We proceeded along a path barely wide enough for the two of us. One side was lined with a majestic forest of dark green pine trees; on the other side the golden meadow sloped downhill. Gradually, I became aware of other white-robed figures on the hillside. There were men and women walking in pairs, children running happily through the fields, small groups gathered beneath the trees. Some of them looked at me and waved.

I recognized my grandparents, whom I knew only from photographs taken when they were young. They died in their native Greece, long before I was born. Yet they recognized me immediately, and although I'm certain they spoke no English, I had no trouble understanding them.

"You're not supposed to be here," said my grandfather, obviously puzzled by my presence.

My grandmother, a much smaller woman than her husband, shook her head and said: "I didn't think it was time for you, Theo."

Behind them stood my mother, who also seemed puzzled to see me there. I started to move towards her, wanting to kiss her cheek the way I used to do when I was a child. But Laura quickly intervened. Apparently touching wasn't allowed at this stage.

A little further down the path, I saw Professor DeBray.

If he didn't call out to me, I might not have recognized him without his vested suit. He, too, appeared younger, and while not quite thin, at least looked to be in better physical shape than when I knew him on earth. It was a relief to see that he bore no trace of the terrible violence that had been done to his body.

"You're early," the Professor said. "You can't be finished with your work yet."

Laura moved me gently along, silently discouraging me from any further conversation with him.

The narrow road turned uphill, leading around a curve beyond which glowed a strange and powerful light.

There were so many questions I wanted to ask her, but through some strange form of mystical discourse, we seemed able to transmit information between each other instantaneously, without the need for forming words. Answers to my queries appeared in my consciousness as fast as I thought of the questions. It was almost as if the answers to everything I wanted to know about the world and the universe were already in my mind, and it was simply a matter of my remembering them.

What I was experiencing was the fabled memory of forgotten knowledge. In the legends of the Hasidic Jews, the secrets of the universe are revealed to infants in the womb, but are forgotten at birth. The recovery of this lost self-knowledge is reported by many near-deathers. In fact, the concept of Forgotten Truths is reflected in the philosophy of almost every religious group, and forms the basis of the spiritual reawakening advocated by them.

For an academic like me, a man who so treasured the acquisition of knowledge, this phase represented one of the most exciting aspects of my journey.

It didn't happen suddenly, in one blinding revelation. Rather, it unfolded gradually, as if the strange light ahead was illuminating portions of my mind that had long been cloaked in darkness. This continuing accretion of mental capacity grew stronger as the light grew brighter. With each step I took on that path, I felt my consciousness expanding.

Soon I knew, I *really knew,* the answers to questions that had puzzled me all my life. I remembered the moment I was born, and I could see the births of my parents and their parents before them. Vast libraries of data raced through my mind, from esoteric mathematical formulae that quantum physicists still didn't understand, to more mundane matters such as the account numbers of the banks in the Bahamas and New York where Harrison Duquesne had hidden the money he stole.

In a stunning burst of knowledge, all of history was revealed to me, from long before man ever set foot on earth. I understood the origins of every creature on the planet, and every star in the farthest reaches of the farthest universe.

By the time the full glow of The Light was shining upon me, I understood the secrets of the Universe. I held the key to mysteries that have puzzled scientists and philosophers throughout the ages. I could look into the future as easily as the past.

But the greatest mystery of all still lay ahead.

Glowing with an intensity so incredible that I was at first convinced it would burn away the pupils of my eyes, was what appeared to be the source of all light in this preternatural world. It was the same unearthly light I had first seen in The Tunnel, the wondrous glow I had seen reflected in the tiniest blades of grass, the radiant energy that illuminated Laura's very being. If we were walking in the rarefied photosphere on the surface of the sun itself, we could not have been surrounded with a light more brilliant. And yet, amazingly, this otherworldly light didn't hurt my eyes. It seemed restful and soothing. I felt its energy suffusing my body, filling me with warmth and wonder and love, drawing me on, inviting me closer, instilling within me an irresistible urge to lose myself within its wondrous embrace.

There seemed to be a central area, a golden nucleus of some sort that was even brighter, if that is possible, than the surrounding area. I thought I saw a shape, but it kept shifting, and it was impossible to tell whether it resembled a human form or not.

Many near-deathers, including not only those with religious backgrounds, but also those who claimed, before their NDEs, to be atheists, describe this encounter as the point at which they found themselves looking upon the Face of God.

Here, as in every other aspect of this account, I must be completely factual. I can't honestly claim that I saw a face, or even anything that vaguely resembled a face.

But this Light which embraced me was so glorious, so almighty, so all-powerful, it could only be that mystical illumination which the oral and written histories of mankind describe as The Light of the World.

And if that was so, then I was here to be judged.

I had arrived at what is certainly the single most critical point in the death journey.

Laura had detached herself from my side, leaving me to stand alone before the Being of Light.

Without actually looking at her, I was aware that Laura had retreated to a bridge of some sort. Although I couldn't see the river it spanned, I knew exactly where we were. The ancient Persians called it the *Chinvato Peretu,* which translates roughly as the Bridge of the Separator. Although most modern Christians have grown up with cartoonish ideas of "the Pearly Gates," such portrayals are religious myths which are as naive as the Christmas travels of Santa Claus. In actual fact, the eschatological traditions of most cultures, including the early Roman Catholic community, recognize a bridge as the final barrier between the living and the dead.

Near-deathers who have traveled this far confirm the existence of the bridge, although their descriptions of this final barrier often vary. In modern NDE research, there is no documented case of anyone ever returning to life after having crossed the bridge.

It is normally at this point, at the entrance to the bridge, that the Life Review takes place. The deeds of the soul are weighed here in the balance before the final, irrevocable decision is made.

Some near-deathers have described the Life Review as seeing their entire life laid out at one time, much like looking at a panoramic vista of a mountain range and being able to see not only the individual peaks and valleys, but also specific rocks and trees on the slopes.

Others have said they saw not only their own actions, but the impact each action had on everyone else who was affected by it. They have described the review as resembling a hologram, a TV documentary, a series of still photographs. Some viewed it from a distance, and some said they actually relived their lives.

I never understood these descriptive discrepancies until my own Life Review took place. That was when I learned that all the descriptions are correct, and yet they are all inadequate. The Review is everything everyone has ever said about it, and more. In a world where time is no longer a linear concept, I discovered events of the distant past had as much immediacy as those of the present.

Every action I had ever taken in my life, everything I ever said, thought or did, was happening to me all over again, all at the same time. The most embarrassing private actions, things I would have been too ashamed ever to share with anyone, were right there beside the most commonplace routines of daily life. Were they really happening to me all over again, or was I recalling them with a stunningly enhanced memory? It was impossible to tell. Yet despite the overwhelming experiential complexity of the Review, I was able to examine each event to evaluate its moral value.

What I was doing was nothing less than reliving a lifetime, and finally understanding what it meant.

At the end of the Life Review, I came to those final moments when I lay dying, watching Laura take the bullet that was intended for me. With my new-found wisdom I finally understood what she really meant by her last words: "It was you I was sent back to save."

In the self-centered manner so typical of mortal beings, I had originally misinterpreted the message. My mind clouded with thoughts of unrequited love, I had focused too narrowly on the romantic aspects of her words. How superficial we humans can be, even at the moment of our death!

In the enlightened state I now enjoyed, I was able to look beyond myself and finally, completely understand not only why she sacrificed her life for me, but why she made her first trip back from Eternity.

Yes, she loved me. Happily, that part was true. But I could see we were only part of a continuum that could be traced back, like Ariadne's thread, to that first anonymous cave-dweller who came back from the dead to tell the strange story of an otherworld journey.

Kings and philosophers, saints and scientists, and uncounted thousands of ordinary people have made the journey since then, expanding humanity's knowledge of the afterlife with their subsequent reports. The territory has been accurately, if not definitively, mapped. The major landmarks have been identified. The hereafter is no longer *terra incognita*.

But the great explorers of the natural world have always brought back proof of their discoveries: silk from China, gold and silver from the New World, spices from the South Pacific, rocks from the moon.

Proof of the afterlife. That was what Professor DeBray and every other chronicler of the near-death experience had been seeking. Although unwilling to admit it openly, that was what I myself had been after all along. Vacillating between belief and disbelief in the concept that the NDE is a preview of life after death, I had wanted to settle the dispute once and for all.

And that, more than getting shot by Harrison, was the ultimate tragedy of my life on earth.

In those final moments, I had in my grasp tangible proof of the afterlife, only to have it die with me. Laura's claim that Harrison was still alive was so contrary to all the available evidence that no one believed her. And yet, it was that very impossibility that would have given her story such impact with the public. Unfortunately, the confirmation of her claim was delivered to me by the very instrument of my death, too late for me to share it with the world.

I could sense that Laura was as saddened by this failure as I was. It was, after all the reason she had originally come back from the dead. Call it metaphysical psychology if you will, but in the presence of The Light, I was blessed with an understanding of motivations that would have forever been beyond human comprehension.

How preposterous it was to think that Laura was forced to leave the bliss of Paradise and return to earth to suffer Zydek's torture, unless some noble purpose was involved. I couldn't conceive that meeting me was a particularly noble event, although the celibacy of our love elevated it to a more sacred level.

There was only one purpose noble enough to merit our relationship. My background and training had uniquely qualified me for the role of Laura's Authenticator, the person who recognized the legitimacy of her proof and could present it to a credulous world.

In the convoluted warping of time that occurs on the astral plane, my role and Laura's eventual relationship with me were probably revealed to her the first time she died. But as the Midrashic legends suggest, such celestial revelations of future events fade away when the spirit returns to the flesh. Only dim fragments of that part of the revelation remained when she was revived, leaving her with the mistaken belief that it was her husband she was sent back to save.

For the briefest of instants, the most miniscule of miniseconds, the thought crossed my mind that I hadn't yet accomplished the mission for which she sacrificed her life.

But in that infinitesimal fraction of time, the damage was done.

The light began to recede.

In a sudden panic, I realized I was being sent back.

I didn't want to go.

Having seen Nirvana, I wanted to stay here, beside my beloved Laura.

I turned to her for help. She had withdrawn to the other side of the bridge. When I tried to approach her, she raised her hands to stop me.

Something had changed between us. The telepathic bond was broken. We had to communicate with words, like ordinary mortals.

"It isn't your time," she said. Her voice had a silvery, ethereal quality. "You must go back."

"I want to stay here," I said.

"You still have work to do."

"I don't want to go back," I protested. "I want to stay with you."

"You must tell people what awaits them."

"They won't believe me. They didn't believe you. I need some kind of proof."

She gave me an enigmatic smile.

"You are the proof, Theo. That is why you must go back."

"But I don't want to leave you."

She reached out her hands to me, but she was already fading from sight.

"I'll be here, my darling," she said. "I'll be waiting for you."

Those were the last words I heard her say before she disappeared.

I felt a sudden jolt and opened my eyes to see the ceiling of the Duquesne apartment. A black man was staring down at me.

"He's back!" the man shouted. "We saved him!"

FIFTY-NINE

I tried to scream, to vent my rage at being separated from Laura, but all that emerged from my mouth was a low moan.

"Welcome back to life," the paramedic said.

They put me on a gurney and rushed me out to a waiting ambulance. An IV bag was quickly hooked up to my right arm, and a plastic bag filled with what looked like blood plasma was connected to my left arm. My chest felt numb. I had no idea what they had done to get me breathing again, but my lungs seemed to be functioning again, although painfully. An oxygen mask was strapped over my mouth, and I could feel the cold metal tank resting on the gurney beside me.

"You're going to be okay now," the paramedic assured me. "Just hang in there, pal."

How could I tell him I didn't want to be kept alive? That I resented their attempts to prevent me from returning to the other side? The anger and frustration I felt was the normal response for those of us who have been taken up into the loving embrace of Paradise, only to be returned against our will to the miseries of the world of the flesh.

"I thought he was dead," I heard one of the policemen say as I was loaded into the ambulance.

"He was," the paramedic responded. "No pulse. No breathing. Full cardiac arrest. But we brought him back. He's damn lucky we got here when we did."

I remember thinking the comment was so typical of the self-important attitude of medical personnel: arrogantly assuming that their intervention was solely responsible for bringing a patient back from the dead. Only in the rarest cases would any of them be willing to admit there might be other, more mystical forces at work.

I began to drift in and out of consciousness. I vaguely remember being unloaded from the ambulance. The pain in my chest was getting worse. People were shouting instructions around me, but I didn't understand what they were saying. All I wanted was to be allowed to die again, so that I could once more be reunited with Laura.

I remember waking up in surgery. The bright overhead lights hurt my eyes. A half-dozen frowning people in green sterile outfits were staring down at me. I felt no pain, the anaesthesia having accomplished at least that part of its work. The only sounds in the room were the hushed comments of doctors and the occasional metallic clink of a surgical instrument being discarded. I closed my eyes, hoping the surgeons would fail in their task, that my heart would stop, my breathing would cease, and my spirit would once again separate itself from my body.

But it wasn't to be.

The next time I woke up, I was lying in bed in a semi-private hospital room. The other bed was empty. Morning sunlight streamed through the window. Looking down at me with unsmiling curiosity was a young man wearing a white medical tunic. He had a flat, moon-shaped face and stiff black hair with no sideburns. His name tag identified him as Doctor Leon Chang.

"You're a very lucky man," he finally said. "For a while there, we weren't sure you'd make it."

"How long was I dead?" I asked.

Doctor Chang gave me a suspicious look.

"Who said anything about you being dead?"

"I was in full cardiac arrest when the paramedics found me. I know I was dead. I just want to know how long I was gone."

"You were never pronounced dead," Doctor Chang said.

"Did you talk to the paramedics?"

"Paramedics don't have the authority to make that determination."

"I know what happened to me," I insisted. "I know the signs. I stopped breathing and I died."

"What happened to you was a gunshot wound to the chest," he said, slipping behind the protective wall of diagnostic jargon. "The bullet shattered your third rib. It missed the major arteries, but it still caused quite a bit of internal bleeding. Part of the rib punctured the pleural cavity, which is the lining between the lungs and the chest wall. That's what affected your breathing. We managed to repair the damage, but you'll have a tube in your chest for the next few days."

"You don't understand," I said. "I really died. My body was dead, but my spirit was still alive. I sort of floated up and I could look down and see my body." Hearing myself, I realized how bizarre it all sounded. Yet I felt a compulsion to describe what happened to me. "Then I went through a long black tunnel towards a brilliant light...."

"You're still a little delirious from the anaesthesia." Doctor Chang brushed off my comments. "What you're describing is a very common hallucination that occurs during periods of oxygen deprivation. That's what happened in your case. It's nothing to worry about. Just be happy you're still alive."

I guess I shouldn't have been surprised by Doctor Chang's unwillingness to take my comments seriously. Most near-deathers report encountering a similar lack of interest and often even derisive comments when they attempt to describe their experiences to their doctors.

I must have lost consciousness again, because the next time I opened my eyes, I found myself looking at a different visitor. He introduced himself as the hospital chaplain, a thin young priest in a Roman collar who obviously patterned himself after the 16th century Spanish clerics painted by El Greco. He had a carefully-trimmed mustache, and a beard that brought his chin to an elongated point. The top of his head was shaved. Circling his skull just above the ears was a thin band of brown hair, cut in the traditional tonsure seldom seen today outside of monasteries. His ascetic appearance suggested a clergyman with conservative views.

But appearances, even in priests, can be deceiving. Father Jack, as he wanted to be called, was a modern priest. Presenting himself as more of a social worker than a proselytizer, he was more interested in lifting spirits than in saving souls.

Like Doctor Chang, he refused to accept that I had actually experienced death. When I explained how my spirit had separated itself from my body and rose towards The Light, he smiled and wondered aloud if perhaps I was taking the Bible too literally. When I told him about the Being of Light and the overwhelming feelings of love and goodness I experienced in its presence, he mouthed some platitudes about the universal human need for love and affection. When I told him how wonderful it felt to be reunited with Laura, he agreed it was everyone's dream to be reunited after death with their loved ones. Never once, however, did he admit there was any possibility that I was describing an event that really happened.

His continued unwillingness to believe my account wasn't entirely unexpected. Other near-deathers reported similar responses from Catholic and Protestant clergy.

Therein lay a paradox that I couldn't get this priest to discuss: how could a religion whose very cornerstone is the death and resurrection of a human being two thousand years ago, and whose most sacred texts tell of so many others who returned from the dead, so cavalierly dismiss the claims of modern near-death survivors? Particularly when their experiences offer such compelling confirmation of the Biblical descriptions of the afterlife?

Perhaps my questions would have been taken more seriously by one of those bearded Greek Orthodox patriarchs I remembered from my youth, one of those austere Old Believers who clung tenaciously to the authentic roots of his faith.

Resenting Father Jack's unwillingness to discuss what I considered questions of profound doctrinal implications, I quickly drew dismissive of him.

What a shame the modern Church should take such an intellectually, if not theologically, dishonest attitude, I told him. He seemed to visibly shrink back, appalled by my outburst. He probably couldn't decide whether I was a harmless lunatic or a dangerous heretic.

I suggested to him that near-deathers should be welcomed as modern prophets, since the visions of Heaven which they bring back from their mystical journeys appear to be every bit as legitimate, and filled with the same exhortations to love one another, as the visions of the most revered of the ancient prophets.

Such comments to a Catholic priest would have earned me death by torture a few hundred years ago. But I was dealing with a modern priest, one who probably didn't even have enough strength of faith to accuse anyone of blasphemy, much less call down the wrath of God upon a sinner. So I blithely went on, comparing theologians who remain mute on the subject of NDEs to the chief priests and elders in Pilate's tribunal, both groups jealously guarding their positions of privilege from the threat posed by anyone who might profess to have been in closer contact with God than they were.

Father Jack had no answers, of course. All he had were the same tired old feel-good cliches that are taught in seminary psychology classes.

Talking to him was pointless, I decided. Worn out by my diatribe, I closed my eyes and pretended to be overcome by the medication. I heard the priest leave almost immediately. He was probably glad to avoid any further dialogue on a subject that obviously made him very uncomfortable.

I was beginning to understand why so many near-deathers are reluctant to discuss their experiences. If the very people who traditionally stand at the entrances and exits of the mortal world were so unwilling to accept my account, then who would believe me?

The problem of credibility has confronted near-deathers since the first human returned from the dead. It is easy, of course, to dismiss the claims of otherwise ordinary individuals, such as those I interviewed for Professor DeBray. But even the most divine beings who walked the earth were not immune from the challenge of skeptics who questioned their claims of having visited Paradise. Thomas doubted Jesus, and the Prophet Muhammad was asked to supply proof before his followers would believe him.

While I dare not compare myself to figures of such monumental religious significance, I faced a similar credibility problem. But I had no open wound in my side for disbelievers to touch, no sacred text from Allah for the dubious to examine.

Other than my own testimony, what proof could I offer that I had truly penetrated the veil of mortality?

The answer, I was convinced, must lie in what I had learned on my afterlife journey.

I tried to remember the details of that moment of incandescent revelation, when, standing before the Being of Light, my mind was flooded with staggering amounts of knowledge. I had become privy to everything that man had ever hungered to know. I remembered learning the secrets of the Universe, seeing the flow of past and future history, and understanding the inner workings of the master plan for the planet Earth. It was knowledge beyond the scope of any human mind, and if I could only articulate one small part of it, surely I could convince anyone I had been to the other side.

But as so many near-deathers before me had discovered, such knowledge cannot be transferred between the two realities. All that remained in my memory were shards and fragments, no better than scattered bits of pottery in an ancient cave. A few fragments, such as the location of Harrison's bank accounts, might prove helpful. But most of what I remembered were details of the journey itself, the very aspect of the NDE that elicits the greatest skepticism.

In what appeared to be the ultimate form of role-reversal, I had become one of those enigmatic beings I once studied. I was now the prototypical near-deather, unshakeable in the belief that my afterlife experience was a reality, and resistant to all attempts to explain it away as some sort of delusion or hallucination.

It was a path I had not chosen.

And as I was soon to discover, it was filled with dangers I could not have foreseen.

SIXTY

They showed up at my bedside shortly before noon.

There were two of them, NYPD detectives in civilian clothing. They introduced themselves with the feigned politeness commonly employed by the police in their often futile efforts to obtain the cooperation of suspects.

The taller one, Detective Oliver Bascomb, was thirtyish, thin and hollow-cheeked, with a pock-marked face. He overcompensated for the facial blemishes by maintaining a meticulously well-groomed appearance, with long, blow-dried hair, stylish designer eyeglasses, a custom-tailored chalk-striped suit, mirror-polished black shoes and a tailored raincoat. He looked more like a lawyer than a policeman.

The shorter one, Detective Francis Wiorkowski, was younger, pink-cheeked and open-faced, his smile revealing a gap between his front teeth. He was the one who shook my hand, and made a joke about the tube in my chest. He was casually dressed, wearing blue jeans topped off with a well-worn brown tweed jacket that could no longer be buttoned across his ample stomach.

It was Bascomb who recited the Miranda warning, trying his best to sound bored, as if it was some trivial drivel unworthy of my attention. I had to admire the ease with which he attempted to downplay the danger his warning represented. Perhaps I should have refused to say anything further, but since I was innocent of any crime, I felt I had nothing to fear.

"Let's start out with Professor Pierre DeBray," Wiorkowski said, giving me a friendly smile. He sprawled himself comfortably in the green vinyl visitor's chair, looping one foot over the wooden arm. "Do you want to tell us what happened?"

"I didn't kill him," I said.

"But you know he's dead, don't you?" Still friendly, still smiling, as if we were talking about the weather.

"I read about it in the newspapers," I said, afraid to admit that I had actually seen the corpse. Technically, what I said wasn't really a lie. During my long conversation with Milton, he had shown me a copy of the New York Post describing the discovery.

"Do you know where we found him?" Wiorkowski asked.

"According to the newspapers, his body was left in my apartment."

"That's right, Theo." He smiled at his own transparent attempt at friendliness. "You don't mind if I call you Theo, do you?"

"I don't mind, Frank."

"Why didn't you come forward when you read about it, Theo?" Somehow he managed to make the question sound perfectly harmless. I wondered how many suspects had fallen for his Officer Friendly routine. "Why didn't you give us a call? We've been looking for you for a couple of days already."

Behind him, Bascomb leaned against a wall, watching me with his intense dark eyes, waiting for me to make a mistake so that he could pounce.

"I assumed whoever killed the Professor left the body in my apartment in a crude attempt to incriminate me," I said. "I was sure the police were smart enough to see that."

"You worked for DeBray, didn't you?" Wiorkowski's voice took on a slightly harder tone. They must have gotten the information from the Professor's files.

"Yes," I said. "But he was more than just my employer. I considered him a very good friend."

"From what we hear, he was the only friend you had," Bascomb interjected in a hostile voice. "We ran a check on you, Mr. Nikonos. You're pretty much a loner. Divorced. Fired from your last two jobs. Filed for bankruptcy. Landlord says you're two months behind on the rent."

"I've been going through a difficult period. But I guess you already know that."

"You were lucky you had a rich friend like DeBray," Bascomb said. "We talked to his sister in Connecticut. She said he had a best-selling book a few years ago, and he earned a six-figure income on the lecture circuit."

"The Professor found an area of specialization that fascinated the general public," I said.

"I bet you must have been a little jealous of him," Bascomb continued his attack mode.

"Not jealous," I said. "The word would be grateful. Professor DeBray was very good to me. He gave me a job when no one else would."

"You ever argue with him about money?" Bascomb asked.

"Never," I said. "He paid me well enough for what I did."

"But it wasn't enough for you to live on, was it? You were behind in your rent."

"The money was getting better. I was doing more work for him."

"You told him you needed more money," Bascomb quickly theorized, demonstrating just how simplistic his thought processes were. "He refused, so you killed him."

"I already told you I didn't kill the Professor. He was my friend."

"Help us out here, Theo," Wiorkowski edged his way back into the questioning, resuming his role of the friendly cop. "The medical examiner estimates DeBray was murdered about a week before we found the body. We have statements from your neighbors who heard shouts from your apartment and what sounded to them like furniture being knocked over on a particular night that week. That establishes the probable time of death as Tuesday night, April twentieth. Do you mind telling us what you were doing on the night of the twentieth?"

"I was in the Poconos, up in Pennsylvania. I was staying in a motel, the Mountain Lake Motor Lodge. You can check their records. I stayed there for a week."

"That's only a two-hour drive from the City, Theo. Do you have any witnesses who can confirm you were actually in the Poconos that night? I hope you're not going to tell us you were alone in that motel room?"

"No, I wasn't alone. I was there with Laura Duquesne."

"The dead woman?" Wiorkowski asked, raising an eyebrow.

"Yes."

Still leaning against the wall, Bascomb grinned and wrote something in his notebook.

"Okay, so you have an alibi that can't be confirmed," Wiorkowski said. He was still trying to be the Good Cop, but there was now a colder gleam in his eyes. "You want to tell us the nature of your relationship with Miss Duquesne?"

"Mrs. Duquesne," I corrected him. "The man who shot me was her husband, Harrison Duquesne."

The two detectives exchanged significant glances with each other.

"So it was a lover's quarrel," Bascomb said, leaping immediately to another faulty conclusion. "That would explain the missing gun. Angry husband comes in and starts shooting, the wife and the other guy go out the window, this guy's bleeding on the floor, and the husband takes off. We'd better send out an APB on the husband."

Wiorkowski nodded his agreement. It was frightening how rapidly these two detectives could come up with such astoundingly wrong hypotheses.

"Can you give us a description of this Harrison Duquesne?" Wiorkowski asked me.

"He's the one who landed on the sidewalk," I said.

Again they exchanged glances, but this time Bascomb was shaking his head.

"The man on the sidewalk was Arthur Hamilton," Bascomb said. "He was identified from his driver's license and credit cards."

"That's a phony identity." I said.

"We've already been to his apartment," Bascomb said. "He had a one-bedroom place, down in the East Village."

"I'm telling you, it's a phony identity. The man was a psychopath. His real name was Harrison Duquesne."

"That's impossible," Bascomb growled. "The man on the sidewalk was Arthur Hamilton. He had a wallet full of credit cards and a New York State driver's license."

"Anybody could get those under a phony name," I said.

"We checked out his apartment," Wiorkowski said. "According to the landlord, he's been living there for almost six years. When we searched the place, we found a ten-year-old passport issued in the name of Arthur Hamilton. We found checking statements, mutual fund records, even copies of his tax returns. Some of the stuff dated back before he rented the apartment. Arthur Hamilton is a real person, Theo."

I was momentarily stunned. All this time I had been working on the assumption that Harrison Duquesne had created a phony identity that he could slip into after the accident. But now I could see that theory was wrong. It was Arthur Hamilton who had created the phony identity. The persona of Harrison Duquesne was a sham. Every document that supported his identity, from the birth certificate in his safety deposit box to his driver's license to his marriage certificate to his condominium mortgage, was obtained fraudulently, and was therefore invalid. The yellow envelope Laura had described to me, the one whose contents Harrison/Hamilton protected so carefully, probably contained documents supporting his real identity.

"I made a mistake," I said, shaking my head in disbelief at how thoroughly I had been misled.

"You sure did," Bascomb said. "The first mistake you made was killing Pierre DeBray. Your second mistake was lying to us about Arthur Hamilton."

"You don't understand," I groaned.

"Why don't you tell us the truth?" Wiorkowski said. "Tell us what you're trying to cover up, Theo."

SIXTY-ONE

One of the basic goals of a skilled interrogator is to elicit statements from the suspect that are contrary to the facts of the case. Whether the result of honest mistakes or desperate lies, such contradictory statements can be used with devastating effect in court to impugn the credibility of whatever else the suspect might say.

And that was the situation in which I now found myself.

After having cut through a seemingly impenetrable maze of carefully planned deceptions, it galled me to find myself enmeshed in the one last obfuscation Harrison/Hamilton had left behind.

Unfortunately, I had fallen into his final trap in the presence of the police. Whatever I said now would be tainted by my foolish insistence that Arthur Hamilton was an alter ego, a false identity created by Harrison Duquesne.

In fact, I now realized, it was the other way around. It explained the one fact that I had not yet been able to answer: why would so unemotional an individual as Harrison Duquesne ever want to get married? For me, the last piece of the puzzle fell into place. It was as much part of his deception as the money he purposely left behind in his safe and his bank vault. It had fooled me as easily as it fooled Laura.

"Don't you see?" I tried to explain. "If Arthur Hamilton was a real person, then Harrison Duquesne must be the phony identity he created."

"Oh, Christ," Bascomb muttered.

"No, I'm serious. If you try to trace back Harrison Duquesne's identity, I'm sure you'll find he never existed until a few years ago."

Wiorkowski was rolling his eyes and shaking his head in disbelief.

"I told you the man was a psychopath," I said. "He planned this all out very carefully, and he killed everyone who got in his way."

"Except you," Bascomb said, with a heavy touch of sarcasm.

"We talked to Hamilton's neighbors." Wiorkowski said. "They told us he was a normal, friendly kind of guy. Very outgoing, a Knicks fan. Even if I believed you about this phony identity stuff, Hamilton sure doesn't fit the profile of a psychopathic murderer. Everyone we talked to said they liked the man, and were sorry to hear he was dead."

"That's exactly what I'd expect them to say," I told him. "If you talk to your police psychiatrist, you'll find out most psychopaths present a friendly and even charming personality. They're smart, talkative, and totally without conscience. That's what makes them such brilliant con men."

"Spare us the psychology crap," Bascomb said drily. "We took some of the same college courses you did."

"If you'd listen to what I'm trying to tell you, you could solve three murders, not one," I fumed, infuriated by his condescension. "And you could also recover over ten million dollars in embezzled funds."

I don't think it was my comment about solving murders that got their attention. They already seemed pretty certain they had their perpetrator. What got them to listen was the mention of the ten million dollars.

Wiorkowski quickly took up the interrogation again.

"Okay, Theo, let's assume for a moment you're right, that Harrison Duquesne and Arthur Hamilton are the same man. Why would he need two identities?"

"Because he was a con man, a psychopath, and a murderer. Harrison Duquesne was an alias Hamilton used when he helped a doctor named Zydek set up a major health-care fraud that operated in three states. But he never planned to share the profits with his partner. He planned all along to empty the accounts and take all the money for himself."

I realized I was talking rapidly, but I desperately wanted to convince them of Hamilton's guilt. If I failed, their next stop would be at the district attorney's office, where formal murder charges would be drawn up against me.

"Hamilton knew if he stole the money, he wouldn't have to worry about his partner calling in the police," I explained. "Zydek would be afraid Hamilton would turn on him and testify about the health-care scam in exchange for immunity. But with the amount of money involved, Hamilton also knew his partner would do anything to find him, maybe even hire a hit-man. Zydek would never stop looking for Hamilton until he was dead. So Hamilton decided the best way out was to fake his own death."

"And when was that supposed to have happened?" Wiorkowski asked, disbelief still evident in his voice.

"In October of last year," I said. "Hamilton staged an accident in Pennsylvania, near the town where the health-care scam originated. He found someone who could match the description of Harrison Duquesne, put him behind the steering wheel, doused the car with gasoline, and sent it off a three-hundred foot cliff. That was murder number one. It fooled the police into thinking the man who died in the crash was Harrison Duquesne. To make it even more convincing, his wife was supposed to have died in the same accident. Everything worked out just as he planned, except that his wife survived."

"The wife, that would be Laura Duquesne?" Wiorkowski asked, his voice flat and noncommittal, wanting me to keep talking, but never once acknowledging that he believed me.

"That's right," I said. "I think he had his plan worked out before he married her."

"You're saying that's why he married her, so he could kill her?"

"Yes. I'm certain of it. All Laura meant to him was a piece of evidence that could make his death more believable. She didn't have any living relatives, nobody to ask any embarrassing questions later on."

"Sounds pretty far-fetched to me," Bascomb said.

"It worked," I said. "He managed to fool everybody about his death. Except for Laura. When she recovered, she was convinced he didn't die in the accident. She asked me to help find him . . . and that's what I did."

"She wanted revenge."

"No. She was in love with him." I paused, remembering the amazingly misplaced fidelity she maintained throughout our search for Harrison. "Really in love."

"Then she wanted the money."

"She didn't know about the money," I said. "She didn't even know her husband tried to kill her. All she wanted to do was to find him."

"You didn't say how she found out he was still alive," Bascomb said.

"She had a near-death experience."

"A what?"

"A near-death experience. They rushed her to the hospital after the accident, but she died on the operating table. That's when she found out her husband was still alive."

"This is getting ridiculous," Bascomb muttered. "If she had a near-death experience, she didn't really die. Near-death means nearly dead, not really dead."

"It depends on your definition of death," I said. "She was officially pronounced dead by the ER doctor. There was no respiratory activity, no heartbeat, no blood pressure, no electrical activity in the brain. They tried defibrillation, they tried direct cardiac injection of Lidocaine, but nothing worked. The body temperature began to drop. A half hour later, her body was sent down to the morgue. She was clinically dead for an hour and twenty minutes before a morgue attendant noticed the first sign of returning life."

"Jesus Christ," whispered Wiorkowski.

"When they talked to Laura later, she told everyone her husband was still alive. She said she looked for him on the other side, but he wasn't there. She asked for him, and she was told he was still alive. But when she came back, no one believed her. They all thought she was delusional."

"Except for you, of course," Bascomb snorted.

"At first, I didn't believe her, either," I admitted. "All the evidence said Harrison Duquesne died in the crash. But now it turns out that Laura was right. Her husband was alive. Whether his name was Duquesne or Hamilton, he was alive. And the only place Laura could have learned that was on the other side. When she was dead. Do you realize what that means?"

I knew I was getting excited, but I wanted someone, anyone to understand and believe what had actually happened.

"She brought back a message from the dead," I said. "She brought back information that she could have learned only on the other side. It's the kind of proof of the afterlife that Professor DeBray had been searching for."

I waited for them to agree with me, as I was certain any fair-minded person would when presented with the facts. I soon discovered the police were no more ready to accept the truth about NDEs than were members of the medical or religious communities.

"Okay, let's say Hamilton really used the name Harrison Duquesne," Wiorkowski nodded. I could almost see his mind working as he developed another faulty hypothesis to fit the facts. "If he embezzled all that money, then maybe the wife was in on everything right from the start. She knew the guy who died in the car wasn't her husband. She was in on that, too. But at the last minute, the husband double-crosses her. He decides to kill her so he won't have to split the money with her. When she wakes up in the hospital, she realizes what happened and she wants to track him down to get back her share."

"That's impossible," I said, dismissing his latest theory.

"Why is it so impossible?" Wiorkowski asked. "It makes sense to me. What do you think, Bascomb?"

"It makes a lot more sense than her coming back from the dead to find her husband," Bascomb said. "That kind of crap only happens in TV movies."

"But it's true," I insisted.

"Then prove it," Wiorkowski challenged me. "If it really happened the way you say it did, give us some proof. Be logical, Theo. You really expect us to believe she found out about her husband when she was dead? Things like that don't happen."

"You can track down the emergency room doctors and nurses and the morgue attendant."

"All they're going to say is they *thought* she was dead," Wiorkowski said.

"And obviously, they were wrong," Bascomb added. "Because she turned out to be alive."

"This sort of thing has happened to other people," I argued. "That was Professor DeBray's life work, proving the validity of the near-death experience. That was what I did for him, interviewing near-death survivors about their experiences on the other side."

"But you never came up with any proof?"

"Laura . . . she was the proof. There was no other way she could have known her husband was alive."

"We've already been over this," Wiorkowski sighed. "If what you told us about a health-care scam is true, then there's a very simple explanation. Let me repeat it for you: Laura Duquesne must have been in on it from the start. She knew her husband was going to fake his death. She wanted her share of the money, that's why she wanted to find him."

"No. It didn't happen that way," I argued. "I know for a fact that she had no idea what Harrison was up to."

"She conned you," Bascomb sneered. "That's all it was. She was using you to get at her husband. You're supposed to be a psychologist and you let her make a fool of you."

They were switching from reasonableness to insults, trying their best to get me to buy into their latest theory. I could see they didn't really care who was guilty of what. All they wanted was to find a logical framework to explain the terrible crimes that had been committed. I couldn't really blame them for trying the simplest solutions first. In their place, I probably would have done the same.

"You don't understand," I finally said. "I talked to her about it, in circumstances where I knew she was telling me the truth. She was a totally innocent victim."

"And when did she tell you that?"

I looked from one to the other of them before answering, knowing they wouldn't believe me, but knowing I had to say it.

"When I was dead," I said.

"Oh, for Christ's sake," Bascomb muttered.

"You can check the paramedics, they'll tell you I was dead when they found me."

"This is ridiculous," Bascomb said.

"My soul left my body and went to the other side. That's where I talked to Laura. She was there, waiting for me."

"It sounds to me like you're trying to lay the groundwork for an insanity plea," Bascomb said.

"Laura wouldn't have lied to me," I insisted. "She couldn't have lied, not where we were, not in the afterlife."

"You expect us to believe this crap?" Bascomb asked.

"I give you credit for having balls," Wiorkowski grinned at me. "It's a hell of a story you came up with. But just like the story you told us about Laura Duquesne, it's impossible to prove."

"That's where you're wrong," I said. "This time, I can prove it. I saw things when I was dead. I know facts that no other living human being knows."

I had their attention now.

Perhaps I shouldn't have gone any further. Perhaps I should have continued to tantalize them with hints of the unknown, and waited for a more sympathetic audience to reveal the few fragments of information I brought back from the other side. But I was eager to prove that I actually had penetrated the veil of death. And although these two detectives seemed prone to over-simplification, they appeared to be relatively objective investigators, unburdened by ideological baggage or preconceived notions.

"What kind of things are you talking about?" Wiorkowski asked in a quiet voice.

"You said you didn't find the gun," I told him.

"Not yet."

"Well, I know where it is."

We were interrupted by a grey-haired nurse who came in, complained that I was talking too much, took my temperature, adjusted the IV drip, checked the tube in my chest, insisted I drink some of the water she offered, and made a face at the two detectives before she left to bother her other patients.

"When a person dies, the spirit usually lingers around the body for a while," I explained. "Most near-deathers report their spirits hover near the ceiling, looking down at their own dead body. With me, it was a little different. My spirit floated out the window, where I looked down at Laura's body on the car, and Hamilton's body on the sidewalk."

"What color was the car?" Wiorkowski suddenly challenged me.

"It was a white Buick LeSabre," I said. "License plate WK7804. She landed on the roof, face down. One of her shoes was on the hood. The other shoe ended up in the middle of the street, where a car ran over it."

Wiorkowski stared at me in startled silence. The accuracy of my response seemed to take him by surprise.

"You could have seen that from the window," Bascomb tried to explain it away.

"Check the carpet," I said. "If I went to the window, there would have been a blood trail."

"Tell us about the gun," Wiorkowski said when he found his voice.

"It's caught in a crevice in the parapet just above the entrance, where the cement is pulling away from the building. You'll have to send someone up on a ladder, because you can't see the gun from the street, or from any of the windows."

"But you saw it."

"I was dead. I saw a lot of things."

"Okay. We can check that out. What else can you tell us?"

"I found out where Harrison, or should I say Hamilton, hid the money."

The two detectives glanced at each other. Bascomb started to smile.

"Who told you about the money?" he asked. "Was it Hamilton, or was it Laura?"

"No one had to tell me. After death, everything is revealed to us. All the secrets of life, the mysteries of the universe . . . " I paused, sadly shaking my head. "But those of us who return to life must leave this knowledge behind. It can't be transferred between the two worlds."

"Now you're going to tell us you forgot where the money is?" Bascomb was sounding impatient.

"No. I remember that part. We're usually allowed to remember bits of information, fragments really, mostly about the way things look on the other side, who we met, things like that. I think the reason we're allowed to bring some knowledge back is to help convince people that there's really something waiting for us after death."

"Tell us about the money," Wiorkowski prodded me.

"He deposited ten million, two hundred forty-two thousand dollars in the Queen's Bank and Trust in Freeport, down in the Bahamas. He deposited the rest of the money he stole, which amounted to sixty-one thousand, three hundred eighty dollars, in a preferred checking account at the Citibank branch on East Fourteenth Street."

Bascomb was writing furiously in his notebook.

"We know about the Citibank account," Wiorkowski said. "We found the bank statements in the Hamilton apartment on East Eighth Street. But we didn't know about any account in the Bahamas."

"The account was opened on March 24," I said. "That was three weeks before Duquesne faked his death. The name he used on the account was Thomas Deaver."

"Wait a minute," Wiorkowski said. "We've got Duquesne, then Hamilton, and now Deaver. You're telling us he had three different identities?"

"There's also a safety deposit box in Hamilton's name in the same Citibank branch. Inside the box, you'll find passports and ID for all three names. They're in the same yellow envelope he used to keep hidden in the closet of the apartment where he shot me."

"You wouldn't happen to know the number for that bank account in the Bahamas?"

"0700032789."

Bascomb quickly wrote it down.

"Anything else you want to add?" Wiorkowski asked. "Anything more about your role in all this? How you knew about these bank accounts?"

"I already told you. I found out about them when I was dead."

"I think you're lying to us," Bascomb said. "I think you're making it all up to save yourself."

"You can check it out easily enough," I said. "You'll find the gun, the bank accounts, the safety deposit box, all exactly where

I said. It'll prove that I brought back information from the dead."

"I'm not so sure about that," Wiorkowski said. "A reasonable man could look at what you told us and say that it proves you were involved in the embezzlement. It was you, Arthur Hamilton, and Laura Duquesne. You were all in it together."

"Don't be asinine. You know that's not true."

"How else can you know so much about the money and where it is? Come on, Theo, you even know the account number."

"I told you, I found out about it when I was dead."

"Doctor Chang told us you were never legally pronounced dead," Wiorkowski said. "Based on what you've been telling us, here's what I think really happened: the three of you were arguing about how to split up the money. You attacked Hamilton, he shot you, and then he shot the woman in self-defense when she tried to push him out the window."

I could see from their self-satisfied expressions that the two detectives found this latest theory of theirs more believable than any of their earlier ones.

What frightened me most was that it sounded plausible to me, too. In fact, it sounded a lot more believable than the story I had just finished telling them.

SIXTY-TWO

And thus we come to what I consider the supreme irony of my life.

I had accomplished a task that scientists and philosophers had always thought impossible. I had penetrated the veil that separates mankind from the deepest mysteries of eternity. I had walked among the dead, and brought back as evidence of my journey information that the man I knew as Harrison Duquesne had taken with himself to the grave. It was factual, verifiable data, the kind of hard evidence of the otherworld experience that no near-death researcher before me had ever been able to produce.

The stolen money turned out to be exactly where I said it was, the balances correct to the last dollar.

When I first heard that the police had found the money, I was elated. The fact that the information I brought back had been independently confirmed by unimpeachable sources served as a kind of personal epiphany for me. It swept away any second thoughts or self-doubts I might have had about the reality of my near-death experience and my extraordinary afterlife encounter with Laura. I was convinced it would finally prove to a skeptical world that another sphere of reality awaits us after death.

But what I saw as information of profound metaphysical significance, the Manhattan district attorney saw as a virtual confession of embezzlement.

With an effrontery that Galileo's accusers would have admired, the district attorney is using the information I brought back from the dead to put me on trial.

After a week recuperating at Bellevue, I was transferred to the prison hospital at Rikers' Island, where I now await trial on charges of accessory to murder, embezzlement, fraud, and criminal conspiracy.

If convicted on all counts, I could spend the rest of my life in prison.

According to Milton, who has volunteered to defend me as part of his *pro bono publico* committment, the basic framework of the case against me is largely circumstantial and ambiguous, relying on unfortunate accidents of timing and proximity.

Any single one of the supposedly incriminating incidents, taken individually, might well be explained away as an unfortunate coincidence. They will be presented, however, in a manner in which each one supports another, like the interwoven strands in a spider's web, so that the cumulative effect is a sense of overwhelming guilt.

For example, although the forensic evidence indicates Arthur Hamilton, a.k.a. Harrison Duquesne, probably murdered Professor DeBray, the body was found in my apartment. Not only does that implicate me in DeBray's murder, it also supports the theory that I was a partner of Duquesne/Hamilton in his criminal activities. My rescue of his wife Laura and the time I spent with her is cited as further proof that the three of us were working in collusion. And the fact that I was found with a bullet wound in the apartment from which Laura and her husband fell to their deaths will be presented as evidence of a conspiracy that somehow went sour.

But by far the most incriminating evidence against me, the foundation on which the prosecution is building its case, is the information I brought back from the dead: the detailed description I provided the police of the location, the dollar amounts, and the numbers of those secret bank accounts.

According to the indictment, the only way I could have obtained such detailed information about Duquesne/Hamilton's accounts was by being involved with him in the embezzlement scheme. My possession of the financial data is the one element that appears to tie together all aspects of the case against me, and provides, at the minimum, evidence of conspiracy.

The trial date is set for next month. The usual pre-trial maneuvering is already underway.

Much to the chagrin of the prosecution, the case has become something of a *cause celebre*. It promises to be the kind of trial ideally suited for exploitation by the New York media and the tabloids. The TV stations have done their usual superficial investigative reports on the near-death experience. And the producers of "Unsolved Mysteries" have expressed interest in doing a segment.

Perhaps for that reason, the district attorney's office has offered a plea bargain. The charges of accessory to murder and criminal conspiracy would be dropped in return for a guilty plea to embezzlement. Under the terms of the agreement, the district attorney would also recommend leniency to the court, citing my help in recovering the embezzled funds, and exposing Doctor Zydek's health-care scam. I have been promised a term of less than one year in prison, the sentence to be served in a minimum-security facility. It seemed a generous offer, and Milton strongly recommended I accept it.

But agreeing to the plea bargain would require me to plead guilty to a crime I did not commit. More important, it would mean disavowing my near-death experience.

To deny the reality of that mystical journey would be to deny everything I now believe in. For the first time in my life, I finally understand the metaphysical reason for my existence.

Some might call it predestination; some might call it karma, some might even call it a strange inversion of the space-time continuum. All I know for certain is all those sometimes pointless years of research and study were merely preparation for the assignment that lies ahead of me.

I was sent back from the dead to be an authenticator, to add my testimony of the Otherworld to the accounts of those astral voyagers who went before me. My role is nothing less than to confirm the existence of life after death.

And this trial is the vehicle through which I hope to do so. Therefore I have rejected any plea-bargain or compromise.

To prove my innocence of the charges against me, I will have to convince a jury that my near-death experience was truly a visit to the afterlife.

It will not be an easy task. But it is one for which my education and training uniquely suits me.

Arrayed against me will be an assemblage of prominent psychologists, scientists, doctors and theologians. They will provide "expert" testimony portraying the near-death experience variously as a cultural myth, a symptom of hypoxia, the result of limbic lobe syndrome, a conversion experience, drug-induced hallucination, religious patterning or any of the dozens of sophisticated rationalizations which reflect the belief systems of their particular professions. In addition, Doctor Chang will testify that I was never officially declared dead, and thus technically did not meet Professor DeBray's threshold criteria for an NDE.

If the jury believes the "experts," I will certainly be convicted.

But if there is any one member of the jury who has ever doubted the infallibility of modern science, or who truly believes that another life awaits us beyond this earthly one, then I will be acquitted.

What sustains me through these difficult times is an absolute and unwavering faith that my beloved Laura is waiting for me on the other side. She will take my hand on my final journey into the Light, and remain at my side throughout eternity.

For if there is one thing I have learned from these extraordinary events, it is that love is a force of such mystical power, it cannot be extinguished by so mundane a human event as death.

ABOUT THE AUTHOR

"I decided I wanted to be a writer as soon as I learned to spell," says author William M. Valtos.

He had his first article published in a national magazine when he was fourteen years old and went on to be a reporter and editor of a prize-winning Air Force newspaper. Years as an award-winning advertising copywriter followed, but Valtos returned to fiction writing "when the last of my four children graduated from college," producing his first novel, *Resurrection* (St. Martin, 1989), which was made into the movie *Almost Dead* for television, and *The Authenticator*.

The author grew up in the Scranton, Pennsylvania, area. He and his wife Rose live in Barrington, Illinois.

Hampton Roads Publishing Company

... for the evolving human spirit

Hampton Roads Publishing Company
publishes books on a variety of subjects including
metaphysics, health, complementary medicine,
visionary fiction, and other related topics.

For a copy of our latest catalog,
call toll-free, 800-766-8009,
or send your name and address to:

Hampton Roads Publishing Company, Inc.
1125 Stoney Ridge Road
Charlottesville, VA 22902
e-mail: hrpc@hrpub.com
www.hrpub.com